TAINTED 3:

THE BOOK OF REDEMPTION

GERALD R JOHNSON

The publisher would appreciate notification where errors occur so that they may be corrected in subsequent printing and/or editions. Please send comments to the publisher by emailing to deeprivers67@yahoo.com Printed in the United States of America

ISBN 978-1-943159-05-5

LCCN 2016948056

TAINTED 3:
THE BOOK OF REDEMPTION

GERALD R JOHNSON

Also available from Gerald R. Johnson

The Tainted Series:

Tainted: the Book of Revelations

Tainted 2: the Book of Retribution

Liquid Eroticism by Gerald Johnson

Pitch Darke: the Poetic Chronicles of Damien Darke
by Damien Darke

ACKNOWLEDGEMENTS

Everything begins and ends with the words… So I want to say thank you for being able to form each of these sentences to create each of these stories. I love what I do and I've been doing it for so long and I think that now that they are getting out for people to enjoy this is the greatest and the most fun part of this. As I write, I get to read and I get to see how my character move about and interact in their worlds, but it's only when I get to share these characters and their worlds with others that it becomes fun. I want to each and every person who has ever taken a chance with any story that I've ever written and given me their thoughts and feedback. I've never shied away any kind of criticism and it has only helped me to grow… so please, keep it coming.

To my family… Thank you all for putting up with me when I get into my writing moods. You know what I mean; headphones on, music in my ears, television playing, and my fingers dancing upon my keyboard at a breakneck speed. I sometimes forget that there are people in the house with me and I want you all to know that I'm not ignoring you, but I do get so wrapped up what I'm writing that the world around me melts away and the world I've created becomes my reality. At times it becomes far too easy to just drop off into the pages of what I'm writing and get carried away with the characters there as they explain to me what's going on and what needs to happen next, a chapter later, or even several chapters later. I hope that you all understand that for me there is a means to an end with all of this insanity I put into all of this writing and I feel that one day the payoff is going to be incredible.

I want to thank some people that I have actually gone in and added to Tainted 3 as characters. I wanted to have a little fun, and whereas I know a lot of people use name brand products a lot, I wanted to include a few people that I know. To my three kids, Nichelle, Le'Keva, and Gerald… my brother Antavio, my brother-in-law Desean "JetEye" Curry, my niece Tranique, and some good friends of mine Netza Rodriguez and Coni Cone… thank you all for allowing me to add you to the fantasy to give it a little more of a personal feel. This is Tampa… This is Florida … This is our home and I want everyone to get a little feel and taste of it from our point of view. Thank you all.

Lastly, I want to say that this is merely the beginning for me. I have so much more to say and I have plans to continue writing for as long as my hands, eyes, and head will allow me to. My imagination is so full of stories of so many genres that I want to share that I am looking forward to the next story(ies) that I am preparing for you all to read. I want to thank Vantage Point Publishing and Dawn Rivers(and I love you) for taking a chance with me and my writings and to let everyone know that you should check out our other authors and poets because you will not be disappointed. So get ready Gang… there's always more to come…

Are you Ready?

TO THOSE I DEDICATE THIS BOOK TO:

I want to dedicate this book to the 3 ladies in my life
My mom Glenda… my lady Anita… and my sister
Kia
Thank you all for always being there for me … I
love you all

I also want to dedicate this to my father Gerald R
Johnson, Sr. After 27 years I still wish I could just
sit and talk to you

To my brother, Antavio
You've become quite the young man and father I
love you

To my kids (all of them)
No matter the time… the place… the issue I'm
always here for you… I will always love you all.

Prologue

Charles "Big Fats" Robins, is a well-known figure in the Tampa Bay area; for some, he's a prominent businessman and philanthropist, a man who has done a lot to build up the black communities in the south Tampa areas down and around Ybor City. If you were to ask around many would applaud and praise him for fixing up a lot of the dilapidated homes and bringing black owned businesses back into the area. Many would toss roses at his feet and credit him with cleaning up Ybor City and making it safe again when the city had pretty much turned its back on that part of town leaving it to be overrun by drug infested buildings and dying businesses. For the prominent, Charles Robins was a household name as a bay area hero, but they were the ones with the wool pulled over their eyes.

That was the Charles Robins for the general public, or as he would put it...

"This is the face them white people need to see because it lets them sleep betta at night," and he would laugh puffing on the expensive, smuggled in, Cuban cigar that he'd have smuggled in every month. "They need to know that the blacks are corralled and cared for and outta they hair. What I do is a public service."

The man called "Big Fats" was not called that because he was a huge man who just towered over everyone. Standing at an impressive six foot five, the man was built like a Mack truck, with a deep resounding voice to match his size. Looking at

him makes anyone wonder who could make a suit to
fit him, but he was always immaculately dressed.
Charles Robins was called "Big Fats" because he
had *fat* pockets; the kind of pockets that just stayed
swollen with all of the different "enterprises"
creating big money that he had flowing in and out of
Florida daily. And, this wasn't new to him; Robins
has been Big Fats since he was a kid running game
in these same endless streets.

"People gravitate to power," he was known
to say quite often, "and I was bound and determined
to be absolutely in power. My goals from a youngin'
was always clear, and anyone out to get in my
way… well, they got ran over."

Big Fats was a powerhouse in the Florida
underground; nothing moved around within the state
without his hands being in it up to the elbow.
Sometime during the late 1960's he had single
handedly come into Tampa and took over all of the
up and rising black gangs organizing them, making
them virtually invisible. He was meticulous, quietly
taking over territory after territory until he had all of
the central counties, Hillsborough, Pinellas, Polk,
and even Orange counties, firmly under his thumb.
Once that was in place he began the "work" of
cleaning up the streets.

Whereas Charles Robins was a respected
public figure and businessman throughout the state
of Florida, Big Fats was a respected a feared man in
the streets. From as far South as Miami to the five
boroughs of New York to even mention his name in
certain circles could and would get you killed. He
was that kind of powerful man that always had

armed men around him to make certain no got too close unless he ordered it, and that was because of the number of threats and times he has been under fire. He could walk through the neighborhoods and the kids would run up to him because they knew he'd give them money for the ice cream truck. It was nothing for him to walk into a wedding reception and give the newlyweds a gift, but what many didn't know is that afterwards he'd been known to have his way with the bride once they returned from the honeymoon.

Big Fats was definitely a lady's man, especially after he'd established himself, and for several years he was never seen with same woman for more than a few months; the story around the neighborhood was that he kept them around until he got them pregnant. It's been said that he has more than twenty children spread out through the Tampa Bay area, a few more in Miami, and at least a set of twins up in Harlem. He wasn't at all shameful of the number of kids he had and proudly took care of all of them.

He'd been heard once telling one of his young soldiers, "No child should ever be held at fault for his parents. If you laid down with a bitch, then she'll be a bitch even after the child is born. You laid with her, and I'll hold you responsible for the life you created."

With the wealth he'd amassed, Charles never felt it was necessary to leave where he grew up, and had him a great home built so that his people could see him living the "struggle" with them. What few people outside of her personal circles knew was that the home in Tampa was one of several he owned around the world; including, a château in Switzerland, a small modest house in Monaco, and an island that included an extravagant villa off the coast of Rio de Janeiro. He kept things like that private, only his lawyer and accountant knew the extent of his wealth and holdings.

To the general public, Charles Robins was just another eccentric bachelor with an eye for business, and a flare for women and expensive toys. In truth; being Charles Robins was nothing more than a high priced ruse, a facade to keep the wool pulled over the eyes of the masses while Big Fats literally ran the city behind closed doors. He had no fears of people in power because he owned them all, from politicians to policemen, lawyers and judges all of them were on his payroll in one way or another. Drugs, prostitution, gun running were just a few things that kept his hands dirty, and he kept all of his secrets to himself refusing to even share any information with his top lieutenants.

That was until a young Sydney Roulette and his best friend were tossed to the floor at his feet.

"Who the fuck is these... lil niggas, Johnny B?"

Johnny B reached down grabbing Sydney by the collar and pulling him to his feet. "Boss, 'memba 'bout t'ree week ago I told you 'bout them lil turks running game on Bill and his crew, takin' dey stash an' shit? Dis is dem, Boss."

The boy couldn't have been more than fifteen, but he stood there beneath Big Fats' stern stare unwavering. His eyes were locked onto Fats much like he would any other kid's on the school yard, and this impressed both Charles Robins and Big Fats. The boy was confident, not cocky, and he had the look of a born leader.

"What's your name, Son?"

"Sydney," his voice waivered a bit as he straightened out his clothes. "Sydney Roulette, Mr. Robins."

"Hm, so, you know me?" Big Fats was intrigued with the boy. "Good. So now that we have that out of the way, why the hell would you steal from me?"

"I wouldn't ever steal from you, Mr. Robins," Sydney stood his ground trying not to appear shaken as he took a quick glance at his partner, "and I'm sorry that that's how you see it."

"You're sorry? So, tell me, Boy… tell me, Sydney, how should I see this?" Big Fats sat back in his chair staring at the two young boys; neither of them looked away, Sydney out of respect, and the other boy stood there with his hands stuffed in his pocket looking more brass and cocky.

"A lesson, Mr. Robins," Sydney answered.

"And to *Whom* is this lesson directed... me?"

"We're not stupid, Mr. Robins," the other boy spoke up.

"Are you sure about that?" He waved the boy off before he could answer. "And your name is?"

"Bobby Johnson, Mr. Robins," his hand was in his pocket rattling around the loose change he had. "They call me Jangles, Sir."

Big Fats laughed out. These two little knuckleheads had balls of steel and he could appreciate that. Right off the bat he picked Sydney as the more rational of the two and Jangles was more like his hot headed muscle. They were a good team together, and if trained properly...

"So tell me, Sydney," he stared down at the staunch young man, "who are you teaching this lesson?"

"I doubt that they would have the balls to tell you that I'd warned them on a number of occasions not to sale that shi… stuff on my blocks. We got kids out there. Those untrained monkeys you have out there trying to set up shop were doing it in an area that I'd claimed as unmarred. I warned them, and they didn't listen. So I had to teach them." Sydney didn't mince words and he kept his eyes on the big man. It didn't look like it, but he knew that Jangles was keeping a watch on everyone else in the room.

"Your block, huh? Are you running game without my say so, Boy? You said you know who I am."

"And I have nothing but the utmost respect for you, Mr. Robins. I say my block because that's where I live, and like I said… we have a lot of little kids on my block. Me and Jangles, well, it's our place to protect em." Sydney put his hands into his pockets looking more relaxed. "I have all of your money and all of your product stashed away safely. I'll pull my boys back... if; you and I can come to an accord about my block."

"Why you little motherfucker," Big Fats released a roaring laugh as he looked around the room at all of his men. "This little bastard used all of you ... Clowns... to pretty much set me up. This shit right here is how a real businessman gains audience with someone well beyond his league. Goddamn, ain't this some shit? How old are you two boys?"

"I'm fourteen," Sydney pointed at Jangles, "and he's fifteen. Why does that matter?"

"It matters because I just got schooled by two little street punks, and that's not good," he sat up on his seat. "Now I have a bit of a dilemma where you two boys are concerned. Do I give in to your little demands, and possibly lose face with my people? Or, do I just kill you both and most likely those asses you've been robbing just to clean up this mess? Of course then I not only lose face with the neighborhood, but I'll have to take care of your goddamn families just to appease people."

"There is a third choice, Mr. Robins, where no one has to worry with any negative fallout." Sydney glanced over at Jangles and nodded before turning back to Big Fats. He smiled at the man before pulling his hands from his pockets and rubbing them together. "The way I see it, Sir, those assholes are a liability... they want to do things big like they holding weight like that, but they were messy and making too many mistakes. So let me and my boys take care of them for you; no blood on your hands. Once that is done, and minus my block we can increase your territory and up your revenue by no less than say... twenty percent. "

Big Fats stood and stalked around the room. "Are you shaking me down, Boy?"

Sydney watched with a smile as the six men watching him and Jangles all stepped back including

Johnny B who seemed really nervous. Jangles had his signature smile on his face, and this was a good thing; the two of them had been the best of friends since kindergarten, and he knew Jangles trusted his every move. Folding his arms across his chest, Sydney watched Big Fats pacing the room.

"A fucking, snot-nosed kid trying to shake me down."

"We're not shaking you down, Mr. Robins. Like Jangles said a bit ago, he and I aren't stupid."

"Then what would you dare call this, Mr. Roulette?"

"This is what you do every day," Sydney hadn't dropped his smile, "this is business, Mr. Robins. This is business how Big Fats would do business."

Charles Robins stopped in his tracks. He slowly turned to face the two teens. There was a murderous look in his dark eyes as he pulled the cigar he'd been chewing on from between his clenched teeth. He stared at the two boys standing there defiantly like they didn't have a worry in the world; Sydney, straight faced with his arms crossed at his chest, and Jangles with his hands shoved in his pockets and a cocky smile. He wanted to rush up on them and slapped some respect into them, but for boys like this... that wouldn't help. He knew these two boys unlike most of the men blindly following him. These two boys were familiar. They were just like him at that age, and it would seem a lot smarter. He stared at his men around the room and recognized the look of fear that he'd become so used to.

Damn, he thought to himself, *there's no life at all in these motherfuckers, no original ideas or thoughts besides the ones I fucking give them.*

Charles turned back to Sydney and stared long and hard at him. The boy had brass, or as the old timers would say, "he got moxy". Then there was the other one; just from the way he held his body standing there, Jangles looked like a loose cannon.

"Business the way I would do business, huh?" Charles Robins couldn't help laughing once more. He could feel his men watching in disbelief as he walked up and clapped both young men on their shoulders.

"We wouldn't assume to know your business," Jangles said. "But, we damn sho' want to learn."

"You two scoundrels are motherfuckers after an old man's heart."

Charles stepped around the two boys and sat down in his chair. He waved for the man standing close to the door. As the man rushed forward, Charles pulled a fresh cigar from his suit coat and bit off the end.

"Yes, Mr. Robins?"

"Macy, run off and make reservations for at least 6 at the Columbia for tonight, and let them know whatever time they can squeeze us in will be fine."

"Right away, Sir," Macy was a slender, older man and he bowed at the waist and hurried off.

Charles watched and grinned. They would both be great at poker holding their looks as they tried not to look impressed. These two are going to make the best students, and if they listened he would show them how to get the keys to the city and so much more.

"I hope that you two boys have no plans because," he smiled and blew out smoke rings, "two things I never do... 1. I never discuss business in my home because you never know who's in the walls listening. And 2. I Never talk business on an empty stomach. So, you two boys hungry?

"Damn," he sat there staring at their clothes. Both began staring at themselves as if they thought he saw something on them. "This shit won't do. Hallowell, contact Pierre and tell him I'm going to need two quick fittings and that we'll be there in 30."

Now they couldn't hold back their looks of being impressed. Hallowell was a tall, bald dark skinned man standing near the bar with a glass held in his large hand. The man swallowed the last of his drink and casually walked from the room.

"Do you need to contact anyone?" Charles puffed on his cigar as he pointed to a phone across the room. He watched as Sydney nodded to his partner and Jangles moved over to the phone. "Very good. I'm not surprised at all."

"It's not that we didn't trust you, Mr. Robins," Sydney began to explain but was waved off.

"You did the right thing, Son." In his head Charles was thinking *Business 101*. "You never walk into a hostile territory without people knowing where you are, or a backup plan."

Both of them looked over at Jangles and he gave the thumbs up before hanging up the phone.

"So here's our itinerary for the moment," Charles said so that the men left in the room could hear. "We cannot go to the Columbia…"

"The Columbia?" Sydney raised an eyebrow.

"Yes, the Columbia down in Ybor, but we cannot go with you two looking like a couple of little street bums, so we're going to start at my tailor... we'll call this Dressing Etiquette 101. You have to learn right off the bat that you should always dress for the position in life that you want and not for where you are. Do you understand what I'm saying?"

Sydney smiled and nodded knowing exactly where Mr. Robins was going with that. In his young head he was already sitting where this larger than life man was sitting. Growing up in a household where his mom was always with some asshole that he didn't like, and never knowing his real dad, he'd looked up to Charles Robins from a distance. He had constantly told his best friend, Jangles, that one day he would be just as big and as powerful as Big Fats. Jangles has never doubted him, and now here they stood with the man he idolizes.

"Let's go my boys," Charles stood from his chair and grabbed the two by their shoulders, "we have a lot of shit to do before dinner. I promise you two that this is going to be a hellava night."

****

Jangles slowly stepped up out of the large Cadillac with the biggest smile imaginable stretching his lips. He pulled on the sleeves and the tails of his new suit coat straightening out the wrinkles. He was almost tempted to pull out a handkerchief and wipe of the new patent leather shoes, but he held that in check because he knew he was being watched. At this point the only thing that felt out of place was the newly growing dreads on his head, but after tonight he'd always keep those twisted and looking clean. He did a quick spin like he was in a boy band and then stepped out the way so Sydney could step out.

"Shit," Jangles popped his collar with the biggest smile on his face, "a nigga can get used to this."

"I bet you can," Sydney punched his boy in the arm.

"Well, Boys," Charles had joined them on the curb, "welcome to Columbia, one of the absolute best spots down here in Ybor. The food is magnificent; I'm pretty sure that you've never had anything like this in your young lives, and it is perfect for letting people see you… one of these days I'm pretty sure you boys will know exactly what I mean by that.

Now, let's go... we have business to discuss."

"Yes, Sir," the two boys bellowed in unison.

Sydney glanced around taking in the sites around him. He'd never been to Ybor City and now that he was standing here in the middle of it... it was hard not to be awed. Running around the streets of West Tampa was pretty all that he knew; he wasn't a banger, although everyone including his mother thought so, but he knew the monsters of the streets. He knew how to hustle, and this brought in some of the little dudes who didn't want to be in no gangs.

Soon he and Jangles had a small bit tight unit and together they all helped to protect their blocks.

Sydney stood staring at the sky. Night was falling and the street lights and the business lights all down the block were slowly popping on. There were a few clouds and fewer stars blanketing the skies as he turned his eyes towards downtown and he smiled.

"What's that look 'bout, Syd?" Jangles tapped him on the shoulder to get his attention.

"You see that, Jangles," Sydney pointed to the skyscrapers lighting up along the horizon, "that's where I want to be, down there doing shit most of these street niggas wouldn't dream of doing. I want more than this."

"Well you know I've always told yo ass that you gots the brains to get us up out these streets. Shit, I mean, look at us now. We 'bout to break bread wit' the biggest muhfucka in the Bay. That's some big shit right there."

"True enough," Sydney stared downtown once more. "This is just the beginning, Brotha, because I see some bigger shit for us coming real soon."

"I'm wit' you all the way," Jangles slapped his shoulder and headed towards the restaurant door. He looked back at his daydreaming best friend and shook his head. They'd been through a lot for just being teens. He'd watched his old man get shot by some smoked out dealer on the block, and they'd found Syd's older brother overdosed in a smack house. Syd's mom worked her ass off to keep him out the streets, but they didn't keep a young nigga from dreaming bigger. Sydney's dreams had Jangles down for whatever, and he was gon' see to it that they reached whatever heights Sydney was reaching for.

"Ay yo, Syd," Jangles called out. "Come on, Nigga, I'm hungrier than a motherfucker, and we can't keep the bossman waiting."

Sydney nodded shaking his friend's extended hand before they picked up their step to catch up to Charles. His mind was still all over the place, and he knew that after tonight everything about him and what he wanted was going to change. He knew that. He was sure of that, and he was sure that Charles "Big Fats" was going to see to that.

"Yea, let's not keep the bossman waiting," Sydney repeated.

Chapter 1

I should be home with Sydnee, Courtney thought to herself before remembering that her daughter and family were in hiding and would remain so until this "war" with Jangles ended. It would end bloody, and one way or another either she would die… or he would.

She stepped out of the Navigator door being held opened by Nicky and looked around. She was standing outside of Club Skyy dressed to kill in a dress that hugged her as only a tailored dress should. It was night, but her eyes were hidden behind a pair of large, rimmed sunglasses. She trapped her small clutch purse beneath her arm as she walked ahead of Nick not waiting for him to catch up. Her heels tapping against the sidewalk was drowned out by the thumping of the music just beyond the building's walls, and the chattering of the crowd of people already waiting to get in.

"This really isn't a good idea, Nicky," she more felt him beside her than saw him as she kept her eyes moving from face to face in the growing crowd.

"Stop fighting me, Courtney," Nick Styles tossed his keys to a young guy that Courtney could only hope was a valet. She smiled as she draped her arm into the crook of his offered arm. "You need to get out and let your hair down. There's a lot of shit going on around you all at one time… you need to just stop and let off some steam every blue moon."

He led them to the head of the line without stopping to worry if anyone complained, and quite a few did vocally. In IXion's name, Nick knew the owner and had purchased a controlling interest in the club as a business tax write off just under a year ago; getting in hassle free was only one of the perps of the deal. Nick tapped the heavily muscular brother standing on the other side of the velvet rope and waited to be acknowledged. He tapped Courtney's hand hoping to calm her down giving her a quick wink as she smiled up at him.

He'd a plan for a night that pretty much included getting her out of that stuffy house for just a couple of hours for a few drinks and perhaps even a dance or two. He just wanted her to relax after all of the craziness that had been happening in their lives. He noticed that since the shooting she was never comfortable outside, and he needed to change that. She needed to become a rock, and that meant getting back out into the world.

"Hey, hey, if it ain't Mr. Nick Styles in the flesh," the large man shook Nick's hand in a traditional manner.

"What's good, Jimmy O?"

"Not too much, my Brotha." Nick moved Courtney so that she could be seen. "Jimmy, I want you to meet Courtney Roulette… Court, this is a long time friend of mine, James O'Bannon. He's as close to a brother as I've ever had; so much so that I even introduced him to my little sister."

"Everyone just calls me Jimmy O, Ms. Roulette."

"Please, call me Courtney."

Jimmy flashed Courtney a million-dollar smile and almost stumbled backwards when she returned it. "So what's a beautiful woman like you doing with an ol scoundrel like Nicky here?"

"Honestly... I think he kidnapped me," Courtney quickly replied.

The three of them laughed as Jimmy unhooked the rope and allowed them in. He cocked an eyebrow at Nick as a one hundred dollar bill was stuffed into his hand.

"What's this for, Bruh?" Jimmy stared at the Benjamin looking up at him.

"Take the wife and kids to lunch tomorrow on me," Nick told him, "tell EmmaJean I said hi."

"You need to bring yo ass by and see yo sistah," the big man clapped him on the shoulder. "Nick, she's heard about the shit's goin' on been worried."

"I promise I'll be by soon," Nick nodded his head before shaking Jimmy's hand. "Give her and the kids my love."

Not giving Jimmy a chance to say anymore, Nick was walking into the club doors with Courtney in tow. The bass from the music vibrated against both of their bodies as the slowly waded through the ocean of people headed towards the first bar Nick could see. Bodies were thrashing around and making contact with them, Nick pulled Courtney into his arms shielding her from the onslaught.

"What are we having, Handsome?" a voice yelled out over the music.

"Give me a Henn straight, and for the lady a tequila sunset. Send it to our booth upstairs."

"Will do," she winked and waved over one of the waitresses.

"You know I'm not good with tequila, Nick." Courtney wasn't sure if he heard her complaint over the music.

"You need to relax big time, Court," he leaned over speaking into her ear. "Look, I just want you to have a nice night out. Take some time away and forget about everything and… everybody. "

Courtney stared around nervously as Nick moved them back off into the crowd. There were so many people, and at this point she couldn't bring herself to trust anyone. Jangles had her completely on edge; everyone was a suspect, even those close to her she believed on the verge of betraying her. Courtney fought back a tear as she thought of her best friend Nina.

"Everyone makes mistakes," sensing what he was thinking about Nick stopped at the foot of stairs leading to one of the upper balconies. "At some point, maybe... maybe you two can talk it out."

"She chose him over me," Courtney wiped away the tear looking around the room hoping to recognize no one. "More than a dozen years, and she chose him."

"No more of this," Nick took her hand and they made their way up the spiraling stairs. He found a table that had his name on a placard and pulled out a chair for her to sit, and as if perfectly timed, the waitress appeared at the table with their drinks.

"Drink, Court," he smiled, "and let's just enjoy one night out… ok?"

"Hey, Nick!"

Nick waved at someone Courtney couldn't see from behind him. His fingers tightened around her hand and she was suddenly concerned as he topped the staircase and turned in the direction the yell had come from. She nervously followed her eyes constantly moving trying to watch every one at once.

"Courtney," Nick had stepped aside, "I need to introduce you to someone."

Expecting something different, Courtney was shocked when the short white man moved around Nick extending his hand to her. The man looked like a short pimp standing there staring up at her over the large rim of his sunglasses. He was dressed in an all-white seersucker suit with a matching hat and white patent leather shoes, and he undoubtedly thought he had the chest to leave his shirt unbuttoned down to his belt.

"It's a pleasure to finally meet you, Ms. Courtney." She accepted the man's hand and had to choke back a groan as her fingers were locked into his clammy hand. "The name's Jackson Legrange."

"Nice to meet you, Mr. Legrange."

"Please, call me Jackson," the man smiled as Nick pointed him to a chair on the other side of their table.

Courtney stared at Nick unsure of his intentions as the man sat down crossing his legs and getting comfortable. Nick took his own seat and grabbed his glass of Hennessey and took a big swallow hoping that she would calm down a bit and just listen to the man sitting with them.

"I knew your husband," Jackson said over the droning music. "Yea, yea him and Jangles. Hell, at one point I was almost a member of the Nine."

Courtney stared at both men. Her confusion was a little obvious under the flashing lights. "So that's what this was about?"

"Courtney, I needed you two to talk." Nick placed a hand on her knee hoping to calm her.

"You could have just told me," she fought to keep her voice in check, "we could have done this at the house."

"Court, you know my paranoid, OCD tendencies; well, I am constantly having the house checked for bugs. The other day I had Tony and Belize do a routine run through the house and they found a ton of them, and if that wasn't enough; there were several more set up at your office."

"Bugs? I don't understand," Courtney stared at Nick.

"Someone is listening in on your home and office, Ms. Courtney," Jackson explained.

"No," Courtney shook her head. "Wait… I know what the *bugs* are Mr. Lagrange, what I don't understand *is* how they got into my home? I've pretty much not left that house since I was shot."

"I honestly don't know," Nick shook his head. "I'm constantly sweeping the inside and outside of the house, so believe me I'm just as shocked. I don't like thinking this, but I feel that there's someone on my team that I can no longer trust. That's why I got a hold of… Jackson here."

"And," she glanced at Jackson, "what do you have to do with this, Mr. Legrange?"

Jackson leaned back against his chair, lacing his fingers behind his head and puffing out his little chest. His smile made her feel completely uncomfortable, but she knew it was best not to show that to him. Their eyes me and Jackson grinned with a wink of his eye that just seemed completely out of character.

"Ms. Courtney, I deal in large, ordinance weaponry and extremely high end security measures, and like I said. I knew Sydney quite well." Jackson filled his glass. "Two years ago I get a call from my old friend telling me that he's calling in an old marker, but he said I'd have to hold the cash in on that marker until I get another call at an unspecified date and time.

"I got that call yesterday from Mr. Nick," he nodded his head in Nick's direction. "It would seem that you are in need of my help, and because I owe a blood debt to your husband... well, I'm here to pay."

"What kind of help do I need from you, Mr. Legrange?"

"I have already put some things in place, Ma'am," again that smile that almost sent a chill up her spine. "Firstly, we'll deal with your security issues, and that may entail a full replacement of your current staff with my men. Between Nick and I, we feel that someone on your payroll has been paid off to keep tab on you. Your trust has been sold out and well, none of my men can be bought."

"Mercenaries?" she faced the one man she trusted with her life, "Nick, you want to bring mercenaries into my home? Around my daughter? "

"I want to keep you and Sydnee protected," Nick answered. "I promised Mr. Roulette I'd watch after you, Courtney, and after that shot I refused to fail him or you. That means that I'll do whatever is necessary to keep you and that little girl safe. You are my top priority, Courtney."

"No offense," she said to Jackson before staring at Nick, "but do you trust him."

Nick leaned forward in his chair making certain she could see his eyes. "Courtney, right now, I trust no one. Sydney trusted this man, and he told me that if I ever needed the help to protect you that I call him. I am trusting in his honor. I am trusting that he will keep his word to Sydney. I am trusting that he knows that I will kill him if he fucks us over."

"Well said, Mr. Nick," Jackson was grinning, "as long as you understand I do not fear dying."

"It's not your fear I'll savor, Jackson."

"All threats and promises aside," Jackson focused on Courtney over the rim of his shades, "I am truly at your services. Sydney not only called in his marker, but the moment I got my call I also received a payment confirmation to one of my private accounts. My man Sydney was always a stand-up guy.

"Now secondly, once security has been reestablished we will be placing in some precautionary measures to maintain that we're putting in place even after I'm gone; the last thing that you need to feel that you still need to walk around looking around every corner and watching every shadow. Your safety is our primary agenda for as long as you need. "

Courtney stood and walked over to the railing and stared down into the crowd. Her heart was racing as much from anger as it was from fear. For the last two years everything she'd done was to bring IXion Industries into a new era, a newer frame of thought that no longer relied on the illegal attitude it was founded on. No more drugs. No more guns. No more trafficking things that could shut them down and get her tossed beneath a prison until her daughter was almost old. She shook her head and then turned back to the two waiting men.

"Have the bugs you found been removed?" Courtney turned staring at the two men as they waited.

"Not as of yet," Lagrange answered. "My thoughts were to not give away our advantage. Whoever you got in the house watching you has gone through some great lengths to do so quietly for whoever he's working for."

"Good," she said over the music," Do what must be done, but I remain completely in the loop. You and Nick report to me and only me. Start by getting the three of us new phones. If my home has been bugged, I can no longer trust what goes on in there is private. Nick, I need for you to sweep my private office building and make certain it's still clean... if not, find me a new building away from downtown."

"I'll get both taken care of tomorrow," Nick answered.

"When will I expect to see this transition, Mr. Lagrange?"

"Immediately," he answered. "From my assessment, you need me and my people around without hesitation. I know your situation with Jangles, and I know first-hand the kind of snake that he is. Your problem goes deeper, Ms. Courtney, and I need to get in to trace it down."

"When we found the bugs," Nick began, "I first thought Jangles, but this shit was beyond him. I called Jackson because Jangles has either put someone new in play that I know nothing about, or we have ourselves a new enemy."

"Thank you both," Courtney felt defeated but she held her composure. "I believe that whatever it is that you do, Mr. Lagrange is a priority. Get you and your men set up over the course of the next two weeks. Somehow or another I need a private room in my house. Someone went through a great deal of trouble to find out what I'm doing, and I'd hate to disappoint them. Things need to be scripted for those bugged areas, but I need an area where we can talk freely.

"Also, and I'm sure that you both have planned for it, but I just need to say it," she was standing there with her hands at her waist, "bug sweeps need to be done, if not daily, then every other day. I need to know where and how many at all times. I need to get ahead of whoever this is pronto."

"I'm already on it, Ms. Courtney," his smile seemed softer as he pulled away his glasses so she could see his eyes. "No matter what, Ma'am I work for you now and you have my complete loyalty. On my word, I am your man."

"Thank you."

"Well you folks have a groovy night," Jackson Legrange stood and shook Nick's hand. He stepped over to Courtney and took her hand into both of his, "I'm an enigma that they'll never expect. Everything about you from this moment forward has my *Full* attention."

"I'll expect a full report in two weeks, Mr. Lagrange," Courtney smiled as he kissed the back of her hand and then disappeared off into the crowded nightclub.

"Are you all right, Court?"

Courtney had sat down and was staring at her glass. There were times when having a drink reminded her too much of her father. He had always been a hardworking man and had built up his own construction company from the ground up so that he could take care of his family. Her mother would forever say that he was a good husband and father, but her family hid a very dark secret from everyone,

Picking up her glass and swishing around the liquid she watched as it whirlpooled creating a small vortex spinning around. There had been so many arguments that had been heard by her and her brother in the middle of the night, and many of those nights she would end up in her big brother's room crying. Bringing the glass up to her lips and taking a sip she wondered once more if she'd ever go off the deep end. She had once despised him for allowing the alcohol to take over and nearly ruining him, his business, and his family. Her mind swam with thoughts of her father beating her mother and her brother just to vent his frustrations, and she prayed often that she wasn't on the same path.

Courtney shook her head and returned the glass to the table. The music had stopped and the club's MC had stepped up on the stage.

"Courtney?"

"Yes, I'm ok. I guess that until now I hadn't taken any of this serious enough. I'll be honest, Nicky… I really don't know what I'm doing right now."

"All right, all right," the DJ was a local out of Polk County named Netza Rodriguez and he was a fan favorite for his old school attitude towards dj'ing. *"I know why y'all are here tonight; I mean we get crowded here at the Skyy, but damn!"*

Courtney turned in her chair and looked down. From her place on the balcony, even though the railing she had a great view of the big man on the stage. The crowd of people were screaming and clapping as he tried to wave them quiet.

"Listen, I've known this Cat since he was like a youngster," Netza was still trying to calm the crowd, *"and I first met him sitting behind a track board over in Lakeland at the age of like sixteen making it look easy as he recorder this trap rapper. He was literally coaching dude through his session and talking to me at the same time. But, what amazed me more was after that session was done he was basically running in and out of the booth recording his own track. That was the craziest thing.*

"When they locked his lil crazy ass up I just knew that when he got out he was going to take the

world by storm, and he has. From his days in a little studio in Lakeland to him being imprisoned for what has now become a cult classic," Netza began bobbing his head as he adjusted his headphone as he slipped on the track *Kill Me a Cop* to play over the speakers for just a hot second to hype the crowd. *"To him releasing what is bound to become top selling album...*

"Ladies and Gentlemen, I give to you the young Phenom... Straight outta Lakeland, from 'Cross da Bridge... The top soldier of ... SKEEEEEEEEE!"

The crowd reciprocated with the word, *"BWOOOOOOOIIIIII!"*

Courtney stood and returned to the railing. The crowd was now chanting *Skee Bwoi* as a young stepped up on stage. She couldn't help but notice him wearing what looked like a bulletproof vest that had the words *SKEE BWOI* on the front and he was dressed in black pants and boots with his head covered in what looked to be a t-shirt. He was smiling big as he stepped up bopping his head and giving the MC a handshake and hug.

"Ladies and gentlemen, I give to you Antavio Johnson or as you know him."

As he passed the microphone, Antavio took and pressed it to his lips and yelled out, *"Ayyyyyyyyy, T. Oooooooh."* The crowd roared.

"I know him," she whispered.

****

"What are you watching, Babe?" Courtney rounded the corner from the kitchen just as Sydney sat up in his chair staring at the television. The news was on and the anchorman was rambling on with the picture of a smiling young man in jailhouse orange on the screen behind him.

"Shit, I know this young dude," Sydney answered.

"And in Polk County, young urban rapper, Antavio Johnson has been sentenced to two years for his song, *Kill Me a Cop*." the anchorman continued with his report.

Courtney sat down next to him watching his face more than the television, and she could see the concern. She glanced at the young man's face; he was so young, but he had the biggest smile on his face. She sat there wondering if he was really that aloof, or just didn't care about the fact that he was being incarcerated.

"How do you know him?"

"I met him through this young football player I'd met a few years ago," Sydney sat back rubbing his head. "He and his brother opened up this little recording studio and I had a couple of guys running with me that just knew they could blow up. We kept hearing talk about this lil, young ass cat who was a beast behind the mix board, and so we went to Lakeland to see bout him. It was crazy, but the kid was everything they hyped him up to be...

"Shit! We was there the night he put that song together," Sydney started laughing. "That kid was recording and mixing the shit on his own as a room full of us sat there talking shit and watching. He was literally running in and out if the recording booth to the mix board. Damn... I can't believe this shit."

****

"Courtney," Nick was shaking her arm, "you good?"

"I know... him," she was staring down at the stage. "I mean... Sydney knew him. Do you think you can get him up here?"

Nick looked down at the young man and his small entourage. The crowd around the stage was already hyped up and screaming the young man's name as he took the offered microphone. His confidence was quite obvious as he stepped center stage waving and smiling at the chants of the group's calling name. Dog tags hung from a chain that he had draped through the snakebite rings pierced through his bottom lip, and Nick wondered if he'd actually perform with them dangling like that.

"Y'all already know," the beat to his first song drummed through the club's speakers, *"My name is Antavio Johnson... I go by the name T.O and this is my band, Pain Killers n the AM. Now you know me, and you know I like to invite my haters to my show. So if y'all down with that lemme hear ya say SKEE BWOI! SKEE BWOI! SKEW BWOI! AY! T.O... HARITE!"*

Courtney didn't know when she'd made it back to her seat, but she sat there staring into her glass as the young entertainer went through his set. She was amazed at how well he could put on a show; she could imagine her husband sitting here pretending to be cool, but inside he'd be bouncing around like a groupie. The songs were upbeat with a sense of cynicism that would definitely be right up Sydney' alley.

Nick jumped up from his seat and stepped back over to the railing laughing. Courtney looked down just in time to see Antavio dive off the stage and into the crowd. She watched as they tossed him around in a wide circle upon the hands of the crowd over their heads before depositing him back onto the stage. The crowd went wild as he began dancing around once again.

"I'll be right back," Nick tapped her shoulder, "his set should be ending after something like that."

Courtney nodded her head and then waved for one of the deck waitresses to come to the table. She smiled as the young lady addressed her name before asking if she'd like another drink. She wasn't big on the club scene, but Nick found it easier at times for them to conduct some of their business away from her home or the office; she often teased him that his paranoid, OCD tendencies were like his own personal Spidey senses. She now understood that he'd known about the bugs. She found all of this cat and mouse play was more than exhausting.

"What's your name, Sweetheart?"

"Tranique, Ma'am," she sounded a little nervous.

"Tranique, I need two bottles of champagne to start, something top self, ok." Courtney smiled watching as she took her order. "And, you'll have to be mindful of the table to know how many glasses we'll need. Keep us comfortable and you'll have one of the best nights you've ever had. You understand?"

"Yes, Mrs. Roulette," she was excited. "I'll be right back with champagne and ice buckets."

Courtney had always liked Club Skyy because the wait staff was always dressed conservatively but classy. The girls wore black slacks, shoes, and black top vest; the blouse beneath was worn to show cleavage, but not to expose their breasts. They all had their hair either short or pulled away from their faces, and the make-up was applied to enhance their beautiful features.

She smiled, this had been one of the best investments she'd made, and very few people, including those in the Nine, knew of this venture and quite a few others she'd made. The plan for the last two years has been to make all money coming into the IXion coffers legal business transactions, and with the help of Mr. Robles and the guidance of Mr. McGregor that's exactly what she'd been doing. During her financial audits she had pretty much scoured out ever thing that the company had its hands in, but she knew Jangles was still conducting shady things that he'd manager to keep from her.

"All of that shit's coming to an end soon," she mumbled to herself as Tranique returned with two bottles of French champagne in ice and six glasses.

"I'll have more glasses ready in case you need them, Ma'am."

"That's great," Courtney smiled. "You stay close, and I'll have Mr. Styles inform David that I'm retaining your services for the night."

"Thank you, Mrs. Rou..."

"It's, Courtney," she interrupted the girl with a wave if her hand. "And trust me; you don't need to be nervous. I have a feeling it's going to be a really good night for you."

Courtney turned towards the stairs at the sound of laughter just as Nick and a small entourage of men made their way up to the deck. She stood as Nick walked up to her.

"Courtney Roulette, I'd like to introduce to you Antavio Johnson," Nick presented the young man from the stage.

Up close he was a very handsome young man, and his smile was infectious. He held out his hand and she accepted the very gentlemanly shake as they exchanged pleasantries.

"My condolences for Mr. Roulette," Antavio his smile had slipped from his face. "I know that kind of loss... I've lost two of my brothers to violence and it's never easy. Dude was a good man."

She could see why Sydney was so easily drawn to him, and she thanked him and offered her own condolences for his loss. She waved to a seat as Nick held her chair. As they sat, Tranique moved forward popping open the first bottle pouring out the first glasses before rushing off for a few more glasses. Antavio made quick introductions of the men with him as they all grabbed chairs to sit around the table.

"So how long have you been doing this?" she asked over the noise.

"Most of my life," Antavio began, "I've always loved music thanks to my big brother, and before I'd messed up enough that I had to spend two years of my life locked away I actually started this Skee Bwoi movement with my two best friends, we're as close as brothers and they know more about me than anyone."

"Are they here with you?"

"Not at the moment," he dropped his head, "Jayy Flyy, that's Eric, he's in ATL... and my little brother Sean, he was All Starr, well he's one of the two that we lost."

"I'm sorry for bring..."

"Naw," Antavio stopped her and his smile had returned, "we good. While I was away my big brother and my boy CJ, he was CeeLock, really got the movement up and running. When I got out things were rolling, and that's when I really started working with my boy there Dee Curry. CJ is the other one that we lost, but in memory of them we kept moving forward."

"Sydney used to talk about you all of the time," Courtney said her smile also returning.

"I didn't realize it," Nick spoke up, "until T.O. said something, but I'd met him on one of those trips to Lakeland with Sydney. I remember sitting in on one of his recording sessions with another up and coming cat right there from Polk County. "

They sat there for a while enjoying the champagne and a few other drinks that kept Tranique on the run, but the young girl didn't complain a bit. Courtney watched quietly as the men took over the conversation as soon it was bouncing all over the place. Nick and Antavio compared people they had in common, and she recognized that as two men who had come up out of the streets to do better for themselves. She felt a part of it all even though she was silent.

After a while it was just the three of them still sitting there. The music blared in the background, but the crowd was not as loud as it had been. Courtney looked at her watch and shook her head.

"Time can get away from you in a club," Antavio was grinning.

"That's for sure," she smiled as she called Tranique over. "I want you to know that you did a superb job."

Courtney reached into her purse and pulled out a roll of money. She quickly counted off ten one hundred dollar bills and passed them to the astonished girl. Tranique took the money thanking her as she folded the money and pushed it into her bra. They watched as the girl walked away trying not to scream.

"That was generous of you," Antavio sat back in his chair.

"Actually, I gave her exactly what she was worth tonight," Courtney explained. "She did an excellent job keeping up with us, and per my promise to her I paid her for a job very well done."

"Not too many people think that way anymore," Antavio was bobbing his head to the song being played. "I can see why Syd wifed you, Mrs. Roulette, strong women are hard to find these days."

The music was still playing but the volume had been reduced. The crowd below was thinning out as most made their way to the doors to exit the building. Courtney took a sip of her last glass and sat it down on the table.

"I want to make a very sizeable investment in the music industry," she stared across the table. "So my question is, do you think you're ready for a very serious partnership with someone who is willing to play the silent business partner?"

"You're serious... aren't you?"

"Quite serious," she answered. "We'll have to sit down and draw up the papers on all of the particulars, but I want to finance your success."

"Shit, when do you want to meet?"

"Can you be back over tomorrow morning?"

"Most definitely," Antavio answered before reach across the table.

"Then you call Nick and he'll instruct you on how to get to the meeting place."

"That's a deal," he stood and stared into her eyes. "This all on the real... no bullshit?"

Courtney grinned as she too stood. "This is all real," she reassured him. "It's what Sydney would have done, and so this is something that I want to do. Are you sure you want to do this... no bullshit?"

Antavio laughed out as he accepted her hand once more. "No bullshit."

He shook Nick's hand and walked off leaving them watching him leave. She looked over at Nick who was smiling at her and she shrugged her shoulders.

"What are you smiling at?"

"Glad I got you out tonight?"

They laughed as Nick pulled her into the crook of his arm and escorted her down the stairs and towards the exit. They both waved at the excited waitress as Tranique waved goodnight to them.

The late night air was cool but not cold as Nick ushered her into the passenger seat of the SUV and closed her in. She was still not used to the kind of power she held, but moments like tonight with the young entertainer always served to keep her grounded. She'd get with Nick and Robles and they'll sit with Antavio and work out all of the fine details and by the end of it IXion Industries would be working partners with and up and coming music label. She was happy.

"Tonight was a good night," she leaned over and kissed Nick's lips. "Thank you, Nicky; you still know how to make me smile.

She kissed him again and sat back in her seat. Nick stared at her for a second longer before slipping the truck in gear and driving off... his heart was pounding in his chest.

Dammit, he thought in happy silence.

Chapter 2

Jangles stood at the office window looking out over downtown Tampa all lit up for the night. It's always amazed him at how beautiful the city looked and the transition from day to night with all of the streets and buildings lighting up. The flow of traffic always fascinated him at night; there was always the perfect amount light for those fast action camera shots where the front and rear lights would blend together. He smiled down at his city with his hands behind his back.

"Yea, Syd," his smile broadened, "you did good with this one. You's a slick muthafucka giving all this shit to that lil wife of yours, and I'll be damned if that bitch ain't done well by you."

He looked out toward the Raymond James stadium, and it was all lit up with some event being held. It was late and there were fireworks going off over the field exploding in a rainbow of colorful designs. He still felt like a king overlooking his kingdom, but he was in the middle of a civil war that had taken a sharp turn against him.

"Remember boys," Big Fats was always schooling them, *"to always think of your business associates as pieces on your chess board. You have to study where each piece and how it functions... is it one you can sacrifice for the sake of the board... is it a piece you can kill off because it has no more value in the game? You have to be five steps ahead of the one across the board from you."*

Courtney had proven to him that she's willing to play the game on his level; hell, she'd upped the playing field with the gamut she had pulled off leaving him standing around looking like a damn fool. Jangles shook his head as he realized that under different circumstances the two of them may have been... friends maybe even business partners of sorts.

"Yea," he grinned at his reflection in the glass, "I know exactly what kind of a partner I'd be to that ass."

As he stood there, he had a stray thought of his wife, Marilene, and their kids. A few months had passed and with all of the feelers that he had out around the world he still hadn't found them. It was pissing him off that the little bitch had managed to not only get away in the dead of the night, but she was eluding him like a fucking professional had trained her. He'd stopped counting the amount of money; his money, he'd given to Dallas Miller and his bullshit investigators to find her, and now he was trying not to think of just putting Dallas bitch ass in a hole.

There were still nights when he wasn't lying beside Nina that he would actually think of her and the way her skinny ass could take a good dicking; shit, sometimes those thoughts were more than enough to get him excited, and of course Nina's ass was the recipient. He loved the fact that Marilene was willing to be as freaky as he needed or wanted her to be with a bat of an eye, but this fine piece of ass he was doting all over wasn't at all shabby either. Goddamn, the woman could take a pounding and she didn't mind where it was location or her body, she'd go the extra mile.

"Bitches," he mumbled staring at his reflection.

He reached down and adjusted the growing pain building in the crotch of his slacks. Damn, the moment he found her that ass was in more trouble than she could handle. The part that kept him smiling went beyond just destroying Marilene's pussy, no, he was looking forward to watching her squirm and beg and plead before he slit her throat from ear to ear. In his wildest dreams, Jangles would bathe in her blood, but in most cases all he wanted to see was her fucking eyes rolled up in the back of her head just after she'd stopped breathing.

"Your lil scrawny ass second on my fuckin' list," he said his smiling face staring back at him. "There's no way you can continue to run around here with my fucking kids thinking that you're going to live on without me. That's pretty fuckin' presumptuous, even for a stupid bag like you."

"You know, J, they put niggas away for talkin' to themselves like that." JC strolled into the office and stood with his back to the door staring at the man who dreamed of running all of IXion.

"Naw, Dude," Jangles turned grinning, "I'm just thinking out loud, ya dig? Too much shit runnin' through my fuckin' head all at one time."

"I hear you, and I have something for you."

Strolling to his desk, Jangles sat on the edge and pulled a cigarette from behind his ear. He nodded to JC as he lit the tip and took in a deep breath holding it before exhaling the thin cloud of smoke over his head. Sometimes he just needed that burn of a lit Newport, the feeling of letting that menthol just mask the angst for just a moment, but when he got to his ride he'd definitely have to burn a blunt to help him relax for a bit.

"What's good, Nigga," he looked up at the man across the room. "Shit, you staring at me like I'm a fuckin' science experiment of some shit."

"I hired a new tech a few weeks ago," JC began, "I just had a feeling that there was something funky going on with our computers and the security.

This kid is like a super hacker or some shit and I figured we needed somebody here to get our shit right."

"Good lookin' out, JC," Jangles pulled on the cigarette blowing out the smoke after a moment. "I was thinkin' that there had to be some kind of way that I could either find out what that bitch is doing or at least keep tabs on how she's running the goddamn company. Did your lil geek find something?"

"Yea, J, and you ain't gon' like none of it," JC rubbed at his head. "Courtney is blowing out a lot of the big money deals we got set up that keep this fuckin' company up. She's setting up some shit that's going to cut times with a lot of our distributors, and from the way she wants to do it… none of them muthafuckas is gon' like that shit eitha.

"Jangles," JC was staring at the pages of information in his hands not daring to look up into his boss' eyes, "Man, she's got some major deal up her ass 'bout taking IXion completely straight; that shit will hang us all out to dry."

"I'll be goddamn… that's that same bullshit that Sydney was hangin' on," Jangles stood from the desk and stomped across the room. "What the Fuck? How does this keep us in favors with the Mexicans and the Chinese?"

"Not too good," JC stepped up handing him the stack of papers he'd been holding. "With the shit that took place with Manciena and now Uncle Yuen has tightened his ranks… it's like we're out here swimming alone."

Jangles threw the papers and slammed his fist into the wall. All of that same bullshit that Sydney had been yammering on about; forgetting all of the street shit, leaving the drugs and the guns alone and taking the Nine legit… For the last two years this

bitch was undermining everything he'd been putting
in place since he'd finally decided that it was time to
put Sydney out of the Nine. He walked back to the
window and stared out over Tampa.

"Fuckin' Murphy's Law, my Nigga," he said.

"What the hell are you talking about?" JC
had walked over to the bar and had fixed him a
drink.

"Murphy's Law, you know, anything that can
go wrong… will straight up fuck you in the ass
raw." He turned away from the window. "Everything
about this shit with Courtney has gone wrong from
the word go. I never played this shit right and this
girl has gone and got the upper hand on me at almost
every turn. I been at this game for too goddamn long
for some little prissy bitch to come into my house
and take over.

"This shit's got to end, JC, and it's got to end
now. Wake all them muthafuckas up… we're havin'
a meeting this morning. I want them all in here
before nine. Time for a goddamn power move."

"Gotcha."

JC walked out without looking back closing
the door and heading to the elevator. He pulled his
phone from his pocket and punched in a quick
number and placed the phone to his ear… waiting.

"Yea, Nick," he stepped onto the elevator
and waited for the doors to close. "I just left Jangles
and slipped him the info we discussed. This shit is
getting crazy, and I'm just about at the end of it. I
gotta think about my wife and kids, ya know."

"I know, JC," Nick answered. "I'm not much
for this war shit either, but it shouldn't be much
longer. I have some things in place for you and your
family."

"That's just it, Nick," JC's voice was shaky, "I need to get my goddamn family out of here because when Jangles finds out what the fuck is going on around him that nigga is going to fuckin' flip. You hear me?"

"Easy, J," Nick kept his voice steady.

"It's no easy, Nicky," JC was trying not to scream inside of the elevator, "that nigga is losing it and he won't just go after me… he'll go after my people."

"We're going to take care of you. I tell you what; let's get the Alecia and kids away from all of this bullshit that way you can concentrate on the task at hand. We need you… hell, I need you in there because I couldn't live with myself if anything happens to Courtney or Nina."

"This is some dangerous shit, Nick. This is some really crazy ass shit we're trying o pull off."

"Just a little longer, Bro, I swear," Nick said. "Courtney and I appreciate everything that you're doing. Just keep your head above water for a bit longer."

"Shit," JC sighed deeply, "I'll be in touch, Nicky, but please tell Mrs. Roulette that I'd really like for this to come to an end. I don't know how much more of this blood I can take, and I don't know how much longer I can keep Jangles in the dark. This is like grabbing a tiger by the tail and hoping he doesn't turn around."

"I know. Just stay safe."

****

"Okay, this shit's serious," Jangles was walking around the long conference table looking at his remaining troops. It was pretty strange to be in this room and at this table without Sydney and Cheecho sitting there.

"For two years now we have been mourning Sydney's death and not handling business."

"What the fuck you want us to do?" D'Marious glared at Jangles.

"That's just it," Jangles sat at the head of the table, "I don't know. When I've sat back and just gone over things it's like Courtney is five steps ahead of us… ahead of me, and I need to get around this bitch and gain control of this shit. We have lost too many people in all of this and now there's the possibility of some power struggles in the Mexican families."

"What about Chin Ti and Jimmy Q?" Darren asked. "Have we heard shit from either of them?"

"Shit has been too quiet with the Chinese," JC answered. "Right now the shit we're dealing with needs to be some in house cleaning shit. We need to get IXion back on track."

"I agree," Jangles said just staring at each man. "I've been on the phone with these two Aussie muthafuckas and they are wanting to get some shit going with our shipping. I still have to iron out the details, but the overall is going to line our pockets big time."

"Wait," D'Marious pushed back from the table. "What the fuck, Jangles? I don't give a good goddamn about money right now. Look at our Fuckin' table, Nigga. First Sydney to a goddamn car bomb and then Cheecho… who the fuck is next man? We need to get this shit right here straight before we deal with any of that other shit. We got our soldiers dying left and right… What the fuck we gonna do 'bout alla that, Man?"

It was out there. Jangles looked down the table and all he could see was the eyes of his men and there was absolutely no trust. After all of these years of being in the trenches with all of these men, and now they have lost faith in him thanks to a goddamn skirt.

"We're in a war that we weren't expecting, Gentlemen," he smiled. "There's not a one of you sitting here that expected this lil girl to come into our fuckin' home and take over shit like she really owned this. I, for one, had no clue that Courtney had the balls to be the ruthless little bitch she's become, and I'll be honest, Boys… I don't think this shit is over yet."

"She can't be doing this alone," JC said. "So where the hell is she getting the help from. I've had our people look into her fuckin' background and she was born and raised in Missouri to some hokey ass family. This woman ain't got no street in her. I mean yea, she got Nick Styles, but goddamn, he can't be all… can he?"

"What can we hold against her?" EJ asked. "Where the hell is her family? We can take them and force her to step the fuck off."

"Gone," JC said looking down at the stack of papers in front of him. "It's like they just fuckin' disappeared along with Courtney's daughter."

"So, flat out you're saying that we have nothing?" Cody looked around.

"No, Cody," Jangles stood, "I think we have something just important as her family and her daughter. I think that no matter how hard she's trying to act she's still just a fuckin' bitch."

"Spill it, Jangles, because we need a fuckin' plan for real man." J-Groove never really spoke during meetings and his voice was kind of a shock. Everyone turned to stare at him as he pulled the blunt that he'd been chewing on from between his lips and laid it on the table. He was Big Bubs cousin

and was the reason the big man was on Jangles'
security detail.

"I want all of you to remember how messy
this shit can get," Jangles had walked up to the
windows and stared out once more over the city. He
found himself doing this shit way too often, but it
relaxed him. "Before we go any further… are we all
prepared to take this shit back into the streets? Are
we all ready to redeem our places here in the Nine?"

"Let's put this shit to a vote," D'Marious
spoke up.

"Do we really need to, D?" JC asked. "This
is our shit… so what the fuck are we voting on? I
say if we gon' do this… then let's fuckin' do this?"

They each turned and looked at one another,
and Jangles stood there watching as his army once
again all got on the same page. IXion belonged to
the Nine and there were no goddamn women
running the Nine under any circumstance. His smile
returned as he stood there watching them rally
together until they were all looking at him waiting
for him to chime in.

"Our motto has always been… From the
Sandbox to the Lockbox. That's how Sydney and I
started this shit before we ever stepped to Big Fats
back when all of us was running the block and
laying waste to those fools trying to run they shit on
our streets. We have always been there for each
other. We have always been strong and right now
it's time to come back together under the banner of
the Nine.

"This ring," he held his hand up showing off
the gold ring that never came off of his hand, "this
ring is what makes us family. It's time for us to take
back what's ours. It's time to teach this female that

she's never been ready to run with the big boys, and it's time to teach her the hard way."

"Where do we start?" Cody asked.

"JC has found out that she's trying to breakdown the company and take this shit legit. So, first things first, I need to go to Ciudad Juárez, we need to find out where the Mexicans are in this shit now that Cheecho and Manciena are both dead. Next, I need a couple of men put on Nick Styles; he's going to be one of our target because that bitch leans on his ass like a crutch. Don't do shit to him now, because when it happens it's going to be loud, hard and fast and it's going to be something she won't ever forget."

"Yea," Darren was grinning. "See that's my nigga right there. I been told you fools that Jangles ain't lost his fuckin' step. Let's get this shit because I'm tired of this bitch diggin' in my muthafuckin' pockets."

"JC, I need you and J-Groove to catch a flight out to Texas," Jangles kept going.

"What's in Texas?"

"Go to El Cenizo and meet up with this brotha named Big Shaw," Jangles sat back down at the table. "I had him in place with Chino, tell him to get his shit together and come back with you. I need someone here that no one knows for some real wet work type shit. This nigga has no fuckin' soul and loves to torture people… I have a job for him."

"I'll have Janice make us reservations as soon as she gets in."

"Cool, go commercial," Jangles added in. "I don't want this shit showing up on IXion books. Yea, from the shit you told me earlier, I don't need her seeing what I'm doing until this shit is too late."

"I'll get it taken care of, Jangles," JC turned and nodded at J-Groove. "Be prepared to leave as soon as I get the tickets put together."

"I'm always ready, Dude," J-Groove had lit the blunt and was sucking the thick smoke into his lungs. "Let's get this shit done… fo' real doe."

For the first time since Sydney had died in that car bombing Jangles felt like he was in control. He still had to deal with that as well because someone had come along and completely took all of his shine with Sydney's death. He'd put out a few feelers trying to figure out who else had a hit out on his brother besides himself and so far everything had come back empty. All of this shit was like some really fucked up gangster movie, but he had plans to change the plot; he had every intention of getting everything that he rightly deserved.

"This is for IXion," he slammed his hand down on the table. "This shit is for the *NINE*."

All of the men sitting around the large oak table slammed their hands down on the top so that their rings struck the wood.

"*FOR THE NINE.*"

Chapter 3

At one time in her young life, Nina Carlton had once considered herself a very beautiful woman. Being American and Asian, her father had been an African American and her mother was Japanese, she was always a gorgeous mix of the two with her mother's soft almond shaped eyes and a much softer shade of her father's cocoa complexion just lightly watered down. Her long, raven black hair hung down her back, and it had always been soft and silky. Her legs and her eyes were always her two best attributes, but most men never made beyond either her ass or her boobs. Yea, at one time she was very beautiful.

But, she could no longer see that in her.

There were bags under her eyes, and that once seductive look they had was gone. The dark rings made her feel like she was a raccoon, and as swollen as they looked she felt like she'd just stepped out of the ring with Lela Ali. Her once high, perky cheeks now slouched and hung, and ever her color looked mottled. The smile that had always lit up her face and made her eyes dance had vanished. Nothing about the woman she'd been was left, and in her place was just the desolate husk of Nina Carlton.

Staring at the mirror hidden beneath the moisture of steam from her shower, and she dreaded wiping the glass and looking the eyes of the woman she knew waited in the reflection. She wanted to cry as she stood there naked and dripping, but she'd run out of tears leaving her emotionless and empty. Wiping away the mist from the mirror she tried to smile at the image staring back at her.

"Who are you?" Nina asked not expecting an answer. She pulled back her wet hair and studied her face. Her brown eyes held no joy, and she'd always been a happy girl.

"You do realize what you have done?" She could hear her own voice, but it was so distant. A tear formed in the corner of her eye, but she'd almost missed it because of the mist covering the mirror. Shaking her head and grabbing a towel to finally dry off, Nina allows herself to softly sob before stepping out of the bathroom.

Her bedroom was cool from the blowing air conditioner, it was a muggy summer morning, and she still hated the way the temperature could be down here in Florida. She slipped into the t-shirt and panties that was lying on her bed and sat on the edge staring off into space. Her life was completely turned upside down, and she didn't even know where to begin to get it fixed. On her nightstand was a picture of her and Courtney on the day they'd graduated from college and beside that was a picture of her and Jangles when he'd surprised her with a trip to Universal Studios.

"I wish that I could make you understand, Courtney," she'd said this so many times that it had become a staple in her mind. She'd stood in front of her bathroom mirror a million times trying to explain; she'd stared at herself a million time in her car's rearview mirror trying to explain how things had developed between her and Jangles. No matter how it all came out the words were unbelievable and her best friend would not listen to her.

Nina was heartbroken.

"I never meant to fall in love with Jangles," she continued to explain. "It just kind of… happened."

In her mind's eye Courtney's face was just a blank mask, and had become one that Nina no longer recognized. It had been months since she'd even attempting approaching the one person in the whole world she would have never dreamed of losing… especially over a man. Their worlds were now a universe apart and all that she wanted was to just hold her best friend again and try to make everything that she'd fucked up right again.

****

"Maybe you should just go to her and trying talking, Nin," Jangles smiled as they were lying in her bed late last night.

"And say what?"

"What the fuck ever comes to mind," he offered trying to be comforting. "Damn, I've never understood women and this shit… when dudes got something to say we just walk up on our boy and let that shit go. We don't sit around holding on to shit for months on toppa one another until it's just too late to say a goddamn thing."

"What if…" Nina stared into his eyes trying not to get lost in them. "What if she doesn't want to talk to me? "

"Then, Baby, it's her fuckin' loss… ya know. You supposed to be her best friend and that shit means you family. Family ain't supposed to get along all of the fuckin' time but they supposed to be able to come together. If she won't talk to you, well, you say what you gotta say and step on."

Nina pressed her head against Jangles chest and held back her tears once more. He wouldn't understand that Courtney felt that she'd been betrayed because it doesn't matter to him that he'd betrayed the one man he'd grown up with as a brother. Jangles loyalties were only focused upon

Jangles and he was willing to step down on anyone standing in his way.

She'd known that he was a cold and ruthless bastard, but when she was with him he was so different. There was so much more to him than what he'd shown to the rest of the world. How could she explain it to Courtney that Jangles had become more than just a "dick" to her? How could she make her best friend understand that she couldn't help falling in love with the one man that Courtney hated more than anything in her life?

"Nina?" Jangles was sliding his fingers through her hair, "I'm always here for you, Ma. No matter what, you always got Jangles by yo side."

Her mind was being tormented as he spoke. His words to her were always so smooth and they always made her feel as if she was floating in the clouds. She would always wonder if he'd used the same words with his wife to have kept her around for so long. She would always wonder how long it would be before he threw her away like he'd done every other person in his life. She knew it was coming, and when it did…

She would be alone.

She laid there listening to his heart beat away in his chest. It was always so slow and so steady, the light thumping like a song that just never seemed to ever to get excited. He was gentle with her and treated her like she was his queen. There had been so many promises made except for the one she knew he'd never commit to. Her heart was pounding away inside of her own chest as she laid there softly crying just hoping things would get better on their own.

"You need to just go talk to her," Jangles voice slipped past everything she was thinking and became the only thing she cared to hear. "Talk to

Courtney and make her listen to you. You have to get this shit off of your chest, Baby, before it fuckin' burst you wide open. Don't even call her ass… just go see her, you know she won't turn you away, but you're gonna have to make the first move."

"Are you just saying this because you want to know what the fuck she's doing with the company, Jangles?"

"Girl, naw," he laughed. "This is all about you, Nina… On the real, I'm worried about you and if you don't go see her then I'll go see her my damn self. For real."

****

Nina stared over towards her closet. The sun was trying to force its way into her room and that slight bit of light gave her an idea of what she had available to wear. She'd promised Jangles last night that she would go see Courtney today and somehow or another she'd keep that promise.

"Coffee," she said aloud. "I need coffee."

She just up from the bed and walked into the kitchen and began preparing the coffee maker to brew her a pot. She fumbled around trying not to make a mess as her head ran through a number of different things she could begin with, but nothing she thought of seemed the appropriate icebreaker.

"Shit," Jangles was in her head again, "just start with 'Hello, Bitch,' I betcha she laughs and y'all go from there."

"Just say, 'Hello, Bitch' and you really think that will be a good opener after not talking all of this time?" she couldn't help but to laugh at him because he was really trying.

"Damn right… Hello, Bitch," he was laughing as well, "and I betcha she'll be laughing."

Once upon a time Nina wouldn't have doubted that because that was the kind of love she and Courtney had for one another. But now… well, now there was no way she'd step to Courtney so casually. The woman she'd known most of her life was not a very shrewd businesswoman thrown into the middle of a war between two men who were like brothers. Courtney was nowhere near that casual, fun-loving girl from long ago, and Nina was downright afraid to be in the same room with her.

She wanted to scream at Jangles. She wanted to tell him that her loving him had taken away the only other person in this world that she could ever trust. She was alone in this world without Courtney. When her parents had died, not only had Courtney's parent taken her in, but they treated her just like she was their daughter; they'd even helped put her through college with Courtney. Courtney's mom and dad were her mom and dad and Bradley was her big brother, and at this point she couldn't face any of them.

She stood in the kitchen sipping at her first cup of coffee contemplating just leaving everything behind and running off. She had enough money saved up from working for Courtney and the money that Jangles had given her over the last two years that she could disappear much like his wife had done. The coffee was strong and bitter, but it was better than going into her purse and pulling out a cigarette… another of those things that were different about her. She swallowed another bitter mouthful and tried to smile.

"Courtney," she said over the cup, "I'm so sorry… I just need you to, maybe, listen to me for just a minute and then I'll be out of your hair… I just need to talk to you, please. I know you won't understand, but I just need to try to make you understand what happened.

"Please?"

Saying it out loud didn't make it sound any better than it had been sounding in her head. How do you tell your best friend that you fucked up, but you don't know how to get out of it? How do you apologize when they are so convinced that you were involved in a plot to have them killed?

"I know you think that I betrayed you, Babygirl," she was standing there crying, "but I would never do anything to hurt you. I swear that I didn't know what he was up to. I swear, Courtney, I need you to believe me."

She sounded desperate, and she was. When he wasn't around and not talking to her it was like her mind was clearer. Maybe she was just in love with his words and lustfully needed his dick, but there was nothing about the man himself that she could say was a good attribute. It was like being under a spell, and he knew it because he'd used it all against her.

"You know damn well that I love you, Nin," he'd say to her the moment she would voice her concerns. It never failed that he could keep her right under his thumb with just a few words, and the moment he had her emotions docile and under control his words would get into her head and she was doing any and everything that he desired of her.

"I just need to know what time she's going to meet you at the restaurant," he'd said out of the blue as he was talking to someone else on the phone.

"I'm not sure… around eleven if I remember right."

"Cool… got that?"

"Who are you talking to, Jangles?"

"Nothin', Bae," he answered over his shoulder. "This just business."

Nina got up off the sofa and walked off into the kitchen and was pouring a glass of wine when Jangles suddenly seemed aggravated.

"Ok, ok, damn," Jangles was sitting on her sofa on the phone as Nina walked back from the kitchen, "I really don't give a fuck how it happens I just want the shit to happen like yesterday."

"What are you talking about?" Nina was silenced by Jangles raised hand.

"No, Callie, you have my permission to do whatever is necessary but I want it done in the morning when she goes to meet Nina at Mimi's. And, I'm sure there's enough room to conceal yourself across the street, but you'll have to go and scout it for yourself."

He'd paused listening to this other person on the phone for a moment. He was not really looking at her, but she hadn't taken her eyes off of him. That slick smile of his was stretched across his lips and he licked them knowing the effect it would have on her before continuing his conversation.

"Yes, tomorrow morning around 11am, she'll be there with an entourage of muthafuckas standing around her so I need for yo ass to be on your goddamn 'A' game because there won't be no second chances."

Jangles turned staring into her eyes smiling and she shook off everything he'd said to whoever this Callie person was. Why didn't she question him more? He'd asked about her meeting with Courtney, and told this Callie about that meeting, so why didn't she ask more about it? Jangles eased back into the sofa and pulled her into his arms and she laid her head on his chest once again listening to his heart.

Why did she just accept his word that it was *nothing*? She should have known better… this was Jangles, and there was just *nothing* with Jangles. The steady beat was always that one thing that made sense to her about him, and she sighed as his fingers slipped through her hair, his nails gently scratching against her scalp. The world always seemed to stop when she was in his arms, and this time was no different.

She was thinking of how she would explain things to Courtney about her change of heart towards Jangles. She was trying to figure out how she could explain to her best friend that this man that she hated was not the monster she had him pegged to be, but she was afraid that Courtney wouldn't listen to her. Finally, he tossed his phone down on the sofa and she looked up into those eyes that had her mesmerized.

"What are you up to, Jangles?" she whispered into his chest unsure if he'd even heard her. "I thought you said you wasn't going to hurt Courtney."

"You trust me… right? I don't need you losing faith in me now, Nina. We're too goddamn close, Baby, but for this shit to move forward I need her out of my way. I have big plans for this company… for us; I need to know that you're on board with me."

"What are you going to do? You promised me…"

"And I will never break my word to you, Baby," his smile seemed larger as he leaned in and kissed her lips. "I won't do anything more than I said to you… you have my word."

"You're just going to scare her; you're not going to hurt her? Swear to Me, Jangles… please."

“I swear…”

****

“Dammit!” she screamed and threw her cup across the kitchen watching as it shattered against the wall.

How do you tell your best friend that you weren’t thinking with your head? How do you explain that you heard the conversation but didn’t connect the dots until it was too late? That you had an idea about what was going to happen, but you believed the man that you’d fallen in love with because he’d fucking promised that nothing would happen.

“I'm so sorry, Courtney,” she dropped to the kitchen floor crying into her hands.

****

“Excuse me,” the knocking on her window startled her. “Ms. Carlton, are you okay?”

Nina rolled down her window smiling at the armed man standing at her door. She recognized him as she put the gear in park gathering her thoughts trying to remember his name.

“Yes, Adam,” she smiled and brushed a stray piece of hair from her face. “I was just coming by to see Mrs. Roulette… is she in?”

“Yes, Ma’am,” she loved his heavy Southern accent. “Would you like for me to call up to the house and announce you’re coming up?”

“No, please…” she shook her head quickly. “No, I’d just like to go on up to the house if you don’t mind?”

“Go right ahead, Ms. Carlton, I believe that Mr. Styles is watching the door. I'm sure he’ll get you in to see her.”

Putting her car back in gear, Nina made her way up the drive from the gate and parked. She sat there watching as the guards moved around the house and it hurt her that Courtney felt she needed so much protection. She laid her head back against the headrest staring at the front door; all of this was her fault. Her heart was racing and she suddenly felt like she was going to be sick to her stomach.

Why couldn't she think straight around Jangles? Why could she see the truth about him when she didn't have him right in her face, but whenever he was near everything around her including the truth didn't really matter?

"Nothing about you is right for me," she whispered. "Why can't I pry myself away from you?"

You know you love me, Baby. His voice in her head made her entire body tremble.

"Yea," she wiped a tear from her eye. "Yea, and that's the problem. I do love you, Jangles. My life is so fucked up because I love you."

She looked up into the rear view mirror wanting to see the Nina she'd always known, but that woman just wasn't there; the eyes were different, the look, the appearance, there was just nothing about that Nina that stared back. That Nina had ran off and left her standing in the middle of that mansion at that party a couple of months ago. That beautiful gown that Jangles had bought for her to wear and that he'd wanted her to feel like the belle of the ball, but the end results was nowhere near that innocent. Again her stomach felt queasy and she turned away from the mirror staring once more at the door to Courtney's house.

"You look ravishing, Nini," Courtney had whispered into her ear. Her stomach dropped as she turned to see Courtney actually standing there with a

smile on her face and her hands on her hips. *"I'd recognize that ass anywhere."*

"Courtney?" she'd burst into tears wanting to reach out and touch her just to make certain she wasn't staring at a ghost.

"In the flesh," Courtney's smile was radiant and a crowd had gathered around the three of them. She didn't need to look at Jangles to know that he was as shocked to see Courtney as she was, and she could see in Courtney's eyes that she relished the looks on their faces.

"Surprised to see me?"

"I... saw you get shot. I watched you fall," Nina walked up and hugged her friend. *"I don't understand, what happened?"*

"What happened is simple, Nini," she could see something different in Courtney's eyes. *"Someone tried to kill me, but as much it hurts where the bullet struck, what hurts me more is... your part in this."*

"My part?"

"I know, Nina." She'd never seen hatred before, and that look in Courtney's eyes scared her. *"I trusted you and you betrayed me."*

Courtney stepped up and grabbed her face and she leaned in and kissing her lips hard. Nina stared into her best friend's eyes as Courtney smiled at her once more.

"You betrayed me, Nina," she stepped back. *"I would have never turned my back on you... I would have never turned my back on family."*

"Shit," she slammed her fist down on the steering wheel. "Shit. Shit. Shit!"

"Nina?" the sound of Nick's voice drew her to the window as she stared into his soft brown eyes. "Nina, open the window."

Rolling down the window she smiled as she wiped her eyes. "Hey, Nicky."

"You good?" he asked as he placed a hand on her shoulder. "What's going on?"

"I really need to see her," Nina said flatly. "I have to talk to her, Nick. I miss her… I need to make this right."

"I can't make any promises," he smiled opening the door. "Let's go inside and see what she's up to."

Chapter 4

Nathan Robles was a wraith. A ghost. He was the invisible man living so visibly amongst people that he simply... vanished. This had been trained into him so thoroughly that he could do it without thought. He could easily slip from one character and right into a new one within a blink of an eye. Each name carried its own backstory that was so intricately woven that there was no way to discern lies from truth. His every life was a complete fabrication that he has to constantly remind himself of who he really is.

He generally thanks the government for being so forthcoming in making him the chameleon that he is. They started with him at an early age, taking him out of the foster care system at the age of ten and dropping him off into a program designed to create "unknown factors"; a flowery way of training spies from the ground up. Through the years he'd come to find out that he was chosen not only because he exhibited some particular, mental attributes that these spooks found appealing, but also because his aptitude test scores were off the charts.

The training was rigorous in many ways. It was composed of a series of mind games and other physical stimuli to push the overabundance of kids that they'd procured, and the endgame purpose was to see just how many of those kids rose to the challenge and the number that completely washed out. He couldn't remember the names of every kid he'd come across in the program, but there were a lot in the beginning and only and handful near the end.

One of the primary challenges was to become someone else completely. They were taught to build these new characters, to bring them to life, and to make certain that their past life was error proof. They were trained in what paperwork would be needed to leave a proper paper trail that could and most likely would be looked up by anyone of authority. They were trained to be unassuming, how to disappear in a crowd with little to no effort and this became something that he excelled in. It became all too easy for him because he preferred being little more than a shadow. But, what he loved most was his training in computers.

He was like a sponge anytime his trainers sat him down with computer techs, geeks, and hackers. He sat there listening, learning and hanging on their every word picking up small tidbits and expanding on it in ways that amazed his trainers; between the trainers and every book he could find he was becoming an expert. By the time he was fifteen, he'd made it his mission to hack in and leave backdoor keys in every major computer system that he could think of including several major banks, the IRS, and systems like the NSA and even the FBI. For fun he even hacked into the financial systems of the New York Stock Exchange and moved around pennies on the dollar creating a mess that took their experts months to clean up.

For that fiasco he was applauded by his mates and reprimanded by his trainers. His overall punishment was a restriction to any computer for two months, thus leaving him to put his mind elsewhere for a while.

"Boredom can lead a man to do one of two things, Henri," trainer Hadley once told him. "He'll either do things of great use... or, he'll do some very useless things. So tell me, which shall you do?"

As an answer, he spent the next year perfecting his ability to disappear. Not being much for make up or prosthetics, he learned linguistics and languages thereby adapting his mind to assume his personas fluently. His focus became studying people and all of their mannerisms. He worked with a number of people who taught him about makeup and more who trained him in cosmetics applications.

"Always remember," Hadley admonished, "to never get so lost in character that you lose yourself in your character."

They were masterful at what they were doing to all of the kids they had in their charge. The overall idea was to turn these kids into automatons; give them their orders and they'd just mindlessly obey. They were dropped off into hostile situations and it would be left up to them to acclimate to their environment until they were "switched" on to carry out whatever their mission was. Infiltrate, learn their prey, eliminate, and fade away into the crowd. Depending on their skill sets, some were merely in their assignments to watch and observe, others were in place to acquire information, and there were those who had been trained to assassinate. He was trained in linguistics and computers… he was in place to gather information and then get out.

There was just one problem with all of this… they didn't take into account that their brainwashing tactics did not work on all of their subjects, and he did the one thing they never expected. No, he did the one thing that they'd trained him to do… he disappeared. There was no malice, but he was bound and determined to be his own person, and what they were requiring of him and the skills that he'd come to own did not fit into his agenda. He wanted out and to get out he began planning for his escape.

The day of his very first assignment had been set, and the objective was just to see how he would react in a real world situation, and he planned for it accordingly. They had no clue what his true potential was because he'd learned to keep his achievement levels low enough to impress, but the truth of what he could do he kept to himself until he was alone on his assignment. Somewhere in the back of his mind he would always wonder if they were impressed that he was able, and has been able to get away from them and stay away for all of these years; there were even days he would still laugh about it.

"A man's successes are not measured by the perceptions of those around him, Henri," Hedley would stress, *"but more so by the force of how hard a man pushed himself to succeed. Are you going to push yourself to be meager, or shall you be an achiever?"*

How does one explain to your superiors that an entire staff of over qualified professionals was outsmarted by a boy who was not old enough to drink alcohol? That was the thrill of it, to plan it so that they were completely baffled and too embarrassed to even search for him. In the beginning he was a lot more cautious, fearful of being caught and returned or worse… killed, but through the years he'd learned to relax somewhat and just plan out his identities with a number of escape clauses.

Trained to just melt away into any crowd, that's exactly what he'd done only days after being dropped off in Tampa, Florida. It was late summer and the weather was beautiful during the day and rainy late evening into the night. He'd been given a small apartment to live in while he got to know his way around the Ybor City area and all of its top players. His target in the area was a man by the name of Charles Robins, and he was being sent in as accountant trainee. They wanted to know everything that there was to know about this black man who seemed to be quite omnipotent throughout most of the South.

"What's your name, Boy?" the man was large and ominous but his eyes were not mean. He was sitting behind a very large desk and smoking a cigar as the sound of children were screaming and playing in the backyard just beyond the open window behind him.

"It's Henri James Thames," he said explaining that his last name was pronounced Tims.

"Where's your family from, Mr. Thames?"

"I don't know, Mr. Robins," he said, "I grew up in the foster system and so never knew them. I ran away at the age of fifteen and put myself through school."

"A self-made man," the man roared with laughter. "I like that. And you've come to me looking for what, Mr. Thames?"

"A job, Mr. Robins, I could really use a job."

Charles Robins sat back in his chair studying the young man sitting before him marveling at how calm he appeared. Not too many full grown men could sit in front of him and not show an ounce of apprehension, and yet this mousy, slip of a boy was sitting here staring him down without so much as a blink of his eyes.

"Tell me," Charles leaned forward over his desk, "what exactly can you do for me, Mr. Thames."

Henri James Thames proceeded to tell this man, this stranger, everything he'd been through in his young life. He told him of the things that he could do with a computer and why he'd been sent down to Florida. He was open and frank about everything that was expected of him by his superiors, and his plans to escape long before anyone knew he'd disappeared.

"And," Charles pulled his cigar from his mouth, "what name do they believe you're using, Mr. Thames, and am I to assume that this name you've given is not your real name?"

"No, Sir," Henri dropped his head before looking back up, "Thames is my real name… the name that I gave them was Roman Peaksmere."

"Hmm, that's a bit different."

"That it is, Sir, but my history is quite thorough."

"I think I could use a man like you, Mr. Thames," Charles stood from his desk and walked to the window looking out at his children playing. "I'm a man with way too many damn kids and it seems like more just keep coming out of the woodwork. This life is not a simple one of playing gangster like they did when Capone and Segal were running around shooting everyone, and now days with all of these computers and all of this other shit that I don't know or understand I need a better way to … hide things."

"I can put things away in ways that no matter what or who they put on you they will never find anything to link your name to anything illegal. I can go through and eliminate your name from anything that they may be investigating and I can set my systems up so that anytime your name or your organizations are flagged… I will… I mean, you will know."

"I like they way you're talking, Mr. Thames,"
Charles pulled on his cigar and blew the smoke out
over his head. "I need you to put together a business
plan and to make me a list of what you need. I'll put
you an office together; I need you apart and away
from all of my other businesses so that I can keep
you private.

"We have a lot of work to do, my young
friend, and I want you to start as soon as possible."

"I understand, Mr. Robins," he stood
extending his hand over the desk. "I'll have
everything together by tomorrow evening."

"I look forward to our business together,"
Charles stood and shook the younger man's hand.

His last night working for whoever those
monsters were that had been training him seemed so
surreal. Sitting in his little apartment thinking of just
the right way to leave things so that they'd know he
was gone for good. He'd surmised that someone
would come looking for him within forty-eight hours
of him not checking in, but that wasn't good enough
for him. He wanted them to know that he was
tendering his resignation… immediately.

*I can travel from there to here by
disappearing… and I can travel from here to there
by reappearing… What am I?*

They'd never get the meaning behind such a
simple riddle, and even if somehow someone figured
out that the answer was "T" they still wouldn't
understand it. It would give them something to work
on for a few years as they tried to figure out the
cryptic meaning of the riddle and where the hell he
would run off to. This would work in his favor as he
planned to remain in the very last place that they

would look… the very last place they' dropped him off in.

To those he'd lived most of his life with; Roman Peaksmere had just dropped off the face of the planet. There was nothing left in the small apartment that would lend a clue as to where he'd gone truthfully; in fact, what he'd left behind would send on a wild goose chase in both the physical and the virtual world all ending in dead ends of virtual loops meant to keep them searching.

"You've been a very fortunate man," Sydney told him once years after they'd met. "Very fortunate indeed."

"I don't know why I would be considered fortunate, Mr. Roulette."

"When you consider that you've been a ghost of a man for more than twenty years on the run from a government agency who I'm sure would love to get their hands back on you just to find out how you've eluded them all of these years… shit, I'd say that you're very fucking fortunate."

"When you put it that way," Henri shrugged his shoulders, "yes, I guess that you're right."

Sydney Roulette had always been a lot like Mr. Robins, and he'd seen Bobby Johnson enough from a distance that he didn't need to meet the man face to face to know that he didn't like him. Mr. Robins had told him once that Bobby Johnson would be the death of him, but what no one had expected was for the young man to actually kill his mentor. Mr. Robins' death and Sydney getting poison would one day become a topic of conversation that would change the way he and Sydney would do business together.

"Henri," Sydney was sitting at his desk in his upscale condo staring out the window at Tampa. "We've been together a long time, my friend."

"Yes we have," he'd answered. "Mr. Robins figured that we could learn a lot from one another."

"And we have, and that's why you're the one man I know that I can trust above all others, and that includes Bobby."

Henri took a seat across from the man and stared at him staring out of the window. Sydney Roulette was a dapper man; Mr. Robins had taught him to dress and speak so that he could go to any high society function and fit right in. It always amazed him that he and Sydney were a lot alike, and from the moment they were introduced to one another a friendship kindled that has run a lifetime.

"I'm dying, Henri," Sydney just dropped that bomb in his lap and still hadn't turned around.

"Does, Ms. Vaughn know this yet, Sydney?"

It was probably the first time that he'd ever called him by his first name, and he stood, walking to stand with his friend at the window. The city was beautiful that night with the moon hanging in the background like the large eye of a god watching the entire city. The light that was coming through the window was a soft glow that illuminated the darkened room without the need of any artificial lights. The two men stood there neither looking towards the other but sensing the camaraderie from the other.

"No, my friend," Sydney answered. "I've decided to wait until we're well away from here on our honeymoon before I tell her."

"How?" Henri reached out touching his shoulder. "When did you find out?"

"Just recently," Sydney finally looked over at the other man. "I've been poisoned. It's a slow acting poison, but currently there's no cure for it. Ain't that like the greatest thing to know?"

His laughter was more a nervous glitch than a sincere laugh. Henri wanted to do something, or say something to make it better but his mind drew a blank. Sydney was standing there and for the first time he actually paid attention to him. His forehead was covered in sweat and he kept rubbing at his brow with the sleeve of his shirt. His breathing wasn't steady, it was at times rapid and shallow, and as he watched he could see Sydney struggling to draw in the smallest sip of air. For a darker man, his face was pale like he'd seen a ghost, and the bags under his eyes were all swollen.

"How did this happen, Sydney?"

"If I was to place money on it… I'd bet it was Jangles."

"Wait, Mr. Johnson, but why would he?" Henri stared at him confused. "You're his best friend, Sydney… why would he kill you?"

"Stop and think about it, Henri, think about when Charles died. Think about how it happened and how it all came about."

The day that Charles Robins had died he was the one who had to break the news to Mr. Roulette, and that was not something that he was looking forward to. Sydney was devastated and it was a good thing that Mr. Styles was right there for Sydney to lean on.

"Charles was poisoned, Henri," Sydney reminded him. "Some exotic shit that the doctors had no cure for even if they had caught it in time, and that didn't make much sense to me back then… but now a lot of things are making sense to me.

"Look at what we've put together, my friend," Sydney pointed to the *big beer can* building downtown Tampa. "When you think about it, why would Jangles do this shit to his best friend? And I'd answer, to become the king of an empire built upon the blood, sweat and tears of a couple of street kids trained by an old man who was an idealist."

An idealist indeed. That was Mr. Robins in a nutshell, and it became Sydney as well. His idea was forcing a bunch of thugs and gangsters to live under the iron will of a woman, and that woman would head a multi-million dollar industry into a whole new world.

"I have an idea," Sydney laughed at the inane joke, "and I'm going to need you to find someone for me because we'll need him to help us with this. She'll trust him because they have a history together."

"Who is this?"

"You may remember him," Sydney grinned, "he worked for us some years ago. His name is Nicholas St. Cloud."

"Nick Styles?" Henri was astounded. "I thought he was dead. I was sure after that ordeal with Mr. Johnson over that deal with the Haitians… well that he'd bought the farm."

"I'm thinking that he preferred the prison sentence over the death sentence, and the moment I found him I made certain that his time inside was short and safe.

"Like I said… we need him."

"I'll find him and bring him to you."

Henri James Thames was a ghost of a man. He was a wraith. A man who knew how to disappear into the crowd of man. He'd made a living making Sydney Roulette a very rich, a very powerful and influential, and a very well informed man amongst the gangsters and businessmen he had an inclination to work with.

He sat at the desk he had in the home he shared with the character Robles' "family" staring at the number he had waiting to dial out on his cell phone. He hated his job sometimes because he hated giving up information he was always ready to find. Grabbing the phone, he pressed the green dial button and he sat there waiting.

"I hate to call at such a late hour, Sir," Henri's tone was quite nonchalant, "but, we have a serious situation concerning Mr. Styles that you may want to address… Soon."

"Damn, why am I not surprised? I should have known better than to put his ass with her. Keep an eye on things, Henri, I'll be home soon."

Chapter 5

Courtney stretched out over the bed staring at Nick's back. It was a vivid display of tattoo art running from his neck to the top of his belt line depicting the anger and struggles of a young man, the ying/yang of a Chinese dragon and tiger emblazoned in color. She'd traced her fingers over each line and memorized each picture and the stories behind them all, including those that were about her. He'd definitely grown up since their previous time together and that runaway stint to California. Standing before her now was a more confident man than that scared kid trying not to get killed over a drug deal gone very wrong.

"I can feel you staring at me, Courtney," Nick was hanging up his clothes in the closet they shared. "I know you're not happy about earlier today, but it was something that needed to happen."

Courtney sat up on the bed pushing her back into the pillows against the headboard. Her mind was at odds with how her morning had begun, and hearing Nick saying that it needed to happen just didn't make her feel any better about the turn of events. Crossing her legs she just stared at him as he continued to undress and hang up his clothes.

"Well?" Nick glanced at her over his shoulder.

"I'm really not sure what you want to hear, Nick," she answered.

"You and Nina have been friends for a very long time, Courtney," Nick walked over and sat on the edge of the bed. "She's lost and she needs her best friend. Didn't you see her today?"

"Yes, I saw her," Courtney's voice wasn't hard or bitter at this point, but after Nina had left earlier today her demeanor was something quite different towards Nick. She was angry and felt that the both of them had been conspiring against her with Nina's appearance and Nick not sending her away.

"We're in the middle of things here, Nick," she tried explaining, "and right now… well, I don't need my head all up in the air dealing with Nina and what ever she's going through."

"That's just it, Courtney," Nick turned towards the bed staring into her eyes, "she is in the middle of this shit; hell Court, she is the middle of this shit because we put her there. From the moment Sydney recognized that Jangles had eyes for her, we began using her."

"So it doesn't matter that she volunteered?" Courtney rolled her eyes.

"Goddammit, Courtney Vaughn, this is not you," Nick couldn't help yelling before choking back on his words. "You're not this fucking cold, Courtney. This is not you."

Courtney dropped her head and ran her fingers through her hair before leaning back once more against the headboard. Memories of her and Nina ran through her head and she fought the tears that threatened to run down her cheeks. They'd been friends for forever and without admitting it to Nicholas, she felt empty without her Nini. Over the last few months all she wanted to do was pick up the

phone and just talk to her, but she'd stopped herself
because there was no getting past one simple fact.

"No, you're right, Nick," she whispered, "this
isn't me, but Nina knew; she knew what he was
planning and she didn't even try to warn me. What
would have happened if we hadn't had her condo
wired and heard that conversation? What would have
happen if I'd had Sydnee with me?

"How do I get past that, Nick? How do I
forgive that?" she was openly crying.

Nick moved up to the head of the bed and
pulled her into his arms and held her. He'd almost
lost Courtney that day; he could still see her getting
struck in the chest and being thrown back against the
car. He could still hear Nina screaming, and him
kneeling down beside her playing his part in yet
another melodrama set up by a Roulette.

"Fuck," he sighed.

****

"Nick," Sydney stood walking out to meet
him with his hand held out, "thanks for coming to
see me."

"I'll be honest, Mr. Roulette," very few
things made Nicholas St. Cloud nervous, but this
man always did, "I was surprised to hear from you."

"No need to be so nervous Nicky Styles, shit,
I remember you from the old days, Man, we got a lot
of history. I know about everything that happened,"
Sydney ushered him to a seat in front of his desk.
"Please, have a seat and I'll explain everything."

They were in Sydney's office away from
IXion in a random building that Nick didn't know
anything about, and from the looks of it, he was

pretty sure that that bastard Jangles Johnson didn't know anything about it either. It was pretty plan, but the building housed several other offices that were all filled with a number of different businesses, and some of them Nick had heard of over the years. Leave it to Sydney Roulette to be a supporter of startup companies.

"To start, Nick, I want to apologize on behalf of IXion, we take care of our own, and you are a part of us. It took a lot of work and time, but I know that you were set up by Jangles in that bullshit those years ago. I couldn't do much about it before now because I needed his hand to be played out, but I had some people in place to keep you safe and out of trouble while you were inside and I tried to keep your books up for you. I want you to know that kept an eye on your moms and that brother and sister of yours."

"Thank you, Mr. Roulette… I guess." Nick looked around expecting some of Sydney's goons to storm out and beat the living shit out of him.

"We're alone," Sydney assured him. "It's just you and I… I needed you to be comfortable because I have something really big to ask of you."

"Mr. Roulette," Nick moved to get up, "I'm not sure what the hell is going on, but please can we get this over with?"

"I'm marrying Courtney, Nick," Sydney dropped it like a bomb in the other man's lap. "She doesn't know yet that you're back home, but when she finds out she's going to want to see you. Before that happens I needed to talk to you. Some things are coming down the pike, Nick, and at some point

Courtney is going to come to you for your help, and I'm going to need you to accept her offer."

"Help? What kind of help? What the hell is going on?"

"Nick, there's no easy way to put this; I'm dying," Sydney sat back and watched the number of expressions that ran across the man's face. "Jangles is trying to kill me."

"What kind of bullshit is this?" Nick snatched up the paper that Sydney slid across the desk and stared at it for a moment before looking back up at the man across the desk from him. He read it again and then laid it back down the desk.

"Is that… real?" he asked Sydney.

"Very… I'm not even sure when it all began or how he slipped that shit by me," Sydney laughed. "But this is not the end. It's just the beginning. I want you to meet someone."

Nick watched as a very slender, white man walked into the room. The man was tall and pale with his stringy hair combed back away from his face. He was dressed in a very well-tailored suit that accentuated his very non-muscular body. In the back of his mind all he could think of was putting a stove pipe hat on this dude and calling his ass Abe Lincoln.

"Nick, this is Henri Thames," Nick stood and shook the offered hand. "He's been with me for a very long time, and Jangles knows nothing about him. I have a lot of shit planned, but in order for any of it to fall through I need to know I have people that I can trust. Can I trust you, Nicholas? Courtney is going to need you."

"For Courtney," Nick repeated, "yes, Mr. Roulette you can trust me. What do you need me to do?"

"Welcome aboard," Sydney sat back in his chair smiling."

****

"I never really had anyone I could call a friend," Nick was stroking her forehead. "My brother and I only had each other and I pretty much raised him because my mom was barely ever home. My sister lived with my grannie because my mom just couldn't handle three kids at one time. Mom's was working two jobs and I never knew who the hell my dad was so it was just me and Tony."

"I guess that's why you never talked about your dad," Courtney said.

"Yea, it was just one of those things I never bring up," Nick sighed. "Courtney, Nina needs you. She's dying inside and it took a lot for her to come here. She's afraid of you, and more she's afraid that you're going to try and kill her."

"I wouldn't kill her," Courtney's voice was barely heard.

"She doesn't know that, Courtney. All she knows is that you think she was a part of the plot to have you killed. You need to figure something out because the two of you are not the same without one another."

"What do you want me to do?" Courtney's face softened and her eyes drooped sadly.

"Talk to her. I don't expect anything from you, but I really think you need to talk to her. Listen to her because she really needs to get this shit off of her soul. All of this business with you, her, and Jangles is eating her alive. She's your best friend… give her that."

Courtney sat up off Nick's chest and stared at him. He was so different than the man she'd run off such a long time ago. There was a lot more to him now, but there was still something she could just feel that he was hiding from her. The hardest thing she'd done was bringing Nick back into her life, and now she'd dropped all of her walls with him again allowing him to share her bed. Leaning in she kissed his lips and then slipped from the bed. Walking to the dresser she picked up her phone and fingered through the numbers until she came upon Nina's.

Her eyes never left Nick's as she waited for an answer on the other end of the line.

"Hello," Nina's voice was tentative.

"Hey, Nini," Courtney smiled at saying her pet name for her best friend, "I'm sorry for calling so late but… we need to talk."

"Now?"

"No, Baby girl. How about breakfast tomorrow morning? Are you busy?"

"You want to meet at Mimi's?"

"That's perfect… let's say around ten?"

She smiled at Nick as he lay on the bed with his arms crossed over his broad chest. He was grinning like a Cheshire cat as he watched the quick phone conversation. Just the look in his eyes let her know he felt as if he'd accomplished something great, but she was not so sure how things would turn out in the morning.

"You need to come here," he said after she hung up and laid the phone on top of her purse.

"Do I really?"

Nick held a hand out for her and sat there waiting. Courtney was such a beautiful woman in anything she wore, but the little sheer nightgown that barely made it past her behind never failed to excite him. He watched as she sashayed across the room and back to the bed.

"And what is it that you want of me, Mr. St. Cloud?"

"I guess that's something that you'll have to bring that pretty ass over to me to find out."

She turned to the side just out of his reach and looked back at him, "Do you really believe that my ass is pretty?"

"In more ways than you'd believe," Nick leaned out and grabbed her and pulled her to the bed laughing as she squealed out.

Rolling her over and pressing her gently into the bed, Nick leaned down staring into her soft brown eyes until their lips met. He'd never found a woman whose kiss ever excited him as much as Courtney; her lips still held on to the innocence he'd always found in her even with all of the craziness she's seen and been through in the last couple of years. As her eyes closed, he could only imagine what could be running through her head, but his own mind was filled with the fact that her body was wrapped around his own.

Her legs laced around the small of his back just above his hips and her fingers were stroking the back of his neck and down the ridges of his spine.

His fingers were holding her face as he deepened their kiss and his tongue slipped beyond her lips and into her mouth. The sound of her moaning was like a bell in his head and he eased more of his body down upon hers. He could feel her breasts flattening behind his broad chest and her nipples were poking at him through the thin gown material. Her body was on fire stroking his own heat as she began to grind up against him.

His lips released hers and he kissed his way to her ear and then the crook of her neck. The lingering taste of her body wash from her shower earlier teased his lips and tongue. He licked his way back up her neck to her ear sucking on the lobe as a purring growl rattled in her throat. Her fingernails were lightly scratching at his neck as he began his trek lower down her body. Her chest was rising and falling quickly and she loosened her legs as he eased down her chest with more licks and kisses until he reached her breast. Licking her through the gown was nothing more than a tease but the moment he sucked down on her nipple he was sure she was going to scream.

Prolonging this method of pleasing her was the only thing that kept his hands from ripping away the gown and apologizing later with a promise to buy her another one just like it. His lips captured her nipple as his hand found and teased her other nipple. Her back arched offering him more of her hidden flesh as he bit down gently and stroked her nipple with the tip of his tongue. He pinched her other nipple and gave it a gentle twist and grinned as she pushed up harder against his pelvis grinding against what he had waiting there for her.

Courtney had her eyes closed as tight as she could. Her mind was exploding into a million fragments as Nick's mouth tempted and teased her. He always knew how to build her up and hold her there until he was ready to push her over the edge; this was one of those things that never left her mind and her body remembered it all like it was yesterday. Her legs held him in place between them as he began to move up and down against the boiling volcano that she held at bay. She wanted to call out his name, but her lips wouldn't move as she held on to the back of his head as he moved from one nipple to the other biting and licking and sucking.

If her eyes hadn't been closed, they would have rolled back into her head as she waited for the next move. His body was smooth and hard all at the same time as the muscles in his back rippled each time he'd leave one nipple to go to the other. She sucked in a deep breath when his fingers began pulling up the hem of her gown, and she bit down on her bottom lip the moment her breasts were exposed and his mouth covered one sucking and licking her heated flesh. The cool air on her near naked body caused her to shiver just a bit but was quickly forgotten when Nick kissed his way down her belly and slipped his tongue into her bellybutton.

"You've always had a way of… killing me," she moaned out as she reached down pushing on his head.

Her legs fell away from his body and his hands were pushing on her thighs to spread them open more. The heat that had been building between her thighs rushed out to meet him as he pushed his face between her spread legs. He could feel the muscles in her thighs quivering as he began to have his way with her through the near nonexistent material of her panties. His tongue was moving all over as she pushed harder on the back of his head and grind up against his face.

Nick slipped his thumbs into the waistband and pulled. The material strained for a moment before ripping apart and he pulled them out of the way tossing what was left across the room. He pushed his face forward and she wrapped her legs around the back of his head locking him in place. She screamed out as she felt his tongue split her open and work its way into her yielding body, her back arched and she thrust crushing his mouth against her.

Her body was losing this battle of passion as Nick's tongue worked to complete his mission to destroy her mind and body. With one hand she was digging her nails into the back of his head, and the other was pulling at her nipple adding to the extreme sensations her body was already experiencing. He bit down on her clitoris and she came up off the bed, her legs tightened around his head and her head rolled back into the pillows as he pressed on.

She was so close… so close that she was seeing stars floating around the room behind her closed eye lids. Her breathing was ragged and burning in her lungs as she cried out over and over. She shook as his tongue pressed back up in her moving in and out at a pace she couldn't quite match at the moment. His head was thrashing as he fed on her body like a man devouring his last meal.

"NOW!" she shrieked out as her orgasm slammed into her body with the force of a tidal wave against the shoreline. Her fingers clutched and pulled at the sheets on the bed as a spasm ran the length of her body and ending with her curling her toes. Her legs dropped away from his neck and he pushed them up at the back of her thighs so that his mouth wouldn't lose contact.

The lights exploding in her head was too much for her to take. Her body had finally become that volcano and she was molting all over this man's beautiful face. Every muscle in her body seized and relaxed and contracted and released as her mind sought the words to beg him to stop. Her breathing was stuck in her throat as her mouth opened into one final silent scream before she slumped down into the bed pushing at his head.

"There's nothing more beautiful in the world than seeing you like this right now," Nick was licking his lips as he sat back on his legs.

Courtney could feel his eyes looking all over every inch of her body like it was the first time he'd ever seen it, but there was absolutely no way she could open her eyes right now. She could feel the bed shifting again and he was moving back over her body as she concentrated on trying to collect her thoughts and slow her breathing. He was easing between her splayed legs and kissing softly on her lips.

"You sure have a way about you, Mr. Styles."

"The night's just beginning, Ms. Roulette."

Chapter 6

Dr. Carol Anne Rosenthal was not at all what most would expect as a doctor. Her long red hair hung loose down her back in wavy curls piled upon one another covering her pristine, white lab coat. Her face was pale, freckled and quite pretty, but it was a little over done with the make she wore taking away from her "professional" look somewhat. Her attire made things worse; the top was at least one size too small hugging her recently augmented breasts and pushing them up and out ridiculously, and her skirt hit just above mid-thigh and she had to pull it down every other step because it rode up her thighs. She was the talk of her office and could be hear clopping down the hall in her four to six-inch stiletto heels which were so inappropriate for a medical office.

She wasn't one to defend her attire or what people thought about her. She never let any of it bother her, her husband paid good money for her boobs because he wanted her to have them, and he loved her dressing sexy... everywhere. She stopped at the door to her next patient and pulled her file to read through it briefly before going in. Nina Carleton was one of her regulars, but her blood work revealed something she hadn't expected to see. Nina was one of her more "careful" girls, but it looked as if this time she'd been caught. Dr. Rosenthal took a deep breath and called for one of her M. A's to verify that all of the recent records were in her file before knocking on the door.

"Come in," Nina answered from the other side.

"Hello again, Nina, it's good to see you,"
Rosenthal liked being formal with her patients. She
stepped into the room with a big smile watching as
the other woman paced. "So, how are you today?"

Nina paused and faced the doctor. She felt a
little better than she had been since Courtney
actually called and said that she wanted to see her.
Her stomach had already been doing flip flops, but
this morning things had gotten worse. This morning
Jangles had found her on the floor in front of the
toilet vomiting like a binge freak coke head trying
going clean. She'd never been this sick, and the one
thing that she was afraid of was that she may be...

"Shit... you're smiling," she'd just noticed the
doctor's rosy grin. "I'm... not... I mean... am I?"

"If you mean pregnant?" Dr. Rosenthal had
sat on her little stool watching as Nina stumbled over
her words. "Yes, my dear, you are very much
pregnant, and before you ask, we ran the test twice
to be certain. We're estimating about ten weeks..."

Everything else said Nina hadn't heard. Her
mind was in a tailspin from just the fact that she was
pregnant. Pregnant. The word repeated itself on a
continuous loop rattling around inside of her head
making her sick to her stomach. She couldn't be.
She'd been extremely careful; for that matter, Jangles
had been extremely careful because of shit with his
wife. Nine sat down in the examination table, dizzy
and trying to catch her breath. She wasn't ready to be
no mom... she wasn't ready for no kids.

Shit... what would Courtney think?

"This can't be... happening," Nina stammered
as the tears rolled from her eyes. She slumped her
shoulders and covered her face crying into her
hands. She wanted to scream. Her stomach turned
and her heart ached as she sat wondering if and

when or how she'd tell Jangles. The very last thing she'd ever wanted to deal with in her life at this time was now the one thing she had to somehow include in her life.

"Dammit," she stood and began dressing no longer paying attention to anything that her doctor was telling her. Snatching up her purse and shoes, Nina fled the examination room and ran from the building to her car. Opening the door she dropped into the driver's seat and slammed her head against the steering wheel as she screamed out in anguish, anger and horror at her newest dilemma.

Wiping her eyes, Nina reached into her purse and pulled out her cell phone and dialed Courtney's number. She held the phone to her ear praying that last night's call to her hadn't been some kind of cruel dream because right now... she really needed her best friend. She found a napkin and wiped her eyes and her nose just as Courtney answered.

"Hey, Nini."

"Hey, Babygirl," she failed miserably in trying to make her voice sound normal.

"Nina? What's wrong?"

"Courtney," Nina cleared her voice, "are we still meeting at Mimi's this morning?"

"Of course. Do you need to cancel?"

"No... God... no. I, um, I really need you, Babygirl."

"Tell you what," she could hear Courtney shuffling around on the other side of the phone, and then yelling at someone, "it's a little early so why don't we just meet there now and grab us some pancakes. I've been feenin' some pancakes for a while now."

"That sounds great. I'll meet you in say... 30?"

"See you then."

Nina hung up the phone and took a deep breath. She sat back in the car seat and looked down at her belly touching it tentatively as if fearful that it would suddenly reach out and grab her. As much as she loved the monster she was involved with, she didn't know if she was ready to start a family with Bobby Johnson. She wasn't certain she could settle down and accept him as Marilene had accepted him, there was just too much baggage to go along with him as the man that he was. She gently rubbed her belly trying to accept the baby now growing there. Her heart was slowly warming to the fact that she would be a mommy, but her head...

That was another story.

She sniffled as her thoughts tripped over Bobby. He was so unconcerned about her, and he'd proven it on a number of occasions. She'd just refused to open her eyes to see it. How could she have missed it? Was her nose that wide open? Was she truly that far up his ass that she was falling for his bullshit left and right? She shook her head as that day Courtney was shot flooded her thoughts, and the tears flooded her eyes once more.

****

Jangles was being an ass, and it was really pissing her off. He'd pretty much demanded to come by her home because he needed to be with her, but they'd been sitting there for about an hour with him just staring at the walls. From the expression on his face his day had been just as bad as hers if not worse. She'd tried talking to him and telling him everything that had been said between she and Courtney; right down to Courtney even threatening to kill her, but Jangles was off in his own world.

She wiped her nose with a tissue and tried to not cry anymore without being successful. Her eyes were red and blotchy and her voice was this high pitch whining that just seemed to bounce around inside of her own head. She wanted him to say something to her, or maybe pull her into his arms and tell her that everything would be ok. She wanted him to pay her some kind of attention, but the bastard didn't even seem to know that she was still in the room.

She sat there trying to block out Courtney telling her that if she ever saw her again that she would kill her; never in all of her life would she'd have ever expected to hear those words uttered from the lips of a woman she saw as her sister and the only family that she had. No matter what she did the words echoed louder and louder in her head, and Jangles was so wrapped in himself that he wasn't paying her any attention. He'd stood and was pacing the room mumbling and staring at his phone as if he was expecting a call.

"Fuck, fuck, fuck," he grumbled shoving his phone back into his pocket after the call he'd made went unanswered. "I guess your bitch ass is dead, Callie."

She stared at him for a moment more letting the words Courtney roll through her head slower. It was all right there in his eyes and she knew it, but refused to believe it. Wiping her eyes, she turned towards him and placed her feet up on the sofa.

"You did this… didn't you?" She could hear her voice; it was like a faint echo somewhere in a small corner of his mind. "Jangles, you set it up for her to be killed didn't you? I thought you were just going to scare her… you were only supposed to scare her."

"I don't have time for you and your shit right now, Nina," he turned and glared at her. "I have so much shit going on right now that you're little sensitive ass bullshit… I don't fuckin' need to deal with."

"Deal with… Why you Son-of-a-bitch!" she'd stood faster than he was ready and was standing in front of him with her fists clenched. Jangles stared down at her as if to dare her to …

"Fuck you, Jangles," Nina swung and struck his face. "Fuck you and whatever bullshit you think is more important than me. I've lost my best friend because of you, you fucking bastard. I've lost Courtney because I fell in love with you… and now…"

Before she could finish her mouthful she was struck so hard that she fell backwards to the floor sliding to stop feet away from him. She was a crumpled mess on the floor crying hysterically and holding her face. Her hair was a mess and strewn all over her face as she looked up at him.

"I hate you, you Bobby," she hissed. "I hate you."

****

"Nina?" Gentle fingers were tapping on her shoulder, but her mind was elsewhere.

Courtney stood there staring at Nina staring off into space. This was the first time she'd taken in how Nina really look, and Nick was right... her best friend did not look like herself. Her naturally straight and glossy hair looked dry and unwashed pulled back into a wispy ponytail dropping down the back of her head. She was wearing makeup, but it was barely applied and did not accentuate her natural beauty. She was dressed in a pair of baggy sweats and a large t-shirt knotted over her bellybutton. She was not her normal flirty self, and this worried her.

"Nina, are you ok?"

"Why?"

"Why what, Hon?"

Nina looked at her for a moment and then her gaze drifted past her once more.

"Nini," Courtney took her face gently in her hands to pulling her to look at her. "Talk to me, Nina, please… Tell me what's wrong?"

"Why did you say yes to see me, Courtney? Why did you agree to meet with me?"

Courtney turned and looked where Nina had been staring and it all rushed back on her for the very first time. No matter how much she'd gone through everything the night before, nothing could prepare her for what was about to happen the moment she stepped up out of that car. Her chest was heavy not only from the weight of the bulletproof jacket Nick had her wearing, but more from her nerves being completely jacked up and she felt like she couldn't breathe. With each breath her lungs hurt, and she was scared out of her mind that this Callie would go for her head and not her heart.

"According to everything that I was able to dig up…damn, I didn't mean. From everything that I could compile on this Callie that Jangles is using," Tytus stood nervously holding out a folder full of papers, *"she loves to go for the heart. Not to get too technical, Mrs. Roulette, this chick loves using high powered rifles and from what I've learned about her… she a dead on shot."*

"So what are we going to do?"

"All I have is this," he handed Nick the bulletproof vest. *"I've reinforced the area around the heart with a piece of five inch thick steel plating.*

Never in her life had she expected to feel anything as painful as the force of being shot. The moment she stepped up out of the limousine door she held her breath. They were not sure exactly where the shot would come from, but they were almost positive that it would be a shot from the front. She took one more moment to get her head right for this performance, but nothing could prepare of for what was about to happen.

Somewhere in the back of her mind she was sure that she heard the gunfire, but that was impossible because of the amount of traffic flying by on Dale Mabry. The pain started in her chest just to the right of her left breast and it ran the full length of her entire body too fast to for her mind to fathom. Her body froze and her fingers gripped the top of the car's window frame trying to keep her from falling back. She'd been holding her breath, but at the moment of contact every ounce of air in her lungs was forced out. Courtney felt her knees give. Her fingers weakened and she fell away from the car in such a dramatic fashion that it all felt like time had slowed down. She wanted to scream, but that was cut off from her head hitting the asphalt parking lot knocking her out.

"I don't understand why you would agree to come here," Nina's eyes were soaked with her tears as Courtney turned back to her. "I'm so sorry, Courtney, I don't know how to say it enough. I was stupid. I was so stupid. I was so stupid to have believed a word that Jangles was saying to me. Oh god, I need you to forgive me. Can you ever forgive me?"

Courtney took Nina into her arms and held her. She was holding back her own tears as her friend slumped against her sobbing. All of the memories she'd been trying to bury of the two of them together flooded her mind and the weight of the anger she'd been holding on to suddenly just relaxed. Her hand stroked Nina's head as she tried to calm her best friend; the woman she'd always known as her sister... tried to let her know that everything was going to be all right.

"Nini, look at me," she whispered in her ear. "Look at me."

Nina pulled away from Courtney's shoulder and looked into the woman's eyes. She was afraid of what she would see as the threat of killing her filled the corners of her mind, but Courtney's eyes were soft and the smile on her lips was the most welcoming sight that Nina had seen in what felt like forever.

"Nini, we'll fix this," she consoled the distraught woman. "We'll fix all of this... I promise."

"I don't want you to hate me anymore, Courtney," Nina replied.

"I don't hate you," Courtney smiled. "I don't think I've ever hated you. I put you in the middle of all of this shit. I was just ... hurt, but everything is fixable. We'll fix this and everything will be ok... Ok?"

"Ok," Nina answered wiping her eyes and nose. "But..."

"But?"

"Courtney," Nina dropped her head, "I don't even know where the hell to begin. All of this shit is so crazy, and everything has just gotten completely out of hand."

"Just tell me," Courtney was still holding her hand. "It's you and me against the world, Nini, it will always be me and you. I promise."

"I've been feeling sick," Nina brushed the loose strand of hair from her face, "really sick, and he found me this morning hugging the toilet and made me swear I'd see my doctor this morning. I did."

"And," Courtney placed a finger under Nina's chin raising her face to look into her eyes. She already knew the answer, but she needed Nina to see that she wasn't going to leave her stranded again. "What did your doctor say?"

"Courtney, I'm pregnant," Nina choked out the words and quickly began crying. Her heart sunk as she waited for her best friend to pull away from her as if she were diseased. Her body trembled and shook, and she felt her stomach getting queasy from the anticipation of rejection that never came. Slowly, Nina looked up and their eyes met.

"I'm going to be an Auntie?" Courtney was a little too excited. "That means Sydnee will have a little cousin to grow up with. Oh, Nini… this is so exciting. We need to get the hell out of here."

Courtney jumped up from the table grabbing her hand. Her eyes were sparkling and her smile lit up her face as she pulled Nina into her arms holding her tightly. For the first time in months something beautiful had dropped into their laps, and even though she was sure Bobby Johnson was the father, her best friend was having a baby, and Courtney couldn't be happier. Now, it was up to her to help Nina find her way back to the girl they'd both known; she wanted her best friend back. "I think

what this calls for is a girls' day on the town… what
do you think?"

"I think that I could really use a girls' day out
on the town," Nina smiled and then wrapped her
arms around Courtney's neck again. "I love you,
Courtney… please don't ever doubt that."

"I know, Nini," Courtney returned the hug.
"And I love you too… you're always my sister."

****

"What the fuck you mean they're together?"
Jangles yelled into his phone. He was racing through
the morning streets headed towards the airport and
the construction on interstate 275 was pissing him
off.

"I'm sitting here watching them, J," the voice
on the phone answered. "Nina had been standing in
front of the restaurant gazing off into lala land until
Courtney showed up. They stood there talking, went
inside for a bit and came back out hugging and
smiling and shit. Now they are getting into
Courtney's car.

"What do you want me to do?"

"Keep a fuckin' eye on them two bitches…
Shit!" Jangles stomped on the gas pushing the large
Hummer through the traffic until he just barely
missed the bumper of some little car ahead of him.
He stomped the brake just enough to keep from
going over the top of the car from the trunk forward
and swerved into the next open lane.

"I'm on my fuckin' way to the airport… you
call JC ass, tell him that I need his ass to get to
Texas pronto and get that shit there handled."

"I gotcha, Jangles."

Tossing the phone in the passenger seat,
Jangles turned up the radio and again stomped on the
gas. He didn't know the rapper that well, but he

bopped his head angrily to Kevin Gates' song, *Believe in Me,* as his turn off onto Highway 60 came up.

"Me taking the background, I was thugging hard... big rod... jumping out of cars, " he was keeping in tune rapping hard as he cut across a river of vehicles. He was feeling bold as he flipped his turn signal and began to make his move over. The music was pumping through the speakers surrounding him in the truck as he glanced up into the rear view and switched lanes again. *"Never gave a name up... murder gang... I am Louie banged up... But I move those thangs. I don't gang banging... Fuck the game up... Passing in the bottom... Everybody hollering... They say Jangles you came up..."*

Jangles cut his wheel slicing through traffic onto the off ramp following the overhead signs towards Tampa International; too much shit to be done. There was entirely too much shit going on and now he was losing his people left and right. He reached into the ashtray and pulled out the blunt and lit it taking a big pull and holding it deep in his lungs.

"Fuckin' women are going to be the fuckin' death of me," he grumbled slowly releasing the smoke. "Goddammit, I need some shit to go fuckin' right for a change."

A car's horn had him looking up into the rear view once more as he cut off a car and the driver had his arm out the window flipping him off. His lip rolled up at the corner as he considered slamming on his breaks just to fuck with the man, but decided he needed to get to his plane. Rolling down his window he returned the gesture with a smile and sped off onto the merge ramp heading towards the airport not giving the idiot a second thought.

His phone rang and he picked it up looking at the screen. Turning down his music he hit the talk button he gave his usual "Yea" and waited for the response on the other end.

"Good morning, Mr. Johnson," it was Janice from the office. "I got the messages from JC about your trip to Mexico, and I've made certain that the August was contacted as you instructed and he's confirmed that the plane will be prepped and ready by the time you get there."

"Good, Janice," he answered. "I need you to get in touch with Quan Tiuan, you'll find him under Jimmy Q in my Outlook. See if he's busy and if not ask him to meet me at the airport, I have August wait if need be. Apologize to him for this being done under such short notice, but that it's important that we meet. Call me back once you confirm."

"Yes, Sir," Janice answered. "I've found his number... I'll call him right away."

"Alright," he said as he hung up the phone. "Time to up the ante just a bit more, Courtney. I've let your ass get away with way too fuckin' much. It's time to end this shit and end it now."

As he was pulling into the private parking to meet his plane, his phone rang again. "What did he say, Janice?"

"He says it will take him about thirty minutes to get there, Mr. Johnson."

"Call the pilot and tell him about the adjustments to the schedule. I'm pulling up to the parking now so I'll be at the plane shortly. I have a few more calls to make before I walk back that way."

"Yes, Sir."

Sitting in his truck with the music turned down low, Jangles stared out over the airport watching a plane landing. His mind was a million miles away as he tried to figure out exactly what he needed to say to Jimmy Q. His alliances were running thin, and he figured that the young Chinese upstart would be willing to get his hands a little dirty… for a price.

The last few months had pretty much wiped the smile from his face and all he could see was blood and fire. He hadn't figure that Courtney would be able to deal the kind of blows to him and his ego as she had and this flight to Ciudad Juárez to speak with Manciena's people was just what he needed to clear his head; or, it would get his head blown off his shoulders.

If Sydney was alive right now he would probably kill him with his bare hands. How could he introduce this female into their business? Why the fuck would he even get his wife involved in…

"Goddamn, you muthafucka," he slammed his fist down on the dashboard. "You knew didn't you? That's why you did all of this shit. That's why you fucked me over like this… You fucking knew."

All of this was making sense now. He remembered the way that Courtney was staring at him that day he picked them up from returning early from their honeymoon. Sydney had told him it was because he'd become sick, but now that he sat thinking about it… as he was gloating because he could see that the poison was working just as it had on Big Fats, what he should have been realizing was that his secret was no longer a secret.

"You set me up," he said. "You took all of that bullshit that Fats told us and you fucking used it all against me, and I was too fucking blind to see it.

Goddamn… that was a slick move, you son-of-a-bitch. It's all about the chess game, right, Syd? It's all about being 5 moves ahead of your opponent, and you trained that little bitch well."

Rubbing his hands together Jangles now felt his confidence coming back. He definitely needed this trip now because his head was clearing and he was beginning to see the road ahead of him again. It was time to get all of his ducks in a row and it was time to get all of these fucking women out of his life. He was going to take his company back… he was going to take his town back… he was going to show his best friend that he truly was the better man.

"You did good, Syd," he grinned, "but you fucked up, Bruh. Yea, you fucked up big time, Nigga… you fuckin' left her alone. I mean who the fuck is Nicky Styles?"

Jangles sat there laughing and staring at himself in the rear view mirror. "There's just one more thing I need to figure out…

"Who the fuck else wanted yo' black ass dead? Who did you fuck over, Syd?"

That was still haunting him. The poison he'd been giving him was meant to take time. He had a sadistic fondness of watching his best friend slowly getting sicker and sicker by the day as the poison was eating him up from the inside. He wanted Sydney to suffer because that's what he'd been doing all of these years following him and Big Fats around like a little lost puppy begging for the scraps. The two of them treated him like he couldn't think for himself, or like he wasn't smart enough to do anything more than run drugs on some fucking street corner while standing there with his dick in his hand. He wanted to show them both, and up until that truck exploded… he was the man.

For the last two years he'd been combing through all of Sydney's papers at the office. He'd had Janice call in a moving crew to bring up files that he knew Sydney kept locked in an old storage building across town, and he'd gone through everything with a fine tooth comb finding nothing. The answer had to be there, and when he returned from Ciudad Juárez he would start over and he would find the answer.

"This shit ain't over just yet, Brotha," he winked at himself in the mirror before getting out and making the walk to where the IXion private jet was housed.

****

"Hello, Mr. Styles," Janice was looking around and whispering to make certain that she wasn't overheard. Every time she made these calls her head hurt.

"Do you have something for me, Janice?"

"Yes, Sir," she answered. "Mr. Johnson is headed to the airport to take the private plane to Ciudad Juárez to meet with members of the Manciena family. Also, I just got off the phone with a man named Jimmy Q and he will be flying down with him."

"Damn," Nick sighed deep. "Anything else?"

"One other thing, but I'm really not sure what he's doing," Janice took a deep breath and looked around once more before continuing. "I had to get some people to retrieve some files from one of Mr. Roulette's personal storage containers."

"When was this?"

"Earlier this week is when they began bringing all of the boxes here."

"I'm not sure what he's up to either," he paused for a moment. "You keep your eyes open and your head low. All of this is just about over and like I promised you… I'll take care of you for everything you've done for us."

"Yes, Sir." Janice hung up the phone and looked around one last time. Her heart was pounding away inside of her chest and she was sweating like she'd just ran a mile, but she was pretty sure that she was alone in the office. She took a deep breath and then a drink of the glass of water she had on her desk.

I am not cut out for all of this cloak and dagger, spy bullshit… she thought to herself.

She laughed out nervously before getting back to work wondering what else she could go through working for all of these monsters.

Chapter 7

When he was younger, Nick used to love jumping on his bike and riding over to Lakeland… to him that town was always so much quieter than the routine hustle of the Tampa streets. Even though he'd had his fair share of run ins with a few of the street knuckleheads roaming around in the dark, he'd always had a good time just being away from the big city. Lakeland had grown up a bit since the last time he'd actually visited, and it was pretty nice riding around traipsing down memory lane.

He'd driven over on his bike and had had a chance to ride around for a while before he had to be at Jackson Lagrange's home for a meeting that the man had called for. Even though there were a lot of things different about the little town that he remembered, there were still far too many things that hadn't changed at all. Cruising around on Tenth Street he'd passed by an old girlfriend's home and was not in the least surprised to see her ass still right there and surrounded by a handful of kids he was sure were hers. He shook his head when she stopped braiding one of the little girl's hair and stared as he rode by.

Laughing, he kept moving hoping that she hadn't recognized him. The pipes of his bike echoed off of the sides of the houses as he sped through the different neighborhoods just taking in the sights. For Nick it was like revisiting a mistress that you hadn't gotten within a very long time, but nothing between the two of you had changed; she'd welcomed him back with open arms. Pulling out on Kathleen he turned towards downtown, but he didn't get too far as he did a quick U-turn and pulled into Country

Chicken & Fish to enjoy some chicken he hadn't had since before he ran off to California. He sat at one of the benches under the trees smiling for the first time in a long time.

Sitting there eating his phone rang and he cursed. "What's going on, Double C?"

"I'm not sure, Nick," he man answered, "but if I heard shit right… you may have a tail on you."

"Interesting," Nick licked his fingers. "Where did you come by this?"

"JC called me into his office this morning. He's being sent out to Texas and Jangles is headed down to Ciudad Juárez with fuckin' quid, Jimmy Q, to see if any of Blanco-Muerto is still around, and I can only imagine what the fuck else they gon' be talking about. It's getting really crazy, Nicky, really crazy…"

"Yea, I know, Cone, but I need you to hang in just a little longer." Nick began looking around. "You wouldn't happen to know what the fuck they're in would you… because my smart ass decided that the day was too fucking beautiful not to be out on my bike."

"Not a clue, Nick," Cone said, "but there's going to be at least two of them."

"Nah, dealing with Jangles there will be no less than three… the driver and two shooters, and they'll be in something big body. If nothing else the man is very predictable."

"Shit. All I can say is watch yo' ass, Bruh, it's like the fucking wild, wild west in Jangles in head. Shit's about to pick up, Nick, and you are definitely in the cross hairs. Jangles feels that if he can get rid of you that Mrs. Roulette will be on her own and she'll finally back down and give him back IXion."

"Right, right." Nick packed up what was left of his food and looked around for a trash can. He grimaced a bit as he looked out at his bike sitting out in the sun, and he couldn't stop looking around to see if there were any cars that just seemed out of place.

"Fuck it," he sucked his teeth. "I'm good. I got my piece on me so if anybody rolls up on me the wrong way they better be ready. Thanks for the head's up, Coni Cone. I'll have to get some extra people on Courtney's ass without her realizing it."

"Good luck with that one. Jus' keep yo' head on the swivel, my nigga, 'cus them fools out there for ya."

"Yea… no doubt." He hung up on the call and made a quick call to Lagrange letting him know he would be a little early.

"Shit," he mumbled to himself, "you've never played by anyone's rules before… why make today any different?"

Nick stepped out of the shadows of the trees and threw his leg over the motorcycle's seat and sat down. He made a big play of looking for his keys and pushing his jacket open so that the handle of the pistol he was carrying in the shoulder harness readily was seen. After getting the bike started and sitting there revving the motor he kicked up the stand and balanced it beneath him while putting on his sunglasses. All of this he was doing while nonchalantly looking around. With no more concerns he pushed off and sped off to meet this man that Sydney had entrusted his wife to.

****

"Aye, yo, JC," JC had his phone on speaker while he walked about his bedroom trying to pack his things for the trip to Texas, "we trailed his ass to

Lakeland and right now he just rollin' around. You want us to do this shit now, or wha'?"

"Jangles wants this shit to be as loud as possible, OB," JC answered. "Give him some time and see what the fuck he's up to… this may be some shit I can use later, ya dig?"

"Cool… we gon' let him ride 'round a bit more and see if he lights up someplace and then we gon' eat. If Jangles wants loud I say we pop his ass on the I-Fo' headed back to TPA."

"Good… yea that sounds real good. Just keep Junior ass on a tight leash and tell Mill that he needs to get that drop box back here and burnt before One Time can sniff it out."

"I hear ya," OB answered. "I'll get back atcha when we at da crib."

JC hung up and called his man Coni Cone to get a message to Nick Styles about the men tailing him. This double agent thing was wearing thin on him and had him wondering just how much more he could do before Jangles caught on to what was going on around him. He wiped the cool bead of sweat from his forehead.

He stood in his bedroom explaining everything he knew at this point that was important so that Coni could get that information to Nick, but somehow he'd forgot to give him the names. The airplane meeting between Jangles and Jimmy Q was nothing short of trouble and for that shit to be nipped in the bud it would eventually mean Courtney would have to have her own meeting with Uncle Yuen once more. There was entirely too much shit happening all at one time and IXion was right in the middle with no closure on this shit in sight.

"Yo, JC," Coni's voice was thick with concern, "what do you know about this dude, Big Shaw?"

"Look, Cone," he said standing at the bedroom window looking down on his empty backyard and missing his kids, "let Nick know that shit is about to get really crazy and from the looks of it… man, none of us are going to walk away from this shit unscathed."

"I hear you, JC," Cone replied. "I'll be honest, Bruh… all of this shit's got me scared beyond words; I mean, all a nigga wanna do is make a little music but all of this crazy shit gots my ass crawling the walls. This is getting me in way deeper than I'd planned."

"Yea, you and me both. I'm just glad I got my family away from here before all of this shit blew back into the fan."

"Yea, no doubt. Yo, be safe out there in Texas."

JC hung up and resumed packing. He had no clue about this Big Shaw character, this was the first he'd ever heard of him, but from the sounds of it he was not someone he wanted to be around for long periods of time. He'd have to see what other information he could find out about this dude so he could get it back to Nick and Courtney before he got back to Tampa.

I'm just not cut out for all of this James Bond bullshit, he thought to himself.

****

Nick stared at Jackson Lagrange and shook his head; even at home this dude dressed like something out of an old, bad movie. He wanted to laugh but he needed the man to stay on top of his game and sitting here laughing and ridiculing the man would not put them at a great starting point. Lagrange had been tapping away nonstop for the first twenty minutes since he'd arrived.

"Jackson," he called out. "What the hell's going on?"

The tap-tap-tapping of the keyboard was beginning to grate on him like someone walking up to a chalkboard and scratching their fingernails across it. He understood that the man was good at whatever the fuck it was that he did, but having him sit there like a student waiting for the principal to finally look up was not boding well for him. He was half tempted to just get up and go slap the man across the back of his head, but he crossed his legs and looked around the very modest home.

"I really need you to say something, Man," Nick popped his knuckles. "This shit is driving me stir crazy and I need to get back to Tampa."

"Just one more moment," Jackson replied. "Almost… there."

"I'm done with waiting," Nick responded. "I have shit that has to be done, and I need to know what this shit is about."

"I've had my people inside your boy, Jangles', house and there's some shit going on that you need to be aware of. I'd say that he's about to pull off some really big things here in the near future. I just got a report that he's on his way to Mexico."

"Yea, he's out to see the remainder of Blanco-Muerto."

"It would appear that you have people on this shit as well," Lagrange grinned.

"I've been at this for a little while now and I kinda know what to expect."

"He's also meeting with the Chinese mafia; did you know that?" Legrange felt as if he were competing with Nick's network.

"Yea, but it's not really the mafia… he's meeting with Jimmy Q and he's the youngest nephew of Uncle Yuen, but here's the thing… we have a relationship with the Uncle. Jimmy tried to have him killed once before and well, Courtney interceded. So he kinda owes us at this point."

"You'll want to set that meeting up with Yuen really soon. The bugs in the house have been moved around, it would seem that whoever is doing this is trying to keep tabs on everything Mrs. Roulette is doing and saying. But, my problem is that they are not hiding them in places where it would be hard to find them. So this morning I set up some nanny cams all over the place to see what we can see."

"This shit with the bugs is weird," Nick sat up in the chair he was in staring at the man across the desk from him. "Are they spying for Jangles?"

"I'm really thinking that they are spying for someone else, Mr. Nick."

"Like… who?"

"See, here's the thing," the man sat back in his reclining desk chair smiling, "I do this shit for a living, Mr. Nick, and I know two things that are facts right now… One, Sydney Roulette is Not dead… and Two, you and Mrs. Roulette are in a relationship. So here's my question to you…

"Did you already know that he's alive, and if so… why are you fucking his wife?"

"Well technically," Mr. Lagrange, "they are no longer married; Sydney supposedly died in an explosion and therefore in her eyes, she's a free woman. It was his choice to make her think what she thinks."

"So you do know he's alive?" Lagrange cocked an eyebrow.

"What's going on between Courtney and I is no one's business," Nick was trying to remain calm, but this man was implying exactly what he'd been thinking for the longest. Sydney was not the kind of man you toyed with, and if it was him trying to find out what was going on inside of the house then the shit was definitely about to hit the fan. He couldn't afford a war on two fronts, and the last thing he needed was Sydney gunning for him when he knew he had Jangles to deal with.

"I'm not trying to get into your business," Lagrange said, "but I need for you to be honest with me. I don't work for Mr. Roulette; I work for you and the Mrs. at this point. I don't report to anyone but her and you no matter who pays the bill. As far as I'm concerned, Sydney Roulette died in that explosion after he'd got word to me to protect his wife."

Nick stared at the man trying to discern the truth in his words, and could find no faults with the man. He had very little trust for anyone, and with all of the shit that he's been dealing with concerning Mr. McGregor he knew that at some point in time it would become known that he knew who this man truly was. The question now was how would this all come to light.

"Courtney and I had a past long before I knew Sydney or Jangles," Nick began. "Sydney knew this before she introduced the two of us together; I'd a meeting with him and Robles, and well I knew what Jangles was scheming, and what Sydney had in mind to fuck him over. I can't say

119

that I'm proud of my part in this whole thing, but I never imagined that all of those old feelings would return…

I love her, Mr. Lagrange," Nick stated flatly. "I always have and I always will and I'll do anything to protect her from anything that will do her any kind of harm… including Sydney Roulette."

Lagrange nodded his head and then turned his laptop around so that Nick could see the screen. Nick sat there watching as one of his men, Davey Sims, moved about the living room pulling out the small listening devices he'd placed around the room and then rearranging them in different parts of the room.

"I take it that you know this one… right?"

"Yes, I hired him myself…" Nick could feel his blood boiling. "Why is he doing it?"

"Damn good question." Lagrange stood and walked over to the small bar in his office and poured him a drink. "So how do you want me to handle this?"

"You don't," Nick answered. "I'll deal with this one myself."

"I was rather hoping that would be your answer."

"And why is that?"

"I really need to see what kind of man I'm working with," Lagrange grinned. "Just that simple."

"I guess I'll do my best not to disappoint." Nick almost laughed. "I need to know… do you have men nearby because I got a call before coming here and it would seem that Jangles has a few men tailing me."

"I'm sure I can help you with that," Lagrange's smile broadened and Nick could tell that the man was a little too excited. "Where do you think they'll try to hit you?"

"All of Jangles people think they're gangsters and watch too many goddamn movies… so they'll go after me on I-4. They'll think it will make a bigger scene so that's what they'll wait for. It doesn't help that I'm on my goddamn bike today."

Lagrange picked up his cell phone and made a quick call. Again Nick took note of how excited the man sounded at the prospect of being a part of something that had to potential of becoming dangerous, not only for him, but all of the people that would be making their way back towards Tampa along with him. He simply shook his head as Lagrange hung up his phone and stared at him.

"Everything is set," he was grinning like a Cheshire cat. "We're ready whenever you are. My men will be in a dark Suburban… we'll watch your back from a distance and the moment they make a move… we'll be all over them."

"Will you be there as well?"

"Oh, I shall definitely be there, Mr. Nick," Jackson Lagrange was all smiles. "I wouldn't miss this for the world."

****

Nick was wiping the Gold Wing Valkyrie through traffic recklessly. He was weaving through the cars in ways he hadn't done since he was a kid flying through the streets on his Ninja. He loved the hard rumble of bike beneath him and the roar of the modified mufflers each time he accelerated to thread his way between the closely packed vehicles. The big Valkyrie was well tuned, purred like a big jungle cat; he'd been working on this motorcycle since he'd got home from prison. After thousands of dollars and thousands of hours of work and modifications there was no way he was going to just let a car full of assholes roll up on him without them earning it.

Nick kept his eyes moving. The traffic was flying by at a breakneck speed, but he was vigilant of every vehicle, or so he thought. The pistol inside his jacket was tapping at his ribs thanks to the wind, and his mind was prepared for anything; it's amazing the shit you get used to when you walk into a war with your eyes open. Jangles never did shit half-assed; if Coni said they'd been sent, he knew they were out there… it was just a matter of when they'd attack.

He'd noticed several large, dark colored SUVs driving by and each one he'd look at expecting some signal that they were Lagrange's men, but they'd keep driving without taking any notice of him at all. He ducked down letting the wind skate across his head and shoulder blades as he revved up and breezed off trying to get back to Tampa with little to no incidents. He'd always felt free in the wind like this, but today… the wind was not his friend.

"Aye, yo, Nigga," the voice seemed to barely reach him over the whistling wind, but he looked over just in time to see a man sticking his arm out of the window of the big body Chrysler 300. "Rememba me, you, sombitch?"

"Fuck…" Nick popped the break watching as the car flew by him; he dropped gears, skirted lanes to the left, and raced off gunning the motorcycle's engine hard. "Too goddamn close."

Bullets whipped and whizzed by his ears as he sped past the car and off into the thicket of traffic. Once again Nick found himself whipping the bike between cars, going from lane to lane and dodging bullets. He was ignoring horning being blown as he maneuvered to keep the 300 at least two or three cars behind him, but the man driving was not to be denied; he was a damn good driver.

He kept his eyes forward only taking quick glances into his mirrors watching for the lights of the car, but they were blending in with every other set of lights behind him. A spark from the window of one car caught his attention just as he dipped back to the left between a set of cars, and he knew now what car to keep an eye on.

The traffic was getting thick just past Plant City and close to Thonotosassa and the 300 was keeping up a little too close for his comfort. Another round of bullets whizzed by Nick's ear causing him to flinch and he almost lost control of the bike, but he steadied her out and dropped back over to the right and then right back up into the middle of traffic before the car could readjust to keep up.

Nick could feel his heart in his throat as he tried to clear his head enough to think. There were entirely too many goddamn cars around for him to get around and those to idiots were shooting without a care who was hit. He'd already seen two cars veer off from to avoid being hit by the bullets and there'd been at least two accidents caused by the shooters.

"Shit," he mumbled as he pulled up in front of a semi and eased off the throttle just a bit waiting to see the car go past. Pulling his pistol and leaning over the handle bars he took off after them as they zipped past him. "Damn good plan, Styles, a pistol versus fucking assault rifles."

Just as he took aim a large, black Suburban pulled up beside him and the passenger side windows rolled down and two men held what looked like AR-15s out of the windows. Nick returned his attention to the 300 and fired off the twelve shots that he had in his gun just as the men in the truck opened fire on the car as well. All hell broke loose when the car began weaving all over the road as it was riddled with bullets from both sides.

Nick saw Macintosh Road coming up and he stuffed his pistol away, this would be his escape. The 300 began careening into a number of cars as the men in the Suburban continued firing. Nick slammed on his breaks bringing the big bike to a stop, and watched as the trucked pushed into the driver's side of the car. The bullets never stopped. He could see the men in the car being jostled around like ragdolls as the large truck moved them around as it felt until the car was scrapping the guardrail. Nick watched in horror as Lagrange's man pulled away from the car and the two shooters opened fired in a big way on the car.

Riddled with bullets the driver and two shooters in the car were now slumped in their seats as the car's wheels hit the shoulder sending the vehicle sailing into the air flipping. Rolling into the roadside ditch the car finally came to a stop smoking with its wheels spinning. Nick shook his head as he heard the sound of sirens coming from both directions on I-4. Not stopping to see what else happened he took off down the ramp and off onto Macintosh without looking back… he would have to call Lagrange and thank him later.
"Fuck you, Jangles," he was pissed. "Your ass is mine, you, son-of-a-bitch."

Chapter 8

Nina almost resembled the Nina Carlton she'd always known, sitting on the sofa with her feet curled under her and a smile on her beautiful face. Her face was again beautiful and not quite the emaciated form of itself that she'd looked upon earlier today. Her eyes were bright and smiling and there were no large bags under them. Her make-up was done properly and accentuated the beautiful features of her long face that was once again framed by her illustriously silky, raven black hair. She felt as if she was glowing.

It had been a good day for the two ladies as Courtney had driven them from Mimi's hours ago and they'd gone and done some shopping at the Westshore Mall and then taken in a day at a small, exclusive spa that Courtney was able to get them into with only a call.

"Greetings Ladies, welcome to The Shangri La day spa," the young lady greeting them as they walked in had a beautiful smile.

"Hey, Keva," Courtney walked up giving her the customary hug and European kisses to the cheeks. "This is my girlfriend, Nina, and we're in need of one of your *Tranquility* treatments each."

"I figured as much when you called," Keva was already walking them through towards a room she'd had set up. "I'll have two of my girls come in for your massages, just pick out your aromatherapy oils and undress. Your robes are there on the tables."

"Thanks, Keva, you're a doll." Courtney was all smiles as she moved towards her table to grab her robe.

"It's been so long since I've been to a spa," Nina grinned, "I don't even know how to act."

"Well strip and enjoy," Courtney joked as they both disappeared behind the changing partitions.

The spa day had done wonders for the both of them with the ladies there giving them both massages and facials that were clearly needed. Kinks and tight muscles that they didn't realize they'd had been worked out, and the oils just seemed to work its way into their souls to completely relax them both. After the facials they'd gone and sat in a sauna for a while just laughing and talking about nothing in particular just like they normally would. For Courtney it was good to not only hear her friend's voice, but to see and hear her laughing.

The sauna ended and they were ushered into a small room that was soaking in the smells of aromatherapy fragrances peppermints and eucalyptus that they were promised would relax them more. There were two glasses of a light, crisp white wine and a tray of cheeses and grapes for them to enjoy as they continued their sauna banter. A young lady came in and checked on them twice, filling their glasses while she was in there, and then they were left alone for more than an hour before being ushered into the room where there was a bubbling hot tub waiting for each of them.

Neither being ashamed of their bodies being naked in front of the other, they dropped their robes and eased into the tubs. The attendants poured bath salts and then a capful of a fragrant oil into the water before leaving the two of them to soak with the sounds of jazz gently filling the room over the gurgling bubbles. For the first time in a while they were both quiet, but both wondering what the other was thinking.

Courtney had so many questions for Nina, but feared running her friend away for sounding callous and uncaring. She wanted to take back that threat against Nina's life, but a part of her wondered just how truthful was she being. She slipped her arms into the water and holding her breath as she slowly moved beneath the surface. The heat and bubbles were just what she'd needed to ease away the last of the tension she'd been under for far too long. As she came back up and taking a deep breath, she looked over at Nina.

"Damn," Nina giggled, "been practicing holding your breath long?"

"What?" Courtney laughed.

"You were under there for a quite a while," Nina replied wiping a wet strand of hair from her face.

"Well remember I was on the swimming team," Courtney stuck her tongue out at her friend. It had been far too long since they'd been this close with one another, and she'd missed it more than she wanted to admit. But, she was still quite tentative.

"Oh I remember," Nina winked, "but I'm thinking you've been practicing something else to be able to hold your breath like that."

"Why you little slut," they both laughed as Nina slipped down into the water and came up a few moments later.

Two attendants returned with two fresh robes and two new glasses of wine. "Your stylist is ready for you both, Mrs. Roulette, if you ladies are ready?"

"I'm ready if you're ready?" Nina smiled.

They stood as the two women walked up with the two fresh and warm, terry cloth robes.

Bundled up they followed the attendants into another part of the building where a host of women were all sitting around being worked on by a number of different stylists and nail technicians. The Attendants lead them to two empty chairs.

"How's everything so far, Ladies?" Keva had walked up.

"Excellent," they both commented almost in unison.

"I haven't had this much fun in a very long time," Nina said as she sat down with her appointed stylist. "How long have you been here?"

"For about two years now," Keva answered after thinking for a second, and then she quickly went into telling Nina how she got the spa started. She and Courtney traded parts of the tale since IXion had actually invested in the company, and Courtney was a bit of a silent partner.

"You've been busy," Nina smiled at Courtney as Keva walked off to talk with some of her other guests.

"Yea," Courtney sat back in her chair to let her stylist take care of her hair, "just a bit, but I can say this… I'm so glad that you're back with me, Nini, I've missed you these last few months."

"I've missed you to, Babygirl."

The day had been really good for the both of them, and now they were sitting at Courtney's home feeling beyond relaxed and enjoying a light meal that Courtney had one of the security men run out and get for them. Nina was talking, but they were both dancing around what really needed to be discussed. Another bottle of wine was being enjoyed; this one was a Moscato, which Courtney knew Nina favored. The sun could be seen setting just beyond a grove of trees, and the fact that they'd spent the entire day together hadn't dawned on them until that moment.

"You should ask," Nina said out the blue.

"Ask… what?"

"I know you Courtney Marie," Nina glanced up smiling. "Probably better than most, and I know you're holding on to something you want to ask. It's like that time you thought I was messing around Jimmy Patton in middle school… you remember that?"

Courtney laughed out as she sat her plate on the coffee table. "I do remember that. I think that's when I started calling you a slut."

"Damn," Nina sat there stroking her chin as if thinking, "you're right."

They were laughing and joking and that was a good thing.

"I'm ready," Nina placed her plate on the table as well. "We have to do this. You know I'm right."

"To be honest, Nini," Courtney stared into her brown eyes, "I don't know how."

"These past few months have been the hardest I've ever been through, Courtney, and I don't even know where to begin myself. But, I don't want to be without you any longer than I have already… so, please, just ask me?"

"Okay," Courtney took a deep breath and then dropped her head. "Why him over me, Nina? I think that's what I don't understand most."

"Yea, I don't understand that either," Nina slipped her foot from her body and slid closer to Courtney. "We always promised one another that no man could ever come between the two of us, and I completely fucked that up. I wish I could say it was just that the dick was THAT good… I mean, shit it was good."

"You're such a slut," Courtney laughed.

"I honestly think that it was because of you and Sydney," Nina explained. "I wanted what you had… I wanted to be that happy, and even though we all knew what Sydney was going through you remained right there. I wanted to be that in *Love* with someone and I think Jangles just came along and he filled up that part of me that I knew was missing. I just don't know why I let it go so completely to my head the way that it did."

"Do you still love him, Nina?"

"I honestly don't know. I think I still love him, but I don't know if I'm in love with him," she stared into Courtney's eyes. "I can say that I know a part of me hates the very ground he walks on. I hate that he lied to me. I hate me that I listened and believed him, but mostly, I hate that he tried to kill you and I did nothing about it.

"I'm sorry, Court, you don't know how sorry I really and truly am about all of that."

"I don't think I ever cried so hard in my life," Courtney's voice was very low. "I'd lost the only sister I'd ever had, and it felt like you didn't even care. That night when I walked up on you at that party I felt so sick to the stomach that I was sure I was going to throw up on the spot."

"Right then and there a piece of me died with that piece of me that died watching you get shot. I think he did that so I could tell him about it. I never knew just how sick Jangles was until that day. When I replay it all in my head, I can hear that conversation he had with that Callie person… but then I can hear him promising me that he just wanted to have you scared and that was so much easier to believe than to believe that he would kill you."

"I've learned a lot of crazy things out about Mr. Bobby Johnson over the course of the last two years. Nothing he does surprises me anymore, and I know he wants me dead... more now than ever before. I've made changes in the company that has given him only limited access to just about everything and it's fucking killing him that I'm in his way. I've cut down his means to do any of his illegal businesses, including using any of the ships that we have or the three different trucking companies that IXion has right here in Central Florida.

"I've pretty much tied up his hands and he and the remaining members of the Nine are stressing."

"Courtney," Nina paused for a moment, "the men that were killed... did you?"

"Yes," Courtney answered quickly. "They were done by my orders, and I have no regrets for any of them. If I had to do it all over again I would in the same way with the same brutality. I need Jangles to see that I mean business and that I'll not just sit here like some scared little girl.

"He tried to take my life, and so I cut off his hands."

"He's been quite fucked up over that... especially Cheecho."

"Cheecho?" she looked at Nina. "What's happened to Cheecho?"

"You didn't have him... that wasn't you?"

"I don't know anything about Cheecho," Courtney stood and paced the room staring out the window into the night sky. Cheecho's death would definitely have to be looked into especially since Manciena was dead as well. This may not be the right time to think about it, but with the two of them being dead that would mean that Blanco-Muerto would be foundering around without a leader. She needed Nick here now.

"What's wrong, Courtney?" Nina asked.

"This whole business is so corrupted thanks to the people that Sydney and Jangles dealt with," she turned away from the window. "I just don't know how to get above all of the bullshit dealing with all of these street thugs and wannabe gangsters. If I know Jangles, he's going to try and fill that hole left by the heads of the Manciena family with someone he can use as his own little puppet."

"If I'm not mistaken," Nina sat up on the edge of the sofa, "Jangles had plans to go to Mexico."

"Fuck," Courtney stomped her foot. "I'll have to have a meeting in the morning. I have a feeling that a real shit-storm is on its way to my goddamn doorstep."

"Courtney," Nina began, "what if you're not completely right about Jangles?"

"What do you mean?"

"I think you may want to sit down," Nina waited until Courtney had rejoined her on the sofa. "Now, I'm not saying that Jangles isn't a bad man, and I'm not saying that he wasn't trying to kill Sydney… but I don't think that he did."

"I'm really not following, Nina," Courtney raised an eyebrow as she stared at her friend. "What are you saying?"

"Courtney, I honestly don't think that he's responsible for Sydney's car exploding."

Courtney's head was swimming as her dreams of being right there and seeing his face before his truck exploded and went up in flames. She

could see the horrified look in his eyes as the flames
crawled all over his body. She could smell the
smoke and feel the heat of the fire. She swallowed
hard trying to block everything but felt it all caught
in her throat and all she wanted to do was vomit.

"What do you mean?"

"I know what he talks about in his dreams,
Courtney, and he's trying to figure out who killed
Sydney before… well before he could."

Courtney jumped up from the sofa and
stormed over to her desk slamming her fists down on
top of it.

"No… you're wrong," she finally managed to
say. "It was that bastard, Nina. I know you're in love
with that piece of shit but … But it was him.

"It had to be him."

Nina stood and went to her friend. She pulled
Courtney into her arms and held her as she cried.
Her heart hurt knowing that what she just told
Courtney not only opened a wound that wouldn't
heal for her, but it most likely took some of the wind
out of her sails. She knew Courtney hated Jangles;
she'd always hated Jangles, but more so because
he'd killed the man she loved.

"I know he's a monster, Court," she
whispered into Courtney's ear, "hell, I know more
about how deviant he is than you'd really like to
hear. But, in some sick way he's hurt that Sydney is
gone… he's been going through everything that he
can find to figure out who killed him since the day
after the funeral."

"But, why?" Courtney asked into Nina's
shoulder. "I don't understand; why does he care?"

"I'm not sure," Nina answered. "I don't really
understand why he's hurt when he was poisoning

Sydney, but he's cried in his sleep about the way Sydney died."

The anger that she felt would not allow itself to be extinguished; she still hated Bobby Johnson for the mere fact that he was trying to kill Sydney. At this point in the game it didn't matter that someone else had succeeded, it just meant that she had someone else that she would have to exact her retribution against. Someone else would pay for the actual murder, and Jangles would take his hit for the initial attempt.

She slowly pulled away from Nina and then kissed her cheek. "Thank you," she smiled and kissed her cheek again.

"For what?" Nina was confused.

"For telling me," Courtney smiled and moved back to the sofa. "It doesn't matter to me that he didn't get to follow through with killing Sydney, but that he didn't actually complete the job means that there's someone else out there that I need to find. I need to know who did this and why? I need to know if they'll be coming after IXion as well and how I need to go about protecting myself and everything I have."

"You're so different than when we were in Missouri."

"Between Nick and Sydney and the shit I've been through," she shrugged her shoulders, "I guess I've kinda just grown up. I can't afford to be that meek little girl that moved here any longer. I cannot pretend that there really are men in this world who have no fear of killing other men."

"But what has that done to you?" Nina asked.

"It's made me… shrewd," Courtney grinned. "I have a multi-million dollar asset that I have to protect by all means and people who have grown to depend on that. It doesn't matter that I'm learning all of this on the fly because with each lesson I learn it makes me that much more of an opponent."

"Do you ever worry that all of this might make you… cold?"

Courtney sat thoughtful and then smiled at Nina. For the first time in months she actually had someone she could share things with. It had been far too long since the last time she'd sat with Nina and they could just talk about everything, and she'd missed that.

"I'm not worrying about becoming cold," she said. "I have Nicholas."

"So you two are, like, back together?" Nina grinned at her like a little school girl.

"Yes, and it's been really good. Nick is so protective him that it's almost too much to deal with, but he keeps my head level in all of this shit. He's the one person I've been able to just put everything on the table with and not worry about him pulling punches with me, and on a number of times he's pulled me back from doing something really stupid or reckless."

"Are y'all sleeping together?" Nina loved asking the personal questions and seeing Courtney blush… and Courtney did not fail her.

"Yes, Ms. Nosey," Courtney laughed out. "And that's not all."

Courtney sat there holding her breath not sure how to say what she was holding on to out loud, but she was almost sure that it was true. She'd picked up a few tests a couple of days ago when her bodyguards were not watching and she had them go wait by the door as she went to pay for the things she'd bought. That night she'd taken the test twice, and both times all she could do was stare at the stick in disbelief.

"What… what is it?" Nina was pushing on her shoulder.

"I'm pregnant too," Courtney blurted out.

She sat there waiting for Nina's reaction unsure how she would respond. Her heart was pounding in her chest, and the only other thing she was wishing right at this moment was that it was Nick she was telling just so she could find out how he felt. She nearly fell off the sofa as Nina began screaming and bouncing trying to hug her and congratulate her. Her chest was still tight, but it felt good actually saying those words out to someone other than hearing them banging around inside of her head.

"Does Nick know? When are you going to tell him?"

"I haven't told him ye…"

"You're pregnant?" the sound of a man's voice behind them scared both of them enough to scream. As they turned to see who it was, Courtney's eyes stretched as they fell upon Nick's.

"Oh shit," Nina grinned knowing that her friend was in a bit of a bind.

Nick slowly moved on into the living room but he didn't realize that he was actually moving. The chase on the highway still had his heart racing and his mind reeling knowing that Jangles had finally gotten bold enough to put a contract on him… but what he'd just heard just about buckled his knees. He made it to the back of the sofa and stood there staring down at Courtney.

"Really?" he asked. "You're really pregnant?"

"Yes," she answered dropping her head not sure how he'd take it. A part of her was waiting for him to scream, and the other part had her crying... just because.

"So, um," Nick cleared his throat and glanced at Nina and then back to Courtney, "I'm going to be a Daddy?"

"That's' right," Nina jumped up and wrapped her arms around his neck. She then whispered into his ear, "Congrats, Nick, and thank you."

"Nick?" he heard Courtney calling his name, but his mouth couldn't move any longer. His tongue hung dry in his mouth and again he felt like his knees were going to just drop away beneath him. Nina let his neck go and he grabbed the back of the sofa to keep him from falling over.

"Nick, please..." Courtney was begging him, "I need to know how you feel. Are you ok with this?"

Shaking the cobwebs from his head he moved around the sofa to stand in front of her. Kneeling down she smiled as she wrapped her arms around his neck and she squealed as she stood pulling her up into her arms.

"I'm going to be a Dad," he yelled out. "You damn right I'm ok with this."

He kissed her lips hard not thinking about anything that had happened or had been said to him all day. At this point right now, Nicholas St. Cloud was the happiest man ever and there was nothing that could knock him off of the cloud he was standing on.

Chapter 9

"Shit! Is that my mans?" the thick, Hispanic accent just seemed to bounce everywhere inside the metal walls of the hangar. "Goddamn, Jingle, Jangles, if it ain't Bobby Johnson... What's good?"

"Everything is everything, Jorge," Jangles walked up to shake the extended hand and hug the man he'd known since high school. They grinned and laughed at one another as they stepped back sizing each other.

Jorge Manciena had been born and raised in the Tampa Bay area, so he was more comfortable around the Americans. He was still a tall, handsome Mexican with the sun darkened complexion, the exotic dark eyes, and he was sporting a mustache with the rugged shaved goatee. He looked comfortable in the blistering Mexican heat in his Dickies and opened shirt showing off his muscular chest covered in a black sleeveless t-shirt.

"Shit," Jangles exclaimed, "I see some things never changed... Muthafucka, you still dressing like a model or some shit. All you missin' is the cowboy hat and boots."

"All to impress all of this pussy running around this dust bowl, but you won't neva catch my ass wearin' that shit... ever."

"Fuckin' fool always," Jangles slapped the man on his shoulder. "This is my boy from back home, Jimmy Q."

The two men shook hands as Jorge's men rushed forward grabbing the bags from the plane and taking it to the waiting limo. The three followed and stepped into the backseat all expressing relief for the burst of cool air. Jorge opened a compact refrigerator and pulled out three beers passing one each to Jangles and Jimmy.

"Here's to old friends, "Jimmy nodded to Jangles and then towards Jimmy, "new friends and continued business. Salud."

They then tapped the heads of their bottles before taking that first drink. Jorge was never one to be quiet so as they drove through the town he'd come to call home, he pointed out small things of interest. It was like driving through an Old West movie mixed with a few modern amenities all surrounding a clay dirt road that the limo and two trucks kicked up leaving the town in a cloud of dust.

"Welcome to Casa Juarez, Gentlemen," Jorge announced after they'd been driving for about hour.

The house was immaculate; it was not only huge but it was also beautiful. It was completely out of place with the mountains in the backdrop and the desert laid out in the foreground. There were those weird shaped cactus trees and in a fenced off areas there was a herd of cows complete with Mexican Cowboys rounding up the cattle. The house was a mansion built in an exaggerated adobe ranch style with a wraparound porch on both the ground level and the second floor. It was a gorgeous sunset color with windows everywhere.

"Come on in, Fellas," Jorge was waving his hands around flamboyantly. "Mi casa es su casa."

The inside was just as beautiful, if not more so, than the outside. The way that it was decorated one could definitely see a woman's hand with heavy male influences. Large tree trunk beams ran the length of the ceilings throughout the house, and the walls all had the log cabin feel of an old fashion lodge. The dark wood floors were buffed to a brilliant sheen and again the furnishings were in place with a man in mind. Jangles walked around nodding his head acknowledging the beautiful setup, but Jimmy just kept pace until they were led into a huge office.

"This was my father's favorite place in the entire house," Jorge walked to the fully stocked bar and poured three shots of tequila. "This is a special blend tequila made in our own brewery from a desert agave plant we cultivate ourselves. We're just waiting a few more months for it to mature, but you have to try this. It's the smoothest shit you'll ever taste."

For a while they sat and talked and enjoying the tequila. But, that was short lived.

"So, Bobby... did you bring me something nice from Tampa, because I know you bein' here ain't no kinda social call."

"Look, Georgi," Jangles sat up on the edge of his chair, 'I want to apologize for your father. I'd only met Señor Manciena once, but he seemed like a fair man. You have to know that I had no say in what happened... here."

"Come with me," Jorge stood and without wait walked out a pair of large, glass French doors.

The patio area was just an empty slab of ornate concrete overlooking the valley beneath the mountains and stretching the length of the back of the house. It was beautiful with the sun sitting high behind them and coloring the area in an array of pale oranges and yellows. There were a few large trees growing off the edge that shaded that corner. Jorge stood in the middle of the porch just looking around.

"My papa was a proud, bastard of a man, always thinking that he was... untouchable. This area right here," Jorge gestured to where he was standing, "he had a very large table and he had all of his meals out here. It's beautiful out here, don't you think? You would think no one would have the balls to even try an attack in a place so open, but so not the case.

"When my mama called me I was in New York visiting this chick I'd been fucking off and on before her ass went off on some photo shoot in Morocco or some shit. She was in hysterics. She and my abuelita watched him die, Bobby, and by the time I got here... Let's just say things here were not pretty."

"How?" Jangles asked.

"It was bold," Jorge laughed. "My mama was screaming how this shit happened, man, a fucking helicopter... goddamn if that ain't some shit I would have loved to have seen. This fuckin' place has always been like Fort Knox, and he got done in by a bitch and a helicopter, right. Mi familia lost not only my papa but a half dozen men in all."

Jangles looked around taking in the entire area trying to imagine the scene. It would be like some shit out of a movie with the helicopter flying in over the copse of trees with some daredevil with a high powered rifle hanging out the opened side door. No one would have expected because a man like Manciena would have a copter flying patrol all of the time. He shook his head; there's no way in hell Courtney could have come up with this on her own, and Nick Styles wouldn't be so open with an attack this elaborate.

"So, not to be rude, Bobby," Jorge placed a hand on his shoulder, "but why are you here, my friend? Again, I know this ain't social and I've been hearing that you are having some sort of internal problems. "

"Yea, that's a nice way of putting the shit I'm dealing with," Jangles retorted. One of Jorge's men was standing in the doorway holding one of the large bags that had been brought from car; Jangles waved the man over.

"I'm here to make amends, Jorge." He took the bag and dropped it to the ground between them. Squatting down he pulled back the zipper and opened the bag to present the neatly stacked bundles of cash held inside.

"The offering is very... appreciated, Bobby," Jorge glanced down at the money and then turned his back and walked off as if thinking. "It is very nice indeed, and if I was my father I would take this and business would continue as normal. But,"

Jangles stood staring at Jorge's back hoping that this shit wasn't about to go sideways. He glanced back at Jimmy and he was looking around nervously expecting a fallout as well with no means of escape for either of them.

"But," Jorge turned to face the two men, "I don't want the money, Bobby... So tell me, what's going on, and what do you need from me?"

Jangles smiled his signature smile and stepped up to face Jorge. He should have known that it wouldn't ever be about the money, but he had to start with that if for no other reason than to break the ice. He glanced back at Jimmy Q and the man gave him the nod.

"It's as simple as this, Georgi," he slapped the man on the shoulder, "the three of us have something in common and her name is Courtney Roulette."

"Sydney's widow?" Jorge raised an eyebrow. "How is a woman going to make all of this right?"

"Let's go inside and talk," Jangles offered. "We have a lot to talk about and I have a feeling we'll have a lot to plan because we have three families here and a merger of some major business to deal with."

"Armando," Jorge called out to the man standing in the doorway once more, "prepare lunch for us… I think better on a full stomach."

The three men laughed as they stepped back into the living room of the large house. Jangles felt in control for the first time in months, and for the first time in months he actually had a plan that he was sure would not fail. He'd have to call JC to make certain he made it down to Texas and once that was in play he could get Jorge and Jimmy Q rolling. IXion was coming back home, and the Bitch… well she was in her last days.

****

"Look, Nick," JC's voice was whispered over the phone, "I'm headed to Texas now to see some cat named Big Shaw… you know 'em?"

"Yea, messy muthafucka… Jangles has used him a couple times before," Nick glanced over at Courtney as she sat there listening to the conversation. They were in the back of one of the company limousines headed towards the Temple Terrace area of Tampa to see a man she thought she'd never have to bother again.

"I had Tytus pull some info on this son-of-a-bitch, and everything that I got back was not shit to sneeze at," Nick was speaking to Courtney more than JC at the moment. "Shit is about to get stupid, and we truly need to prepare. You be careful with this dude, JC, and you gots to play your cards close to your chest because this man can smell a cross a mile away. He's a hitman in its most dangerous form."

"Well that's only part of the bullshit we have to deal with," JC sounded stressed out. "Like I told you earlier, Jangles and Jimmy Q are together and they've headed down to Mexico to see the Manciena family."

"I know exactly who he's going to see, and I'll have to get that shit checked quick."

"What do you mean?" Courtney stared at him and winced at the frown on his face.

"Manciena had two sons that are in the business, his oldest boy is Michael… they call him Miko, but we don't have to deal with him yet because he's locked up in prison on a murder rap that's going to keep him away for at least fifteen more years. Then there's Jorge, I always called him the pretty boy of the family. He's flashy, calculating, and a bonefide hot head… but he's as dangerous as his daddy ever was.

"I remember one of the first times I met him and that was because I was kept pretty close to Sydney and Jangles in the beginning after they got off the streets… before they truly got the Nine underway. This dude came in with his father and he recognized someone in the room that Sydney was working a deal with, and it just so happen that the man was a UC DEA… Jorge walked up on him sitting at the table and shot him in the back of the head. The shit was gruesome and the boy didn't bat an eye."

"Goddamn," JC mumbled. "What the fuck are we getting into here, Nicky?"

"It's almost over," Nick was staring at Courtney. "Jangles is reaching and he's hoping that he can pool his resources in a final play. He's pretty

sure that we're in the dark and that this will give him
the upper hand. JC, you need to keep your eyes
open… all of this is going to start happening pretty
fast. His first strike will be with Shaw, that will be
his calling card, and that's what we need to
concentrate on firstly."

"We're headed to talk to Uncle Yuen,"
Courtney announced. "The hope is to bring him in
more up front to keep the Chinese out of this for just
a little longer. I'm hoping that us putting our illegal
nonsense on the board as a barter along with his son
joining Jangles will sway him to side with us until
this shit is over. With a lot of the deals that I've put
together without the knowledge of the Nine that
should stabilize IXion as a founded business with no
need of the illegal stuff we'll be losing."

"Well I'm with you and Nick all the way,
Mrs. Roulette," JC offered. "I'm just ready for this
bullshit to be over so I can bring my family home. I
just want all of us to walk away from this with our
skin intact."

"JC, when the final nail is beat into the coffin
of this war," Nick spoke up, "I'll personally send
you and Nicole and the kids away on a long
vacation."

"I'm going to hold you to that, Nicky," the
two men laughed and Nick hung up.

"How bad are things… really?" Courtney
asked.

"Really… they are bad, Darlin'" Nick
answered. "If we cannot convince Uncle Yuen to
step up in this war we will be alone with Jangles,
Jorge, and Jimmy Q coming at us from three sides. I
will have to speak with Jackson and see how many
people he can bring in, and then I'll have call in a
marker or two."

145

"I want to get Janice out of this as soon as possible," Courtney added to the plate of things to worry and deal with.

"Agreed, and I'm already taking care of that and her family."

Nick took a deep breath and turned towards his window staring out at the cars passing by. After leaving prison he never thought that he would be in another fight to stay alive. Those two years was like spending time in a war torn country and trying to hide in the bush to stay alive because you're completely cut off from anyone who could faintly help. Jangles had him trenched in with his back against the wall, and he was constantly on full alert.

He couldn't count the number of times he was attacked in the shower by a gang of men with shivs, and the fight was always for his life. Several times he got help, and it wasn't until he was out and in that meeting with Sydney that he found out that his former boss was actually watching out for him. But, there were still those times when he was completely alone.

"What kind of markers?" Courtney was pulling on his shoulder trying to get his attention.

"I know of a few people from when I was locked up," Nick explained. "They're always up for a fight and shit like this is right up their alley."

"Can you trust them?"

"To be truthful," Nick wrapped his arm around her pulling her to his chest, "who can we really trust? But, these are the kind of men who live this kind of life on a daily basis, this is all they know. We have to play this game by their rules, Courtney, and everything that you've done thus far you're going to have up the stakes."

146

Courtney pressed her ear to Nick's chest and listened to his heart beating. Her mind was all over the place, and she was tired. Never in her weirdest nightmares would she have dreamed that she would be caught up in a war for the control of a business that a bunch of street thugs started. She missed her daughter, who was only God knew where, to keep her and her family safe. She missed her husband, and still hated the man she'd thought had killed him for the last two years. This was all too much to deal with; she was a guppy swimming with a bunch of sharks pretending to be a shark, and always so close to being eaten alive.

"Call them, Nick," she said softly. "It doesn't seem we have any choice but to surround ourselves with as many people just like them as we can. Time to fight fire with fire and show them that I'm not bullshitting anymore. I want this over, Nick; like JC, I want my family home.

"Trust me," Nick said laying his head back on the seat, "I know you do."

His conversation with Jackson about Sydney filled his head, and for the first time he wondered just how this was going to play out. Not only would he have to deal with Sydney about his relationship with Courtney and the fact that she was now pregnant with his child, but he'd also have to deal with Courtney about knowing Sydney had not died in that car explosion. There were just too many lies in the air, and all of them were now surrounding him. He took a deep breath and turned his head back towards the window as he continued to hold her.

"I have to keep you safe," he said hoping she heard him. "That's all that matters… protecting you and our baby."

The house that they pulled up to was larger than the house that Courtney owned, and the large red door just seemed to stand out from the dark wood color of the front facade. The limo stopped and Nick opened his door stepping out and reaching in for her to take his hand. As Courtney stepped out, she stared once more at the Chinese mob boss' home and wondered for the first time if this was really worth it; she could always just give Jangles the company and disappear with the help of Nick and Mr. McGregor and Tampa would never hear from her again. But, would that really solve anything... for that matter, would Jangles just allow her and Sydnee to just live?

Even as she thought about it the answer was simple...

"Doubtful," she whispered to herself.

"What's doubtful?" Nick asked her.

"Nothing," she smiled and gave him a quick kiss before walking up to the door. Taking a very deep breath she knocked and stood there waiting.

"Good day, Mrs. Roulette," the older Chinese man answering the door addressed her bowing upon opening the door.

"Good day," she returned the man's bow and smiled.

"Yuen-san, is expecting you... I shall escort you and your company to his greenhouse."

Courtney bowed again and she and Nick followed him through the beautiful home and into the backyard where a huge greenhouse stood. She was floored by the size of it and upon going in her awe increased as they walked through a lustrous botanical garden. There were flowers and trees growing that she'd never seen before, it was the most beautiful thing she'd ever laid eyes on, and just

148

being there took her mind off of everything else that was going on around her.

"I see you love what you see," the familiar voice called out.

"I do," she exclaimed. "This is absolutely gorgeous. I thought the inside of your house was great, but this, Mr. Yuen, is absolutely magnificent."

The two met, bowed and then hugged.

"It would seem that every time we meet," she began, "is under ominous circumstances."

"And yet, even under those circumstances I enjoy our meetings," Yuen smiled. "Come let's look around and talk. Being out here always has a way of keeping me centered… keeping me calm."

"Thank you," she smiled once again taking his offered arm to be shown around the greenhouse. She glanced over her shoulder to make certain Nick was following and she prepared herself to bring this man back into her family business.

Chapter 10

Nick stepped into the office expecting a moment to get situated for this meeting, but he was met at the door by Sydney with his hand stretched out. As he shook the man's hand, all he could do was stare at the difference in how he looks now and the way he looked when they'd first met when he got back home from California. By the time they'd met that initial time Sydney was still the buff man that Nick remembered from when they all ran the streets together; you could see that he still worked out to keep his weight in check and to keep his body in shape without looking overly muscled.

But, this man standing before him was something completely different. His eyes were sunken into his head, and the skin to his face was drawn back over skull like a bad mask. His body was slender in a very sickly way and the muscles he had had were gone. He looked emaciated and siphoned of everything that made him the man he'd once been. He was limping towards his left leg and every time he drew in too deep of a breath you could see that it hurt. What had once been a very powerful looking man now looked like a frail cancer patient.

"What's good, Nicky Styles?"

"Shit, I should be asking you that," Nick responded as they moved to sit down. Nick took note that Sydney's shadow was present as he nodded his head in the direction of Henri Thames.

Sydney laughed as he moved behind his desk and took his seat pointing to the seat in front of the desk for Nick.

"For real, Syd," Nick settled into the chair staring at the man, "you're not looking too damn good. What are the doctors saying?"

"Well the doctors here can't do shit for me, but," Sydney glanced over at Henri, "I think we've found someone who can help. I've been having blood samples sent out to leading doctors around the world who have studied poisons and there's this one cat over in Switzerland who feels he may be able to help. The only thing is I have to get there soon or there ain't shit out there that will save my black ass."

"So, whatcha gon' do, Syd, and have you told Courtney?"

"Well see, Nicky," Sydney stared at him with a weird smile, "that's where you come in at my friend. No, I haven't told Courtney and I don't plan on telling her because we're going to do something really extreme."

"Why?" Nick broke in. "Why not just tell her? Why keep her in the dark, don't you think you've put enough shit on her shoulders?"

"Yea, I have and that's why she has you, Nick… you're going to keep her sane and pulled in. She's going to need you in a pretty major way."

"What are you up to, Sydney?" Nick sat there trying to read the man's face but getting nowhere. "What are you two planning to do?"

"I'm going to die, Nicky," Sydney said flatly.

Nick jumped up from the seat and leaned over the desk. "What the fuck do you mean, Sydney? Goddamn, what the fuck's going on?"

"Easy, Nicky, easy," Sydney took a sip of the glass of water sitting on his desk. "This shit's going to be pretty simple to get through, but you're gonna have to be on your p's and q's for a while longer to see Courtney through everything. I need you to listen and I need for you to keep an open mind because I'm going to lay out everything for you. Cool?"

"Sure," Nick hesitated for a moment before sitting back down. He glanced over at Henri and man pretty much hadn't moved an inch from where he'd been standing. There's always been something about the man that made him nervous, but Sydney seemed to trust him with everything.

"So, what's really going on?"

"Like I said, shit's going to be simple. I'm going to kill myself off. I refuse to give that bastard the satisfaction of being the death of me; so I'm a dead man here really soon. I need you, Nick… I need for you to take care of Courtney for me because what's going to happen is going to do one of two things to her."

"Destroy her," Nick interrupted.

"Yea…" Sydney hesitated. "Or, it's going to give her the drive to end this shit with Jangles. She's got everything in place, and she's already preparing for me to die."

"So you just gonna play fuckin' god and do it a little sooner?"

"It's not like that, Nick," Sydney sat up and leaned on the desk. "If I tell Courtney that I'm going to fucking Switzerland then she's not going to be concentrating on what needs to be done here. She'll forever be wondering and worrying about what's going on with me, and I need her mind here in Tampa. If she loses sight on Jangles even for a minute he will eat her alive, and I refuse to let that happen anymore than I refuse to let that bastard have IXion.

"That son-of-a-bitch was supposed to be my brother," Sydney's voice dropped to a hiss, "I trusted him with my fucking life and his bitch ass tried to take it."

Nick sat there for a moment before rubbing his hand over his head. He couldn't begin to explain to Sydney how frustrated he was that he was going to be implicated in a ruse to lie to Courtney. He'd promised that he would never lie to her again and yet there was no way Sydney would let him tell her what he was planning; he had to stay near her, and protect her.

"Fuck," he finally said as he stood and walked over to the bar. He reached up and grabbed the bottle of bourbon and poured a glass. He stood there and took two big swallows draining the glass and then refilling it.

"Can I think about this shit?" he finally asked.

"Ain't no time, Nicky," Sydney sat there watching him with a nervous smile on his face as he wiped a bead of sweat from his forehead. "I need an answer, brotha, because me, you, and Henri have a of planning to do before I get this shit underway."

"You know I'm in, Sydney," he announced as he took a sip of the second glass. But, you know she's not stupid and all of this is bound to blow up in our faces. When that happens, we're all fucked."

"Trust me, Man," Sydney was laughing, "I've been trying to come to terms with that as well."

"So what's the plan?"

"Like I said already," Sydney had walked over the bar and poured him a glass of the bourbon, "I'm going to die. It's going to be something big and not this pussy ass poison shit that Jangles got me going through. Henri and I were thinking of something like some dude just walking up on me and shooting me in the chest."

"Not big enough," Nick bluntly responded. "If you're going to do this then we need not only Courtney all fucked up, but we need Jangles thrown off his game too. You need to think bigger… a lot bigger."

"Bigger? Hmm." Sydney began pacing the floor thinking. He would look up at Henri and shook his head before continuing to walk. Nick stood there watching and sipping at the second glass.

"What are you thinking?" Nick asked.

"You say we need to go bigger, so," he looked over at Henri once more. "Can you make me blow up?"

"What do you mean?" Henri cocked an eyebrow.

"Well the way I see it I need to completely disappear and Nicky is right we need to go bigger, and I need to make it something that fuck with Jangles' head in ways that throws him way off his game; it'll give Courtney time to recover and move forward. So, if I'm going to die I want to make it something explosive. I think it should happen right there in front of the IXion and it should be over the top theatrical."

"Given enough time I'm sure I can get one of the vehicles wired for an explosion. What would we do about a body?"

"Good question," Sydney turned to Nick. "I need you to find me someone to take my place. Make them whatever promises you have to and we'll make certain that they are kept. I'll also need at least two men I can be assured can keep their mouths closed."

Nick sat his glass on the table and stood there with his hands on his head. The headache that was suddenly pounding between his ears was enough to make him want to empty his stomach. This was absolutely too much to deal with, but as he's standing there listening he knows what has to be done and what he has to say to Sydney.

"Look," he cleared his throat, "if you're going to do this shit then you need to do it right."

"Speak your head, Nicky."

"Ok, I'll find you someone to take your place, shit, I think I know a dude right off; similar body size, dying of cancer, and I think with the right amount of money to his family I can get him in the seat. But, there can be no one left standing to let it slip that you're alive. If you're going to die, then everyone involved, except for the three of us, has to die as well."

"I didn't know your ass could be so cold blooded, Nick Styles."

"This game we 'bout to play is going to be putting all of our asses in slings," Nick stared Sydney, "last thing I need is some nigga running off at the mouth and then I not only have Jangles all up my ass but this will put Courtney in more danger... not fuckin' happening."

"I agree," Sydney responded. "Can we make this happen, Henri?"

"Without a doubt," Henri answered nonchalantly. "I'll need no more than a month to get it all together. Mr. Styles will have to keep Mrs. Roulette in the dark while you and I put this in action."

"Once we get a day together I'll have Courtney off taking care of things until after I know the shit's happened." Nick could feel his stomach lurch and rumble.

"Then it's settled," Sydney announced. "We conspire to kill off... me."

****

"Time for the last play, Syd ol boy," he whispered to himself.

He pulled opened the doors to the huge conference room and looked inside. Some things never seemed to change from how you remember them, and this room was one of those things for him. He remembered that very first meeting that he and Jangles had put together when they pulled all of their friends together to initially create the Nine. That was one of those great moments in his life and he could still picture the faces of every last one of them the moment he told them of the kind of money they would all be making over the course of the next few years, and now here he stood.

He was at the precipice of the end of a lifetime and for the first time in his life he didn't feel like he was truly in control. He glanced down at the threshold and walked inside.

"So," his voice suddenly getting everyone's attention, "what's all of this really about, does anyone know?"

His men stood and all stepped up to him with a chorus of "Hey, Boss," and "how's it going?" as he was hugged and handshakes given. He kept moving taking in all of their faces as if it would be the last time he'd ever see them, and for most of them it most likely would be. He kept his smile up but deep inside it was killing him inside. As he looked around, he wondered who among them he could still trust, and how many had sided with Jangles and was looking forward to the day he would finally just roll over and die?

"Where the hell is Jangles at?" he asked causing everyone to look around at each other shrugging their shoulders.

"Well it sounds like everyone is here,"
Jangles opened the doors to the conference room and
walked up with his hand out towards Sydney.

"Nice of you to drag your lazy ass outta the
bed." Everyone laughed.

"Well, shit," Sydney slapped him on the
shoulder, "someone had to come here and show you
how to run a meeting."

"Well then we should get started."
Jangles flashed his signature smile as he walked
around the table then down to the opposite end that
Sydney would sit at.

Sydney moved to his seat at the head of the
massive table set up in the center of the room. The
expanse of Tampa was at his back in a panoramic
view from the large windows that covered the back
wall of the room. He could feel the power of the
streets below as his men settled in and they were
beginning to ask about what was going on and what
this meeting was all about.

"Time to bring the Nine up to date on all of
the shit that's happening," Sydney began with a
wave of his hand. Everyone in the room turned to
him as they quieted down their stares going between
him and Jangles.

"You mean there's more?" Cheecho sat near
the end of the table close to Jangles and he was
looking back and forth between Jangles and Sydney.
"What have you not been telling us?"

Jangles pulled out his phone and placed it on
the table, "That I've been getting text messages from
whoever is doing this shit, and well, I got another
one today."

Cheecho picked up the phone and looked at
the phone and the passed it on.

"The thing I don't know is who they are talking about." Jangles watched as they passed his phone around staring the text message without a word being said amongst them.

"The one thing we are almost sure of," Sydney said as he re-read the message before passing the phone on to the next man, "is the killers are the Vasilevich Brothers, but what we do not know is who the fuck hired them or where the fuck they are hiding."

"Yea, no shit on that one," Jangles said, "I've had JC working on that for the last two weeks and so far we've come up with nothing. These bastards are slicker than pig shit."

"So what's next?" JC asked leaning in and looking from Jangles to Sydney. "I mean whoever the fuck this is from is saying someone is going to die."

Sydney was almost impressed with how well this was all going. For the most part they were all soaking in this threat just like a bunch of scared kids all trying to play the part of big touch gangsters, and the only one he couldn't rightly read was Jangles. He sat there staring down the table at the man he'd always considered to be his best friend; his brother, and he wondered if he'd done right by Courtney by placing her in the water to play with these sharks. The worst thing he could think that they would still swallow her up whole no matter how much he'd

prepared her and that meant he'd have to find a way
to keep her ahead of the Jangles and his bullshit.

He made a quick mental note to speak with
Henri about setting him up with a new identity so
that if anyone was bold enough to investigate him all
they would run into was a bunch of impenetrable
walls and dead end paths. He toyed around with
names as the Nine continued to talk about the
inevitable threat against them as a whole. Nick was
right when he said that all of this was bound to just
blow up in their faces… there was just too much shit
to deal with.

As they were all talking at once he had to
pull his handkerchief from his pocket to cover his
mouth as he began coughing. The pain in his chest
felt like someone had taken a knife and was slipping
it in and out of his lungs between his ribs one bone
after the other over and over. He wiped his mouth
and tried not to open it to see how much blood was
there. His forehead was soaked in sweat as he slowly
found the strength to pull air back into his lungs

"Damn, you good, Nigga?" Malcolm asked
before everyone around the table began laughing.

"Yea," Sydney laughed as well. "Damn cold
got my ass good." He stared down at Jangles who
was watching with a very cold, interested look in his
eyes. The urge to pull the pistol he had in the small
of his back and shoot his ass between the eyes was
strong, but he just glanced around the table keeping
up his act.

"Didn't you know that's what pussy is for,
Fool," Malcolm continued and the room was filled
with laughter again.

"Shit, they say pussy keeps you from getting
ugly too… but then look at yo' ass." Everyone stared
at Malcolm and the laughter echoed in the room

It was these moments that reminded him why they had put the Nine together, and as he looked from man to man it was funny how there were more than nine men involved with those considered the Nine. There had been a few deaths amongst the original and there had been several who had proven that they deserved to be at this table wearing that one ring that made them all part of the same. IXion had become more than just a group of men trying to make it rich in a business front for a bunch of illegal shit; they were a fucking family.

A family that had betrayed him.

"So," Sydney spoke up over the talking and laughing men, "who are we assuming they are talking about; this person they are going to kill that will change your life?"

"The only one I can think of," Jangles cocked his head looking down the table at him, "is you."

Everyone got quiet.

"Then I guess it's Mr. Sydney who needs the extra security," JC offered.

"Fuck that, just make certain my wife is protected," Sydney feigned an argument.

"NO fuck just that," Jangles looked down the table, "I think I got it all covered and that's why I needed your ass to come in here today. I need for you to stop taking this shit so goddamn lightly, Syd. We got some major shit going on and for the first time in a long time we have actually lost people. Good fuckin people.

"You top dawg, and you out there walkin' 'round like you Billy Bobo somebody. You gotta be real on this shit. They got people gunnin' us down left and right and we ain't got no eyes on none of 'em yet."

Sydney wondered how Nick would get his people into the building as his security, and Jangles pretty much just let him know. Everything was going smoother than he'd figured it would. Now he just needed to get the fuck out of here and put these final pieces into play.

"Alright, goddamn," he answered. "Alright, Jangles, where are these new guys? Let's get this shit over with so I can get home to my wife and get me some pussy for this cold."

"The main ones I'm concerned with are downstairs waiting in the lobby," Jangles stood and walked down to his end of the table, "and, then another set will follow you back home and remain outside with the guys you have posted. I have one more set who will go up and guard the hallway just to be on the safe side, and yes I know you don't like this shit… but deal with it."

"Sounds good," Sydney chuckled. "No more arguments from me, Bossman. Fellas are we done for the day; I need to get outta here."

****

"Is everything in place?" Sydney asked the two men on the elevator with him.

"Yes, Mr. Roulette."

"Good," he put his Bluetooth back on and made a call to Nick Styles to give him the go ahead signal. "Nick, I'm on my way home from this meeting so let my wife know that I will be there shortly and to wait up for me."

"As you wish, Mr. Roulette," that let Sydney know that Nick was with Courtney at that very moment. "Is everything ok, Sir, is there anything I need to take care of?"

"As long as everything is in place when I get home," Sydney stared at the two men and they both nodded, "everything will be perfectly fine. Just tell her that I was being sappy and said, 'I love you.' You got that, Nicky?"

"I got it, Sir, I got it," this let Sydney know that Nick was ready for his part in this game they were going to be putting in motion. "I will take care of everything."

As the elevator came to a stop, Sydney was ushered off. He was not on the first floor but in the basement and being hurried out towards a door towards the back of the building. He had Henri on the Bluetooth just as he came back out into the warmth of the sun. He stopped and stared own at his watch.

"Keep a close eye on my wife, Henri," he said, "you are responsible for her from this point on."

"I understand, Sir," Sydney stared at the man to his right as he pulled out a small device and pressed a button. The ground vibrated and from the front of the building Sydney could see the flash of fire as the sound of the explosion finally made it to him. He stood there a moment longer before walking away from everything he'd put together. His whole life had been this business, and thanks to Big Fats he'd been groomed to be the leader of this ragtag bunch of street thugs to make them more than what they'd always been. Everything that he' come to understand no longer made any sense.

"We have to go, Mr. Roulette," one of the new security men said.

"Gentlemen, from this moment on, Sydney Roulette is dead," he plainly said. "The name's Evan McGregor."

"Yes sir, Mr. McGregor," the man answered. "We have to get you to your plane."

"Excellent." Evan McGregor looked around one last time before being escorted off to his waiting car. His mood was a little melancholy, but his spirits was a little high. This new game he had in play was going to be exciting… very exciting.

Chapter 11

JC opened his eyes with a groan. His head felt like it had been bashed in by a baseball bat, and he had the taste of blood in his mouth. He stretched his eyes open but all he could see was black. Feeling was slowly returning to his body and he almost cried out as he pulled at his arms and his shoulders felt twisted in their sockets the wrong way. Taking a deep breath, he attempted to assess his situation.

Easy, he said to himself, *don't freak out yet.*

He closed his eyes and slowly opened them once more hoping something different, but was still in the dark; there wasn't any kind of light to give him an idea of where he was. He could feel the scratch of something covering his head leaving him blinded. His knees hurt from him kneeling and he could feel the rope around his wrists pulling his arms up behind him. He could tell from the heat and moisture on his body that he was naked, and that it was some kind of concrete under his knees.

"What the fuck's going on?" he called out not knowing who was listening.

His head felt like a fire was smoldering on his brain, and on top of swallowing blood he could smell it. The thick, iron tinged smell was enough to make him gag. His stomach turned. He was trying not to vomit, but the smells of the blood and something else in the air was making that very hard. He could feel his body swaying nervously, and he was trying to keep his breathing steady as he knelt there listening to his surroundings. He was getting anxious and angry, but at this point… what the fuck could he do?

He was in more pain than he cared to ever
feel. The back of his head was the most obvious, but
his stomach and especially his ribs were throbbing.
His lips were swollen and he was sure that his nose
was broken. He felt like he'd been through a war and
was on the losing end of the last battle. He pulled at
his arms and groaned out once more at the way they
were twisted back and pulling in the socket.

"Hello, goddamn," he called out once more.
"What the fuck? This bullshit ain't funny."

JC tried to clear his mind, but nothing was
clear at this point. He was beyond trying to remain
calm and was about ready to start screaming out. His
head was pounding and he wanted to vomit, but as
he knelt there retching there was just nothing coming
up. He tried to relax against his restraints; he was
hoping for something to let him know what was
going on.

"Oh damn," D'Marious groaned to his left.

"Ay, yo, D? You good?"

"Naw, I feel like I been cracked ova the head
by a fuckin' semi or somethin'. I can't see shit.
Where the fuck we at?"

"I'm not sure, Bruh." JC was trying to
remain calm, but he had a feeling that they were
being listened to. "Do you remember anything?"

"Not, shit," D'Marious moaned out again.
"All I know is I can't really breath, J. My chest feel
like I got a goddamn elephant sitting on my heart,
know what I mean. Something's all fucked up here,
JC. I'm not liking this shit at all, Bro."

"Yea, I'm feelin' ya, D," JC shifted on his
knees trying to remember anything since they'd got
on the plane, but everything was so sketchy. They'd
made it to Texas and found the man Jangles had sent
them for, and from jump there was just something

off about the dude. D'Marious kept making comments about the way that Big Shaw was staring at them like they were marks or something, and JC tried to wave it but he felt it to. The flight was okay, but they could feel him behind them and both men were nervous. Once they were off the plane and in the IXion car that had been waiting for them… everything after that was a blank.

"I know you there, Nigga," JC finally said. "Let's get this shit ova with."

The light hurt the moment the potato sacks were pulled from their heads, and both men had to shut their eyes and slowly re-open them to adjust. Once they were able to see again they were staring up at the brutish monster they'd met in Texas smiling down at them. D'Marious immediately began babbling and looking back and forth between JC and Big Shaw unable to say anything that made a bit of sense, but JC just knelt there staring up at the big man not saying another word.

Big Shaw was massive; he was like staring at a walking mountain of a man with a head full of dreads. He had to stand close to seven feet tall and as wide across the chest as a semi. The man had hands the size of two small pigs but they weren't fat; his fingers were long and slender like those of a basketball player. He had arms and legs that looked like they belonged on an elephant and the muscles seemed to stretch his shirt and pants like they were trying to escape. He was a scary man.

****

JC couldn't help thinking of how his face must have looked when they first met the man. They'd made it to Texas and sat around two days before they finally received the call to come meet the man at his Texas ranch. The drive from the city out into the middle of nowhere had been long and arduous and by the time they'd made it the sun was setting. Walking around the small rustic home gave JC the impression of some small fragile white dude who was trying to play cowboy, but when they walked into the office and were met at the door by the huge man all JC could remember was staring up like he was trying to see the top of the Empire State Building.

"What's good, Boys?" his voice was as deep and heavy as he was large and seemed to echo through the room. "I just got off the phone with Jangles and he told me to be expecting you both."

"Did he tell you why we're here?" JC asked as they all exchanged handshakes and he marveled at how his hand was swallowed up by Shaw's hand.

"Yea," the man had a smile that made JC nervous, "some shit going on in Tampa and he wants me to come out of retirement to deal with her."

"Out of retirement?" D'Marious asked.

"Yea, Jangles and I have done some business in the past," Shaw kind of offered. "He knows that I enjoy doing certain things and if the end result is a muthafucka dying well that kinda shit just makes my dick hard."

The three men all laughed, but JC was convinced more than ever that something wasn't on the up and up.

"Check it," Shaw said as he moved around to the back of his desk, "as you can see I'm a big mug, so I got some steaks being grilled out back and my cook is putting together some shit for my men… so let's eat and then we can discuss more about what's goin' on in the TPA."

"Sounds good to my ass," D'Marious said. "I could use a good ass steak."

Sitting on the plane and thinking about that right now JC had a feeling that he'd just enjoyed his last meal. Staring at the back of Shaw's head nothing about any of this trip was making sense. The man just seemed to aloof about just packing up at the drop of a dime from Jangles and coming to Tampa.

"Whatcha' thinkin', JC?" D'Marious asked.

"Not sure," JC wished he could keep the man calm, but right now his nerves were all fucked up. D'Marious sat there running his fingers through the oily curls on his head. "Something about that nigga got me all fucked up, ya know. I can't put my fingers on it but there's something about this man that I can't…"

He sat there trying to think, but whatever it was eluding him. He pulled out his laptop once they were in the air and put his earphones and pulled up his Skype program. He'd told Nick to be waiting for him so that he could report in once they were in the air. He wouldn't be able to talk but he needed Nick to check on some things while they were in the air.

"Hey, JC," Nick was sitting at his desk in the office of Courtney's home, "are y'all on the way back?"

Yea, but something is wrong, JC typed out. He sent a picture of Shaw to Nick and waited for it to load and the man to look at it. *Do you know this nigga?*

Nick sat there staring at the picture for a moment and JC could see that Nick recognized Shaw. He sat calmly, but his insides were like jelly. He glanced at D'Marious and his eyes alone told the man that they were in some serious shit, but they needed to keep their heads about them. D'Marious sat back in his seat and played look out as JC continued to talk with Nick.

"Where is Shaw at now, JC?" JC nodded his head indicating that he was ahead of him. "Cool. Okay listen, this shit just went sideways and you need to get the fuck out of from under him as soon as possible and I mean that. You're being set up and all I can think is that D'Marious is either in on it or they're going to kill him too."

What the fuck is going on, Nicky?

"I don't know but Jangles has either put it together that you're working with me and Courtney or he's fucking fishing and trying to see who alls loyal. I don't know how we fucked up, but we gotta get you outta there for real."

JC sat there just staring at the screen of his laptop and then he glanced over at D'Marious and the man was scared and nervous sitting beside him. He was able to sit there and talk to Nick without D'Marious paying attention to him because he couldn't take his eyes off of Big Shaw.

I don't think D is in on this shit Nicky, on the real. Dude is sitting here trying not to trip the fuck out. Tell me what you know about Big Shaw. JC typed out.

"He's old school, JC," Nick began. "He's a killer, but he loves to torture his victims. He has no love at all for guns… this man loves to tie people up and take his time. He's on some of that Vietnam bullshit. This cat is beyond dangerous and if he's coming to Tampa I need to get him taken care of quick. Where are y'all supposed to be taking him?"

That's just it… JC looked up and looked around, *I have no clue where we're going when we land. He said that he had it all take care of through Jangles.*

"Shit," Nick rubbed his head. "I'll have some people there to follow you once you land. Most likely Jangles already has a spot in place."

I think I know where, JC typed. *You remember that old warehouse spot they had out in the stix? I thought Sydney got rid of it, but I heard from Bubbs that Jangles been keeping it for some of his shit.*

"I think I know where you talkin' 'bout," Nick said. "I'll get a call in to Jackson and get some men out there ASAP."

Thanks, Nicky.

"JC," Nick sat up close on his camera, "I got you man. I won't let you down… you got my word. You two be safe."

****

JC groaned out as he slumped forward too far and his shoulders let him know to pull back. He was still groggy on how he actually got into this situation, but at least he had Nicky's word to depend on. He was putting all of his trust in a man that he at one point didn't even know existed. What he remembered of Nicky Styles was that he was just a lil street kid that Sydney kind of took under his wings until the boy double crossed the Nine in a deal that went south bad.

"I'm waiting," he said more to hear his own voice than speaking to anyone.

"Waiting on what, Nigga?" Jangles voice was right in his ear causing him to shiver. "Waiting for more of this ass whooping that my boy been givin' yo' bitch ass? I can't believe this shit."

"What's this about?" JC mumbled.

"This is about you siding against the Nine, JC," Jangles pulled the black sack from over his head so that they were staring in each other's eyes. "Goddamn, Boy, you all fucked up."

Through swollen eyes JC stared up at the man standing over him and he shook his head. He tried to think back over the last several months and he couldn't think of anything that he had done to fuck up.

"I don't know what the fuck you talkin' 'bout, Jangles," JC groaned from the pains in his chest.

"Why is when a nigga gets caught up in his bullshit he wanna pretend he don't know what the fuck he in?" Jangles stood up laughing as Shaw came into JC's view. "Look at this bitch made nigga right here, you thought you was playin' me, JC?"

"Playin' you about what, Muthafucka?"

Jangles walked back up and reared his hand back and swung forward striking JC across the jaw. JC screamed out as his jaw popped and he was thrown to the right enough to force his shoulder to pop as well. The ropes holding his arms behind him didn't give much as they bit into his wrists and he slid and was pulled back into place on his knees. JC bit down on his teeth as he forced his body up right to take the weight off his shoulders so they were not being pulled from their sockets.

"You… betta watch yo fuckin' mouth, JC," Jangles was all in his face. "I got yo ass, Bitch, and I promise you that every fuckin' thing is about to change."

Shaw stepped forward once more holding a pair of jumper cables. His hands were in a pair of thick, insulated gloves and there was a nasty smile on his face. JC wasn't sure which would be better, to try and hold his breath or to just wait it out and scream. His muscles reacted and contracted from the contact of the jumpers and then the pain was like lightning searing through his entire body. His teeth slammed down and his jaws locked as he tried to open his mouth to scream. He was jerking against the ropes holding him in place as he floundered around until Shaw pulled the jumpers away.

"Now, Nigga," Jangles was standing over him again, "let's try this shit again. How long have you been running back to that bitch and telling her my fuckin' business?"

"I… I," JC was slobbering and trying not to cry like a baby. "I don't know what you're talking about, Jangles."

"Too much of my shit been fuckin' up for no reasons, JC," Jangles had walked behind him and slapped his hand down on his head. "I got a rat in my house and I'm thinking that it's you, Nigga."

"Why?" JC began. "Why would I go against the Nine? I've been there with you since day fucking One, Jangles. I'm the one who found out that they was locking up yo' fucking money, Nigga. Goddamn, Jangles! I'm the one who been making sure that all of this shit with Courtney is getting planned. Nigga, I got Callie ass here… I just went and got this big nigga here. I been with you through all this shit since you decided to poison Sydney. Why turn on you now?"

Jangles stepped back and began walking around. Big Bubbs walked up with a bag of chips and a bottle of Henny. He took the bottle and swallowed down a mouthful before handing the man back the bottle. JC was right about a lot, but this shit wasn't making any kind of sense. Courtney was always ahead of him and that could only mean one thing… she had someone feeding her information.

He turned and nodded his head to Shaw, and the man touched JC with the jumpers once more.

JC's screams echoed off into the darkness of the hollow warehouse. His body was pulling at the taunt ropes harder this round than the last and somewhere in the back of his mind he could feel his shoulders popping out of their sockets and all of the feeling in his arms going somewhere between knives being constantly slammed into the muscles… to absolutely no feeling at all. His eyes were closed, but he saw all manners of lights and stars and his life flashing in a mish mash of colors that made him sick enough to empty his stomach all over Big Shaw's shoes.

"Little bitch," Shaw kicked him brutally in the stomach.

"Oh!" he could hear Jangles voice up over his screams. "My nigga… that's gonna leave a mark."

Big Shaw stood over him laughing as he held the jumpers in his huge, gloved hands. "We're gettin' nowhere with this som-bitch, Jangles… whatcha wanna do?"

"Yea," Jangles stood back watching Shaw slam his fists into JC's face, "this shit ain't working for me. Get that bitch in here and hoist him up."

JC screamed as his arms were pulled up over his head and the rope tightened around his wrists. With each pull, his weakened body was hauled up from the cold cement until he hanging with just the tips of his toes just barely touching the floor. Gritting his teeth and trying to breathe through his nose to ease the pain he watched through swollen eyes as Jangles and Shaw walked around him as if studying a piece of artwork.

"Body bag, Shaw," Jangles nodded at JC.

Each time Shaw swung his heavy fist it was like being hit with a sledgehammer drawing out a weak grunt or moan to slip from JC's lips. Two punches to the gut… Shaw moved around. A shot to the kidney. One to the lower spine… Shaw moved around. A right cross to the jaw… JC felt the bones pop again. A quick jab to his eye. His body shook and trembled held in place by the ropes. He could feel the blood drooling from his mouth. Each breath was labored as he tried to draw air into his lungs. His eyes were blackened and swollen but he still managed to look up at Jangles.

"This... is... so fucked up... Jangles." JC could barely move his mouth, but still spit that out through his swollen lips. "I am fucking Nine... You hear me, I am fucking Ni..."

He stopped as D'Marious was tossed to the floor before him. The man looked as bad as he felt. D was not a big dude and they had him stripped of his clothes and beaten to a pulp.

"Why, Jangles, why?" JC couldn't help but tear up as he stared at his friend

"Someone is lying to me, JC," Jangles reached down and pulled D'Marious up to his knees by his hair. "There's no way Courtney could be out running me without someone inside giving her information. I'm thinking it's yo bitch ass, but it could be this nigga right here."

Jangles reached into his jacket and pulled the Glock out pressing the muzzle to D'Marious temple. He looked crazed as he kept beating at the man's head with the gun, but JC could see the seriousness shining in his eyes. He was enjoying this as he pushed D away to sprawl out on the floor. Standing over the both of them Jangles pulled back the slide and let it cock back in place.

"You fail to see the problem I have, JC. I have worked hard to pull off this shit, and I was sure all of y'all was with me. He was going to change everything... everything, Muthafucka, and what do I get for making this shit right?

"One of you two niggas is stabbing me in the back." His voice was deathly calm as he squatted down grabbing D'Marious and pulling him to his knees once more. "I want the truth, JC... did you sell me out?"

JC stared out D'Marious who was just barely able to stay on his knees. The man was babbling incoherent words that he was sure were an apology.

"You're wrong, Jangles," he looked up staring into his eyes. "Neither of us betrayed you. We're nothing like you."

"The fuck you mean?" Jangles swung out striking him across the mouth with the pistol. "Everyfuckinthing I did was for IXion and the Nine. Y'all have no idea what Sydney had planned for all of us... all of this bullshit talk about going completely legit because that's what Big Fats always wanted. Shit, I don't give a fuck about what people think I'm a fuckin' hustla... my life is them streets and he was trying to take that from us. Millions of dollars lost because he wanted to be a muthafuckin' pillar of the community. Well fuck that shit"

JC was staring down the barrel of the pistol. He was unable to be afraid any longer because he was surely going to die. He looked at D'Marious and he offered his beaten friend his own apologies.

"I'm fucking touched," Jangles spun the gun and fired into the back of D'Marious head. "This is on you, Nigga... All of this is on you."

With blood splattered all over his naked body, JC slumped forward sobbing over his friend.

With his eyes closed he never noticed Jangles
stepping behind him and his only relief from the
sight of D'Marious was being knocked unconscious
by the clubbing blow from the butt of the pistol
Jangles was holding.

"Well this shit was a fucking waste," he
stepped around and buried the toe of his boot into
the side of D'Marious' dead body.

"Whatcha want done?" Shaw asked as he cut
the rope holding JC up.

"Fuck 'em both," Jangles shrugged his
shoulders. "Just leave them where they lay and let's
go."

Chapter 12

Nick snatched up his cell phone and looked at the screen. He'd been waiting for this call for the last couple of hours, and was pretty sure that it would be a bunch of bad news. He'd promised JC that they would find him… He'd promised the one man he was sure he could trust that everything would work out, and now he was sure that he was dead.

"Fuck," he said as he hit the talk button. "Jackson, what do you have for me?"

"It's not anything good, Mr. Styles," Lagrange answered. "We found the place that you sent us to, but there was nothing there. There are three warehouses out here and I had my men search all three and the most that we did find was recent blood concentrated in this one area. I'd have to say that one or two people were pretty much tortured there."

"But no bodies?" Nick asked feeling almost hopeful.

"No, Sir, no bodies," Lagrange answered. "But, Nick, don't get too hopeful. One of those splatters was definitely the result of a gunshot wound. Without going all CSI on you… I'd swear that it was a headshot."

Nick stood from sitting and walked off towards the kitchen. He could use something stronger than coffee, but he'd been drinking a lot more here lately and the coffee helped to ease up that need for the alcohol. He needed to figure out something because this shit was all going downhill and at some point Courtney was going to get completely caught up in it.

"What do you want us to do?" Lagrange asked. "Do we keep… hold that thought."

"What's going on, Jackson?"

Nick stood there holding the coffee pot waiting for Lagrange to say something. It had to be more trouble coming and right now he had his fair share of all of that and didn't need anymore.

"Mr. Styles, one of my men picked up Johnson and he's headed your way in a big hurry."

"Great. I'll let Courtney now so we can be ready for his bullshit. You keep your men on full alert… I have a feeling that things are going to get really messy really quick and I don't need her in the middle of a bunch of bullshit."

"You're not telling me something, Nick," Lagrange said. "What's going on there?"

"I had a run in with Henri this morning."

****

Nick took a deep breath as he stepped to the door of the kitchen and looked around; his mind was all over the place, but Courtney was nowhere to be seen and that was good. He glanced in the direction of the front door and he could see Henri walking through just as he walked out of the bedroom with just his slacks on. He shook his head knowing that this could go wrong in a lot of ways, but the man just glanced at him as if nothing was out of the ordinary.

"Good morning, Mr. Styles," his voice had a very condescending tone that Nick picked up right away.

"Good morning, Mr. Robles," Nick always found it weird calling him by this fake name, "did we have a meeting this morning, or is this a social call."

"No, not a social call," Henri answered. "We do have a situation that needs to be taken care of and soon, Sir."

Nick stared into the man's deadpan eyes. "What's going on, Henri?"

"He's in town, Nick," Henri answered, "and he's wanting to see you post haste."

"I really don't need this shit right now," Nick had walked to the windows and was looking out over the backyard. "I have so many fires I'm putting out at one time all thanks to *Him* and now he wants to see me? Well you can tell *Him* that I'll have to call when I can fit him in because right now I'm in the middle of a war and the shit just hit the goddamn fan."

"I'll let him know, Nick, but from what I've gathered… he's come back to get everything that he says is his and that includes…" Henri glanced towards the closed bedroom door.

Nick stepped into Henri's face stopping him before he could say another word. The man didn't flinch as they stood nose to nose staring each other down in dead silence.

"I am not your problem, Nicholas," Henri said calmly. "But, your problem has returned to Tampa, and he's none to happy about things. He's told me things, Nick; things that are going on in here that he could only know if he was actually in here. I'd say that your home… I mean Mrs. Roulette's home has been wired."

"Well there you have it," Nick feigned surprise, "just one more thing to have to deal with. You tell our enslaver that I'll be in touch as soon as I can. Better yet… I'm sure he already fucking knows."

****

Nick poured him another cup of coffee while waiting for Jackson to take in everything he'd just told him. He'd been expecting Sydney to return, but now with Courtney telling him that she was pregnant the last thing he needed was him returning trying to reclaim everything he'd pretty much abandoned… including Courtney. Their past wasn't the best thing to sit and think about, but he'd never stopped being in love with Courtney, and if anyone had asked him they would have found out that that is why he returned to Tampa after being release.

"He's back," Nick dropped the news in Jackson's lap, "and he wants to meet."

"Damn," Jackson finally said. "You know how long or where?"

"Naw," Nick sat his desk and just stared off into space. "But there's more."

"More as in… worse?"

"I guess it depends on how you see it," Nick chuckled half-heartedly. "Courtney's pregnant."

"I guess," Jackson whistled, "congratulations are due. Do you think he knows?"

"I'm pretty sure now that it wasn't Jangles that had the house bugged."

"Yea, I agree, or else he'd be trying to use this against you."

"So tell me, Jackson," Nick looked around again, "where do you stand now?"

"Like I said before, Mr. Styles, my loyalties lie with whom I've been paid to stand by. He may have made the payment, but the Mrs. is my charge and I'll stand by her against whoever decide to ride up against her and that now includes him."

Nick sat there nodding his head. "I need to get her ready for Jangles shady ass."

"I'll be in touch," Lagrange said. "You have about twenty minutes according to my people."

"Good." Nick hung up his phone. With a deep breath he stood and went to get Courtney ready for the day they had ahead of them.

"Fuck me," he exasperated through gritted teeth.

****

"So what's the game plan?" Big Shaw asked Jangles as they sped along 275. "Do you think this fool remembers me?"

"Nicky Styles don't forget shit," Jangles grinned. "That's why I always like that nigga. I had to convince Syd to bring his ass into the fold because he thought that Nick was just a little hood rat looking to make a come up, but the boy is a thinker like Syd in a lot of ways. And, the boy is conniving."

"What you mean?"

"When that shit fell through with that buy," Jangles glanced up into the rear view and dipped over two lanes, "I just knew he was planning to take that money and run because he was with some bitch he had looking to get out of the game. Word had got to me and that's why I set his bitch ass up. Shit you was with me when I laid the shit out… remember?"

"Yea, I do," Shaw nodded his head.

Shaw sat there staring out the window as the city and other cars zipped by the window. He'd never been a fan of Tampa; he'd gotten into too much trouble in this city as a kid, but he and Jangles were family and he would do anything for family. He was a warrior and so was Jangles and that's why they were always close.

"So this nigga holdin' a grudge on, Jang?"

"Yea, most likely, especially since I've recently found out that the bitch he was with is the same on Sydney ended up marrying… now ain't that some bullshit.”

“Goddamn, Cuzo y’all live in some drama down here fo’real.”

“No kidding, but I'm getting my fuckin’ company back. I’ve put in too much shit to let some fuckin’ woman run it.”

“So what’s the plan?”

“Playin’ it by ear, big Cuz’,” Jangles turned up the radio and grinned. “Playin’ it by ear. Right now I need to get a feel for the game these two up to, ya feel me… so we headed there.”

Shaw was never a dumb man, and even though he loved to tear people apart piece by piece he never went into a situation without a plan of action. He’d dropped everything to come back home because Jangles sent word for him, but he was not much for all of this spur of the moment bullshit. Even as kids, Jangles had ways of getting them into the kind of trouble that he would always have to find them ways out of, but it never stopped him from loving or following his crazy ass cousin.

“Your cousin is going to be the death of you and your stupid ass,” his mother would constantly tell him, and she was almost right on a number of occasions.

****

“I want you there, Shaw,” Jangles said slapping the big man on the shoulders. “I want you to tell me what you see in Nicky’s eyes the moment them fuckin’ Jamaicans load his ass with bullets.”

“You sho’ this shit ain't gon’ go sideways, Jangles?” Shaw was pacing the floor thinking of the plan Jangles had in place to get rid of Nick Styles. “What this nigga do to you that you want his ass merc’d?”

"Nick too goddamn smart for his own good, ya feel me?" Jangles was sitting in his chair with his feet kicked up on his desk. "See I've heard he's planning to cut out with a fist full of my money and run out to Cali with some bitch and start over all clean and shit. Ain't nobody cut on me like that… shouldn't neva bought that nigga to Syd ass in the first damn place. Neva can trust these niggas."

"Yea, but them Jamaican muthafuckas, Jangles?" Shaw argued. "You know them bastards don't give a fuck who they merc, and you want me there."

"I need you there, Cuzo'," Jangles sat up in his chair. "You and Bubbs, cuz you two the only ones I know gots my back in this shit. You let Nick handle the deal and once the product is laid out just know to duck down because all shit's going to break loose."

"No doubt, Fool, no doubt," Shaw shook his head nervously.

"I'm serious, Shaw," Jangles lost his smile. "This shit's gon' be like the Wild, Wild West and I don't need you and Bubs gettin' blooded."

"You playin' dangerous, Jang," Shaw grinned for the first time, "but let's do this shit."

"That's my nigga."

****

The drive out to Courtney's home took longer than he thought but it gave him time to sit and think. It was shortly after that fire fight that he'd gone to Jangles and told him that he needed to be someplace else. Shaw sat there actually missing his ranch and for the first time he was fearful for his life. No matter the shit he'd ever gotten into with Jangles he'd always managed to find a way out unscathed,

183

but he had a different feeling about things this time around; he just couldn't put a finger on why.

"I appreciate your loyalties to your cousin, Shaw," Sydney had once told him, "and I love that fool like a brother, but we don't need to keep doing all this street level shit. I want more for all of us, but Jangles wants to stay a soldier. I need people around me who want more than just this minor league bullshit that we're in to. I want to take IXion and the Nine into that next phase of evolution."

"Meaning what, Syd?" he asked knowing exactly what Sydney was talking about thanks to a conversation he'd already been through with his cousin.

"I want to take the company completely legit, Shaw," Sydney took a sip from the glass sitting on his desk. "I want our money to be completely clean. I want us to be up there running with all of the other companies you see running game all over Tampa. I'm tired of hiding in the shadows and this city not knowing just how much money we put back into her.

"Look at the number of people we've helped to either rebuild their homes or update their homes in the last few years. Look at the number of businesses that have started because we've given entrepreneurs the seed money to start but they cannot say shit because they don't trust where the money has come from. This is bullshit."

"I hear whatcha sayin', so whatcha want with me, Syd?" Shaw stared at the man sitting across the desk from him. "Jangles is gon' do Jangles and there ain't shit neither of us can tell him to make that change."

"True enough," Sydney laughed knowing that Shaw was more than right but it was more about trying to get everyone to see more than the little bit of money that they were making and the way things were being done. "I just want to get all of y'all on board for some new shit coming down the pike… some new deals I got under my belt that's going to clean up IXion and line our pockets in some major ways."

Shaw sat in the car and almost shook his head. Jangles had set him up in South Texas and being out there on his ranch was a good life for him because it kept him out of the all of the drama and the bullshit here in Tampa. His life had become quiet and docile with him doing very little other than checking in with the Mexicans that Jangles was running shit with. He had no hand in any of the business matters and he was pretty much left alone to run his cattle and ride his horses. But, now he was back in the middle of everything and this was the last place he wanted to be.

Pulling his phone from his pocket he pulled up the last text he'd gotten from Cheryl and smiled. They'd been together for a few years now and he even had a daughter… for the first time in his life he was a happy man.

I love you David Crenshaw…

What the fuck have I gotten myself into? He thought as he read and reread the message.

"Alright," Jangles had turned down the radio, "this how I'm gonna run this shit. I'm gonna go inside and tell them about JC and D'Marious being taken. I gotta get ahead of these fools and after that botched attempt on Courtney thanks to Callie"

"Wait," Shaw turned in his seat to stare at his cousin. "You had Callie here, and you say she fucked up?"

185

"Yea, royally too. Bitch was supposed to blow the fuckin' heart outta Courtney and somehow… she missed."

"Bobby," Shaw never called him by his real name unless shit was deadly serious, "we both know that Callie never misses. What the fuck is really going on down here, Cuzo? What are you into with Nicky Styles and this woman?"

"That's just it, Shaw," Jangles slung his head back tossing his dreads away from his face. The disgust was obvious. The uncertainty was obvious. He looked lost and confused as he sat there staring at the house of this woman he'd come to hate. "This shit shouldn't be this hard… I mean, I was sure it was JC givin' Nick information and now I think we beat the shit outta two loyal soldiers and I killed one. Everything's all fucked up because of Syd and this woman, Shaw, and I don't know what I'm doing wrong. She should have ran by now, but she holdin' in there better than most dudes we know. She gots to be gettin' help other than Styles, but I don't know who."

"And you fo' sho' Sydney dead?"

Jangles stared at the big man for a second. It wasn't the first time that same crazy thought had run through his head, but he'd replayed the explosion a million times in his head. The coroner had confirmed the body. The autopsy had confirmed the body. Everything had confirmed that what they'd buried had by Sydney's remains. Jangles shook his head to clear away the craziness of that idea.

"I'm going in. Pretty sure I'm not going to be welcomed. Gimme about ten minutes then call the boys to roll up and toss JC out. Got it?"

"Got it." Shaw stared at the message from his girl once more. "It's better you decided not to leave his ass layin' there. Let's get this shit over with."

Jangles slipped out of the driver's seat and ran up to the door punching the doorbell over and over until the door was finally opened. As he walked in past the guard watching the door, he plastered his game face on to look frantic as hell and rushed into the living room.

"Good," he said as Nick and Courtney turned to stare at him, "the gang's all here."

Jangles stared about wild eyes taking in everything in the room. Once again that strange white dude was present, and as he stared at the man he tried to remember just why he was always around; one day he'd get all of the answers to all of the questions, but today the agenda was clear.

"What's going on?" Courtney stood from her desk.

"Why are you here, Jangles?" Nick was reaching for the small of his back.

"Whoa, whoa, Nicky," Jangles stood there with his arms stretched out, "I come in peace, Nigga, real deal."

"In peace," Nick stared at him his brow furrowed. "What the fuck do you want?"

"We got a problem," Jangles wiped his forehead. "JC and D'Marious were taken."

"What do you mean… taken?" Courtney stood from her desk and walked up to Jangles. He almost grinned at the look of hatred and contempt he could see in her eyes.

"I asked them to go to Texas to find out what the fuck is going on there, you know with all of that shit with that driver, and I got a call from some fool I don't know saying he had our boys. He was making threats to kill them, Courtney. He was making threats to kill key members of the Nine."

"What did he say he wanted?" Nick asked as he came to stand beside Courtney.

"What do any of these muthafuckas want," Jangles shrugged his shoulders. "He just didn't give me a price."

Courtney stepped away turning her back on Jangles. The last thing she ever wanted was to see him in her house again, and it was taking everything in her not to just grab the mail opener on her desk and stab him in the throat. The conversation between her and Nina about Jangles not being responsible for Sydney's death played in her head once again and she stood wondering… if not him, then who?

"All of this shit's out of control," Jangles said. "Members of the Nine is dying left and right and we need to get ahead of this right now."

"We don't know they're dead," Courtney said but knowing from what Nick had told her the likelihood that those two men still being alive was not at all possible.

"Mr. Styles," the guard at the door had run up with his fingers at his ear, "we have a situation outside, Sir."

"What now?"

"A car just broke through the gate and is heading up the drive, Sir."

Nick ran off leaving everyone standing there staring at the man. Just as he opened the door the car in question skidded to a stop in front of the house and a body was tossed out of the backseat. Shaking his head not wanting to see what he was seeing he ran out into the yard as the car sped off. The body was barely moving as it rolled to a stop at his feet.

Kneeling Nick turned him over and stared down into JC's bloody and beaten face.

"Fuck," pulled the man's head up. "Goddamn, JC… goddamn."

"Nicky," JC's voice was barely heard, "I told them nothing. IXion is good 'cus I told them nothing."

"Don't talk, JC," Nick looked back over his shoulder. "Call a fucking ambulance… NOW!"

"Tell my wife and kids that I love them, Nicky," a tear was streaming from his eyes. "Promise me that you'll tell them."

"You ain't dying today, JC," Nick sat on the ground gently cradling the man's head in his lap. "You hold on. You hold on."

"Promise me, Nicky, please."
"You have my word… I promise."

Chapter 13

"I'm here to see James Charles Williams," Nick watched as the older lady typed the name into her computer. If everything he'd demanded had been taken care of he would almost have to go through a security check.

"Mr. Williams is in a secure room," she informed him. ""I need your name and ID to verify against the list if names."

Nick pulled out his wallet and slid it to her with his driver's license showing. He watched as she looked from her screen to his license to his face a few times before handing back his wallet.

"Mr. St. Cloud, there are officers at Mr. Williams' door and they'll require your ID as well," she informed him. "He's in room 212, I'll have an orderly show you the way."

"Thank you, "he answered walking off not needing the orderly.

Nick proceeded to the elevator and punched the button to go up and waited. He'd heard about this medical facility several years ago and thought it better to put JC here under watch to make certain no one could take a second crack at splitting his head. He got off on the second floor and made it through the two cops guarding the door because they were his men; he remembered Mr. Robins telling Sydney that it was always prudent to have cops willing to work off duty for you, and he knew quite a few willing to make extra money.

Stepping into the room was like stepping into a sci-fi nightmare. There were machines all around the head of the bed beeping with flickering lights. Monitors were flashing vitals and plastic bags with varying liquids were dripping into tubes all connected to different parts of his body. A sick thought of Darth Vader suddenly sitting up and that ominous hissing breathing apparatus starting up filled his head.

"See, JC," he placed a hand on the man's shoulder as he softly whispered, "I told you that you wasn't dying on me. I got the wife and kids tucked away safe and sound waiting for you to get out of here and I'll make certain that y'all get away for at least a good month for you to recoup.

"Damn," he tried to stifle a sniffle, "I'm so sorry for all of this, JC. I'm so sorry."

Hospitals of any kind had always made Nick nervous, and being in here with JC hooked wasn't helping his phobia at all. The room was dimly lit, and all of the beeping echoed and vibrated annoyingly around one another. He took a deep breath and stepped back staring at the man just lying there. His face was still swollen, his eyes and lips were puckered closed, his nose had been reset and they'd taped it to keep it in place, there were bruises everywhere, and yet somehow… JC was still alive.

****

"After all of this shit settles down, Nicky, you get with JC," Sydney advised him. "He's not a part of that group and he'll see the big picture."

"You sure he can be trusted, Syd?"

"It was in his eyes, Nick," Sydney's voice sounded a little muffled, "he knows what's going on but he ain't down with it. He'll make a damn good ally because he's part of the Nine's board. He can keep an eye on things when you and Courtney cannot be in the office."

"How long?" Nick's question was blunt.

"How long for what?"

Nick was downstairs away from the condo letting Courtney rest. He'd taken her to see her doctor after the explosion to get her something to make her relax, and he'd stepped away leaving two of his men upstairs with her. He was pacing just outside the parking garage trying to figure out a way to talk sense into Sydney.

"We can't do this to her, Sydney," he argued. "Goddammit, she thinks that you're fucking dead. How long do we keep this shit up? How long do we keep her in the dark?"

"All you have to do is keep her alive, Nick," Sydney stated hard. "She's your responsibility from this point on, and I'm entrusting her life into your capable hands. I have to get ahead of this poison, Nick, and I need her to concentrate on the Nine and not me. Jangles will be gunning for her... do you understand? "

"I get that," Nick stared up at the moon hanging just behind a flotilla of clouds. "None of this is going to end well, Sydney, and I'm telling you now she's gonna be fit to be tied when this all blows up in our faces."

"Yea I know," Sydney exhaled heavily." We'll deal with that then... for now get with Henri about JC and I'll be in touch soon."

"Yea... right."

****

Nick reached out to touch JC's arm. "He was so right about you."

Unable to look at JC lying there hooked up to all of those tubes and machines Nick turned away to stare at the window that looked out into the hall. Davies and McDaniels, his two cops, were standing just outside and he could see the shadow of one of them as they stepped aside and the door opened. A young nurse smiled at him as she walked up checking on the bags of liquids.

"So, um, how's he doing? "

"He's responding well, Mr. St. Cloud," she answered. "He's not out of the woods yet, but he's getting stronger. We're watching him closely... I promise."

"I trust you," Nick smiled." It is in your notes that I'm to be contacted if there's any kind of change."

"Yes, Sir... with three numbers if I'm not mistaking."

Nick nodded and allowed the young lady to complete her assessment without any more of his questions. She seemed capable as she moved about the bed checking his vitals from his blood pressure to his pulse and heart rate. She was talking to him as if he were awake, and Nick wondered if anything she said was getting through to him.

"Not too long, Mr. St. Cloud," she nodded as she left the room.

Standing next to the bed he dropped his head. "I'm exhausted, JC," Nick said more to hear his voice than anything. "I'm so fucking sorry this happened. This wasn't supposed to happen, and I swear I had men on the way to get you. The moment we hung up I was on the phone with Jackson and he had men on the road to find you.

"He's going to pay, J," he placed his hand softly on the unconscious man's forehead staring at his closed eyes. "On my word, that nigga's gonna pay with his life. I'm going to rip his fucking heart out,"

"Not if I rip it out first."

Nick didn't turn towards the voice but he did rise up off the rails of the bed. He would definitely have to have a word with his men, but it didn't surprise him that this one man could get in with little to know effort.

"You're making me feel unwelcomed, Nicky... Come on, turn around and greet an old friend."

"What's good, Syd," Nick turned towards the room door, "or should I call you McGregor?"

"Ha! Jokes, you got me laughing, Nicky," Sydney stepped into the room and sat in the only chair available. "I figured since you wouldn't come see me that I'd just drop in on JC until you showed up."

"How did you know I'd bring him here?" Nick folded his arms across his chest. "I didn't even tell Henri or Courtney where I have him."

"If I don't know ya," Sydney grinned shrugging his shoulders.

"Why are you here, Syd?"

Sydney stood and walked to the opposite side of the bed looking down at JC; Nick wasn't certain, but he actually looked concern. He watched as Sydney gently stroked the man's head and then leaned over to kiss his forehead much like a father would his son. Nick stepped back from the bedside and leaned against the sink counter behind him.

"We have a problem, Nick," Sydney looked up, "you and I."

"We do?" Nick kept a straight face.

"Yea," Sydney's eyes were hard but there was a smile on his lips. "You see... I've been hearing things, Nick. The kind of things that's got me feeling some kind of way."

"Be real, Syd," Nick pushed his hands into his pockets his hide his fists, "don't you mean you've been seeing things. Or maybe the word I should use is … spying things?"

"Word it as you will, Nicky, this shit's real and that means you and I have some real problems."

"This is neither the time nor place, Sydney," Nick said nodding his head at JC. "We need to deal with this shit someplace else."

"Oh, my brother, I agree," Sydney walked around the bed to stand in Nick's face. "I came here for two reasons... I needed to see JC, because I heard about this shit here, and now we have to decide on what to do about Jangles. Oh and I needed you to see me.

"You can't continue to avoid this shit, Nigga," Sydney was nose to nose with Nick staring into his eyes before slowly backing away. "We gon' have that talk, Nicky, and I won't be asking so nicely the next time... ya dig?"

"When and where?" Nick stood his ground staring at a man he used to fear and admire.

'The office... you remember how to get there, right?" Nick nodded his head never dropping the eye contact. "Be there tomorrow... after, say two."

Sydney turned and walked off to the room door. As he turned the handle, he looked back first at JC and then to Nick with a very unfriendly smile.

"And, Nicky, be there... ok. Don't make me come looking for you this time, because if I do… it won't be so pretty. Don't you forget, I put you up on this shit, and I can take you down at any fucking time that I'm ready to."

"I'll be there, Mr. McGregor." Nick answered.

"Haha! Cool." Sydney strolled from the room leaving Nick staring at the door.

"Damn." He stepped to the window watching as Sydney pressed a wad of folded money into each of the guards' hands before walking off without a care in the world. "Son-of-a-bitch… I should have known."

Sitting in his car moments after Sydney had left, Nick reached over and pulled his pistol from the glove box and laid it on the passenger seat. Once again Nick found himself looking around nervously. He could hear his heart pounding between his ears and the sweat was draining down the back of his head drenching his collar. Pulling out his phone and dialed Jackson Lagrange.

"How did I know you'd be calling?" the noise in the background let Nick know that Jackson was in some kind of club. "People always tend to call me when Tangerine is about to dance."

"A strip club in the middle of the day?"

"We all have our vices… now don't we?" Jackson laughed before realizing that Nick was quiet. Just as he was about to ask what the problem he was cut off.

"Jackson, he's here," was all Nick said and then he sat there waiting as the man walked off to get somewhere quiet.

"If you don't mind," Jackson said as he closed his truck door, "but can you please repeat that?"

"We were just face to face, and this shit is about to really blow up in my face."

"Does the Mrs. know?"

"No," Nick's voice dropped.

"Pardon my asking, Nick... but how much does Courtney really know about Sydney's death?"

"Up until about a week or so ago, she'd thought Jangles had decided that the poison wasn't

fast enough and decided to blow him up. To tell her
now is not going to go over well, but that's what I'm
going to need of you."

"Explain."

"He's demanded that we meet tomorrow,"
Nick said, "I doubt this will go well at all and I think
it's time she knew the truth about all of it. I'm going
to text you some information in a bit, I have a safety
deposit box with some things you'll need to get for
her."

"Why not just talk to her, Nick?"

Nick took a deep breath and slid his hand
over his bald head. "Everything I'm leaving you," he
released another exasperated breath, "it will go over
better after I meet with him. Either we can give it to
her, or you can. Either way I need you to get that
together and have it ready.

"I have a guy that I use that I'll have looking
for Sydney," Nick continued. "You'll be busy with
her if anything happens to me and he's damn good.
I'll have Tytus contact you in the morning so you'll
know who he is. Tomorrow will be a turning point...
I have a feeling that she's going to be facing shit
from all angles with Sydney, Jangles and all the
thugs involved."

"Do you truly believe that he's out to kill
you, Nick?" Jackson asked.

"Courtney is pregnant, and I'm pretty sure
that it was Sydney who had the house bugged now.
There was something in his eyes that's got me pretty
sure that Sydney not only wants me dead… he needs
me dead because that will put Courtney back into his
arms."

"So this all ends up back to being about the
woman?" Nick could almost see Jackson shaking his
head. "A fucking pissing contest just to see who has

197

the biggest dick, and you're going to just walk right
into it because you have to show Sydney that you're
not afraid of him any longer."

"It's more than that," Nick sat in the car
trying to convince himself now. "If I don't go, I put
Courtney in the middle of the two men she knows
she loves… she's going to hate me, Jackson. She's
going to hate me because I've known for over two
years that her husband is still alive, and she's going
to hate me more because she now has my baby
growing inside of her. I have to talk to Sydney, and
he and I need to get this shit settled between us."

"You're right about one thing, Nicholas St.
Cloud," Jackson said.

"Yea," Nick chuckled, "and what's that?"

"None of this will end well." Jackson sat in
his truck staring out at the flashing lights of the strip
club he was sitting in front of. He'd been doing this
business for several decades, and he'd never run up
against a man like Sydney Roulette until now. There
was something almost honorable about Nicholas St.
Cloud; the man was trying to make things right
without concerning himself with how it was going to
make him look in the end. He rubbed at his rough,
unshaven face and let out a heavy sigh.

"Don't forget to send me the information for
the security box, and I'll get that taken care of in the
morning first thing. I'll have men posted closer to
Mrs. Roulette until we find out where Sydney is held
up and I need to get a better handle on Mr. Johnson
because this shit with all of you men has gotten way
out of hand. You may want to send me the
information on where Mr. Williams is set up and I'll
make certain that nothing else happens to him.

"Nick, this shit is crazy… you know that,
yes?"

"Yea, and it's bound to get crazier," Nick stated flatly. "I have a feeling that everyone is gonna have to die for her to be safe. I have some people I'm going to send to you. I knew them when I was locked away and I'll be honest… these fools love crazy. Also, I'll contact Yuri Vasilevich and I'll let him know what the hell's going on so that I can find out where his allegiances lie."

"I'll have to miss my girl Tangerine tonight," Jackson laughed. "Too much shit to be done. We'll talk in a few hours, Mr. Nick, go get your ducks in a row."

Nick ended the call and sat for a moment longer before punching in the number into his phone and waited for the other end to be picked up. He reached over picking up the pistol and he laid it in his lap.

"Mr. St. Cloud?" Janice seemed surprised. "You're calling my cell and not the office phone… is everything… everything alright?"

"No, Janice," Nick answered, "everything is not alright. I need you to listen and do everything that I tell you with little to no questions. I want you to go through everything and make certain that you're not leaving any traces of what you've been doing for Courtney and I. Once you get that done. I want you to just leave the office. Don't say anything to anyone you just get up, walk the hell out. and you don't look back. From there I need you to go home and get you some things together because I need for you to leave Tampa."

"Leave," Janice was whispering into her cell phone, "and go where? What's going on, Sir?"

"Things have taken a very bad turn, Janice, and I don't need you and your family caught up in things. Jangles had JC beat to within an inch of his

199

life and I'm pretty sure that D'Marious is dead. I need you out of there ASAP. Do you understand? And I'll take care of money for you so I don't want you to worry about that."

"Yes, Mr. St. Cloud," she was breathing heavy. "Where do I go?"

"Drive to Atlanta, and I'll make certain you have enough money in place to not only get you to wherever you want to go, but to take care of you and your family for a very long time.

"I just need you to hurry, Janice. Oh, and keep calm… don't let them see you panicked."

"I won't, and thank you, Mr. St. Cloud, thank you very much."

"Text me your bank information once we get off the phone and then you move out quick. Don't make any calls from the office phones, but contact who ever you're taking with you to get ready so y'all can leave today."

"I will." Janice was looking around to see if anyone could have heard her conversation before she hung up her phone and began doing exactly what Nick had said.

Nick stared at his phone and went through his contacts; he made a quick call to Yuri Vasilevich and told him that they needed to meet at the house today. The man had no problems with the meeting and told him that he and his brother, Tomas, would be there. With that done he made one last call as he finally began the drive back to Tampa to see about Courtney.

"Tytus," Nick said after the phone was answered.

"What's good, Styles?" Tytus never was one for a business conversation.

"I have something big I need you to work on for me, but," Nick glanced around before pulling out into traffic and noticed a car that just seemed out of place. "But, I need you to keep this one close to your chest."

"Alright, Nicky," the man answered. "What's up?"

"Sydney Roulette is alive," Nick said bluntly, "and I need you to find his ass for me."

"The fuck you mean; Sydney is alive?"

"Look, I can't go into everything right now, but Sydney was not in that truck when it blew up. He's alive and well and he's here in Tampa. I need you to find out where and to get that information to Jackson Lagrange, I'll text you his contact information when we get off the phone."

"Nick, what the fuck is really going on? You pawning this info off to anotha muthafucka that I don't even know."

"Some things are coming down the pike, Ty, but I need you on your up and up. I just need to make certain that if anything happens to me that nothing…" he hesitated, "nothing happens to Courtney. I need you to make certain that you and Jackson are on the same page."

"Nick, you know I'm here for you in whatever you need, Bro," Tytus said. "You sound worried?"

"I'm just worried about her," Nick tried to make his laugh convincing. "This little war with Jangles is about to get really sick; so you keep your head on the swivel."

"No doubt… no doubt. I'll get to work on Sydney and I'll get in touch with this Jackson as soon as I know something."

"Cool, I'll get you his number once I get a moment to text."

Nick hung up on the call and glanced up into the rear view. Nodding his head, he spotted the same car from where he'd pulled out of the hospital parking lot. He'd never seen the car before, but the jet black vehicle with its dark tinted windows just looked out of place. Currently, it was about three cars behind him so Nick flipped on his flasher and slowly eased into the passenger lane. Glancing up just in time, he smiled as he watched the car move over into the same lane.

"You overplayed your hand, Syd," he said to himself as he turned up the radio. "So let's get this shit started."

Punching the gas Nick sped off into traffic keeping an eye on his follower as he decided that today he needed to have a little fun. His thoughts were on Courtney and the shit he'd put her through during their run to California, and here he was still doing stupid shit by listening to Sydney about lying to her.

"Courtney," he said as if she was sitting beside him, "I wish I could take all of this shit back. I wish I'd listen to those voices in my head that said I needed to tell you what Sydney was fucking planning. Shit… shit, you should have known. I hope that someday you'll find a way to forgive me."

He slid his thumb along the surface of the pistol in his lap and then looked up into the mirror with an evil smile across his lips. The car was still keeping its three car pace, and that was good because that meant they were only back there to keep tabs on him.

"I'm so done with all of this shit… so fuckin' done," he said out loud.

Chapter 14

"So, Mr. St. Cloud," Courtney crawled up into the bed and laid her head on his bare chest, "how was your day?"

"Every day is an adventure," he chuckled. "And just what did you do that kept your day exciting, Ms. Roulette?"

"Oh you know me," she was running a finger up and down the ridges of his abdominal muscles, "I spent time trying to keep myself five steps ahead of an egomaniac by getting my hair and nails done and listening to the sexual exploits of my best friend."

"Well damn that sounds like a typical day for a woman who owns and runs a multi-million dollar business… living vicariously through the sexploits of her nymphomaniac best friend."

"Hey now!" she laughed as she punched him in his stomach. "I don't need to live through her sexploits… I just don't share with her the way this man I know tends to put it down on me."

"This man huh," Nick was now an active player in her little game. "Damn, so that means you have sexploits of your own? Are they as juicy as hers, because we both know that Nina can be a little sluttish."

"A little, ha! That heffa is a straight up slut," they both laughed out. "And as for my own sexploits… well let's just say that one thing about this man… he always leaves me feeling like I'm being put away soaked."

"Soaked definitely sounds like a good thing."

"Oh it's really good," Courtney allowed her finger to trace further down to slide around the edge of his bellybutton. "I think though that I haven't been showing him how much I appreciate him."

"Hm," Nick grinned as her finger slipped under the sheet that was pulled up to his waist, "that doesn't sound too nice of you, Woman. Why would you not appreciate this man who provides your sexploits?"

"It's not that I don't appreciate him," her hand was now sliding up and down the top of his thigh, "because I really do, but I think I need to show him more… often."

"Well if I was this 'man' I'd definitely appreciate more often."

Courtney leaned over his chest and began to slowly kiss her way down his body paying attention to his nipples as her fingernails lightly dug into his thighs. There was something magical hearing Nick groan out that always tickled her, and he was never fearful of her putting her nails into him… it always seemed to excite him more. It was these moments when he would just lay there and allow her to tease him that she loved the most. Her fingers would come close to that ominous lump in his boxers without touching him until just the right moment, and he allowed her to dictate when that right moment was.

Her tongue slipped between her lips and circled his nipple before sucking it into her mouth to nibble at it before she leaned over to tease the other nipple. She'd found out a long time ago that Nick had sensitive nipples and he was quite prone to having them licked and sucked, and she was more than willing to comply.

Nick was running his fingers through the curls of her hair watching as she began licking her way down his stomach. There was always something so sexy about watching her tease him; she may have come from a very strict upbringing, but the girl had definitely learned a few things after leaving Missouri. There had been a number of times that he'd been tempted to ask her where she'd learned some of the things that she knew, but decided it was better to just let her do what she was doing… and enjoy it.

"There's just something about the way you taste, Mr. St. Cloud," she licked at his belly button before looking up at him, "that always makes me horny."

Nick moaned out as her tongue dipped into his bellybutton and her fingers grasped his dick stroking him through his boxers. This was the time when he had to fight with himself to keep from just grabbing her and having his way with her. Her fingers were small as they pressed the fabric around as much as it allowed and the silk of the material created just enough friction to make him groan out.

"Well you know me, Ms. Roulette," Nick grinned, "there's just something about you being horny that just makes me smile."

"I love your smile," Courtney whipped away the sheet. Her smile broadened as she stared at her filled hand. Things had been too hectic lately for her and Nick to enjoy themselves and she'd planned to spending a very intense night with him after having to listen to Nina about her night with Jangles.

Moving down the bed Courtney straddled his legs. Grabbing the waistband of his boxers she pulled on them until he pressed up his hips for her to pull them away from her prize. Her eyes widened like they always do when Nick was finally exposed; from that very first time to now, it always amazed her with what he kept hidden away from the world. Her mouth watered as she pulled his boxers to his knees and released them to take him into her dainty hands. She could feel Nick watching her as her fists slid up and down his length.

Nick was indeed watching. He had his hands clinched behind his head as he waited to see what she would do next. There was something very sexy about watching her kneel over him with his dick in her hands and licking her lips.

"What have you found there?"

"Something… tasty," her voice was raspy as she leaned forward to kiss the head. "Something I've been thinking about all day."

Nick sucked in a deep breath as she let the head slip between her lips and into her mouth. The warmth and the wet was enough to make him want to pound his fists against the bed as her head eased further down his shaft. She'd come such a long way from that little girl fresh out of college he'd met all of those years ago to this woman he was in the bed with right now, and goddamn if he wasn't the happiest man on the planet for it. Her tongue swirled around the head as she pulled back and the down the belly of his dick as she pushed her mouth back down.

All of the bullshit of his day vanished into the fog as he reached down to pull her hair out of the way so that he could continue to watch. He loved seeing her lips stretched around in a tight "O" holding him into her mouth. Her teeth lightly grazed his heated flesh as she began to bob her head up and down with a slight twist each time she had just the head trapped. Her eyes were closed and he could feel little puffs of air burst from her nose each time she took in as much of him as she could.

The first time Courtney had ever done anything like this had been with Nicholas, he happened to be her first in a lot of things, but most especially everything sexual. She'd never told him that she was a virgin the very first time he made love to her, and that had remained a secret to this day. She once thanked Nina for all of her talk about the things she'd done with her male friends and for introducing her to pornography, but Nina had teased her so badly that she never brought it up again.

He was very wet thanks to the way she was drooling and her hands were slipping up and down his length keeping up with her mouth. She stopped and gently chewed on the spongy head as her fingers cupped and fondled his dangling testicles. Nick was holding back and she could tell… the muscles in his thighs were jumping around as he was curling his toes to keep from just fucking her mouth until his release. She loved this power she held over him right now as she slowed down her attack on his dick. She eased down until the head nudged the back of her throat and she pushed down harder until he felt her gag reflex trigger.

"Goddamn, Court," Nick groaned out.

Holding her breath and swallowing she took a bit more of him into her throat. Tears were forming in her eyes, but she was bound and determined tonight. Pulling back just a little she swallowed again as the breath she held in her lungs eased from her nose. Sucking another deep breath, Courtney pushed down again feeling him ease into her throat until at long last she had all of him trapped inside of her mouth. Opening her eyes, she stares up his body and into his eyes as she slowly pulls back.

"Damn," Nick breathes out as she's stroking him and smiling a very big smile. "You out to kill me tonight?"

"Oh no, Baby," she licked the head, "I'm just trying to show my man how much I really do appreciate him."

Unable to think of anything to say, Nick pulled her head back down as he thrust up. He groaned as Courtney took him back into her mouth. His eyes closed and all he could see was stars as she bounced her head up and down taking him all the way in and then releasing just enough for her to take in another deep breath. This was a first for him and all he could do was restrain his impulses to fuck her mouth until she was unconscious.

"Enough," he finally tapped out with a laugh as he pulled her head up. Looking down his body he watched as she slid her tongue over her lips in a very suggestive manner. "Yea, someone is in some trouble tonight."

"Oh yea?" she teased. "And who could that be?"

Nick sat up and then pulled her body up his until she was lying on his chest. Staring into her eyes and then looking at her sweet lips all wet from drooling all over his dick he couldn't resist kissing her any longer. Their lips met in a powerful, hot kiss that had them both pawing at the others face in an effort not to lose the connection. Holding her to his body, Nick rolled them over until he was on top of her with her looking down.

Courtney loved the look in her man's eyes; they were as hungry for her as she was for him. His hands were gently stroking her face, then down to her neck and then she took in a deep breath as he pinched her nipples through the thin material of her nightie. She watched as Nick grabbed the satiny gown into his fists and she almost screamed as he ripped the material in half.

Once the ruined gown was pulled off and thrown across the room, her panties were treated to the same caveman brutality and they too joined her gown on the floor. Her body was on fire as Nick began to kiss and lick her all over starting at her neck and working his way down. Her breasts and nipples were giving the same teasing treatment she'd given to his nipples and then he was on his way further down her body. Everything about her was on a low boil as he didn't stop at her navel but licked his way down her legs and even treated her toes to something he'd never done before causing her to squeal and squirm all over the bed.

Again he had her thinking about all of the firsts she'd experienced with him as he licked and kissed his way back up her legs. She was burning up and the fire was only getting hotter as he stretched out between her legs. His tongue was doing things to her that had her cursing under her breath as his mouth finally made contact with the hottest point on her body. Courtney screamed out and thrust up as he slipped his tongue as deeply as his mouth and face would allow.

Nick could only imagine the way she looked with her eyes rolled into the back of her head as he took her into his mouth. He'd always loved the way she tastes and the feel of her legs wrapped around his head locking him between her thighs so he couldn't get away. His mouth and tongue were in constant movement as he reached up to grab that thick ass of hers to keep her from getting too far away from his ravenous mouth.

He could feel the muscles in her thighs twitching around his head as her feet locked and pulled him down tighter between her thighs. He stiffened his tongue as she began to grind and gyrate against his mouth and face and her moans and screams began to bounce off the walls. Her hands were on the back of his head and her fingernails were starting to bite into his neck as she pushed down. Her body was beginning to shake and shiver and Nick knew it was time to apply the pressure. He wanted to push her over the edge… he wanted her to explode… he wanted her body to be amped up and ready for the rest of the night, and he attacked her with all that he had.

Courtney's mouth fell open in a silent scream as Nick's mouth assaulted her in a way she'd only dreamed about. Her toes were curled as her feet were locked at the ankles behind his head. Her stomach muscles were rippling like the waves of the ocean from an approaching storm and her breathing felt like it was caught in her chest. Her eyes were squeezed closed, but she could still see Nick trapped between her clenching thighs with his head bobbing up and down and his tongue captured deep inside of her. She was so close to her orgasm that she could almost taste it.

She was moaning and calling out his name over and over as her body moved in queue with his mouth until the end flashed before eyes. Her body stiffened and her legs fell away from his shoulders as she pushed up as hard as she could against his face. Her head pressed back into the pillow as her hands kept him right where she needed his mouth and face to be. His tongue was ravenous as he feasted upon her like a starving man, and she fed him all that her body could.

Slowly Nick eased his face away and stared up at Courtney, he grinned as she was just lying there her whole body twitching and she was breathing erratic. He eased up onto his knees between her spread thighs staring down at her beautiful body as he waited for her to come back to the world of the sane. As her breathing slowed, he lowered his body over hers until she could barely feel him. Moving his hand between their bodies he pressed his dick against the lips of her pussy.

"So tell me, Ms. Roulette," he leaned forward kissing her lips, "are you ready for round two?"

Courtney giggled and slowly began to grind against him, "More than you'll ever know, Mr. St. Cloud., now… give it to me."

"As you wish."

Nick pushed down and then forward watching as she threw her head back. He'd never met another woman who ever made him feel the way that Courtney did, and at this point he could die right now and go to hell and he'd go with a smile on his face. He leaned down again and pressed his mouth to hers in a passionate kiss that always took their breath away. Her legs had wrapped around his back and clamped down and her hands were sliding up and down his back as he began to slowly ease in and pull out in long strokes. She was moaning in his mouth as he pushed his tongue between her lips and his hands were squeezing her breasts as their bodies moved in sync.

Courtney had her eyes closed again as Nick pushed up into her. No man has ever filled her or even made her feel the way he had a way of doing, and that included Sydney. The passion she had for her husband was on a totally different level, but what she had with Nick was always completely consuming. He hadn't moved yet other than to make them "One" being and she was waiting… preparing herself for the inevitable to come. She wanted him,

and if they were already expecting she'd want him
right now to place his baby in her belly so they
would have one more thing in this crazy world to
share.

"I love you, Baby," she pulled her mouth
away and mumbled as he pulled back between her
thighs.

"And I love you more than words,
Courtney," Nick pushed forward filling her as their
lips met once more.

Soaked and pressed against one another Nick
made love to the only woman in the world he'd ever
wanted to be with. He tried not to think of the
bullshit that he'd put her through as he laid his body
down in her arms and she held him as tightly as she
could. Her moans filled his ear and sent trembles
down his spine. He groaned in her ear and gently bit
her neck as her fingernail sunk into his shoulders to
the point he was sure she was drawing blood. With
each stroke she was screaming out his name and this
amped him up to make it hurt as good as he could.

Their bodies were pounding up and down
against one another as he reached up with both hands
grabbing and pulling her head deeper into the pillow.
The heels of her feet were digging into his ass as his
thrusts became deeper and harder pushing her down
into the mattress with each cry out she made begging
him for more. They were taking no prisoners tonight
as what began as a night of loving making because a
powerful night of heated fucking. The more she
screamed, the harder they beat at each other's bodies
until as last both of them were pushed over that edge
they'd been racing towards.

"No matter what ever happens," Nick had
pulled his weight up off of her allowing her to catch
her breath as he worked towards catching his own, "I

want you to know that I have always and I will always love you Courtney… more than you'll ever know."

"And I will always and have always loved you as well, Nick," pulled his head down and kissed him hard. "Always… no matter what."

Chapter 15

Nina couldn't take her eyes off of the huge man that Jangles had introduced as his cousin Shaw. The man was like staring up at a mountain, but to her he was like a giant teddy bear. He had the biggest brown eyes she'd ever seen, and his face was covered in a wooly mass of facial hair. He had a clean shaven head making him look a little like Rick Ross, and he kept flashing her the biggest and friendliest smile.

"I can see why this nigga always talkin' 'bout you, Ms. Nina," he grinned glancing over at Jangles. "I've told him a couple of times that if I didn't have my Cheryl waiting for me back in Texas… I'd steal you from him."

"Hell, I doubt his ass would even miss me," Nina giggled as Jangles cut his eyes at her. "I'd almost say that you could have me."

"Yea," Jangles glared at the both of them as they started laughing, "the two of you can kiss my ass. Talking about me like I ain't even in the goddamn room."

"Aww," Nina rushed over taking his face in her hands and kissing his lips, "it's ok, Baby, we still love you."

As Shaw moved to come towards him, Jangles raised a finger, "Don't even think it, Nigga… you kiss me and I swear I'll shoot you where you fuckin' stand."

Shaw dropped onto the sofa laughing so hard that he began snorting and this stopped Nina and Jangles from making out to stare at him. Looking up the big man could see their weird expressions before

they both began laughing and pointing at him
causing him to laugh once more.

It had been a long time since the last time he
and Jangles had gotten together for anything other
than business, and just sitting here laughing was
something he'd missed. As shorties running around
West Tampa, neither of them had known their dad's
and they'd always depended upon one another.
Jangles had taught him to fight, and he'd kept
Jangles from failing out of several of his classes.
They were inseparable from the moment they
stepped out the door of their homes until that last
second they split to go in for the night.

Jangles met Sydney in kindergarten, but
Shaw hadn't met him until they were in junior high
because he'd been sent to live with his granny. Shaw
was always surprised how Jangles and Sydney
became so close so quick, especially because Sydney
wasn't the typical street kid. Sydney, for all of their
junior high years and the first two years of high
school, was a stellar student. He was never late to
school, and he even made certain that his sister and
brother got to school on time before he rushed off to
where he needed to be.

"You kinda pussy huh," Shaw had asked
Sydney once when he'd walked away from a fight
with a couple of the school's little wannabe street
thugs.

"What did you say, Muthafucka?" Sydney
was in his face before he had time to react.

"Naw, naw, Cousin," Jangles was laughing,
"you don't wanna do that."

Being so big, Shaw always played the
"bully" card. "Shit… I gots this, Cuzo," Shaw
laughed as he turned from Jangles and back to

215

Sydney. "Oh I know yo' lil bitch ass heard me, you kinda pussy?"

Sydney stood his ground and smiled up at the large boy standing over him. It was like he was working out just what he needed to do before he said a thing or made a move. Shaw looked back at Jangles and laughed as Sydney finally turned away and began to walk off once more. Jangles was standing with his back against a wall and his foot propped up watching as his cousin continued to bait the kid from around the block.

"Yea, just walk on… pussy," Shaw yelled out as a group of kids began to gather around him. He always loved being the center of attention and it was never hard because he always towered over everyone he'd gone to school with.

"You think," Sydney stopped and dropped his book bag to the ground and turned around, "that because you're so big that you're something impressive? I think you're a moron with an influx of testosterone and no goddamn brain between your huge ears. More like a big gorilla looking for a tree to swing from to show off for the people standing around."

Of course didn't go over well with Shaw as he watched Sydney slowly making his way towards him. Because it was now such a natural thing to do, he quickly dropped into a defensive posture with his big meaty paws balled up in front of his face. He looked back at Jangles once more who gave him the nod of approval as he stood watching with that smile of his on his face.

"Come get some, Pussy boy," he grinned at Sydney.

With his own grin Sydney made his move. He quickly stomped down on Shaw's foot and as the boy yelped and hopped on the one foot he kicked out at Shaw's knee. With another scream Shaw reached out towards the smaller boy who scurried out of the way to get behind him as he stumbled forward. With just the side of his foot, Sydney kicked the boy in the ass and watched as he slid forward on the ground with the circle of kids screaming out their laughter and taunts.

Dropping into his own defensive stance, Sydney waited patiently for Shaw to stand and turn to face him. As the boy turned, Sydney struck out with two quick right hand jabs and then a wide over hand left that all connected with Shaw's jaw and nose. Blood spouted from his nose as Sydney bounced to his right and struck once more with his left and then a right to the larger boy's chest that knocked the air from his lungs.

As Shaw dropped to his knees, Sydney glanced back at Jangles and then back at his defeated opponent. "Never mistake my walking away for being pussy, Bitch," he got close enough for just Shaw to hear, "because next time I'll be more inclined to really whoop yo' stupid ass than just embarrass you."

Shaw sat on the sofa watching as his cousin and his pretty little lady did the kissy face thing as he thought about all of the shit that he, Jangles and Sydney got into after that fight. Sydney continued to do his thing in school, but it was who he'd become away from the school that got them all noticed.

"Ah yo, Nigga," Jangles barked out. "What the fuck you over there dreaming about?"

"All kinds of shit, Cousin," Shaw smiled.

"Well after that rousting we put up man I need a goddamn shower, a piece of ass, and a fuckin' drink."

Nina slapped him on the shoulder as he reached around and grabbed a big handful of her butt. "What makes you think I'm that easy?" she teased.

"Well," he grabbed her again and then winked at his cousin, "mainly because you ain't got on no drawls."

The two men burst out laughing as Nina punched Jangles shoulder and walked off into the kitchen. As she stood in there watching the two of them, she pulled her phone from her bra and turned on the voice recorder. Her loyalties were back in check, and as such she was feeling good about herself again. Jangles had commented about her looking like the woman that caught his attention all stretched out on Sydney's sofa and had him wanting to fuck her brains out right there in front of all of them. She was no longer that shell of a woman who had betrayed the only person in this world that loved her, and now she was back on the job.

"I think we got Nick on the ropes," Jangles said as he sat down on the sofa. "That shit we pulled with JC has got that nigga reeling, and now I want him done."

"Whatcha got in mind?" Shaw asked as he watched Nina pouring her a glass of wine in the kitchen.

"I want you to get some of your people on him. I want to put him through the rack, but I don't want him to roll away from it."

"Yo," Shaw stared at him and then nodded his head back towards Nina, "we good, Nigga?"

"Yea, that's my ride or die bitch there, Cuz," Jangles smiled and looked up at Nina as she stood in the kitchen sipping her wine. "No worries, Fool, she got zipped lips and we can talk freely here."

"Cool," Shaw pulled out his phone and dialed a number. "Shit I ain't talked to his fool in forever, but I know I can depend on him being down."

"Who?" Jangles stared at his cousin.

"Ay, yo, E.L., what's good?"

"Everlast?" Shaw smiled and nodded his head as Jangles sat back.

"I need some work done, Brotha, you game?"

****

Nina strolled into the living room where she found Courtney and Nick staring down a desk full of papers. As she approached, they both looked up and Courtney smiled and Nick kind of waved before he walked off into the kitchen. Courtney stood from the desk and walked out to meet her and they hugged before moving over to the sofa.

"Oooo, somebody's in a really good mood," Nina teased. "You got lucky and got you some last night?"

"You're so nasty," Courtney laughed.

"I may be nasty," Nina responded, "but I saw the way you was walking all bow-legged and shit. Looks like Mr. Styles laid that dick down on ya."

"You sound jealous, Nina," Nick poked his head around the kitchen door.

The two women looked up and both began laughing as Nick slipped back into the kitchen most likely to get him a cup of coffee. Courtney slapped Nina on her bare knee as they continued to giggle for a moment more before Nina pulled out her cell phone.

"I have something for you, Court," she said as she pulled up the recorded conversation between Jangles and Shaw.

"Nina," Courtney placed her hand over the phone before her friend could start the recording. "Nina, I don't want to put you in the middle of this shit any more. I don't want you to feel as if you have to make a choice between Jangles and me."

"There's no choice to be made, Courtney," Nina smiled softly. "I hadn't told you that he hit me, have I?

"Well I will one day, but just know that he did, and well things are a lot clearer for me now. I keep saying I'm sorry to you for the things that have happened, and I know I'll never be able to make things completely right… but I have to try."

Courtney started to comment, but stopped as she looked into her friend's eyes and could see there was no need to try and argue her down. She accepted the fact that Nina wanted to be responsible for her part in how things ended up happening, and she was slowly accepting her fault as well. At some point she knew she would have to make an effort to sincerely apologize for expecting so much from Nina and not recognizing that she was completely wrapped up in Jangles' lies.

Nick stepped out of the kitchen managing three cups of coffee and passed one to each of the ladies before taking a seat to see where this little meeting was going. His mind was already at the office meeting with Sydney and Henri, because that slimy bastard was definitely going to be there. His primary concern was how this was all going to play out and most assuredly… when. Taking a sip of his coffee sat there trying to keep a stern look so that Courtney could not see his true concerns written all over his face.

"So," Courtney finally said, "let's hear what you have."

"Jangles came over to my place last night
with a guy he says is his cousin. He's a big ol' bear
of a man named Shaw, and I swear there's more to
him than meets the eye." Nina hit the play button
and laid the phone on the coffee table between them.

"I think we got Nick on the ropes." They all
quickly recognized Jangles' voice even though the
sound was a bit hollow. *"That shit we pulled with
JC has got that nigga reeling, and now I want him
done."*

"Whatcha got in mind?" They heard Shaw
speak for the first time, and it was a voice that Nick
instantly remembered.

*"I want you to get some of your people on
him. I want to put him through the rack, but I don't
want him to roll away from it."*

"Yo, we good, Nigga?" Nina explained that
while she was in the kitchen Shaw was asking
Jangles if they could talk with her in the room; with
a smile, she told them that she was standing there
pretending not to be paying attention.

"Yea, that's my ride or die bitch there, Cuz,"
Jangles answered. *"No worries, Fool, she got zipped
lips and we can talk freely here."*

*"Cool. Shit I ain't talked to his fool in
forever, but I know I can depend on him being
down."*

"Who?" Jangles asked his cousin.

"Ay, yo, E.L., what's good?"

"Everlast?" Jangles sounded surprised.

*"I need some work done, Brotha, you
game?"*

"Stop right there," Nick said as he stood up
from his seat and began pacing the floor. "Dammit."

"What's wrong?" Courtney asked him as she and Nina traded looks of concern.

"I told you that I knew some people, remember," Nick looked over at Courtney and she nodded her head. "This cat, Everlast, is one of them I was talking about. I've known his ass for forever… and when I was locked up in California it was Everlast that was there watching my back. Damn… I didn't know that Shaw knew him."

"Ok, so what does this mean?" Nina asked.

"I'm not sure, but if Shaw has Everlast working with him things are about to go from bad to worse." Nick responded. He stood there thinking about the bugs that they knew were in the room and he wondered if Sydney was hearing this.

A conversation one day out for PT in the yard E.L let him know that Sydney was looking out for him. He remembered E.L smiling when he said Sydney had called him into his office to ask him if he had a problem doing a little time to keep an asset of his safe.

"'Shit, why would I mind keeping Nicky Styles safe?' I asked him," E.L pulled on his skully as he looked about the yard. "That crazy muthafucka has saved my ass plenty of times."

"I don't get why Sydney Roulette would give a damn about me," Nick sat down on some steps away from the crowded yard waiting for Everlast to explain. Any time the man would look at him with his one good eye, it was always hard not to stare at the scar that disappeared under the skull cap and then ran the length of his face over his left eye.

"All I can tell you, Nicky, is that the man feels like he owes you a debt. He told me that by the time he found out about that deal with the Jamaicans it was too late to stop it… said he was hopin' that

Shaw was going to side away from Jangles, but it would seem that he decided blood was thicker than money."

"Yea, no doubt," Nick stated before spitting. "That muthafucka was there when them Ja fools began blasting. All I could think was grab the money and the blow and run… that's exactly what I did."

"What happened to all of that smack and dough?" Everlast asked.

"I got it put away," Nick gave Everlast a sideways glance. "I figured at some point that I might need an insurance policy one day. I figured that if push came to shove that I could talk to Sydney and maybe would could come to some kind of deal."

"Oh I get it," E.L grinned. "And no, Nick, I'm not here to find out what you did with that shit. Sydney didn't even bring it up… I was just curious.

"We got two years to keep you alive because Sydney is almost sure that Jangles is out to kill you. What the fuck did you do to his bitch ass anyhow?"

"Damn good question, Bro… damn good question. One of these days that nigga is going to answer it for me because I'm going to step to him and ask before I blow his fool head off his shoulders."

Courtney sat there her eyes bouncing from Nina, who was just as confused as she was, and up to Nick who was pacing the room talking to himself. She wasn't sure what she should do as she and Nina sat there waiting.

"There's more, Nick," Nina finally said.

"Yea… yea," Nick shook his head to get out of those memories; there'd be time later to deal with all of the why's and shit like that. "Go ahead and play the rest, Nina."

✳✳✳✳

"Look, E.L," Nina stood there watching the man on the phone, "it's been a long time, my Dude, but I got some serious paper for you to snatch up that nigga Nick Styles and bring him to me."

Nina had to put her wine glass up to her lips to keep from showing any kind of reaction to what she'd just heard. She looked at the face of her phone once more just to make certain it was still recording and then she turned her back on the conversation to pull something out of the fridge. Once again she was putting herself right in the middle of shit… but, she owed this to Courtney.

"Naw, naw," Shaw said into the phone, "I don't give a fuck his condition other than still being alive, but I need it done tomorrow. I got no less than ten stacks sitting here waiting for you to get this shit done for me."

Nina pulled out a tray of cheese and grapes and sat them on the counter as Shaw continued his phone conversation a few moments more before finally hanging up. She took the tray into the living room and placed it on the coffee table in front of the two men and then she went back into the kitchen for the bottle of wine she'd been drinking from.

"So, we good?" Jangles asked as he leaned over for a handful of grapes.

"Yea, E.L sounded excited about getting his hands on Nick for me," Shaw responded as he again watched Nina walking around the condo.

"He didn't suspect that I was involved… did he?" Jangles pressed back into the sofa and crossed his legs.

"Nigga didn't even ask, but he ain't a stupid dude. Check it… I'm here in Tampa and everyone knows my place is now Texas… he's bound to put two and two together."

"Right," Jangles winked at Nina as she poured him and Shaw a glass of wine. He licked his lips as his woman bent at the waist putting that fine ass of hers into the air. He'd been taking notice of Shaw watching her, but he had no worries that his cousin would try him like that… shit, niggas gon' be niggas and that's the simple truth of it.

"Cool," Jangles smiled. "Cool… now we need to take care of Styles because that's some shit that's a long time coming. And then after we got him outta the way… lil Miss Hotpants is next. I want my fuckin' company back. I've played long and hard to get this shit to the point of finally getting IXion under my control. Don't nobody understand how much I hated that long, slow process of poisoning Sydney… that nigga was a lot stronger than Big Fats, but I just wanted to see him wither away into nothing before finally choking on his own blood.

"I want to know who fuckin' blew his ass up… I deserve to know who stole that moment from me just so I can find them and put my fuckin' hands around his throat and squeeze. But, to make matters worse… he gives my company away to his bitch. Goddamn nigga had some balls on him."

"So do you have any idea who?" Shaw stopped as Jangles looked over at him with an expression he'd never seen on his cousin's face before.

Jangles sat there with tears in his eyes and a look crossed between grief and contempt. He was still pissed that Sydney's death was taken from him, but he missed his brother. Sydney was always the thinker in their little operation; that fool could have shit planned out and mapped out five ways to

Sunday and for years they never lost a man. Now he was losing people left and right, and IXion was still not his.

"Naw… no ideas, Cousin," Jangles began popping grapes into his mouth, "but I'm gonna find out… believe that."

****

"So he really didn't do it," Courtney sat there shaking her head. She looked up at Nick and immediately noticed that he didn't seem surprised by Jangles revelation. "Nick?"

"Huh?" Nick was staring at the phone and then looked over towards Courtney. "Yea? What?"

"Do you know what he's talking about?" She asked. "Do you know what happened to my husband?"

The word "husband" almost made him gag, but he corrected himself before answering. It was the longest few seconds of his life as he considered telling her the truth that Sydney was not blown up in that truck, but alive and kicking and somewhere in Tampa. He rubbed his hand over his head and sat down once more; there was just too much to take in, another mark on his life and now Courtney questioning him about Sydney's death.

"Sydney? I know what you know, Courtney," he lied. "And now we both know that we've been wrong for the last two years."

"This changes everything… doesn't it?" Courtney looked at Nina and then at Nick who was sitting with his head in his hands.
"Dammit, I need to call Lagrange and the Vasilevich brothers," Nick jumped up from his seat and walked off towards the bedroom. "We're going to need everyone here for this shit… Everyone because the shit's definitely about to hit the fan."

Chapter 16

"You want to tell me why you lied?" Courtney walked into the bedroom and sat down on the bed watching as Nick rushed around the room.

"Lied about... what?" Nick stepped into the walk-in closet to keep from seeing her face.

"What the hell aren't you telling me about Sydney's death, Nicholas?" Courtney did little to hide her frustration. She'd known this man for the majority of her adult life, and knew a lot of his quirks.

"I was completely surprised by Jangles admission," Nick lied softly from the closet.

"No," Courtney shook her head, "something's not right, Nick. Something's different, but I don't know..."

"Ain't shit changed," Nick stepped out of the closet and walked up on her lifting her face to look into her eyes. "I've been looking forward to killing that fool myself for what he's done to you. Hell, for what he's done to us... I mean, look at the shit he did not just now but all those years ago, we could have still been together, Courtney if it hadn't been for that motherfucker. I have lived hating Bobby Johnson and can't nothing change that."

Courtney refused to push, but she could hear something wrong in Nick's voice. In her mind she's replayed everything over the course of the last two years in varying angles and degrees. Flashes and images of Sydney played from the moment the he told her he'd been poisoned and he knew that Jangles did it, up until Nina had first told her that Jangles hadn't been responsible for Sydney's death. She loved all of the stress she'd been causing that sick, son-of-a-bitch, and had been planning the overture to this great symphony. Now everything felt different.

Just as she was about to ask him about the conversation they'd just heard, Nick's phone rang. She sat on the bed listening as he stepped away. His body language had changed. Nick was normally a very confident man, but right now, everything about him was stiff and unsure. He would take a quick glance at her and then look away, and that alone was very unlike him. All of this would have to be address soon, but right now… it was back to business.

"Everlast, my man," he turned on the phone's speaker and laid it on the bed between he and Courtney, "you caught me running around the room so I gotcha on speaker. Long time no hear... what's good, Son?"

"Nicholas St. Cloud, my man," the man on the phone sounded very cordial, "yes, yes, it has been a long time, Yungsta."

"I keep telling you, EL," Nick was laughing, "I'm not that much younger than you."

"Yea, you keep telling me, but you still younger, Yungsta. You need to see 'bout me, Nick, 'cus I've picked up a contract on you."

"Would it surprise you if I said that I know?"

"Not wit' you, Nicky, not wit' you," Everlast answered with a chuckle. "You always was on top of shit like that."

"Would you be surprised if I told you that the contract is from Jangles Johnson?"

"Fuck!" they could hear him slamming his hand on a table or something. "I should have known wit Shaw calling on me like dat. Dat sombitch know what I say about workin' for him afta dat shit him wan put my people in... On my name."

"So that was on you?" Nick was more just said aloud than asking the question. "You never told me that."

"Long time gone, Nick," Everlast remarked. "I 'ave no fucking love for Jangles and dat sombitch knows dis, and to try an use me 'gainst you... Dat fucka him gots dem balls."

"No doubt." Nick took a deep breath and looked up at Courtney. He smiled hoping that this would calm Courtney down some.

"They are wanting you dead, Nicky," Everlast said stating the obvious.

"Not the first time from that prick," Nick grunted. "What are you going to do, E.L?"

"I want to kill dat nigga Shaw and send pieces of him back to Jangles."

"How many people you got with you? "

"Me, Vert and 'bout 'alf dozen soldiers... W'atchu t'inkin', Nicky?"

"Lessons to be learned, my friend," Nick winked at Courtney before leaning over to give her a kiss. For the first time in the last couple of weeks he actually felt at ease. He stood and went back into the closet and pulled out his gray with black and white pinned stripes.

"Look, E.L., let me get a few things taken care of and I'll call you back in say ten. Cool?"

"I be right 'ere waitin' on ya, St. Cloud."

"What's going on, Nick?" Courtney asked as he hung up the phone and began getting dressed.

"Jangles tried to kill me the other day when I went to see Jackson," Nick began, "and it looks like he brought his cousin in to finish the job."

"Wait a goddamn minute," Courtney put up her hand shaking her head. "What the hell you mean

he tried to kill you the other day and you didn't tell
me?"

"Stop and think about that day, Courtney,"
Nick was pulling on his pants as she sat staring with
a dangerous glare in her eyes. "What did I walk in
on between you and Nina? That was the day I found
out about the baby and well that shit concerning
Jangles just went right over my head."

Courtney's hand went to her stomach and
then she glanced back up at Nick. He was buttoning
up his shirt and back in the closet to find a tie.

"Ok so… what's the plan?" she asked him.

"I'm done with all of this running and hiding,
Courtney," Nick said as he turned around, "and after
this shit with D'Marious and J.C. I want to put this
nigga in his place."

"You're not telling me something, Nicholas,"
Courtney stood and stepped to help him with his tie.
"So what is it that you're not telling me?"

"Let me do it this way," Nick pulled her into
his arms, "let me survive today and I promise you
with all that I am I will tell you everything that you
need to know. Can you let me do that?"

"You promise to tell me everything?"
Courtney asked.

"I promise to open the flood gates and let it
all come out, but," he stared down into her eyes
before giving her a kiss he felt like might be his
last.'

"But… what?"

"I have a feeling that you're going to hate
me."

"Nick St. Cloud," Courtney's fingers slid
along his jaw line, "I could never hate you."

Nick's smirk, his attempt at smiling, didn't
slip Courtney's notice, but she didn't say anything.

As they walked towards the front door, her mind was on a million other things including how Nick said, *"let me survive today,"* and this put knots in her stomach. For as long as she'd know him, Nicholas St. Cloud had never been vague; he's always had a bad habit of just saying how he felt or what he thought. She was truly concerned.

"You be safe, Mr. St. Cloud," her kiss was soft and pleasing leaving him standing there with a goofy smile on his face. She stroked his full lips and then across his mustache and goatee before kissing him once more.

"I promise that I will, Ms. Roulette," she smiled at his grin. "You have my word."

"Nick," Courtney called out as he pulled out of her arms and headed towards his car.

"Yes?"

"I want you to know that I love you," she said not caring if the guards walking by heard.

"I know," Nick winked and slipped into the driver's seat closing the door.

Slipping his Bluetooth into his ear, Nick dialed Everlast and waited for him to pick up. Backing out of the drive he wanted to let down his window and tell her that he loved her too, but that would have to wait.

"Good to 'ear from you again, Nicky," Everlast's voice filled his ear as he hit the gas and pulled away leaving Courtney watching him drive off.

"Ok, here's the deal, E.L.," he turned down the radio with no fear of his car being bugged thanks to Jackson's security measures, "I'm off to a meeting with Sydney Roulette and I'm pretty sure that at some point he's out to kill me."

231

"What da fuck a minute," Everlast interrupted, "I taught dat nigga him dead."

"That's something I'll have to tell you about another time, and that's if I survive when I tell Courtney. But, that I'll deal with later, right now I need to know if I can get you to keep some men on me today because I need to survive this shit if I'm going to keep Courtney alive."

"What's da deal with the wife, Nick?"

"She's pregnant, E.L., and it's mine." Nick said those words aloud and for the first time he actually thought of himself as being a… Father. "I have to keep her safe, E., you know how I feel about her."

"I get it, and what are we going to do about Jangles and that bitch nigga of his Shaw?"

"I want Shaw dead," Nick said dryly "I want it big… really big and I want Jangles to know that I had it contracted, but I want your name out of it for now. I know you got men who ain't Jamaicans and I need it done with them."

"No worries, Yungsta," Everlast sounded a little ecstatic. "And after Shaw, when do we go after Jangles?"

"As soon as I know what the fuck Sydney got on his mind, then we'll figure out Jangles part in this dance."

"You still a thinkin' muthafucka," Everlast laughed out. "It be good to see you no longer running but standing tall"

"I told Courtney that I am tired of running. I've run from Sydney because I thought he wanted me dead. I've ran from Jangles because that bastard tried to kill me back then and here recent. I'm done with running… time to show them why I got the name Nick Styles."

"Wit' you, Nicky, e'ry t'ing's always good."

"I'll be on 275 in about ten minutes," Nick said, "have your men meet me and I'll let them know when they need to hang back."

"Dey on da way. You be safe out dere, Nicky, and after dis meetin' I need for you to come right to me and get met caught up."

"Will do," Nick answered before hanging up.

****

"Mr. Lagrange," Courtney had stepped back into the house once she could no longer see Nick's car, "I need something from you."

"How may I help you, Mrs. Roulette?" Jackson Lagrange was being driving to see her and was waiting for this call.

"I need to know if you have private investigators?"

"I do, Mrs. Roulette, and they are at your disposal." Lagrange was watching the city flashing by out of the passenger window. "How can we be of service to you?"

"I've been trying to find out what truly happened with my husband's death," she began, "and I've been using my own private detectives and from the beginning they've been hitting nothing but wall after wall. I need to know what happened… how it happened and who's responsible. I need a fresh pair of eyes looking into this."

"I understand, Mrs. Roulette," Jackson glanced down at the attaché case in his lap. He hadn't looked through everything but the bit that he had had him convinced that Courtney Roulette needed to see what Nick had stored away in that deposit box.

"I'm actually glad that you called," he finally said. "I'm on my way to you as we speak and I think

I have some things that you need to see…
personally.”

“Things like… what?” Courtney was walking circles around the sofa.

“Things that are best seen and then talked about, but only face to face,” Lagrange responded. “I’ll be there in about twenty minutes and we’ll talk then.”

“I’ll be waiting.” Courtney stood in front of the sofa and just dropped down exhausted.

****

“Well it’s about time,” Nick kept a straight face as he stepped into the office where Sydney was sitting behind the desk waiting on him. “It’s good to see that you didn’t forget where the old office was.”

“Well it is your momma’s old house and I've been here more times than I can count.” Nick took a seat but not after taking notice that Henri was not in the room. “So where’s your lapdog?”

“Damn, Nick,” Sydney grinned as he reached across the desk with an open hand, “no need of being so hard on Henri. Shit, both of you was just doing as you were told.”

“This shit is getting old, Syd,” Nick again looked around. The office hadn’t changed since the last time he’d been there. That meeting had set the tone for the last few years of his life.

“Yea,” Sydney’s demeanor changed, “you keep saying that. So you tell me, Mr. St. Cloud, what do you feel needs to change?”

“All of this,” Nick was trying to keep his voice from getting high. “We’ve been lying to Courtney for almost three fucking years… and you know she hates lying.”

"You don't need to worry about Courtney," Sydney sat up in his chair. "She's my wife and I'll do all of the worrying about her."

"Oh really?" Nick sat up in his chair as well. "You mean like you've been doing? Oh… wait no the fuck you haven't, but I have, every goddamn day since you 'died'. Me, Syd, I've been by her side, I was the one there as she cried herself to sleep. I had to tell her that things would be better. I had to help her take care of *Your* daughter, you son-of-a-bitch."

Sydney sat back in his chair. He'd always known that Nick St. Cloud was not the pussy that Jangles swore that he was. He'd seen Nick put down a little banger back in the day so fast that the boy never saw what was coming at him. He always figured that Nick ran because of him and not so much any fear of Jangles; he was always positive that if put in a room together that Nick would hand Jangles his ass.

"Goddamn, grown a set a balls, have we? Looks like we're at an impasse, Nicky," Sydney reached up on his desk and pulled out a cigar from the humidor, "I know you know that I want your fucking head right now… how could you, Muthafucka?"

"How could I? You are one sick fuck, Syd," Nick stood and walked behind the chair to stare at the man as he took the time clip and light his cigar. "Goddamn, you knew it was her, didn't you? You fucking knew that it was Courtney I ran off to Cali with when Jangles dicked me over? All of this fucking time and I never stopped to see it… you fucking knew it all this time. And since you know that then you have to know that I never stopped loving her… right? You asked me to do this and you promised me that it wouldn't be for too long. You

235

fucking swore that six months are less you'd be back
and we would deal with your boy and get you back
with her.

"Almost three years later, and I'm still
walking around with this goddamn lie. I was the one
with her when Jangles had her shot at, and I was the
one with her when she found out Nina had betrayed
her. I was the one who wanted to talk some sense
into her when she order all of those hits… Me,
muthafucka… Not you but me!"

"You feel better, Nigga," Sydney sat there
casually smoking his cigar. "Shit you sound like a
whiny little bitch right now. I need to get up from
here and just kick yo ass.

"You slept with my *WIFE*, you pussy ass
Bastard."

"Yea, now who's whining," Nick grinned as
he walked over to the bar and fixed him a glass of
bourbon. "Say what you really know, Mr. Roulette."

Sydney stood and walked over to the bar
facing Nick. The two men stood toe to toe staring
into each others eyes. Sydney was amazed at how far
Nick had come along since they'd met. He was no
longer just some little hood kid trying to make a
come up anymore… naw, this nigga had become a
fucking shot caller, and to be truthful, he was rather
pleased. He actually felt responsible for the change
in this man because he knew that it was all hidden
inside.

"We got a big problem, Nicky," Sydney blew
the smoke he'd inhaled out just over Nick's head,
"naw, we gots a big ass problem… you and I."

"Yea we do," Nick stood his ground. "So spit
it out so I can get gone."

"Get gone? Boy, you just got here." Sydney laughed as he walked back to his seat. "Nicky, you got my wife pregnant."

"She's not your wife, Sydney," Nick pointed out the obvious. "The moment you played your card and blew up that truck you fucked up. You're dead, there is no longer a Sydney Roulette in the picture, and that means you gave Courtney back her life. You did this shit. You did it."

"NO GODDAMMIT!" Sydney slammed his fist down on the top of the bar taking notice that Nick didn't flinch at all, and he almost smiled. "Do you actually believe that she'll pick yo' bitch ass over me once she finds out that I'm alive. We was destined to be together, Nick… do you fucking understand that?"

"And yet," Nick set the empty glass down, "you've allowed her to believe that you're dead for nearly three years. She deserves better than that, Syd. She deserves better than you… and she definitely deserves better than me.

"You left her to deal with that triflin nigga knowing the kind of shit Jangles would pull. Her life has been dangling by a thread, and do you know what he's recently done? You don't do you?"

Sydney was seething that Nick was literally standing there going word for word with him. Give a nigga a couple of years of feeling a little power, and he'll think he's the master of his own world.

"Jangles has brought in that sick ass cousin of his, Big Shaw. Yea, yo punk ass didn't know that… did you?" Nick stood there staring as Sydney sat back down. "So you tell me… Mr. McGregor, how is Mrs. Roulette supposed to deal with all of this? We put her in the middle of this bullshit, we turned her entire life upside down, and here you sit still trying to play fucking King Dick."

Sydney was lost for words; he hadn't planned on Shaw being a part of any of this. He didn't think that Jangles had the pull to bring that big fuck out of Texas.

"When did he get to town?" He finally asked Nick and his tone had completely changed.

"J.C. and D'Marious was sent to get him," Nick answered, "and I didn't recognize his name at first to warn J.C. about his ass. That's why a good man is laid up in a hospital out of Tampa hanging on to his life by a fucking thread."

"This isn't good at all," Sydney walked back over to the bar and fixed himself a drink. "We got a serious problem with his ass being in town, and I've found out that Jangles had a meeting with Jorge Manciena and Jimmy Q; Jangles is getting ready to unleash hell on everyone."

"Welcome back to Tampa, Sydney," the facetious tone in Nick's voice was obvious.

"I know you have a plan," Sydney smiled. "So tell it."

"Well for some reason Shaw reached out to Everlast and offered him a contract on my head," Nick fixed another drink "What Jangles don't know is that Everlast and I did that time together and well, E.L. called me this morning. Shaw is going to be dealt with and a message will be sent to Jangles. I'm ready to end all of this bullshit, and at this point, that includes you and I."

"Yea, I'm hearing ya'," Sydney was walking back to his desk with his thoughts a million miles away from this room. "When are you planning on dealing with Shaw?"

"I'm going to see Everlast… well, that's if I'm walking out of here." Nick swallowed the last of his drink as Sydney stood with his hands on the edge of the desk talking to himself. "Am I walking out of here, Sydney?"

"We good for now, Nick," Sydney turned and faced him once more. "You have to take care of our girl. Shaw ain't a nigga to fucking play with, and if you have E.L. in play, well, we need to let that shit play out."

Sydney stepped back up into Nick's face and again he admired the man for not backing down. "It wasn't supposed to go down like this, Nick. I think I fucked up… I think we fucked up royally."

"No doubt," Nick responded as he took Sydney's extended hand.

"Well we have a mess to clean up," Sydney puffed on his cigar. "You're the man, my Friend, and I'm following your lead… for now."

Nick nodded his head before backing out of the room. As he turned to leave, he walked out into a room full of men including Henri Thames and all of them were armed. He looked over his shoulder as the men hadn't lowered their guns and waiting for Sydney to signal them to allow him to pass. Sydney stood there leaning against the door frame just watching as he stood there not showing an ounce of fear.

"Goddamn, Nigga," Sydney laughed. "Nicky Styles has grown the fuck up to become a hardened O.G. like muthafucka. Lower your guns and let my boy walk on… and No One is allowed to touch this man… if anything happens to him I will personally merc the fool who did it and anyone who knew and didn't tell me."

“I’ll be in touch,” Nick said before turning and leaving Sydney’s childhood home.

“Henri,” he heard Sydney as he was closing the door, “change in plans… we need to talk.”

Chapter 17

Courtney stood in the bathroom mirror staring at her naked body. She turned to the side and rubbed at her belly, she was only a few weeks pregnant so she wasn't showing yet, but it did make her miss her baby. Sydnee had been the reason she'd remained sane after Sydney's body was laid in the ground. Being pregnant and having Nick around made her life make some kind of sense. She'd cried on Nick's shoulder so many times that she was pretty sure it had become waterlogged, but he never complained.

Sliding into the tub filled with water and bubbles she let out a deep sigh as the hot water scald her skin. This was exactly what she needed after her meeting with Jackson Lagrange, and now she had more fucking questions than answers. She slapped her hand into the water causing it to splash all over her and out onto the floor. She was angry… she was angrier than she'd ever been in her life and that included her anger towards Nina.

"Damn," she said just to hear her voice, "you're alive."

As she sat with the water right at her chin, her mind kept questioning her…

Am I madder because Sydney is alive… or because Nick knew all this time?

"So this is what you've been keeping from me, Nick? Why would you do this to me, why would you let me continue to think that he's dead?"

She sunk under the surface of the water holding her breath as the heat covered her entirely.

Her head was hurting and she felt sick to the
stomach as her afternoon with Lagrange just took
over every inch of her mind

"Thanks for letting me come see you, Mrs.
Roulette," the funny dressed white man stepped in
past her and just walked towards the living room.
Courtney followed as he made his way to the sofa
and sat down

"So what is this all about, Mr. Lagrange?"
Courtney was unsure of what to expect about
anything anymore. "You definitely have me worried
now."

Jackson Lagrange pulled a small box from
his pocket and placed it on the coffee table. There
was a small red light flashing on the top of it and he
watched until the light turned green and he smiled.

"A little something I put together so that we
could sit here and talk," he informed her as she
stared quizzically at his actions.

"And that was for what?" Courtney finally
asked since the man didn't seem inclined to just
offer to tell her what the hell he'd just done.

"Oh, forgive me," Lagrange grinned, "that
little box will allow us to talk freely without worry
of being recorded or overheard by anything planted
here in the room.

"I see," Courtney smiled. "Okay?"

"Well I had a meeting with Mr. St. Cloud
and well shortly after that conversation he and I had
another discussion and I was instructed to go retrieve
this case from a private safety deposit box."

"Ok, Nick knows about you coming to see
me about what's in this case?" Courtney was
curious.

"Well not entirely," Lagrange took a deep
breath, "What's in this case is documents that you

242

really need to see because they pertain to your deceased husband, and well Nick sent me after this after your dead husband confronted him."

"Wait," Courtney was looking the man in his eyes, "what did you just say?"

"Mrs. Roulette, Sydney is not dead."

"No… no… that's not possible," her voice cracked and it felt like she had a knot stuck in her throat. "They played the explosion on the news. The coroner showed me the burnt body…

"I FUCKING BURIED HIM!"

"I know, Ma'am." Lagrange laid out a handful of papers on the coffee table. "But everything in this case says the opposite."

"I've had nightmares about him for two years," Courtney dropped her head trying not to cry in front of this man that she barely knew. Picking up the papers and thumbing through the pages she asked without looking up, "Mr. Lagrange, Nick got this because… he had someone investigating Sydney's death, right? He didn't know? You have to tell me that Nick didn't know that Sydney was alive all of this time."

"I'm sorry, Mrs. Roulette, as far as I can tell," Lagrange picked out a few pages of what she had in her hands and laid them on top of everything else, "he was a part of it. Mr. Nick kept some very good records. I would say that he knew that this day would eventually come."

Courtney sat back as Lagrange took all of the papers and began organizing them. She couldn't bring herself to say anything as the last two years began to flash before her eyes. She couldn't count the number of times she'd called Sydney's name because she was missing him… needing him. She couldn't count the number of times Nick held her whispering words of courage and encouragement to keep her going. She couldn't think of the number of times where Nick had told her that if he could he would have taken Sydney's place just to keep her happy.

She sat with her head swimming… they'd both betrayed her.

"I think," Lagrange broke into her thoughts, "Nick was planning for this day, Mrs. Rou…"

"Ms.," Courtney stopped him. "Vaughn, Ms. Vaughn."

"Yes, Ms. Vaughn," Lagrange smiled as if understanding her pain and anger. "If you look right here… Nick left a note to you."

Courtney,
You wont understand the number of times I had to keep myself from telling you this, but I'd promised Sydney that I wouldn't and that I would keep you safe. If you're reading this well that means things have gone really wrong and that means I owe no more loyalties to Mr. Roulette, but I do everything to you. I don't know if what I did was right or wrong, but it kept me close to the only woman I've ever loved in my miserable life. I would have done anything to make certain nothing happened to you, and the shit that you've been dropped off into was just shy of a death sentence to niggas who've been in this lifestyle their whole lives. I hate Sydney for pitting you against that egomaniac Jangles, and I swear my whole intentions was to find a way to kill him before he could ever did anything to hurt you. I know that what I'm going to ask is more than I ever should of you because no matter how you cut this up… I have been lying to you for a long time, and I'm sorry.

If you can, Courtney, please find a way to forgive me

With all of my love,
Nicholas Xavier St. Cloud

Courtney looked over at Lagrange and all he could do was nod at her.

"I think it was sincere, Ms. Vaughn," he said to her. "He's gone to meet with Sydney and he was not sure if he'd walk away from that meeting alive because we are almost positive that it was someone working for Sydney who bugged the house."

"Nick thinks Sydney knows about me being pregnant, doesn't he?"

"Yes," Lagrange dropped his head. "Nick is almost positive of it. Sydney told him that the two of them have a problem. From a man like Sydney that cannot mean too much other than the most obvious. Sydney left him here to protect you because he thought if nothing else he could trust a man who loved you as much as he loves you."

"Two years," Courtney whispered. "He's been gone for over two years, what did he expect to happen. Did he think that I'd sit here by myself for the rest of my life waiting for a ghost to return home to me and our daughter? What kind of man does this?"

"According to this," Lagrange handed her the compiled papers, "Sydney wasn't thinking he'd be gone no more than six months. Nick has been keeping record of every phone conversation between the three of them."

"Three?" Courtney look puzzled for just a moment and then her eyes widened. "Robles… that bastard was in on this as well wasn't he?"

"His real name is Henri Thames and he was the one who orchestrated Mr. Roulette's demise. From what I've been able to get from a lot of what Nick has wrote, there's a lot of smoke and mirrors involved, but Nick had always assumed that Sydney was going to let you know what was really going on. Right here," he pulled out another paper to show her, "this is a conversation between him and Sydney…"

Sydney: Look, Nick, it won't be much longer. You just keep an eye on my wife for me and you keep me informed on what's going on with Jangles. The doctors are saying a good six months… so keep your head about you.

Nick: Goddamn, Syd, I hate lying to her. You said six months ago almost a year ago. I'm beginning to think that you like this behind the scenes bullshit. She's going to see through that McGregor crap and when she does it's not going to be pretty at all.

Sydney: I'll deal with that when it happens. She's pretty smart but I've been doing this shit a long muthafuckin' time. Just keep your wits, Nigga.

Nick: No… fuck that, Sydney. She's too good for this, and this shit is eating up inside. I hate the shit that we're doing and yet you and Henri seem to think that she's going to take this laying down. You've created a fucking killing machine. She's become as ruthless as all of you if not more so. This woman is a gangster and she's being swallowed up in this Nine bullshit you've thrown her into.

Sydney: You throw some to the wolves and they get eaten up… I threw her to the wolves and she's come back leading them. That's my muthafuckin' girl.

Nick: You keep that shit in mind.

Courtney felt sick to the stomach.

"I need a drink," she said standing up slowly. Her head was spinning and it was like her feet didn't want to move from where she was stood. Forcing her legs to bend she made her way to the bar and poured her a glass of tequila because it was the first thing she grabbed. The alcohol was harsh going down and burned not only her throat but her stomach which was already gurgling. Coughing just a bit, she poured another and sipped this one.

"I feel…" she began after choking down another swallow. "I feel… set up."

"That's understandable," Lagrange acknowledged. "Please, Ms. Courtney, your… condition."

Courtney stared into the near empty glass and her hand went to her belly which was still gurgling and turning causing her to feel sicker by the second. She set the glass back down on the bar and took a deep breath as she stared across the living room towards the smiling man nodding his head.

"It would seem that Sydney was preparing to do this to you before your marriage. From what I've read in Nick's notes, he knew you would go to Nicholas because he'd made certain that your friend Nina Carlton found out he was back from his prison sentence. Nick had been home for almost a year, but he'd heard that you and Sydney were together so he stayed away."

"So why did Sydney marry me? Did he even… love me?" the words burned more than the alcohol had.

"That I do not know, Ms. Courtney, but it seems that Nick has never stopped loving you. He wanted me to tell you everything in case he didn't make it out of that meeting with your husband alive. He wanted you prepared for what was to come next."

"And that is?" Courtney had made it back to the sofa and slowly sat.

"This war for IXion is about to pick up, and now with Sydney back you almost bank on him thinking that you're going to just give him back the company without blinking an eye. The question… is that what you want to do after all of this?"

"That is the question indeed."

Jackson Lagrange could see the change in her eyes, and finally understood why Nick said that Sydney had created a monster. This man had taken a young lady who didn't know a damn thing about the ruthless end of gangsters and he'd molded her to be just like him… if not worse. He could see in her eyes that she was now considering all of her options and it intrigued him.

"I've gone through a lot in the last two years," she sat back against the sofa and crossed her legs. "I had to bury a man I thought loved me, but now I'm finding out that his idea of love is throwing me out to the wolves, as he said, just to see if I could survive. I had to send my daughter and family away after my life was nearly taken from me. I've ordered the deaths of people because I needed to use them as leverage against a man who is completely sick in every way and I needed to show him that I am not afraid of him.

"And the truth of it, Mr. Lagrange, is… I am deathly afraid of Jangles and I always have been."

Her stomach was no longer making noises, and her head no longer seemed to hurt. She was angry. She was angry with everyone… that was not a good thing.

"I'm done," she whispered. "I thought I was playing this shit right, but I was being played as a fucking pawn. I'll not be led around by the nose any fucking more. Time for all of them to realized that I'm the Queen of this goddamn empire and I'm in a mood to step on some necks.

"Now, Jackson," she said his first name letting him know that she felt in charge, "where do you wish to stand? And I want you to know… you're either with me or you need to leave Tampa."

"Damn," Jackson Lagrange whistled, "I love your style. I'll tell you like I told Mr. St. Cloud, I am your man. The hire and the pay may have come from Sydney, but you're my charge and I'll not leave your side until you release me."

"Then until I talk to Nick, you are the only one I trust," she held out her hand. "Please, Jackson, do not make me regret this."

"On my word… I am in this with you until the end. Besides," Lagrange grinned a mischievous grin, "I want to see how you want to play all of this out. You have three men to deal with; two of them have said that they love you, and the third is out to kill you. It's like none of these men have never heard that age old adage… Hell hath no fury…"

"Like a woman scorned," Courtney finished for him.

Courtney stood and walked over to her desk and picked up her phone. She quickly punched in Nina's name and then hit the call button on her number. She was smiling again and feeling like this was now more in her favor whether Nick was still alive or not. The ball was in her court because at this point Sydney did not know that she knew he was still alive.

"Hey, Nini," she responded to Nina finally answering, "we have a lot of work to do. They played me like a bitch and I'm done with it."

"What's going on, Babe?" Nina asked. "What do you need me to do?"

"I don't want to do this over the phone," Courtney said, "I need to see your face. Can you come here to the house?"

"Give me a few to put back on my face and I'm there."

Jackson stood and made his way to the bar. For the first time in his career he actually had a cause he could truly believe in. He'd only skimmed through all of those papers Nick had told him to get, but from what he'd read he definitely couldn't see dealing with Sydney any longer. He'd never had a wife because of his crazy lifestyle and all of the ridiculous traveling he'd done, but never had he been inclined to just feed a woman to a dog like Bobby Johnson. Sydney has always known what kind of man Jangles was, so now he wanted to know… why?

He'd done a lot of research on the kind of man that Bobby Johnson was. He knew about his life running the streets. He knew about all of the drug dealing and the fact that this man had never spent a day in jail, which was amazing considering that even Sydney had spent about two years locked away. Thinking about it now, Jackson began to wonder if during that time that Sydney was away is when Jangles got the bright idea that some day he would try to kill off his best friend to take over the business they would create together.

"Looks like I'm starting everything from scratch," Courtney said as she sat back down. "Once Nina gets here I'll have to let her in on everything that's going on. She's been trying to find out what Jangles knew about Sydney's death, and well, that's unnecessary at this point.

"What you may not know is that Jangles talks in his sleep," she informed him, "and she's willing to give me any and all of the information he's babbling about. We recently found out that Jangles has brought a man into town named Shaw, and when Nick heard the name he was none too happy."

"Yes, I know about one Mr. David Crenshaw aka Big Shaw," Jackson reached into his attaché bag and pulled out another folder. "He's a dirt bag of the worst caliber. Killer. Assassin. He believes in torture, and Jangles loves to call him in when he's wanting to send a very messy message to his enemies."

"Hm," Courtney smiled, "looks like I have my first casualty of this new war."

"He's already being dealt with," Courtney turned to glare at Nick as he walked into the living room. "My friend Everlast has men out there looking for him right now."

Courtney walked around the sofa in a rush. Her hand was moving faster than her feet and by the time they were face to face she'd reared back. Her knuckles cracked as her fist made contact with his jaw and she almost fell into him as the momentum of her punch slung her forward. She watched in horror as Nick took what she had to give and his face followed through with a sickening grunt, but he didn't fall.

"You know," his hand was at his jaw as he erected himself to face her. "I'm sorry."

"Fuck you, Nicholas St. Cloud," her teeth were grinding together as she stood ready to deliver another blow to his face. "You should have just told me."

"I know, Courtney," Nick was still rubbing his chin. "And I promise to tell you everything… you have my word; I'll never lie to you again." "You better not," she fell into his arms as her legs suddenly gave way. "Never."

Chapter 18

Jangles sat up in bed watching Nina sleep and smiled. Since that bitch of a wife of his ran off with his kids Nina had been his ride or die and that's what he's needed with all of this shit going on with IXion and Courtney. He reached over and ran his fingers along her hip that was naked and exposed as she lay on her side. Her skin was always so soft, and here lately she'd returned to being that sexy ass bitch he'd fallen in lust for the moment he saw her at Sydney's. Licking his lips, he slid up behind her and pressed his body to hers.

He caressed her leg at the knee and began dragging his fingers up to her hip. She moaned in her sleep and pressed back into him grinding that ass of hers against his growing dick. He pushed forward sliding between her thighs as his fingers traced around her bellybutton. She giggled in her sleep like she was having a really good dream, and he continued to softly tease her body. As she pushed back and gyrated her hips, he smiled as her heated wetness coated this shaft.

He tickled his fingers up her rib cage and cupped her breast gently squeezing it in his large hand. She took a deep breath as his finger circled around her nipple before he lightly pinched it. Jangles leaned into her neck kissing and licking his way to her ear as her hand reached up grabbing at his dreads to pull him deeper into her neck. He was slowly sliding back and forth between her legs and she was pressing down and back against him wetting him with each stroke.

"Damn," she moaned again as he pinched her nipple once more, "that's a hellava way to be awakened."

"Well laying here with your ass all poked out like that gots a nigga feeling some kinda way."

Nina giggled grinding harder against the dick stuck between her thighs. He was the bad guy in her mind, but she was still in love with him and in the back of her mind that sickened her. She'd seen what he was capable of and she could no longer trust him. Her heart was pounding in her chest as he palmed her breast and squeezed again, and that magnificent piece of him between her legs always made not just her mouth drool.

Jangles slid his hand down her body and between her legs. She almost screamed out as his fingers sought and found her pearl and pressed. Her top leg moved back over his and as he pulled back he adjusted his angle waiting for that little sound she always made.

"Goddamn, Bobby," she called out his name followed by a grunting moan as he pushed his way into her yielding body. He always stretched her to the point of pain but it always felt so goddamn good; he was never forceful and with each push in he would pull back allowing her a moment to recover before pushing in deeper.

Nina was in a mood this morning and began pushing back on him not waiting for his thrust forward. The head was flared and just felt like it was trying to collapse her walls to make more room, and as she flexed her muscles she could feel all of the veins snaking along the shaft. His fingers were rubbing and tweaking her clit adding just enough stimulation to her over sensitive flesh that the pain of him pushing forward faded away in her clouded mind.

Grabbing her by the waist Jangles pushed forward giving her what she seemed to want because she pushed back taking more than he'd been able to give her. Her heat was exhilarating and as he looked down between them he marveled at how wet he was. His thrusts increased and her moans were louder as they moved together. She was begging and crying out for more and he was more than willing to give her exactly what she was calling for. Thoughts of Marilene slipped into his head and he remembered how that little skinny ass loved a good pounding.

"You gon' gimme that pussy baby? Can I take it like I want it?" he was growling in her ear and grinned as her body shivered against his.

"Fuck me, Bobby," she kept moaning out. "I want to hurt, Daddy, I want it bad."

Kneeling up behind her Jangles rolled her over and maneuvered between her thighs. She was quick to wrap her long legs around his waist and lock him in. He leaned over her body and kissed her hard as he pushed up filling her once more. Grinding against her clit as his tongue pushed into her mouth. Sliding out he grunted into her mouth because of her fingernails digging into his shoulders.

"Time to give you the *LD*, Baby." His voice was a rolling grumbled that had her entire body wiggling underneath him.

"The LD?" she managed to finally say once he'd pulled back until just the head was being squeezed and sucked locked inside her pussy.

"Damn right," Jangles thrust forward grinning as she screamed out and her body just seemed to lock up around him. "That's that long dick, Bitch. Now take this."

Nina's grip tightened as Jangles thrusts increased to the point that it felt like he was beating the air out of her lungs. He was up on his knees his hands on either side of her head and his elbows locked and his hips were pounding between her thighs nonstop. He was staring down at her with an animalistic glare that only excited her more and she licked her lips between screams. Her breasts were bouncing violently on her chest in tuned with his brutality. But, she begged for more.

She wanted to be as sore as he thought he could make her. She wanted another reason to try to hate him, but the way he was using her only made her desires for this ruthless bastard strengthen. Her fingernails dug deeper into his shoulders and his thrusts were now being punctuated with him grinding against her clit each time he pushed up into her stomach. Her feet had been separated due to his movements, and they were going to leave the muscles in his hips bruised from the way she was pressing the heels of her feet down into them. She was trying to move with him, but he was a powered machine banging and grinding her body down into the bed.

"Gimme that pussy, Babe," he was chanting over and over. "Who' pussy this? Huh? Who pussy?"

Nina stroked his ego between breaths telling him it was his. His sweat was dropping down on her body like a light rain and all she wanted was… more. She was squeezing and releasing her inner muscles slowing his motions a fraction and creating a friction that pushed her closer to the edge of her building orgasm.

"Take it, Daddy," she begged. "Fuck me, Bobby, fuck me harder."

Dropping his body down onto her and pressing her deeper into the mattress, Jangles bit on her neck as he picked up his pace. She was babbling incoherently into his ear and her arms were locked around his neck keeping his head trapped into her neck. Their bodies were slick with their perspiration and it was soaking into the sheets. The headboard was beating hard against the wall and the rail was screeching like it was straining to maintain the punishment it was currently under.

He was in love with her voice. The strained screams. The near pitiful begging. All it did was give him that drive to push and pull… thrust and grunt… bang her through the mattress until she finally begged him to stop, but she didn't. He pulled back up off her body and leaned in to capture her nipple into his mouth and he sucked giving her body a bit of a break grinding and churning his dick deep inside her pussy making certain he pressed against her clit. She was literally squirting her thick, syrupy juices all over him and the bed and her body was going through spasms.

"Yea, you are one hot ass bitch," he'd caught her nipple and was talking through his teeth, "gimme that fuckin' cum. Cream that big ass dick like a nasty little slut for me."

Nina felt her mind explode. She'd had men talk dirty to her, but with Jangles it was different. He was so deep in her mind that nothing about what he truly was saying really seemed to matter to her and her love for him burned her alive with every breath she took. His thrusts were beginning again, and his teeth biting into her nipple ignited a brand new fire in her body that covered her from the top of her head to the soles of her feet. She couldn't even scream

anymore because her throat felt like it was closed
and only allowing her to breathe in gasping breaths.

And then he just pulled out.

"No," she pleaded as he knelt up between her
spread thighs. "No, Bobby, don't stop… please."

Not listening to her Jangles sat back on his
legs stroking his hand slowly up and down his length
staring between her spread thighs. His mouth is
watering and he has a wicked grin spread over his
lips. The lips look like the petals of a flower
puckering and kissing at him dripping that glistening
line of morning dew. Leaning forwards he slid his
tongue up from the clinching muscle of her little anal
bud and up over the sweet mound of her pussy. Her
moans were louder than before and her hand was
pasted to the back of his head keeping him in place.

"Oh you, nasty ass bastard," her voice hissed
through her clenched teeth as his tongue tapped at
her clit before dropping back down between her lips.

Dipping his tongue deep into her welcoming
hollow, Jangles pressed his face forward making
certain that his nose nudged against her clit. Still
stroking his dick, he began to tease her with his
tongue and her body responded nicely. Her ass was
bouncing around beneath his face and he from the
corner of his eyes he could see her toes clenching
and grabbing at the bed sheets. Sliding his face up he
sucked in her clit and again teased it with the tip of
his tongue, swiping and dancing all over the
sensitive bud.

"No," her voice is a hollow echo that vibrates
around in his head. "Stop, stop goddamn you!"

She's wailing but her hand is not moving
from his head and she's pushing harder against his
face. Her hips are whipping about and he can feel the
muscles in her thighs contracting around his ears.

Her legs are locked at the knees at the back of his head making it hard for him to breathe, but Jangles didn't care as he bit down on her clit to keep her from pulling out of his mouth. Her body was all over the place as his teeth and tongue torture her.

Nina screamed out something between his name and a gurgling cry for help. Her body felt like she's being tossed against a tidal wave and her orgasm destroyed what remained of her mind. Her hand fell away from his head and her legs dropped away from his neck and she stretched out beneath him with her body quaking and quivering.

Not allowing her a moment to regain her senses and being so close to his own need to release, Jangles is back up between her legs thrusting forward as hard as his hips will allow. He's staring down at the wasted woman grinning at her the moment her eyes flash open at his entrance. Reaching up he grabs her breasts and squeeze hard, mauling the tender flesh and once again he's pounding her with his body.

Unable to speak… unable to utter a sound, her mouth is just hanging open and she's taking a beating beneath this beautiful man of hers. He's being as brutal as he can be, and her body is still wanting more. She's feeling dirty. Incomplete. But, she feels whole with him especially when they're making love. Her hands won't move and neither will her legs, but none of that matters to either of them.

Somewhere in the back of her mind she's begging him to finish. Somewhere in the back of her mind she keeps telling herself that she asked for this, and he was just being himself. Somewhere in the back of her mind she was berating herself for her stupidity where this man was concerned, and with each puffing gasp from his body jogging thrusts she knew her conscious was right.

He's no good for you, Nina... the voice was screaming over and over, but her mind and body were working well together to block away that voice.

"I love you," her voice was a weak whisper in his ear. His body dropped down upon her and she could feel every muscles on his frame jumping like he'd been struck by lightning.

Jangles heard her saying she loved him, and this triggered the intense orgasm he'd been holding on to. His toes curled and he buried his face in her neck and he could feel her pussy jumping around his dick with each spurt of his seed pressure washing her insides. He screamed into her neck allowing his body to jerk until at long last he was empty.

"I love you too, Nina," he growled into her ear.

****

The shower was just what his body needed after that morning with Nina. Jangle was sitting in the living room having a cup of coffee, and she was still sleeping. It was tempting to go back to bed and get her started all over again, but she was exhausted and he respected that. He sat down on the sofa and wondered what had happened to prompt the change back into that sexy, cocky woman he'd seen stretched out on Sydney's sofa, but in truth, it didn't matter because his baby was back.

The television was on and the news was playing but he wasn't paying it any attention. He had the newspaper and was wrapped up in reading about some new nonsense happening down in the hood concerning some new drug sweeps to come in the following weeks. This news would mean that he would have to talk to all of his boys and get the trap houses cleaned up and the stash houses cleaned out. He'd always planned for things like this, and he would have to dock his insider at the sheriff's department this month for not giving him a heads up

He moved on and began laughing at the idiots getting all caught up in a prostitution sting between Tampa, St. Pete and Clearwater, Polk, and even Orange Counties. It always amazed him at the number of sick ass men who were willing to travel with the hopes of running up in some young pussy. Sickly Jangles shrugged his shoulders as he considered that as a possible business venture once he'd gotten IXion back under his control.

"Damn fools," he muttered with a laugh as he tossed the paper aside to pick up his phone. "Yo, Cuzo, what's good?"

"Ain't you, Nigga," the voice wasn't one he recognized, "but this fat fuck is still alive."

"Who the fuck is this," Jangles sat up on the sofa, "and where's my goddamn cousin, Muthafucka?"

"Easy, easy there. Wrong question, Jangles," the man responded. "I'll let you try once more."

"What do you want?"

"What I want is for you to bleed, Nigga," the man sounded like he was having fun, "but I guess I'll settle for Shaw to do so in your stead."

"In my stead? What the fuck you mean?" Jangles was up and stalking around the room. "You know if you do something stupid when I find you I'm gonna make you fuckin' hurt?"

"I'm really not worried about that, Jangles," the man was now taunting him. "I'm already looking for you, Muthafucka, and you're a fucking dead man."

Jangles stood frozen where he was standing as he heard a man screaming in the background.

"I'M GOING TO KILL YOU!" Jangles screamed. "DO YOU FUCKIN' HEAR ME?"

Nina had been standing at the door listening in, and she ran out with a sheet wrapped around her body to see Jangles standing in the middle of the living room. His eyes were stretched in horror as he held the phone to his ear. His face was a mask of anger and sadness leaving Nina unsure of what she should do. She reached for him but he brushed her hand aside.

"Shit, talk to me goddammit." He was trying to ignore the sounds of the man screaming in the back. He refused to believe that Shaw could be crying out like that… not at the hands of any man. Whoever he was kept screaming at the top of his lungs begging them to stop doing whatever it was being done to him.

"Listen to him scream like a stuck pig, Jangles," the voice was back, "soon that will be you. Soon I'm going to have you begging and pleading with me to just kill you, but I want to see you crying like a little bitch."

"That's not Shaw, you piece of shit," Jangles spat into his phone.

"Wrong, Nigga, check your text," the man was laughing just as Jangles got the notification that he had a new text message. "I just sent you something."

Pulling the phone from his ear he opened the message and stared at the thumbnail of the picture. Small it resembled his cousin, but he wasn't sure and he was too afraid to enlarge to be certain. He heard another scream and the man's laughter once more with him saying over and over to look at the picture.

Pressing the thumbnail to enlarge it, he heard Nina gasp as she stepped away and he almost dropped the phone as he stared at his cousin cut up and dripping blood in more ways than he could count. His eyes welled.

"You're going to regret this," Jangles hissed into the phone. "I'll find you and when I do … you're a fuckin' dead man."

"Promises, promises, you, fuckin' pussy. You was never the man of the operation, naw, naw, Nigga. You always needed Sydney's bitch ass and now I hear y'all actually have a woman running the show better than either of you two ever could. I'm loving this shit."

"Fuck you," the screaming in the background was now closer to the phone. Jangles could hear the man breathing heavy. "Shaw? Goddammit, Cuz, is that you? Speak to me, Nigga."

"Bobby," Shaw could barely get his name out. "Bobby, I'm so fucking sorry. I'm so fuckin'…"

Jangles sunk to his knees as Shaw's voice was suddenly gurgling and he could only assume that his throat had been cut. In his head he could see his cousin on his knees with his hands behind his back and his head flopping on the muscles remaining in his neck. Tears burned his eyes and he tried to drop the phone.

"You're next, Bobby," the voice whispered into his ear. "I'm coming for you right now you, sorry son-of-a-bitch, and when I find you… what I did to Big Shaw is nothing compared to what I have in mind for you."

"Fuck you," Jangles slung his phone across the room watching as it shattered against the wall. "Fuck you, Muthafucka… fuck you."

263

Nina was kneeling beside him and he fell into her arms sobbing like a baby.

Chapter 19

"Something's happened," Nina rushed into the living room after Nick let her into the house.

"I'm sure it has," Courtney turned from the window and walked up to her friend. "As a matter of fact, quite a bit has happened in the last several hours."

"What do you mean?" Nina was looking into her friend's eyes and there was something different about them… something cold… something she'd never seen before.

"Come and sit, Nini, we have a lot to talk about."

****

Jangles stood over the covered body of his cousin trying to keep calm. The body had been thrown out at his stash house in West Tampa. Two of his small time boys, Bobo and Junebug, had called him the moment the body was tossed out of a speeding car. He'd left Nina's condo and raced through the streets to get to the small, two-bedroom house just down from Busch. If the chain link fence had been closed when he pulled up, he would have driven right through it.

They'd dragged the body into the house before anyone in the neighborhood had seen what had happened and had him lying on the dining room table. He was as naked as JC had been and just as beaten, but it was his neck that Jangles couldn't take his eyes off of. Standing there he could still hear his cousin gurgling his last words to him, and he'd known that whoever had called him had cut the big man's throat. But, actually seeing his throat slashed and split open was more than he was ready for.

"What do we do?" Bobo stepped up touching his shoulder.

Before he knew what he was doing, Jangles spun and hit the skinny man with a solid blow across his jaw. He watched as the man flipped head over heels landing some few feet away from him and he stepped forward as the man scrambled to get away.

"Don't you touch me," Jangles looked at his shoulder and then down at the huddled man. "Don't you ever fuckin' touch me!"

He glanced over at Junebug who was backing away from him with his hands up. Everything was wrong right now, and as he ran his fingers through his dreads pulling back from his face, he stood there trying to catch his breath. He could hear his lungs thumping inside his chest and his pounding a drum's tempo in his ears. He unclenched his fist and slowly backed away until the back of his legs hit the table.

"What did you see?" he asked without looking at either man.

"It wasn't much, Bossman," June walked over and helped Bobo to his feet. "We was here in the house and I was walkin' by da window ova there and I saw this black van runnin' up da road, so I stepped to the door wit' dat choppa. I thought it was gon' run right through da fence… but instead da van skid to a stop and the back doors open. I yelled at Bo and we watched as they tossed da body out."

"We really didn't know who dis nigga be," Bobo added as he glanced between Jangles and his little brother Junebug. "We ran out as they drove off not really sure what to do but he was layin' dere naked and shit. We had to get him inside before dem nosey muhfuckas began to call One Time. My first thought was to call you wit all da shit been goin' on, right."

"You did good," Jangles had turned back to the body and gently laid his hand on the man's forehead. "This is my cousin… since you didn't know. Thank you for getting him in and covering him up like this. You did good."

The two men kept their distance unsure how safe they were at the moment. Jangles looked like a man about to crack or meltdown. They'd never seen Jangles emotional even at the loss of someone he was close to, but this man looked like he was about to start crying or throwing a tantrum.

"Anything in particular about the van?" Just as he asked his phone rang.

"I see you got my package," the man on the other was taunting him again.

"How did you get this number?"

"Looks like ya boy has all of your little stash numbers in his phone… I just dialed until you answered." The man began laughing.

"You have no idea what you've done," Jangles hissed into the phone.

"Oh, Bobby Johnson, I know exactly what I've done, but the thing you just don't realized is how fucked you really are. Even now, Nigga, if I wanted to I could launch this rocket and blow that lil piece of shit house you're in sky high. You're mine when I'm ready for you, Bobby."

Hearing the man call him by his name sent a eerie shiver up his spine. He walked to the window of the stash house and looked out hoping to see someone. His free hand had pulled the Glock .40 from the shoulder harness under his jacket and he felt ready for anything.

"That's like bringing a knife to a gunfight, Bobby," the man was laughing. "Yea, I'm watching you, Boy, I can see everything you're doing. I can

see those two crack fiends behind you standing there
like they are about ready to piss their pants. I can see
everything."

"Who the fuck are you? What is it that you
really want, huh?" Jangles turned away from the
window. "You want money, huh? I can pay you
whatever you want. You want drugs, huh, is that it?
You want drugs… 'cus I can get you whatever you
fuckin' want."

"I love an ol' beggin' ass, hard nigga. Keep
begging for your life, Bobby. Matter of fact… get on
your knees and beg, you weak ass piece of shit."

"I don't beg no man," Jangles responded. "I
am going to find you and when I do… I am going to
rip your throat out with my fingers."

He hung up the phone and glared at the two
men standing shaking against the wall. "Is this house
cleaned?"

"Yea, Boss," Bobo answered. "We got the
word and emptied the monies and stashed at the
MLK house."

"Cool… burn it."

"Jangles?" June stepped forward. "Um… the
body? What about the body?"

Jangles leaned forward and kissed his
cousin's forehead before turning to walk away. His
heart hurt because this was the last man in this world
he would ever trust. He didn't have a clue who the
man on the phone was, but he'd find him and he'd
make him pay. At the door he glanced at the body
once more and then at Bobo and Junebug.

"Burn it all." He walked out leaving them
standing there staring at the dead body on the table.

****

"Are you serious?" Nina was sitting on the
sofa with Courtney. Nick was standing back near the

bar with a white guy she didn't know. The Vasilevich brothers were also there and they just seemed to be waiting for some kind of big fallout. "Sydney is alive?"

"Yes, he is," Courtney looked more perturbed than hurt. Nina wondered if she'd actually had time to process that or if she was just running on some pent up adrenaline.

"But, I don't understand… why?"

"He wanted to see if I was strong enough to stand up to Jangles and keep his company safe while he was off being treated for the poison."

"But, why not just tell you? Why keep this shit a goddamn secret when he knew the kind of shit that Jangles would put you through?"

She turned and glared at Nick, "And you fucking knew?"

"That's a host of demons I'll have to deal with, Nina," Nick didn't offer any apologies to her. "I'm not proud of it, but I did have my reasons."

"Yea," Nina spat out, "it was all because you love her… right? You, Sydney, and Jangles are all cut from the same goddamn cloth. You're all pieces of shit with no care or concern other and for yourselves."

Nick stood there listening unable to say a thing… because she was right. He could have stopped this a long time ago. He could have told Sydney to fuck off and told Courtney the truth, but he didn't. He'd allowed himself to be used by these men continuously and he was sick with himself. All of this had to come to an end, and somewhere he needed to find out who he was as a man.

He turned away and walked off into the kitchen to fix him a fresh cup of coffee. He needed to be away from everyone for a moment so that he could think and figure out his… no, their next move. He could still hear them in the living room as Nina continued to bash him along with Sydney and Jangles.

"What are you thinking, Mr. St. Cloud?" Lagrange had followed him into the kitchen.

"I never wanted to be anything like Sydney… let alone Jangles," Nick said pouring the coffee into his mug. "I just wanted to make certain she stayed safe. I just wanted to be close to her because I was… shit, I am still in love with her. I never intended for her to be hurt."

"That is the power of lies, yes," Lagrange stated. "But there's still time to put all of this to bed. We don't know exactly what Sydney has planned, but I'm sure that we'll not have to wait for too long. He is going to make himself known that much we can be sure of. You need to start thinking like these two men because we need to get back ahead of them."

"Yes we do."

Nick was leaning over the counter staring down into his coffee mug when Courtney walked into the kitchen. He didn't have to look back at her to know that she was standing there with her arms crossed and her hip popped to the side, but when he did finally stand and looked over his shoulder… that's exactly how she was standing there. He couldn't help his thoughts of how beautiful she looked staring at him with a look that was somewhere between contempt and concern.

"We need to talk," she announced and as Lagrange moved to leave she stopped him. "No, this is for the two of you."

"I'm not going nowhere," Lagrange smiled as he leaned back against the counter

"I'm done with being a puppet for anyone, and for us to move forward I need a couple of things to happen right quick. First, I need to know who bugged my home, and I need to know yesterday," she glanced at Lagrange and he nodded his head. Nick stood waiting his turn and she didn't make him wait too long. "Next, from what I've been reading, Robles… Henri was a part of this little conspiracy and I need you to get him to me. Since Sydney thought it was such a grand idea to make me his own little experiment… well I think that it's time for the Monster to call out the Maker."

"What do you have in mind?" Nick cocked his head watching her eyes.

"I figure that the only real way to make Sydney play his hand is to force his call. I want Henri… dead."

"You do understand that we're dealing with a very dangerous man?" Nick asked.

"No, Baby," Courtney's smile was cold, "I'm dangerous thanks to you and all of them and its time to show just how dangerous I am. This game is ending Nick and I need you to pick your side or you need to pack up and run… now."

"Run? Run where, Courtney?"

"Anywhere that I cannot find you," Nick couldn't help but to grin at her answer.

Stepping up and placing his hands on her shoulders and leaning down into her face, he moved in to kiss her lips and then pulled back. "I'm not going anywhere unless you kill me. I can't apologize enough for my hand in this shit, and no matter what I say from this point on, you're going to have to decide if you believe me or not. Like you… I'm done being a puppet. I'm done with letting someone else dictate what I do and that's why I had Everlast grab Shaw.

"I want Jangles and Sydney to know where my allegiances lie… and that's with you. I've done everything wrong in all of the wrong ways, but Nina was right and it was because I do love you. I have always loved you and I will always put my life on the line to protect you."

"It's not that I don't believe you right now, Nick," Courtney pulled back away from his face, "but I need time. I need to see that this is not just a mouth full of fucking words."

Nick smiled and moved back to pick up his coffee mug. He'd broken her trust and that needed to be repaired and he knew he'd be willing to do whatever needed to get back into her good graces. Pulling out his phone he dialed Henri's number and waited for the man to answer.

"Yea, Henri," his eyes never left Courtney's, "no worries I'm outside and she's not around, but she wants to meet. I believe she wants to put Yuri and his lot back into play because of what happened with JC. I think she's about done with all of this bullshit and you need to let him know that she's breaking, but she's a fighter."

Nick stood listening to the other man talk for a moment. He could feel Lagrange eyeing him and it was making him uncomfortable, but he never looked away from Courtney.

"Look, Henri," he stopped the man in the middle of a mouthful of bullshit, "I'm barely holding her together by a fucking string, and I have a feeling that she suspects something. Also, I'm dealing with Jangles and he knows all about that, so I really don't need all of this extra nonsense. We need to get this bullshit taken care of and it needs to be done soon.

You need to meet us here at the house and tell him to expect a call so that she can get his thoughts on a new game plan.

"I'll see you in an hour."

Turning on her heels and leaving the kitchen, Courtney walked back into the living room. "Ok, kids," she announced, "we're about to have company and we need to be prepared."

****

Henri Thames had never been a superstitious man, but there was something about the way Nick sounded that had him on edge. Nick was always that soft spoken, follow any orders kind of guy that really disgusted him, but today he spoke like he actually had a backbone.

"I'm really not sure if now is the right time for Mr. Roulette to be on the phone with her, especially with what he knows of she and your relationship now. He may say something that she will…"

"Look, Henri," Nick interrupted him, "I'm barely holding her together by a fucking string, and I have a feeling that she suspects something. Also, I'm dealing with Jangles and he knows all about that, so I really don't need all of this extra nonsense. We need to get this bullshit taken care of and it needs to be done soon. You need to meet us here at the house and tell him to expect a call so that she can get his thoughts on a new game plan."

"Maybe I've been wrong about you, Mr. St. Cloud," Henri said into his telephone. "I'll be there within the hour and I'll call and let him know what's going on and to be expecting our call."

"I'll see you in an hour," Nick answered before hanging up on him.

"Good to see you're finally stepping up to the plate, Mr. St. Cloud," Henri said as he grabbed his coat and headed towards the door. As he was turning the knob his wife walked into the foyer from upstairs.

"Are you leaving for the day?"

"Yes," he answered without turning around. "If you need me I'll be back before dark. You can call my phone"

Not waiting for an answer he pulled the door and stepped out into the daylight. This was a life he was longing to be away from because this woman was becoming too much like a real wife. He didn't see the need for such an elaborate background set up, but Sydney had insisted and he was following orders.

The sun felt good on his face as he pulled off his unnecessary glasses and made his way to his car. He walked around the car as he's always done checking for anything out of place including the markers he'd laid out to let him know if anyone had been around his vehicle. Satisfied, he got into the car and began the trek to see Nick and Courtney.

"Good morning, Mr. Roulette," he'd dialed his boss the moment he sat down, "I'm on my way to see your wife. I just received a call from Mr. St. Cloud that she's needing Mr. McGregor… to consult on a new plan of attack."

"She never fails to impress, does she Henri?"

"No, Sir," the man answered as he was pulling out into traffic. "But, I am concerned about Mr. St. Cloud."

"Don't worry too much about Nicky right now because Jangles and Shaw will be keeping him busy. I have it on damn good authority that Jangles has put a rather high marker on ol' Nick Styles' head and thanks to a couple of calls I've made… well there are quite a few of those young thugs out there who will be gunning for his ass as well."

"As you wish, Mr. Roulette," Henri answered. He pressed back into his seat as he allowed the conversation with Nick roll through his head and something still felt… different.

"You call me once you get there and they let you in on what's going on," Sydney instructed the man. "I think that Nicky is right, I think that it's time for all of this shit to come to an end; I think that McGregor will make his last vocal appearance before I finally let Courtney see that I am alive. This game is almost completely over and Jangles is coming to end of his rope."

"I think everyone involved will be happy to see the end of this," Henri said and he pressed the button on his Bluetooth to end the call.
"But I fear that all of this is going to end quite ill," he said to himself as he sped off to this meeting.

Chapter 20

"Hey you," Sydney was sitting in his favorite chair as she walked into the living room. He was smiling, but his smile was weak and forced and he looked frail. He called her to him and held his arms out for her to slip into.

Courtney was careful how she sat on his leg because everything was hurting him now. She'd watched the steady downward spiral of his health and she felt helpless because there was nothing that she could do to help him. She'd been researching a number of doctors and hospitals across the country thanks to a list that she'd received from Mr. Robles, but so far none of them were equipped to help her husband in this advanced stage.

All she could do was sit and watch him die, and a piece of her died with him every day.

"I need to talk to you," Sydney wrapped his arms around her as she lay back against his shoulder. He giggled just a bit as her hair tickled his nose.

"What's up, Babe?"

"I need you to remember something," he began, "something Big Fats would always tell me and now I finally understand."

Courtney sat up a little and faced him because he sounded so serious. The last few months had been extremely hard on him with Jangles coming around and smiling in his face like he'd done nothing wrong, but all the while they'd been getting reports from Nina about the things he'd done and was planning from his sleep talking. Her own personal loathing of the man had increased by a thousand fold, and that was increasing with each day she had to looking to Sydney's eyes.

"Big Fats would say, 'The troubles you'll mostly face will never come from those you don't trust, you can always depend on them to do what they do… but the ones you need to focus on are those that you trust. It's the ones that you will love like your family that will bring about your ruin. You watch them, and you watch them close.'

"And I get it now. I get it."

Courtney sat on his lap and leaned in kissing him softly on the lips. Her husband was trying to be strong and she knew it was because of her, but he spent too much time in the restroom on his knees vomiting up more blood than his body held. He rarely slept and it showed by the dark circles under his eyes. He barely ate because foods didn't sit well on his stomach. His smile was so weak that it no longer made it up to his eyes, and his muscles were getting weaker by the day.

"I've been learning to keep my eyes open to everything around me," she whispered into his ear, "and with Nick and Nini around they will help to keep me grounded."

"I feel like shit," he turned his head coughing into a handkerchief and then staring at the blood spittle. "I shouldn't have ever introduced you to all of this. I should have been a bigger man and kept you out and away from Jangles ass. I trusted him. He was my muthafuckin' brotha and to know that it was his hand putting this shit in me"

"I've never trusted his trifling ass," Courtney gently leaned over and grabbed a glass of water and handing it to him.

"You keep it that way," Sydney took a sip. "There's nothing about Jangles that you should ever trust."

She could see the discomfort that he was in and quickly stood. She watched sadly as Sydney stood and walked as quickly as his weakened legs would allow towards the bathroom. Once again she stood at the door listening as he heaved and soon the sound of his stomach emptying into the toilet. Tears filled her eyes and her stomach turned as she walked off to get a towel wet with some cold water from the refrigerator.

"Are you ok, Babe?" she asked upon returning to the bathroom door

"Yea, I'm still alive," his laughter was weak, but she laughed as well.

"Well, that's a damn good thing, Mr. Roulette," she giggled, "because I'd hate to have to kill you for dying on me."

Sydney opened the door, "I knew that there was a damn good reason that I loved you, Mrs. Roulette."

"And I love you too, Mr. Roulette," she smiled rubbing the cold towel across his forehead as she led him back to the sofa.

****

"Good day, Mrs. Roulette," Henri had on his Robles glasses and carrying his ever present briefcase. He was dressed in yet another boring black suit that pretty much hid the wiry man underneath, but upheld the weakly persona he was portraying.

"Thank you for joining us, Mr. Robles," Courtney offered him a smile hoping that he didn't see a difference in her… just yet. "Nick and Nina are here and as soon as you're settled I'd love for you to get Mr. McGregor on the phone. There's been some crazy things going on with Jangles and I really think its time to push forward our efforts."

278

"That sounds good, Ma'am."

Henri walked into the living room and acknowledged Nick with a nod of his head and Nina by kissing the back of her hand; it was something that had always made her nervous, but she'd always just accepted it. Nick was standing with his back against the wall holding a cup of coffee which was his norm and Nina had been standing by the desk. As he sat down, he suddenly felt nervous but he shook it off and proceeded to open his briefcase.

"Mr. McGregor wanted me to get an idea of what you had planned, Mrs. Roulette," he pulled out a stack of paper and laid them out on the coffee table.

"I'll be honest, Mr. Robles," Courtney began as she sat down on the other end of the sofa, "I've already explained myself twice now, so if you don't mind I'd just rather explain it once more to you and Mr. McGregor one last time so that I can get things underway. "

"As you wish," the man answered with a nod and he pulled out a speaker that he connected to his cell phone before dialing McGregor's number.

"You're early, Mr. Robles," McGregor's harshly disguised voice rolled through the speaker. Courtney glanced up at Nick and shook her head as he stepped away from the wall.

"I'm sitting here with Mrs. Roulette, Mr. St. Cloud, and Ms. Carlton," Henri announced. "Mrs. Roulette said she wanted to just talk to all of as one, Sir, so that she could get her plans underway."

"I understand," McGregor responded. "Hello, Mrs. Roulette, how may I be of service to you today?"

Courtney stood and began to walk the floor in front of the coffee table. Her mind was full and

she was fighting the urge to just start blurting things
out about what she'd found out over the course of
the last few days. Looking up at Nick, who gave his
nod, she began.

"I've come to the conclusion, Mr.
McGregor," she took a deep breath, "that my
husband had no faith in me."

"I'm not sure I… understand," the man
stuttered.

"All of this," she waved her hands around
more for those there in the house with her and the
man on the phone. "All of this that he's put me in,
was merely… a set up for failure. Sydney didn't
trust me at all, and he knew that Jangles was going
to eat me alive. I think that he was banking on me to
fall on my face."

"But," McGregor began, "that's why you
have all of us in place. Mr. Robles has been there
giving you advice either from his own experiences
or after conferring with me. You have Mr. St. Cloud
and Ms. Carlton there to keep you grounded. You've
proven yourself again and again over the last two
years."

"Yes, you're right," Courtney almost
coughed listening to this man, "but its all been
bullshit, wouldn't you agree? A ruse. I have proven
myself, not just to all of you but to myself as well,
and I've made a decision. I'm done with being a
puppet hoisted around and dancing on these invisible
strings. I'm sick of doing everything that's expected
of me."

"You have me at… a… um loss, Mrs.
Roulette," McGregor was again stammering.

"This is where my head is, Mr. McGregor,"
Courtney moved over and sat on the edge of her
desk. "I've come to see the truth of everything and I

accept that my husband didn't believe in me. So, I've decided that it is time to deal with all of this shit. I've had my life threatened… I've had to send away my daughter and family… Nick has had his life threatened and Nina has put her life in danger. It's time to cash in for all of that we've put into this … game."

Courtney was watching Robles as he sat there expressionless and seemingly unsure what he could say. He was on the edge of the sofa and just listening the conversation going on before him.

"I think that the time has come for everyone to see that I'm no bitch and I'm not to be played with any longer… and that means everyone."

"I can understand that," McGregor answered. "So what are you thinking, Mrs. Roulette?"

"It's already began, Mr. McGregor," she announced.

"In… what way?"

"Big Shaw is dead," Nick had stepped up behind the sofa just behind Robles. "I had it taken care of after he and Jangles thought it was a good idea to put out a contract on me."

Courtney waited for just a moment letting that soak in.

"That's not all," Courtney continued "I've come across some information that's given proof to me that my husband thought I was nothing more than a … umm."

"A mark," Nick offered the word that she was pretending to be looking for.

"Yes, a mark," Courtney glanced down at Robles.

"I would never say that Sydney thought of you as a mark," McGregor was trying to calm a situation that he felt was going completely sideways.

"I know for a fact that your husband loved you, and that was one of the main reasons that he contacted me…"

"Contacted you?" Courtney laughed. "And he loved me huh? I beg to differ. First off, the son-of-a-bitch lied to me the moment he told me that he loved me, and then again the moment he decided that he wanted me to be a part of this little game of his."

Courtney could hear the man on the phone moving around and assumed that he was up pacing whatever hotel room that he was hidden away in. Her brow furrowed as she waited to see if he would say something, or if she should just continue and drop the hammer.

"You've completely lost me now," his voice was strained. "I'm not sure where this is going or how I can continue to help you."

"I have something I want you to hear, Mr. McGregor," Courtney stepped behind her desk and fumbled around with the mouse of her computer. "I think that once you hear this you'll see why I feel about my husband the way I do."

Sydney: Look, Nick, it won't be much longer. You just keep an eye on my wife for me and you keep me informed on what's going on with Jangles. The doctors are saying a good six months… so keep your head about you.

Nick: Goddamn, Syd, I hate lying to her. You said six months ago almost a year ago. I'm beginning to think that you like this behind the scenes bullshit. She's going to see through that McGregor crap and when she does it's not going to be pretty at all.

Sydney: I'll deal with that when it happens. She's pretty smart but I've been doing this shit a long muthafuckin' time. Just keep your wits, Nigga.

Nick: No... fuck that, Sydney. She's too good for this, and this shit is eating me up inside. I hate the shit that we're doing and yet you and Henri seem that to think that she's going to take this laying down. You've created a fucking killing machine. She's become as ruthless as all of you if not more so. This woman is a gangster and she's being swallowed up in this Nine bullshit you've thrown her into.

Sydney: You throw some to the wolves and they get eaten up... I threw her to the wolves and she's come back leading them. That's my muthafuckin' girl.

Nick: You keep that shit in mind.

"Just from that conversation," Courtney was staring right at Robles, "you can tell that my husband lied to me... that he's still lying to me because...

"Because Sydney is still alive," she swallowed the bile that was trying to rise up in her throat.

Henri looked around as the sound of more footsteps was coming from behind him, and as he went to move he was suddenly staring at Courtney Roulette holding a pistol in his face. For years he'd been damn good at keeping himself out of situations where his life was back in the hands of other people, but as he slowly sat back down, he could see that he'd failed today.

"What pisses me off beyond words," Courtney began, "is the number of people in on it,

wouldn't you agree, Mr. Robles… or should I call
you Henri?"

"Either works for me, Mrs. Roulette," the
mousy white man looked pale as a ghost. "I just
want you to know that I was merely following
orders."

"Yes, I know," Courtney smiled as the
Vasilevich brothers stood behind the sofa beside
Nick, and Jackson Lagrange was seated behind the
desk.

"What's going on there?" McGregor asked.

"Oh right, I forgot, you can no longer see
what's going on because there are no more of your
little cameras. So, what's going on, my dear, dead
husband," Courtney's eyes never left Henri's, "is
that I'm about to up the stakes on this little 'game'
you've dropped me in to. I'm calling your hand,
Sydney, and I'm moving to take what is now
rightfully mine."

"Courtney," his true voice almost buckled
her knees, "I can explain, Baby, but you just have to
calm down a little and give me a minute to do so."

"Oh, I am very calm, and I don't need your
explanation, Sydney," Courtney wanted to cry but
she refused to do so. "I know everything that I need
to know thanks to Mr. St. Cloud. We've had a very
long conversation the last few hours and well…
thanks to him, I've finally decided to sack up… isn't
that what you boys call it?"

"Sydney sat there and listened as it sounded
like someone was being grappled and then he could
hear Nick screaming at someone to get the fuck off
of him. He was frozen in place as he listened to
furniture being overturned and glass being broken.
The fight was fierce and Nick seemed to be holding
his own for a moment until it all ended with the loud

"POP" of a gun being fired. His heart sunk as he
heard Henri scream out.

"I cannot stand liars, you fucking son-of-a-
bitch," Courtney suddenly said. "Thanks to you,
Sydney, throwing me to the wolves has taught me
that you deal with everyone one way… hard, and so
I've dealt with Nicky Styles. If they can't go the way
I'm going, then I'd just as soon kill them than to deal
with them."

"COURTNEY!" Sydney yelled. "What the
fuck is wrong with you? What the hell have you
done? Courtney, Baby, talk to me… please."

"Talk to you," Courtney couldn't help but to
laugh at that statement as she stepped up to Henri
staring down at him. "That is truly funny coming
from you now, Sydney. You could have *talked* to me
in the beginning. You had two years to *talk* to me
and you refused to do so. Now you want me to talk
to you."

"Courtney, you don't have to do this,"
Sydney was pleading with her over the phone. "We
can fix this, Baby… you got my word..."

"Fuck your word, Sydney," Courtney was
standing in front of Henri once more with the gun
leveled between his eyes. "Tell him what's
happening right now… Henri."

"Mr. Roulette," Henri confirmed the obvious,
"your wife is standing here holding a Glock .40 to
my head. I must say that I never in my life would
have dreamed this would have ever happened, but I
just watched her shoot Mr. St. Cloud and I do not
doubt that she is about to end my life as well."

"What is it that you want, Courtney?"
Sydney's voice was pleading.

"I want Jangles head on a stick," she
laughed. "But, what I want more than that is to tell

my husband good bye and to kiss him one last time… no wait, fuck that, what I truly want is your head right beside Jangles, and…"

Sydney slammed his fists down on the table as the gun fired off once more. His heart was in his throat and he was sweating profusely.

"This ain't how this was supposed to be," he said. "Nicky warned me but I didn't believe him. Goddamn, Baby, I'm so sorry."

"I'm not your baby," Courtney hissed. "I don't know who you are, but you're not the man you're pretending to be. Good bye, Mr. McGregor."

Courtney stood over the dead body of Henri Thames. His head had been thrown back violently against the back of her sofa, and the hole in his forehead leaked the grotesque fluid that slowly streamed down his lifeless face. She stared at the Vasilevich brothers watching with smiles on their faces, and then she glanced around towards Nina and Jackson. They were all on the same page and each gave her the acknowledging nod to let her know they were ready for the next move. Using the back of her hand, she wiped away the dots of blood that had managed to splash back into her face and then she sat down on the sofa.

"Wait, Courtney," Sydney said softly hoping to calm her. "Wait, please…"

"I'm done with the bullshit, Mr. McGregor," she went back to using the name she'd known him by for the last two years. "My husband is dead, and IXion belongs to me. Jangles is going to know this very soon… the Nine is going to know this very soon… and if you get in my way…"

Courtney watched as Nick stood up once more behind the sofa, and their eyes met as he slowly walked around to stand in front of her. He reached out and eased his hand around the pistol and gently tugged it from her hand; there was something in her eyes that he didn't recognize, but it wasn't anger, hurt, or fear and this worried him. Placing the gun on the table, he ripped open his shirt and pulled off the bulletproof vest he'd been wearing underneath; she placed her hand over the bruise left by the impact.

Courtney dropped her eyes from his and placed a finger to her lips to silence him.

"If you get in my way, Mr. McGregor, then you'll '*Know*' very soon as well."

She hung up the phone before he could say anything and then she looked over at Lagrange. "Find him… now."

****

Sydney Roulette couldn't move and all he could do was stare at the phone. He couldn't believe what he'd just heard, and how all of it had come about. This was all his fault and he couldn't just walk away from it. His beautiful wife had become what he'd been his entire life and now she'd even taken a life… no, two lives.

"FUCK!" he grabbed the phone and slung across the room and it exploded against the wall into a dozen pieces.

He sat back in the chair he was in and rubbed his hands over his bald head. His stomach felt worse now than he ever had while that poison was swimming around in his blood stream. He slammed his fists down on the table a couple of times before standing and flipping it over. He was beyond being angry and he room would pay for it at this present time as he completely destroyed the furniture around him.

287

"Goddammit, Courtney," he'd dropped to his knees in the middle of the mess he'd made. "I'm so fuckin' sorry… so fuckin' sorry."

Chapter 21

"Ay, yo, Bobby," Jorge Manciena walked into his office all smiles, "look who made it back to Tampa."

"It's about time, Bro," Jangles stood from his seat behind his desk and walked up to his old friend. "I got a lotta shit that I need you and your men to deal with. I'm fuckin' losing people left and fuckin' right… and now… now someone has killed my goddamn cousin. I'm pretty sure that it was either that bitch, or that nigga, Nick Styles, who had it done."

"Do not worry, Bobby," Jorge clapped his friend's shoulder, "I got this shit all figured out and I'm starting at the source."

Jorge walked over to the desk and pulled one of Bobby's cigars from the humidor and took in its fragrance with a smile. He'd had a long trip from his hacienda in Mexico and was looking forward to the difference in heat from home to the tropical humidity of Florida. He stood there staring at Jangles and took note of how frazzled the man seemed.

"Tell me about your cousin's death," he said. "I knew Big Shaw and he was a damn good man, worked with him a few time… I loved his killing style."

"Yea, that nigga knew how to fuckin' torture a bitch," Jangles laughed for the first time in days. "He died how he lived and I still need to call his girl and let her know. This shit is getting crazy, Bruh. This shit is gettin' really crazy"

Jimmy Q was not a man of many words and even less since partnering himself with these two egomaniacs. He'd sat back patiently waiting to take over business from his Uncle for long enough; he'd hoped that this would be his opportunity to finally do so. He was standing by the large office windows overlooking the city and he could see their reflections and for the first time he began to wonder… would he have to eventually kill these two men.

He was a proud man and he'd been taking care of the street soldiers of his family since he'd turned twenty because he was being groomed to take over. He had a meticulous manner about him that often times made people wonder about his leadership qualities until they crossed his path the wrong way. Beneath his calm and quiet exterior raged a monster of a temper that's seen more than a few men flayed at his hands. There were a few men in his family who knew just how much he enjoyed his work.

Folding his arms across his chest he turned and pressed his back to the window as Jangles and Jorge continued their very animated conversation about a man who was dead, and to him that was such a waste of time. He'd been planning his Uncle's death for nearly as long as he'd been told he was being groomed to take over; at that point, he wanted it all right at that time.

"I want her dead," Jangles just said out of the blue. "I don't want her scared off any longer… I don't want her to just leave my company. I want this bitch dead. Do you understand?"

"I know, my friend," Jorge dropped his own smile. "Like I said, I'm taking this fight to the source. I have men on the way there as we speak and they'll let me know when things have been taken care of."

"Good. Good. I want this shit over," Jangles rubbed his hands together. "This has been going on for far too long and too much has been lost to the point I haven't been concentrating on business and we're losing more. I have little street demons out there trying to operate without guidance because I've been M.I.A and that shit needs to stop right now.

"I need to regain my control."

"Trust me, my friend," Jorge's grin was ominous, "you'll have more control than you'll know what to do with, and once we get this shit settled… it's back to business for all of us."

"What are we going to do about my uncle?" Jimmy Q chimed in."

"I say we kill them," Jangles stared at the small Chinese man. "We killed them all."

"Good, because I'm tired of that tired old man."

The three of them all began laughing.

****

"We need to get the hell out of here," Nick was stalking around the bedroom as Courtney casually sat on the end of the bed.

She'd been quiet ever since she'd shot Henri in the head and made everyone leave the house, but he had refused to leave her alone. He'd upped the number of men circling the house thanks to the additional people Jackson had provided, but he still didn't feel safe. Word had gotten to him from IXion that Jangles was meeting with Jorge Manciena and Jimmy Q which meant that shit was about to get really ugly with the angry drug lord in town. He knew how Manciena operated and he was just as ruthless if not more so than his father, and he was bound to strike quickly.

"Courtney," he stepped and grabbed her by the shoulders to look up at him, but her head slumped forward.

"You have to get over this shit," he was concerned because she was reacting how he thought that she would. "Courtney, goddammit! Get over this shit… we need to get the fuck out of here now."

Courtney looked up in to his eyes and he didn't see the emptiness he was expecting; all he could see was anger. She shrugged out of his grip and stood to face him. Her hand went to his chest where he'd been shot and she rubbed that area causing him to groan out a bit because it was still tender. Her eyes filled with tears as she looked back up at him.

"I didn't think," she began. "I'm so sorry, Nick, my God can you please forgive me?"

"For what, Baby?" he pulled her into his arm and held on to her.

Courtney could feel her entire world pull away from her and exploding. She hadn't signed for this kind of madness when she married Sydney; this was not the life that she'd imagined with the man who had become her knight in shining armor after Nick had been locked away. She wanted to scream but there just wasn't enough air in her lungs to do any more than whimper against Nick's chest and listen to his heart.

"I wanted to shoot you because I was still so angry with you for lying to me," she explained through her whimpering. "I wanted to shoot you because Sydney is not here for me to shoot and then when the gun exploded and you fell… I was so sure that you were dead."

"But I'm not, Courtney, I'm right here. I'm right here with you and I'm not going anywhere."

292

"What is wrong with me, Nick?" Courtney pulled away and looked up to the man she'd never stopped loving. "How could I just shoot you and then turn and kill Mr. Robles?"

"There's nothing wrong with you," Nick brushed a strand of hair from her face and leaned in to kiss her forehead. "I'll be honest, I wasn't sure if were going to be able to do it, and I wanted to say something when you suggested it. But, watching you turn that gun on me and to see your finger pull back on the trigger, well, I knew then that you're ready to do what needs to be done to end this war."

"I'm so tired of all of this, Nick, and now knowing for a fact that he's still alive... I... I don't feel anything for him other than hate."

"I know, and I know that you still don't trust me." Nick pulled her back into his arms and held on to her for a bit longer. "Just give me a chance to prove that I love you, Court. I don't want to lose you."

"It hurts," she pulled away once more and went to her closet and began pulling out her clothes. "You're right; we need to get out of here. Get the men outside to load up and let me grab a few things. We'll need to get a few rooms and let Jackson and Yuri know where we're at. I'll call Nini when we're out of here."

"I'm on it as long as you're sure that you're ok."

"It would be a lie to say that I am," Courtney gave a half smile, "but I will be."

Courtney watched as he walked out of the room carrying the bag of clothes that he'd already packed up. Her head was beating a painful pattern against her temples and her stomach was still doing flips up into her throat; she was trying to keep what

293

little she had in her stomach from rushing up and out, but it was quickly becoming a losing battle. Running into the bathroom she dropped to her knees just in time to hold on to the sides of the toilet. She grunted and groaned as she vomited until she felt dizzy. As she flushed, she sat back on her legs and screamed out.

Sitting on the bathroom floor she cried. She cried as the feel of that gun firing in her hand felt as if it vibrated through her body once more. She cried as she watched a bullet strike Nick in the chest and flipped him backwards onto the floor and he laid there not moving. She cried as she turned the gun towards the man she'd known as Robles and watched his eyes stretch in horror, and she pulled the trigger once again. She cried as she watched in slow motion as the bullet bore through his forehead and seemed to explode from the back of his head in a shower of blood, bone, and brains all over her sofa. She cried as that scene played over and over in her head.

Never in her life had she known resentment… until now.

"I hate you," she cried. "I hate you."

Pounding her fist against the side of the tub all Courtney could see in her head was the explosion of her husband's truck. In her dreams she was always right there at the moment he sat down and turned the ignition. She could feel the heat of the blast as she was thrown backwards and the concussive blow would explode all around her. Her ears would hurt and her screams would be muted from the roar, but she could see everything as if she were sitting in the truck with him. She could do nothing to save him and she watched as he was burned alive screaming and fighting to get out but the metal had already fused together leaving him trapped. She was always right there with him and their eyes would always meet just before the truck would explode once more causing it pounce up and flip over.

Through it all she could hear him screaming out her name. She would always cough and gag at the smell of his burning flesh. Kneeling all she could do was watch helplessly as her husband and truck were consumed by the hungry fire until the fire department finally made it to the scene.

But now… now it was all lies.

Pulling herself together and she stood from the floor. Washing her face and staring at the woman in the mirror she could definitely see a difference. Defiance. Gone was the innocent girl she'd once stared at hoping against hope that her life would become some kind of great adventure. Gone was the girl she'd watched growing up starting out with little pigtails and missing front teeth only to be replaced with a woman who is no longer afraid to pull out a gun and shoot a man. She shivered and splashed water in her face once more.

"Are you ok?" Nick's voice startled her.

"Yea," she answered, "you know me, I've been tossed to the wolves… I'll survive."

"It's more than just surviving, Court," Nick offered as the words she said stung. "You've done something that you were never meant to do, and that's something you'll have to find a way to come to terms with. We are in a war, and it has gone so far away from just being about a muthafuckin' company because they've made it about our lives. So now, you must ask yourself one question, Courtney… is it going to be you, or is it going to be all of them?"

"I'm done being some little Pinocchio on a string for everyone's amusement," her voice was cold. "I'm tired of dancing around with no clear path of where I'm going or what I'm doing. Sydney started this shit, and I'm going to end it."

"I'm with you all the way, Courtney," Nick walked into the bathroom and stood in front of her. "I don't want you to ever worry again that I'm deceiving you. I'll never lie to you again."

Nick leaned in and pressed his lips to hers. The kiss was hot and needed as he held her in his arms hoping that she could feel the need in his touch. His heart was pounding and thankful that she was responsive.

"If you do, Mr. Styles," she pulled away from his lips, "I will shoot you again."

"I'm sure that you will." They both laughed.

****

The cars in the front of the house were the first clue that no one inside was aware of the danger that they were in. The six men moved around outside under the stealth of night. They were all dressed in black with their faces covered just in case one of the men who were normally patrolling the house would never know who had cut them down before they died, but those men were missing and it was like having the entire house to themselves. They moved like a well-oiled machine. Silent. Quick. They kept to the walls of the large home and at what they'd considered, strategic points, they dropped and partially buried small packages pulled from the packs on their backs. Twenty minutes later they moved back out to the large van parked down the road from the house.

"Senor Manciena," the man in the passenger's seat spoke into his Bluetooth, "we are ready."

"Good, Paco, good," Jorge was sitting in a large leather chair staring out of the window of his condo at the lights of the city below. "I just may see the light show from here."

"Let me know when you're ready," Paco sat listening to the other man's laughter. He saw nothing humorous about what was about to take place because he was a consummate professional and he kept his men profession until they were all back to where ever they'd made their base safely.

"Are you sure that they are there?" Jorge finally asked.

"We didn't go into the house, Sir," Paco answered, "but the key vehicles we were told to look for are in the drive way and there's sound and movement inside."

"Excellent," Jorge struck a match and lit the cigarette between his lips. "Then light it up."

Benito "Paco" Morales pulled the switch from his pocket and stared at the toggle switch. Nodding to the man behind the wheel to drive off he pushed up the switch and finally smiled. There was always that rush the moment he heard that first rumble of bombs going on before their concussive blasts ruptured something causing the explosion to go nuclear. It was always the most beautiful thing in the world to him. Turning in his seat he watched as the house was mangled by the large bright ball of fire that splinted wood and brick and mortar into a million pieces.

"It's done, Senor," Paco announced into his Bluetooth. "Emergency vehicles should be on their way."

Paco had his driver pull over to the curb and stop; he was the typical "firebug" and loved to watch his work as it burned the house to the ground. The fire was a thing of beauty, even from the distance they were, and he loved the way it lit up the night sky; flickering blades of orange and yellow dancing against the black sky. Standing there he began to wonder about the bodies that would be found. Had they suffered as the bombs blasts ripped through their unsuspecting bodies? How much of them would be left after the fire was put out?

He wanted to be there. He wanted to be a part of the crowd standing there staring in awe at the destroyed house. He wanted to hear all of the questions and comments as they all stood around watching and waiting for that last flame to be extinguished. Even standing there he could feel his heart pounding away in his chest and he was breathing heavy from the excitement of the fire.

"Paco," he could hear the driver Darren calling his name. "Goddamn Fool… Paco, we gotta get the fuck outta this bitch. Shit, we stick out like a sore fuckin' thumb."

He hated working with idiots like Darren, but he was there because of Jorge's business partner, and the black man needed a black man here with him to make certain the shit was done. He reached behind him and wrapped his fingers around the grip of his pistol hoping that this motherfucker called his name one more time.

"Oy ye, Hefe," Chico had opened the sliding side door. "Time to go. The last thing we need is for Jorge to catch wind of us sitting around in this neighborhood after he said get in and get out."

"Right," Paco smiled once more before putting back on his death mask and slipping back into his seat. As his door closed, Darren gunned the van out of the neighborhood just as the first of the emergency vehicles were making their way to the house.

If he'd been alone he would have pulled over and stripped off his clothes and sat there enjoying himself watching them fight the fire. As it was, he shifted in his seat uncomfortably as Darren drove like a maniac to get them back into the city.

****

"How did you know?" Courtney asked Nick as they sat two houses down watching as the van drove away.

"Jangles went down to Mexico to see Manciena's son and he took Jimmy Q with him, and I'd heard that Jorge Manciena is here in Tampa… this is what he does. He doesn't play with his food, per se, he likes things to happen quick, loud and messy." Nick didn't take his eyes off of the house he'd once felt that Courtney and little Sydnee was safe in. "This is what I would do. The way Jorge sees it, even if you're not dead this is a way of letting you know that he can get to you whenever he wants to."

"So he thinks that I should feel threatened and ready to run scared?" Courtney sat there watching Nick watch the fire. For her it was a house, something she could buy again… what pissed her off the most, Jangles and Manciena's son thought this would frighten her.

"Nick?" she tapped his shoulder to get his full attention.

"Yes?" he turned away from the front windshield to look into her eyes.

"With all of the shit that I've been through so far," her eyebrow was arched, "do they really think that something like this would scare me?'

"You're a woman, Courtney," Nick said with a crooked smile on his lips, "and they're counting on you to react as a woman would react. You're not supposed to fight them and yet that's exactly what you've been doing. You're supposed to be frightened and ready to jump ship, and you're doing the exact opposite. Jangles is pulling out the big guns."

"I think I'm ready to pull out some guns of my own," Courtney grinned, "and I happen to always keep mine on retainer. So where do we start?"

"According to some of my conversations with JC," Nick could see this new glimmer in Courtney's eyes, "Jangles still holds a lot of stock in his drug deals and he has stash houses all over from Ybor to New Tampa."

"Excellent," Courtney took a deep breath, "I want all of the money and drugs… we can stock pile it all in one of the dock warehouses, but I want all of those stash houses destroyed. He blew up my home and so I want to take everything he holds important from him. I want Jackson to find out the name of Jorge Manciena's second and I want that man brought to me, and lastly… I want the man who blew up my home found and I want him dead."

"Sounds like a plan to me, but," Nick glanced out once more just as the fire trucks were pulling into the housing development, "what about Sydney?"

"We'll deal with him… once Jackson has found him, but he won't remain hidden for long. He's a chess player and now that I've outted him and

I know he's alive… he'll have to readjust his play and if I were him, well, I'd go see Jangles."

"Why?" Nick looked confused.

"Because now they have something in common again…"

"Yea?" Nick's eyebrow cocked. "That being?"

Courtney's smile broadened. "Me."

Chapter 22

Sydney stared at his reflection in his bathroom window; the wisps of steam from the shower distorted everything, but he could still make out his face. He looked older than he remembered and he needed to shave, but other than that… nothing had changed. He'd grown out his mustache and goatee into a full beard, and his eyes looked tired, running on exhaustion. He tried to smile, but that man staring back at him refused to turn his lips up.

"Dammit… dammit." He slammed his fist into the mirror not feeling it shatter around his fingers. He could see the blood dripping down into the sink, but there was no pain.

Pulling his hand away from the broken glass he pulled out the few shards that were stuck in his fingers and he stared at the bloody mess. The moisture from the shower's steam made the scene a bit more than it actually was as the blood spider webbed his hand running down the back of it and dripping into the sink. It was pretty much like the mess he'd made of his life and now he had to figure out how to clean it up.

"Why am I not surprised to hear from you, Mr. Styles?" he always called Nick this when he wasn't in the mood to be lectured about his wife, and that seemed to be the only reason Nick would call. *"I'm not in mood tonight. We have too much shit going on."*

"Are you sure that this is the road you want to take?" Nick had a way of sounding frazzled even

302

in the best of situations, but this was why he wanted him close to Courtney.

"She'll come out of this a lot stronger for it, Mr. Styles," he sat back in his desk chair and lit a fresh cigar drawing on it to pull the fragrant smoke into his mouth. He could sit and just listen to Nick go on and on about how he was fucking Courtney up more and more, but he could only see it differently thanks to all of the reports from Henri.

If only he could get Nick to understand that everything that he was doing was only going to make Courtney that much better… that much stronger a wife for him. He had it all planned out and soon, very soon, he was going to let Courtney know that he was alive and that he'd been cured of the poisons that Jangles had fucked him up on. He was going to kill that son-of-a-bitch for her and they would be able to take IXion into new and greater avenues of prosperity.

She'll be stronger… he whispered to himself.

"Yea," Nick hissed into the phone, *"and if she comes outta this shit broken, who's going to fix her… You?"*

"You goddamn right, Motherfucker, I'm going to fix her," but he was already speaking to the dial tone.

Sydney shook off the thought. There was too much to do and now he'd clearly made an enemy of the one person he actually loved. His mind was in a twist; did he try to make things right with his wife, or did he just go back to his original plan of getting his company back. A shiver raced down his spine as the thought of completely abandoning his wife spiked in his head.

She'd become as calculating as he was, and that impressed him; that alone put a smile on his face. Everything he'd taught her, everything that he and Henri had trained her to do, she was doing with the practiced ease of someone who'd been in this life for the majority of her life.

Sydney stood there shaking his head. Had he truly created a monster? Courtney wasn't supposed to change, just become stronger.

"Is there a way to fix this shit?" he turned away from the shattered mirror and moved into the bedroom area of his hotel.

Sitting on his bed, Sydney rubbed his head trying to get rid of the headache that was beating a pattern against his brain. For the last two years he'd been pretending to be someone other than himself to keep his wife protected, but to keep him close… in a manner of speaking. He'd become her sounding board and her voice of reason in a world of gangsters, thugs, and drug dealers, and the last thing he wanted was for her to become tainted by all of the shit he'd placed her in. Maybe Nicky was right, and if that was the case…

He'd fucked up.

****

He'd been sitting almost comfortably on the IXion company jet waiting for the Vasilevich brothers to make it onboard. To keep his identity hidden for the flight, he'd had his personal physician, who was making the flight with him, bandage his face. Sydney was sipping a glass of Hennessey when he'd received the call from Henri that it would be good to call Courtney. His heart was pounding in his chest as he contemplated the number of ways this rouse could go bad not only for him with his wife because of the number of lies he would have to tell… but with her life for having to deal with Jangles.

Keeping Henri on the phone, he dialed his wife's number and switched over to three way advising the other man to keep quiet through the call. The moment she answered his concentration was shot, and he had to remember to use the voice he'd been practicing for this new persona.

"Good evening, Mrs. Roulette, and thank you for taking my call," his voice sounded deep, somewhat raspy and very distorted. "My name again is Evan McGregor and I want you to know right off the bat that I am here to help you."

"How did you know my husband, Mr. McGregor?" Courtney asked. "I've never heard him mention you before."

"We were in the same businesses, Mrs. Roulette," the lies began. "I have a very private interest holding in IXion Industries; he and I have a very mutual respect for one another and we've done quite a bit of business together. He contacted me shortly after it became evident what Mr. Johnson was doing to him."

"So you knew about the poisoning?"

"Yes, and I was the one who suggested to him that he needed to find a better person to put at the head of his company, but," he paused for a moment, "I was mildly surprised when he suggested that we groom you for the position."

"Why is that, if I might ask?"

"Because," the man stopped and coughed away from the phone, "the business that we're in is not usually the place for women, and then for you to be a woman of culture and not the streets… well, I just didn't see you being the right person for the job. I must add though, Sydney had been keeping me in

305

the loop with everything he'd been teaching you, and I am very pleased to say that I was quite wrong about you.

"It would seem that you have a natural knack for this, and from what Sidney had been telling me… you seem to enjoy it."

"I wouldn't say that I enjoy it," Courtney responded with a bit of an attitude in her voice, "but, I do have a bit of an axe to grind with Jangles. I want to see him fall on his face and when he looks up… I want him to be looking up at me. I want him to know that he was beat by a woman before he crawls away with his tail between his legs."

"My biggest fear, Mrs. Roulette, is that he will not just crawl away." Sydney took a deep breath. "Consider this if you will; Mr. Johnson was willing to poison the man he'd believed to be his best friend and brother since before they were both kids. I have a feeling that this man would be willing to sacrifice everything, including his life, before he allows himself to be outdone by a woman.

"So my question to you is simply this… How far are you willing to go?"

"You consider this, Mr. McGregor," Courtney was angry at this point, "this man not only tried to poison my husband to death, but he went as far as blowing him up alive in his truck. So you tell me, how far do I need to go?'

The silence between the two at that moment was tense. As McGregor, Sydney couldn't be more proud of his wife as she was undoubtedly prepared to go as far as necessary, and this would allow him to use her to get rid of some key people that will impede him from finally getting to Jangles.

****

"I guess," Sydney took a deep breath, "if anyone is going to stop you, Courtney, it will have to be me. Damn… I'm sorry, baby, with all of my heart I swear that this isn't what I wanted."

Sometimes you have to make a deal with the devil you hate, Big Fats voice was floating around in his head, *to deal with the monsters you've created.*

****

Courtney had never imagined being on the run again so soon after the last time she was caught up in a hotel hiding out from Jangles. But, she sat in a chair at the small dining table staring out the window and across town to where she could barely see the building that housed IXion Industries. From the very beginning, the business was never really a major concern of hers, and the only reason she'd continue to play this cat and mouse game with Jangles was because Nick, Mr. Robles and Mr. McGregor had her convinced that her playing would keep Jangles off his game trying to deal with a woman who held a seat of power over him. At one point she wanted this to be some kind of fun, but it always just seemed like a chore that she longed to do away with.

But now her entire perception had been changed. She could hear Nick moving around the room behind her, but she had no desire to look at him at the moment. She'd found a way to forgive him for his part in Sydney's little melodrama that was being played at her expense thanks to him being the sounding board that what they were doing would and could all go wrong… and now, for them it has all gone wrong. Nick had spent the last few days after the destruction of her house trying to explain his part on more than one occasion to the point that she'd heard his reasoning from every angle and now she just needed a break from it all.

Thanks to the three men that she had placed all of her trust she now had no trust for anyone anymore. Everyone had failed her and she felt like she was floating on this cloud of destruction all by herself; she couldn't even trust Nina any longer at this point, and that saddened her to the point of making her feel sick. She sat there rubbing her belly half expecting the baby growing there to move or kick or something give her some kind of hope, but it was way too soon. She grabbed her phone and dialed a number that only she and Nick knew and waited for an answer on the other end.

"Courtney?" his voice sounded concerned.

"Hello, Dad," she smiled for the first time in what felt like months. She'd sent her daughter and parents away after Jangles had tried to have her killed.

"How are you doing, Baby girl?" she could hear the excitement in his voice now as she'd confirmed that it was her. "Is everything ok? What's going on there?"

"Dad," she tried to keep herself from exploding emotionally, "things here are ok for the moment, and I promise once I get everything's settled I'll explain everything to you and mom. Right now… right now I just needed to make certain that all of you was safe and away from all of the shit going on around me."

Courtney almost covered her mouth because that was the first time she had ever used any kind of profanity around her father, but she noticed that he hadn't said anything. Taking a deep breath and wiping away a tear that was sliding its way down her cheek, she listened to him sitting there breathing and the sounds of things going on behind him. Then she heard her baby's voice.

"We're all good, Kitten," her dad answered, "as long as you're good. You know I could always come back and help with…"

"Oh my god," she whispered over her dad. "Is that Sydnee? Can I talk to her, Dad, please?"

She was so nervous, her daughter had been away too close to a year now and she missed her cute, little baby doll face. Courtney could hear her in the background squealing and laughing undoubtedly having fun until her dad called out her name. She sat waiting with bated breath until her dad informed the child that her mom was on the phone.

"Mommy, Mommy…" her voice was like that of a cherub singing in her ear.

"Hi, Cutesy bear, how's mommy's little handful?"

"She wants to see you," Courtney could hear her dad's voice speaking up for the little girl.

"I know, Sydnee, and mommy promise that I will see you really soon. Ok?"

"She's all smiles," her dad answered. "When, Courtney, when will you come?"

"Soon," Courtney laughed and turned just a bit catching Nick standing there smiling as she talked to her daughter. "I want you to make me a promise, ok, I want you to be good for Nana and Papa. You be mommy's big girl, ok?"

"Oh she will, Kitten, she always is."

"Good… I love you, Sydnee," she was holding back the tears. "Dad?"

"Courtney?"

"Everything is good, Daddy," Courtney was smiling to the point of tears. "Do y'all need anything?"

"Courtney," her dad began again with his authoritative voice, "what's really going on? You sound so… different than my little girl. Is this still about Sydney's death and his company?"

"It's gone way beyond that, Daddy," Courtney stood and walked over to where Nick was standing. "I promise, I'll explain everything really soon, ok?'

"Ok, Baby," he wasn't really accepting being brushed off, but he didn't push. "We love you and if you need me you know that you can always call me."

"I love you both too, and thank you. I'll be in touch really soon… I promise."

She hung up the phone and fell into Nick's opened arms crying against his shoulder. For the first time, in a long time, she felt weak. All she wanted to do right at this moment was find herself a hole and just bury herself in it. She never asked for any of this and now she was neck deep in a war that she hadn't started. What made all of this worse was that the man she'd fallen in love with and had given her soul too had completely deceived her, and now he was pretty much as much her enemy as his best friend had been for the last two years.

"We could always just leave, Courtney," Nick's voice had a way of soothing and calming her when she needed it most. "We have enough of IXion's money hidden away that we could go find little Sydnee and we could live abroad without ever worrying about Jangles and your husband ever again."

"I don't have a husband," she said into his shoulder. "And if I were to run now, he would try to find me. No matter how I do this shit, Nick, it's not going to end well. There'll be no happily ever after's, but, if I end it on my own terms I'll never have to worry or deal with either of them again."

"Court, I'm with you to the end. I know I have to reaffirm your trust in me, and that's my fault, but I'm not leaving your side ever again."

"I know." She wrapped her arms around him and held on. She wanted to feel safe with Nick again, but at this point it was going to take a while. Yea, she'd found a way to forgive him, her problem was she hadn't found a way to forget.

Nick's phone ringing was the only reason she pulled her body away from his. He pulled the cell from his pocket and glanced at the screen before answering.

"What do you have for us, Jackson?" he switched on the speaker.

"We've found Mr. McGregor," Lagrange answered using the name that Courtney accepted for the man who had once been her husband. "He's walking into IXion building as we speak."

"I'm not surprised," Courtney smiled. "Mr. Lagrange, had you been able to get into the offices and change out the listening devices?"

"Yes, Ma'am," Lagrange answered. "I have a young tech we call Pixell that was able to get into the offices shortly after Mr. St. Cloud told me about that meeting with Mr. McGregor. What I did was leave in all of the ones that he would know about and Pixell place more strategically placed microphones where neither man would think to look."

"Excellent," Courtney's smile broadened. Sydney may have taught her how to play this little game of his, but his biggest mistake was telling her to play this as one would play chess.

311

"Yes, the kid is really good at what he does, and I think we'll have enough of what you need to put all of this to rest shortly." Lagrange sounded quite proud of himself and this caused Courtney to laugh lightly.

Always remember that you have to keep your head about you, Sydney would beat this into her by repeating it constantly, *you play this shit like you'd play chess. You watch your opponent with little to no emotional expression, and as he's making his moves you're already making moves five places ahead of him. You keep him on the edge of his seat while you're sitting comfortably in the cat-bird seat.*

"But why would he go to IXion?" Nick asked.

"Because he and Jangles now have something in common once again," Courtney walked back over to the window that looked out towards the building. It was a beautiful night and the full moon had risen just behind the building lighting it up in an almost ghostly light. "They both need to get rid of me."

"So you think that they'll patch up all of their own bullshit just to fight you? This is not good, Courtney, not fucking good at all. Jangles, Sydney, Jorge Manciena, and Jimmy Q… shit, with all of their resources that's pretty much an army."

Staring at IXion with her hand on the window tracing its outline, Courtney nodded her head. This was exactly what she'd expected to happen the moment she found out his ass was alive and she'd told him to fuck off. They'd started this and now that she'd cut her strings and was no longer playing the part of the willing puppet it was her intention to end this shit. And when the smoke cleared… she'd be standing on the top of the pile.

"True enough, that would definitely give them an army," she turned from the window to face Nick. He was still standing there holding the phone with Lagrange quietly listening. "But, I am not without my own resources and at this point there's nothing holding me back from unleashing all hell out on Sydney and Jangles and anyone that they'd want to bring to this little party.

"I told you, Nick, I'm done with all of this bullshit. He thought it was such a good idea to drop me off into the middle of this, he put me and his child's life in danger and for him it's was pretty much an experiment. Well, its time that I show him everything that I've learned thanks to him."

"It's going to be really messy, you know that right?"

"Nick, I'm looking forward to being messy because I plan to be standing on top of the bodies… My husband is dead to me, as dead as he was the day his truck exploded. I've buried him and I'm moving on to bury the rest of them."

"What do you want me to do?" Lagrange spoke up.

"For now," Nick answered, "watch him. Find out where he goes after he leaves there and we'll go from there.

"Understood."

****

The moonlight coming through the tinted windows was the only light illuminating the large conference room, and that's how Jangles liked it for the moment. He'd been sitting there staring at nothing for hours now and he was smoking his last blunt. If it wasn't for the fact that he knew where the weed had come from he'd swear he was smoking some skunk shit because he didn't have any kind of buzz from the shit tonight. He was sitting slumped down in the chair puffing on the tightly rolled joint and blowing the smoke into the air trying to make sense of everything thing going wrong in his life… and he could only come up with one answer.

Courtney Roulette.

"Bitch," he grumbled. "I hate that bitch."

The door opening caught his attention because he was supposed to be alone.

"Whoever the fuck you are," Jangles pulled his Glock from the shoulder harness and slammed it on the table, "I've no time to be fucked with."

"Oh trust me, Jangles," Sydney stepped into the room his face hidden by the shadows until he was standing at the end of the long table and he too slammed his pistol on the top, "I'm definitely not here to fuck with you, but… you ready to redeem yourself, Nigga?"

"No fuckin' way," Jangles sat up in his seat and leaned over the table staring down its length at the man standing there. "Sydney?"

Chapter 23

"Nigga," Jangles stared at the blunt he'd been smoking, "is you a ghost? You supposed to be dead."

"Shit," Sydney laughed, "I've been called worse by worse."

"How's this shit even possible?" Jangles watched as Sydney pulled out a chair and sat down. "I saw your truck. I saw what was left of you… of the body. How is it you standing here right now?"

Sydney sat for a moment just looking around and taking a deep breath feeling like he was back home… back where he belonged.

"Do you remember when we first bought this office?"

"Yea," Jangles chuckled. "You said some shit about buying the whole floor and we barely had enough to buy the first room."

"Right," Sydney laughed out. "But you looked at me and said, 'Shit, Syd, I give you a good year and you'll be good on that.' And that's what happened. One year later we bought out this whole floor and IXion finally had a home. We started from nothing and look at us now… we the kings of this fucking city, Jangles. Everywhere we look out of those windows or any of the windows in this entire building and we got our hands in something out there."

"How are you here, Syd?" Jangles asked again dropping the blunt on the table not trusting to take another hit.

"I was never in the truck, Bruh," Sydney stood and pulled off his suit jacket and sat back down. "I stood there and watched as the bomb

315

ripped that muthafucka apart with some dude in it that I promised I'd take care of his family. I stood watching as you and all them otha niggas ran out screaming and acting like it was such a bad fuckin' thing I was dead, but none of it, including you… none of it was real."

"Bullshit," Jangles pushed back from the table and stood. "That's that bullshit, Muthafucka, that's that bullshit. All of this time I've been looking for some otha nigga who coulda killed yo bitch ass, and you fuckin' alive."

"Looking for…" Sydney laughed and then caught himself. "Looking for what reason? I'm not sure where we went wrong, Bobby… from the sandbox to the lockbox… Remember? You was my brother, I loved you because you was all I had. All the shit we did together… and you was trying to kill me."

"You… *CHANGED*!" Jangles slammed his hands down on the table and glared down the length at the man staring back at him. "You changed, Syd. All this bullshit talk 'bout going legit and leaving all that street shit behind."

"We had gotten bigger than street hustles, Bobby, and I wanted you to see that. I wanted us to make bigger money doing shit that we didn't have to keep under the covers." Sydney stood and paced the floor just behind the chair he'd been in.

"Street hustles is what fuckin' made us, Syd," Jangles shook his head in disgust. "That's that shit I know, Nigga, and you wanted me to act like I was better than that? You wanted me to act like I was one of these stuffed suited white dudes and that shit ain't me… it was neva fuckin' me."

"Not better than that, damn, Man," Sydney rubbed his hand over the top of his head, "you just don't get it… you don't understand this shit at all."

"Explain it to me," Jangles dared him. "Make me understand, Big Man."

"We had become so much more than what the streets had made of us, Bobby," Sydney forced himself back into the seat and he spun the pistol on its side on the table watching it twirl in a tight circle. "Look at us, Bobby. Look at all that we have and not just you and me… all of us in the Nine are fucking richer than we'd ever be just running shit in the streets. What we have is bigger than drugs and guns and the direction I was leading us in would made us fucking pillars of the community. We were at a stage in our life where we were more than Big Fats could have ever drea…"

"Fuck that, Sydney," Jangles spat out. "Fuck that! Fuck Big Fats! And fuck you too, Syd. I didn't want to be some kind a city celebrity. How would my people look at me if I sold out to those fuckin' suits that we spent years trying to become better than? You wanted me to fall to my knees before them kissing they asses.

"That shit ain't fuckin' happenin, Nigga. Nope. Never."

"See, that right there is your problem. That right there." Sydney couldn't disguise his aggravation with the man he'd always looked at as his brother. He sat there trying to think of where they'd started walking down such different roads. They'd spent hours talking and planning to become men who would make Big Fats look like a common street criminal, and now he was listening to this fool basically tell him that he was ok with being a common street criminal.

"What, Nigga, huh… what?"

"You think too small, Bobby," Sydney answered after thinking for a moment longer. "For you it's always been about the next small score, but I'd been building IXion and the Nine to grow beyond that."

"You say that like you've been building IXion by yourself, Muthafucka," Jangles picked up the blunt and lit it taking in a deep breath of the burning smoke and holding it in his lungs for a moment before blowing it out over his head. "If I remember right, Mr. C. E. fucking O, I've been a part of this shit from the beginning. I was there by your side when Big Fats had us brought before him that first time, and you stood there with your goddamn knees bangin' together so loud I'm sure he heard them. I was there then and I'm still here, Nigga… I'm still right fucking here."

"Yea you're here alright, but you're going nowhere." Sydney just sat there smiling, but he was exasperated. "Goddamn, Bobby, we've had this same discussion a million fucking times."

"Well make it a million and one, Bruh," Jangles sat down taking another pull from the blunt. "And I'll be honest… I'm sick of havin' it too."

"That's the muthafuckin' problem," Sydney slammed his hand down on the table making certain that the band of his rings struck the wood, "you're so sick of having a discussion about progress, but yo ass ain't sick of running game in the hood. How the fuck is that possible? We've outgrown this small, piddly shit, Bruh. We could be doing shit that would make the Cartel look at us… make the Chinese and the Jamaicans look at us… make all them look at us because we would be doing big things and making that big spread and it would all be on the up and up.

"There would be no need to hide from the 'One Time' and the jack boys. We wouldn't need to have all of those fuckin' stash houses to hold on to money that we have to launder into the banks… shit, Nigga, think about that one for a second. Think about all that money we lose to the cleaners because they have to have their cuts off the top and then hit again when we go to put the cleaned shit into the banks. We losing on both ends, Jangles; everybody's turning a goddamn profit but the Nine."

Sense was sense and sitting there having it all explained to him again was making a whole lot of sense. They had money stretched out all over the city and were paying niggas almost a dollar on the dollar to have that shit washed up. Then there were the fees for the homes, utilities and paying either a family to stay in them or some of them lil young cats to stand guard. They were blowing money hand over fist, but, it was all that he knew.

"What about them lil niggas we got holdin' shit down? Or the families we got making shit look clean?"

"We deal with them," Sydney responded. "We find places for the jits so that they keep on working and it takes all of that shit they be goin' through about taking a little here and there… or pocketing some of your product and tweaking out later out of the question, and we don't have to deal with it. We get outta the hustle and take IXion to a whole new playing field."

"A whole new field huh?" Jangles signature smile split his lips. "Well there's only one problem I see with that, my Nigga."

"Yea," Sydney sat back thinking Jangles actually had something to bring to the table. "What's that?"

"You gave all our shit to your bitch," his lip turned up as he leaned forward. "Neither one of us own this shit no mo' and that's on yo ass… so whatcha wanna do?"

"No," Sydney stood and began walking down the table towards him. Jangles was tempted to reach for the Glock sitting just in front of him, but Sydney had left his still laying down on his end of the table.

"Our problem is a lot bigger than that."

"Meaning… what?" Jangles pushed back in his chair as Sydney sat on the edge of the table in front of him.

"I trained her, Jangles," Sydney crossed his arms over his chest and took a deep breath. "Courtney ain't no fuckin' soldier, Bruh, I trained her ass to be a fuckin' General. She works this shit like me and that makes her more dangerous than a little bit, and she ain't alone."

"Nigga, I ain't worried about Nicky Styles bitch-made ass." Jangles almost choked on the smoke the moment he began laughing.

"Nick is dead, Jangles," Sydney's face was like stone as his best friend tried to force himself from coughing.

"What? When, Nigga, shit… how? Because he escaped a little road kill I had planned out for his ass."

"Not even two days," Sydney said, "and it was her."

"No fuckin' way." Jangles began laughing again and this time harder. "Boy, get the fuck outta here with that ol' bullshit."

"Him and an associate of mine… while I was on the phone with her."

"Wait, Courtney?" Jangles looked amazed. "You tellin' me that she shot Nicky Styles? Why?"

"Yea," Sydney looked disgusted. "Nick was working with me, Bobby. I needed him close to her because of you. I needed her safe because I know the kind of nigga you are."

"Shit, I appreciate that," Jangles laughed as he stood and walked over to the windows and stared out over the city. The moon was higher now and it was brighter lighting up shit in a way that the street lights never could. He's always loved the city like this; Sydney had taught him a long time ago to appreciate small things like this because you just never knew when a nigga was poppin' off bullets that had your name written on them. Looking upon his little kingdom gave him a moment to reflect on the shit he'd just been given by Sydney.

"Shit," he could see the man standing a few feet away in the window, "that definitely explains a lot. I thought that she was just a shot calla, looks like baby girl is a down ass balla. This is what you set on me to what, huh? Teach ol' Jangles a lesson?"

"Yea, that's it in a nutshell," Sydney stood there trying not to laugh at the fool before him, "I wanted to teach you a lesson. You was trying to kill me over some bullshit and money, and I was trying to teach you a lesson. I hope that you learned something, but I'll be honest I've learned a lot about you and Courtney."

"Yea, what's that?"

Sydney stepped up to the window and he too looked out over Tampa. He'd missed doing this in the two almost three years he'd been gone. He'd always found peace in watching the city move beneath him; they'd become something like insignificant insects there for him to crush under the

heel of his patent leather shoes. Such small people
going about their small lives and never knowing
what it felt like to hold and feel… power.

"Power," he whispered before looking over
at Jangles. "Neither of you was used to holding on to
that kind of power and it's nearly destroyed you
both. The only difference is that she had me and a
few other people holding her in check, but all you
had was the Nine and they're just like you."

"A lil cocky, aren't we?" the blunt was
burning close to his fingers but he still took a hit and
offered it Sydney. "So fuck all that... what is it you
thinking?"

"First," Sydney stood and reached under the
lip of the table and yanked down, "we have to get
ahead of my smart ass wife."

Jangles stared down at the small microphone
that Sydney dropped on the table in front of him.
Picking it up he studied from every angle as if he
was expecting it to change and become something
other than what it was. Sliding back from the table
he stood and dropped the small listening device to
the floor and stomped it until it was several small
pieces beneath his foot.

"Are there more of them?" knowing Sydney
would understand what he was truly asking.

"Yea I've got a few floating around, but..."
he'd walked over to a picture of the first members of
the Nine. He slid his fingers along the edge of the
frame pulling out a second device and tossing it to
Jangles. "But, it won't take much to weed them out
and cut 'em off at the nuts."

"See that's the muthafuckin' Sydney I know."

The two men slowly walked the room
checking all of the obvious spots for more of the
microphones and finding three more. Upon finding

them they dropped them on the floor and crushed them until nothing was left that could possibly send a signal.

"You know she's going to know?" Jangles was close to laughing as he looked from one crushed microphone.

"I want her to know," Sydney pushed his hands into the pockets of his slacks as he glanced around at the trash on the floor. "I want to blind her before going to pay her ass a visit at home."

Jangles broke out laughing as he walked across the conference room to the table holding an assortment of alcohol bottles and poured him a glass of bourbon. "Well you may want to change those plans, Nigga."

'Why," Sydney stood perplexed. "What's happened?"

"Well... My boy, Jorge had some of his boys go and turn her little palace into firewood. "

"FUCK!" Sydney grabbed the chair nearest to him and he threw it across the room. Grabbing the next chair, he began beating it over the table until all he was holding the back rest.

"Goddamn, Syd, calm the fuck down."

"You just don't get it," Sydney dropped the piece of chair and leaned forward over the table, "she's in the wind now. The lil bitch has a tactical advantage and at this point she can strike from any point and we can easily find ourselves at her fuckin' mercy."

"You think too highly of her, Syd," Jangles walked over and placed a glass of bourbon on the table under his nose. "You just need to do your chess moves shit and tell me what needs to be done. It'll be just like the old days"

"Yea," Sydney grinned after taking a swallow of the alcohol, "just like the old days. If I'm the brains, then you're the..."

"I'm the muthafuckin muscles. "

It was like finding that one missing piece of a puzzle, and it was soon just like they'd not missed any time, or like the thought of one trying to kill the other was no longer an issue between them. They shook hands and hugged before sitting and sharing that bottle of bourbon and forming a strategy against their common problem.

"Hey, Brain," Jangles was forcing his voice high to sound like the little skinny, lab rat from on of their favorite childhood cartoons, "what are we doing tonight? "

"The same thing we do every night, Pinky," his voice was slow and deep with a very non-black accent. "Try to take over the world."

****

Some things never change, Courtney thought to herself, *boys will be boys.*

"So what's the play, Courtney?" Nick walked into the living room with Jackson and Yuri in tow.

"We have a lot of shit to get done and in a short period of time," Courtney was sitting at her computer watching the screen. Jackson's man had done a better job of wiring IXion than she'd even thought, not only was she getting sound, but the man had the entire office covered in cameras. She was tapping her fingernails on the table as she watched Sydney and Jangles sitting around gabbing like the last two years hadn't happened. She almost felt insignificant, but she shrugged her shoulders and turned to face the men standing before her.

"Mr. McGregor has found out about some shipments that I have moving about the state,"

Courtney stood from her chair and walked across the room to where the coffee pot was and poured her a cup, "and at this point he thinks that he is a step ahead of me, and I want him to keep thinking that."

"What do you need us to do?" Jackson was sitting comfortably on the small sofa.

"I need a couple of things." Courtney felt like all of this was a bit too second nature for her now as she plotted and schemed. "Firstly, I need all of those routes changed to more secure routes, but I need for the trucks that he knows of to stay as they are scheduled. I want them armed and I want them ready. According to Mr. McGregor, if they are able to discredit me with my suppliers that will begin my spiral downward… I don't want anything to fuck up these shipments because they are only the beginning of getting IXion out of the bullshit we're currently in.

"Second, Mr. Lagrange, I need to know if your computer guy, Pixell, is anywhere nears as good as Mr. Robles was?"

"I only hire the best," Jackson said with a big smile. "I pretty much got him fresh out of MIT and he was at the top of his class. The boy is worth every cent that I pay him because he can get in and around any computer no matter what wards of security that they have in place."

"Excellent," Courtney grinned. "I want you to have him do two things, the first one is to freeze all of Mr. McGregor's and Bobby Johnson's personal accounts and then I want to begin moving IXion accounts into some new accounts away from everything Robles set up."

"I'm on it," Jackson pulled his phone out and made the call to his man as he stepped away from the group to talk.

"How many trucks are we talking about, Courtney?" Nick asked as he fixed him a fresh cup of coffee.

"There are three trucks running today, but we also have one freight carrier that should be docking in the next two days." Courtney answered. "I need this done quickly, Nick, because the trucks are supposed to roll out first thing in the morning. That means we don't have a whole lot of time, but I don't want anything to happen to those drivers or their cargo.

"I spoke with Captain Ponzi on board the Nine Seas, and he's already prepared for anything that could possibly happen. He told me that he never leaves port without a few good men who can handle any kind of business that needs to be handled."

"Good, that's one less thing I need to get taken care of, but I'll have everything set up for the drivers," Nick pulled his phone and he too stepped away.

"Yuri," she walked over to the large Russian man she'd come to depend on since he'd been allowed back into Florida.

"I know you've worked with Sydney for a lot of years," she began, "are you sure that you wish to remain with me?"

"Of all the things I've done," the man ran his fingers through his greasy looking hair, "but da one thing my brother and I have never done is wage war on a woman. You've been a good… employer, Ms. Courtney, you have my brother and I for as long as you need us."

"Good," she smiled as she deciphered what he'd said thanks to his heavy accent, "we have a lot to do and there are going to be a lot of bodies to deal with."

"Killing is truly our specialty," Yuri grinned.
"I'll get Tomas on the phone and have him get our
men ready."
"Then it begins," Courtney walked over to the
window and looked across town at the building
housing her company. She was more than ready to
end this, and starting tomorrow that's exactly what
she was aiming for… to end all of this.

Chapter 24

Charles Speed was yawning and stretching as he pulled his car into the fenced in area and parked in an open parking space. He glanced at the clock on the radio in the car's dash and shook his head; it was too fucking early to be up. The sun wasn't even attempting to come up because it was so fucking early and the moon was still hanging around in the sky.

"Goddamn," he grumbled before forcing himself from the car, "I need some coffee or I'm not going to make it."

"You's say that same shit e'erytime, Speedo," his riding buddy Mac, a large smiling Cajun, was at the trunk of his car stuffing a duffle bag with enough guns to start a war. "Why yo' ass not stop and get a cup before gettin' here?"

"Running late, Mac," Charles stretched again and then stepped to the trunk of his car. "The old lady was feeling frisky this mornin' and well the pussy is always too goddamn good to say no to."

Mac laughed as he slammed his trunk closed and dropped the heavy bag to the ground. He walked around to his driver's side passenger door and reached in pulling out a large thermos. He shook it up and then tossed it the parking lot after whistling to get Charles' attention.

"The wife made it fresh t'is mornin' 'cause she knows how you's love her coffee."

"I'm going to marry that woman one of these days," Charles joked. "You better keep a close eye on her."

"You better have a bigger dick dan me, 'Chere" Mac was laughing so hard that he began coughing. He was standing beside his friend now with the strap of the duffle bag over his shoulder, and they walked off making more crude jokes about his wife which didn't surprise any of the men standing around the parked semi.

"So the boss lady thinks we gon' be hit today," Charles slipped into the driver's seat of his big rig and glanced over at his shotgun rider. "You ready fo' this shit, Mac?"

"You's know I'm always good fo' a fight," Mac tossed in a large duffle bag before climbing up into the passenger seat. "We got 'bout ten men in da' back all armed to the gills. I hope these niggas do show up. It been far too long since da last time, ol Eloise got to sing."

"Shit," Charles laughed as the heavy breathing man squeezed the seat belt around the girth of his belly, "you would say some crazy shit like that. You know who we 'sposed to riding against?"

"Do dat muthafucka pays my check, 'Chere?" Mack tried adjusting his belt to make it sit more comfortable over his stomach and away from his neck. Being short and big was always an issue in these fucking semi-trucks, but none of that slowed him down when it came to a good fight, and he didn't care if was with his hands or weapons. "I wish a muthafucka would try to jack this shit today."

"You say that shit now," Charles turned the key and smiled as his rig growled to life once again, "but if that nigga Jangles was to walk up right now you'd shit yo' funky ass drawls."

Mac laughed as if he'd just heard the best joke of his life. He'd been working for the Nine a lot longer than Charles and he'd had the "privilege" to meet the great, in his mind, Jangles Johnson and he was not impressed. The dude was definitely full of himself, and he was sure that the world stopped and revolved at his command. He'd once told a buddy of his that he wouldn't be surprised if Jangles wouldn't one day try to kill the real muthafucka who ran the company.

"You got jokes, Nigga," Mac reached over punched the man in the shoulder and laughed out when Charles grabbed his shoulder wincing in pain. "That nigga ain't 'bout shit, but they say Ms. Courtney is a muthafuckin' kingpin. She da real boss, and ol Mac… he only follows da boss."

"Well no matter if she a boss or not," Charles dropped the rig into the first gear and she lurched forward, "we 'bout to knock some heads today and if'n them niggas thinkin' we some push ova driver…"

"They got anotha think comin'," the two men laughed as they pulled out of the garage area they'd been parked in. As Charles looked into his side view mirror he watched as two loaded Suburbans pulled out behind them.

The run was to be a short one compared to many of the road trips that Mac and Charles were used to. They'd both got the call from Nick Styles that where were needed special for this run because of some information he'd received that a few of the IXion shipments were going to be high jacked by some of Jangles' men.

Both men knew of the rivalry between Jangles and the new owner of the business Mrs. Roulette, but neither of them went into the main offices enough to know what the real gossip around the old watering hole. What was known to almost every one of the men was that Jangles was not going to be pushed out by no skirt and that he'd been trying to get rid of the woman now for almost three years. But, Ms. Courtney was proving that she was no easy target, and with Nick Styles standing at her side she'd easily proven that she can run the company and all of its men.

Mac had a lot of respect for the woman because she was tough as nails. He'd never personally met her, but for the last couple of years she made it her business to get to know him and every other man who worked the shipping and the docks. Every year for every birthday of the men and their family members and for every Christmas she made certain that the gifts were plentiful. If asked, he didn't know a man in the company, besides Jangles and his ilk, who didn't love Courtney Roulette.

"Did they have an idea of when and where this jack move was going to take place?" Charles asked as he shifted gears pulling back out into traffic after exiting the weigh station. They'd been out for a few hours headed north on I-75 outside of Ocala headed towards Gainesville and so far it had been all open road with no incidents.

"Not a clue, but knowing how dat fool Jangles he thinks," Mac was staring out his side view mirror, "I'd keep an eye open."

"Not paranoid… are ya?"

"Speed," Mac turned and glared at his friend, "no bullshit, but Jangles he a maniac and word has it that he's working with some crazy fucka from Mexico."

"Yea, talk around the yard," now Charles found himself looking out of his mirror more often, "the Mexican is responsible for the boss lady's house going up in flames."

"So that shit true?" Mac grimaced and turned
back towards his mirror. "The old lady said that
there was something on da news 'bout it, shit, she
was afraid dat Ms. Courtney'd been hurt. Dat was
until Nicky Styles called."

The two men sat in silence as the motor
growled over the sound of the music blaring from
the truck's speakers. The morning fog had burned
off and the sun was peeking through the heavy
clouds leaving a near brilliant glare on the blacktop
as other vehicles flew by heading towards
destinations unknown. The two SUVs that had
pulled out with them from the shipping yard were
still back there, but traveling in two different lanes to
not looks so conspicuous.

Mac had reached into his duffle bag and
pulled out the loaded .12 gauge he'd named Eloise
and had her laying on his lap. Afterwards he passed
the Dessert Eagle that he loved to his boy with the
safety off and the hammer locked back. He'd pulled
the bag close so that he could reach into with little to
no effort and then he was back on mirror patrol.

"Any word on what we should be looking
for?" the voice was over the CB on a private channel
from one of the SUVs.

"Not a fuckin' clue," Mac had grabbed the
microphone before Charles could and answered the
question. "There's a lotta fuckin' road out there to
keep an eye on, but I have a bad feelin' that it's gon'
be something big."

"Why something big?" Charles asked as Mac
hung the mic back on the dash.

"That's what I'd do," Mac turned back to the
side view mirror. "I'd want to make as big a
statement as I could to teach da lady a lesson. A race
down the highway with two or more rigs battling on

da road and the big 'I… X' on the side of one, well her name will get white washed all over the news and in da worse way."

The big black rig was racing forward at breakneck speed, and from the way it was moving Mac could tell it was a bobtail. Hauling no trailer was allowing it to catch up with no problem, and judging the speed they had maybe two minutes before the men in the truck pulled up alongside of them. He reached for the CB mic without looking and hit the comm button.

"Like I said," he glanced at Charles and nodded his head, "it's gon' be somethin' big. There be a black, bobtail chasing down on us right now. I would not be surprised if there was another trailing it that I can't see. Hang back and let 'em get side us and watch for more."

Mac grabbed the walkie-talkie that he had sitting on the dashboard and informed the men in the trailer to be ready. He smiled as he wondered what the reactions of the assholes running up on them would be the moment his men opened fire on them. The trailer had been specially made just for a moment like this when Mr. Roulette was alive and running things because of a few incidents IXion had had with a rival "shipping" company… this was back before the Mrs. had come in and cleaned up shit. He checked his shotgun locking it in place and pulling back the dual hammers; the barrel had been sawed off right up to the stock and he'd practice long enough to handing the severe kick it dropped upon firing.

"This shit is about to get nasty," Charles watched as the truck was now at the corner edge trailer. "Should we call Nicky, or do we wait to let them know how things went?"

"Already on it," Mac could no longer see the first truck, but he was now watching the approaching second truck as he hit the call button on his phone. "Shit's 'bout be get poppin', Mr. Styles."

"Yea, Mac," Nick answered, "we're getting the same report from the other trucks as well. Keep your men safe, but we need this shit handled and I need to make certain that Jangles know that he fucked up."

"We on it, Mr. Styles," Mac flashed a smile at Charles. "Tell the boss lady this shit it be as good as done."

"There's a big bonus for all of you once you return to Tampa," Nick said before hanging up the phone.

"Let's do this shit, Speedo," Mac pressed the comm button twice as a signal to the men in the trailer.

The bobtail slamming into the driver's side shook the entire truck and Charles had to act fast to make the adjustments in steering to keep from weaving all over the road. He glanced over at Mac who was sitting there with the same excited look a kid would have walking into Toys 'R US and that look always scared the shit out of him.

"I ever tell you that you's a sick fuck?" Charles laughed out as he stomped on the gas pulling ahead of the weaving bobtail before it could hit his cab again.

"Yea, but that's why yo' wife loves me," Mac reached across Charles and stuck his shotgun out the opened window. "Fire in the hole, Muthafucka!"

The sound of the gun firing rung in the two men's ears as it vibrated through the cab of the semi. Charles could barely make out Mac whooping and hollering but he could see it in the man's face that he was having more fun than he should be. They'd been partners since they'd met in the Marines almost fifteen years ago, and it never seemed to get old to Mac them finding themselves in a shitload of trouble; hell, the man seemed to thrive on the chaos.

"I'm getting to fuckin' old for this shit," Charles screamed out as the bobtail swerved in for another hit at the side of his rig. He glanced into the side mirror and the second and third trucks were on his ass end. "Tell em to pop the fuckin' trailer and let's take care of this bullshit. Fuck, I'm done with it already."

Mac tapped the comm button twice more and reloaded his shotgun. He looked over beyond Charles and saw the bobtail preparing for another ramming, and as he turned to his right he watched as another rig slammed into his door. He felt the bones in his body jarring against one another and his knee popped soundly as he yelped out in pain.

"Sons-of-a-bitches," he howled. Glass had shattered from the window. Mac watched as the driver of the new rig eyes spread in horror as he pointed the shotgun at his face.

"Yea, take that…" he pulled the two triggers and the window of the rig exploded into the face of the driver.

The second rig swerved and veered away from their rig and hit the shoulder going full speed. Mac watched from his side view mirror as the nose of the truck plowed down into the grass and the rig flipped over onto his roof before rolling down away from the highway. Glancing over at Charles, he gave the thumb's up, and laughed as the big truck lurched forward.

"Time to get the second team in on the fun," Charles down shifted and pulled into the middle lane. The road was pretty clear and there was no other traffic on the road to get in the way of the huge trucks battling down the highway.

Mac grabbed the CB mic, "Alright, Muthafuckas," he yelled into the microphone, "time to take all of these fools out. We've dropped one and Charles is going to lead the chase… let's tear all these bastids some new assholes."

Charles had found his groove and was pushing the big truck down the road at a little close to ninety miles per hours, and she was humming like it was nothing. Mac had unbuckled his seat belt and was leaning his fat body over to pull something new from the big bag he'd brought on board. As he looked out the mirror he could see that the men inside of the trailer had slid aside the plates of siding and had the muzzles of their weapons pointed out and waiting. He could see the two SUVs had switched lanes and were now behind the two trucks that were remaining.

"Time to party," Mac said as he opened his door and stepped out of the cab.

The sound of automatic gunfire was suddenly rattling around inside of the cab and Charles found himself ducking even though he was in no danger of the shooting. He glanced out of his window as the rig on his left began to approach only to swerve back away as the bullets from both the trailer and Mac riddled their side. He could see the faces of the two men in the truck and they were not prepared for the barrage of bullets that was now hitting the truck.

One of the SUVs peeled away from behind all of the semi-trucks and pulled up on the far side of the truck being fired on. Charles could barely make it out but he watched as the truck began to swerve all over the road and noted it was in his best interest to get out of the way. Smoke was billowing from the hood and the bobtail was floundering to the left side, and Charles was sure it was because the front tire had been shot out. The two men in the truck could be seen through the windows but neither man was moving, and as he watched the truck careened off the road and nosed into the median before rolling into the oncoming traffic of the South bound lanes.

The last semi had slowed down and appeared to be pulling off of the road. This was nothing that they'd prepared for, and with the loss of two trucks it would appear that the two remaining men were not up to fight any longer.

"We need to get da fuck outta here," Mac had managed to get back into his seat and was slamming the door closed, "before the goddamn po po get here. Take the next exit and get us off this fuckin' highway."

"Gotcha," Charles was moving over to the far right lane preparing to turn on to the next off ramp. "You think they got the message?"

"What?" Mac was putting away his guns. "Not to fuck wit' da boss lady?"

"Yea," Charles flipped the turn signal and adjusted his gears and speed. "This has to be a major upset to Jangles ass."

"Man, fuck Jangles," Mac sat back in his seat and buckled his seat belt in place. "I wish Ms. Courtney would let me just walk up and merc his bitch ass. Dat nigga has always thought he was a gangsta... I got his fuckin' gangsta."

"Fall back a bit," Charles had grabbed the CB mic to speak to the men in the SUVs, "make certain that last truck don't get no ideas of following us. Meet us back in Tampa at the docks and well get all of this shit cleaned up.”

“10-4,” one of the men responded, and Charles made certain that they pulled off before he made the turn to get back up on I-75 going South towards home.

His heart was still pounding and his hands were shaking from the adrenaline rush. He took a deep breath when his boy pulled out a blunt and lit it up. The smell of the marijuana filling the truck’s cab was almost refreshing, and he wished they hadn’t lost the windows on the truck to keep that plume of smoke from escaping, but he’d make up for it when he took his first hit.

“I think that this is my last run,” he announced to his partner as he accepted the blunt. “I'm really getting to old for this shit.”

“Yea, I know what you mean,” Mac was grinning as he laid his head back slowly letting the thick smoke slip between his pursed lips. “I think I need to retire to an island, maybe down in Jamaica or some shit… right.”

“Right, I can see yo Cajun ass in Jamaica.” Charles passed the blunt back and tried to keep from choking as the smoke burned his lungs. “You need to call this shit in. Let Nick know that we was hit by three and that two are down. Tell him we on the way home and keepin’ an eye on that last truck.”

“Roger that,” Mac took another toke of the blunt and pulled out his phone to call Nick.

****

“Courtney?” Nick walked into the bedroom to find Courtney just sitting on the bed. “You ok?”

“Yes,” she answered but not looking at him. “I think I am.”

Nick moved into the room and walked to the bed and sat down beside her. As she turned to finally face him he reached out and wiped away the tears in her eyes. She didn't resist as he pulled her into his arms and held her.

"How much more, Nick?" she was crying openly. "I cannot do this anymore. I don't want my daughter to ever know the shit that I've been pushed to do. Why can't I just end this and walk away?"

"Is that what you want to do?" Nick was gently sliding his fingers through her hair. "We can walk away anytime you're ready. I've got things set up for us to leave at any point."

"But then they win," she was trying not to scream into his shoulder. "If I do this all of the shit that Sydney has put me through with Jangles, and all of the shit I've had to endure with Jangles trifling ass. All of the bullshit and deceit… I walk away and I went through all of the last two years for nothing."

"Then let's end it, Court, and then you let me take you away from here for a while just to rest." Nick pulled her face from his shirt and kissed her forehead. "I just heard from Mac and they've made through everything without a loss and they are on their way home. Sydney sent three trucks after them so I'm figuring that the same happened with the other fake loads as well… I'm just waiting for everyone to check in."

"Then our next step is to get with Uncle Yuen." Courtney smiled for the first time in a long time. Nick was still with her even though she'd shot him in the chest, and even thought it felt good to do that, she was glad he wasn't hurt.

"I'll get him on the phone," Nick smiled back and made his way towards the bedroom door.

"Oh, Nicky," Courtney had been watching him walk away and as he turned, "I love you, Mr. St. Charles."

"And I love you more, Ms. Vaughn."

"That sounds good."

"What?" Nick stood staring at her a bit confused.

"My name, Genius. I love the way it sounds when you say it," Courtney giggled. "Besides, I was never truly a Roulette, I feel like everything about my marriage was a lie. So my name is Vaughn, Courtney Vaughn, as it always should have been."

Chapter 25

Jimmy Q was tall by stature of most Asians and he'd spent a lot of time in the gym making certain that he was as big as he was tall. He kept his hair cut short with just a tuft of spiky hair on top and he always kept a clean shaven face. He was not a hard man to look upon, but to his pleasure most people avoided his stare for fear of what could possibly come… a beat down by any number of men who were always at his side.

He'd taken over the place of being his Uncle Yuen's second after the disappearance of his cousin Chin Ti; the number of stories running around about Chin Ti never mattered much to him because he was just as soft as the old man. He'd always had plans of getting rid of both men since he'd first been allowed to partake in the family business, and there were many who he knew would stand with him when he was ready to take over. At last, that time had finally come and within the next couple of weeks… he would be running the Chinese family business in the South.

As he sat in the back of the upper level of Club Skyy waiting for Jangles and his newest business partner to show up, he was sipping at a glass of vodka listening to the music and the jabbering of his men over the thump of the music. He was rarely ever without these four men and it was because he not only trusted them, but he'd handpicked them to be a part of his personal crew. These were the men he could tell everything too and they were right there with him, and each of them had stressed a number of times that he should be running this branch of the Triads.

"Jimmy, are you sure we can trust this
Jangles dude?" All of them were pretty much
Americanized and had little to no accents of their
Asian descent.

He turned and glared at his second, Jackie,
and nodded his head. This was the first time he'd
been questioned about their trusting an outsider, but
he'd known Jangles since Chin Ti had introduced
them years ago.

"And this Mexican that he's running with,"
Jackie wasn't one to give up, "you know we've had
a lot of shit go down between us and the Manciena
family. None of them motherfuckers can be trusted."

"Jack," Jimmy took a sip from his glass and
set it back down on the table, "you worry too much,
but that's why I keep you around. All of this shit has
been worked out between the three of us and by the
time my Uncle finds out what's going on it's all
gonna be too late."

"You know I'm with you, but this shit's got
me on edge, you know what I mean? Jimmy, if
Uncle finds out…"

"Trust me, Jack, trust me… I know and I've
got this shit in the bag. Just keep your eyes open and
you watch my back."

Jackie took a swallow of his own drink and
began looking around the club. He'd picked this
back table because it gave him the best view of the
club and the best chance of keep this fool alive.

"Everything's all in order, Jack," Jimmy
grinned and that was always a dangerous thing to
happen, "I need you to trust me."

"I trust you," Jack was watching the crowd,
"I just don't trust them."

The group of women walking up the stairs
had caught Jackie's attention and he was no longer

concerned with whatever deal Jimmy had set up with the black man and the Mexican. There were six of them, and each nothing short of a model looking for a runway to swing her ass down. It was like having all of your favorite kinds of candy come to you, and Jackie ran his fingers through his hair, making himself more presentable before elbowing Jimmy in the side nodding his head towards the approaching skirts.

"You ordered some pussy, Jack?" Jimmy took his last swallow and slammed to glass on the table. "I can use a piece of ass because that bitch at the house seems to always be on the fucking rag."

The two men laughed as the women stepped up to the table all standing with a hand on a hip. Jimmy was more taken with the blonde and the redhead, both women were pretty much all legs and tits that he was positive were well paid for. The blonde was obviously interested and moved to where he was sitting to give him a better view of her ass just to let him see that she was well stacked in that department as well. Her blue eyes were like staring up at the sky on a beautiful summer day and she had her lips painted with a thick, deep red lipstick that just made his pulse jump.

Jackie stood and took the hand of the brunette and pulled her around the table towards him. She was shorter than the blonde and that worked well with the short skirt that came just below her full ass. Her eyes were a gorgeous hazel green that just seemed to call out to him and what she lacked in tits she more than made up for with her full lips and her full figure. He spun her around taking every inch of her in right down to her pedicured toes. He didn't pay any attention to who the other girls partnered off with as he quickly turned all of his attention the beautiful woman before him.

"Goddamn," he whistled before pulling her close and doing a quick little dance step with her as she giggled like a school girl.

Jimmy welcomed the distraction of the women, and it was apparent that his men did as well. All of them were hugged up with a woman of their own and now watching as Jackie and the brunette were dancing just off from the table and it was like watching some Lambada type dancing that had all of them making enough noise that they could be heard over the music. The girl was throwing her ass back into Jackie's crotch and he was pretty much dry humping her in front of a crowd of people that were now circling the table. Jimmy had pulled the blonde down onto his lap and was cheering his boy on.

The crowd of people was increasing by the second, and the drumming of the music was as intoxicating as the alcohol as Jackie and his new friend's dancing became increasingly raunchy. He'd pulled her up against his body and his hands were squeezing and fondling her tits as her ass gyrated hard against his growing dick. The sweat was dripping from his forehead and down into his eyes as he spun the girl around and planted her pussy down on the leg he pressed between her thighs.

"Drop that ass, Bitch," Jackie was screaming out. "Drop that ass."

The crowd began chanting with him as the girl dropped down on his leg and began humping against him with reckless abandon. Her dark hair, which hung down past her shoulders, was whipping about her head hiding her face and her hands were high about her head with her fingers snapping in beat with the song playing. She did a move that was so quick but she once again had her back to him and she was up further on his leg and riding him like horse.

The excitement in the air was beyond anything any of them had ever experience, and it was getting wilder by the second. Jimmy was having a ball watching and cheering on Jackie as much as the rest of the crowd. He'd waved over the one of the bar waitresses and order a few bottles of *Grey Goose* vodka and had the girl pour rounds to everyone standing in the circle around the table until what was at least thirty people were all holding shot glasses.

Jimmy's eyes stretched wide as the pain struck him in the throat the moment he raised he had to swallow his shot of vodka. The fire of the hot lead seemed to cauterize his esophagus and he was choking and trying to breathe before he dropped the glass. The girl sitting on his lap was dumped to the floor and she scrambled away into the crowd before anyone even noticed that he was in trouble. The next two shots followed quickly hitting him in the chest and slamming his body back against the cushioned seat.

A woman in the crowd screaming stopped everything. As Jackie turned to see what was going on, the girl on his leg tried to run off but she didn't get far as she ran into someone in the rushing crowd and fell to the floor. She screamed the moment someone grabbed her by the hair pulling her up from the floor. That man was hit with two bullets just as quickly as Jimmy had been and he dropped pulling the girl back to the floor with him.

"Find whoever did this, goddammit! Find them now… move it." Jackie ordered as he crawled over to where Jimmy had finally fallen. He knelt over his friend and checked for a pulse at the side of his neck and looked up as the crowd of people quickly thinned and were rushing towards the stairs.

The fourth man that had been in their group was hanging over the railing swaying back and forth at the waist, and Jimmy knew that he was all that remained. The club was in total chaos as people were screaming and shouting and forcing everyone out of their way to get through the two main doors of the building. With a look of defiance, he stood and reached into the small of his back pulling free the Glock .40 he had nestled there.

"Where you at, Punk Bitch?" the club music had died down and his voice was echoing through the building. "Come out and show yourself… COME OUT!"

The red light caught his attention as it flashed across his eyes. He blinked and turned his head for a split second. The moment he turned back towards the direction the light had flashed, a brighter flash caught his attention for a split second. He had wanted to scream out, but before he could make a sound his head was tossed back and his body flipped over landing on top of Jimmy's.

"This is T.J." He was sitting atop a building about five hundred yards away pulling his face away from the scope. The night air was cooling and comforting as he sat down and began breaking down and packing up the high powered rifle. "Targets at Skyy are all down. Contract has been satisfied."

"You know where to rendezvous, T.J.," Jackson responded. "I have this last series of contracts on the docket before I'm there with all payments."

"Copy that," T.J. sat there a moment longer staring at the city around him "Rendezvous point in thirty."

Dressed in all black the man on the rooftop stood and stared across the way towards the night club. People were still trying to get away and in the distance he could hear the sounds of sirens; that was music to his ears as he reached down and picked up the expended cartridge shells and tossed them into the carrying case for his rifle.

"I love working in this fucked up city," he slung the straps of the rifle case over his shoulder and disappeared into the shadows.

****

"I need everyone to check in," Jackson spoke into the boom mic at his ear.

"This is check point one," a voice answered, "I have target E.J. confirmed and waiting."

"This is check two, and I have target Cody confirmed."

"This is check point three… I have target Darren in sight and confirmed."

"This is check point four, and I have target J-Groove confirmed and ready."

"Stand by all," Lagrange responded, "prepare to take out all targets on my command."

****

"Ay, Bobby," Jorge was sitting in the back of a stretch limo watching two girls he'd paid good money for dance with one another. "I hadn't heard from you and I wanted to know how the truck hits went?"

"I'll be honest, Bruh," Jangles exhaled deeply, "I haven't heard shit yet and this shit is fuckin' with me."

"What the fuck do we need to do; I mean, this goddamn woman is worse than a fucking cockroach. I was sure the house thing would send her pretty, little ass running."

"Yea, I've thought the same thing on a number of times," Jangles responded. "Shit, I've been sure a couple of times her ass was dead and she just rises back up and continues to fuck me over."

"So you're sure that she is alive?"

"Oh, I'm positive," Jangles sounded aggravated. "I spoke with Syd…"

"Wait… Sydney is alive too?" Jorge waved the two girls off as they tried to get close to him. He reached over and grabbed a *Corona* from the small refrigerator and popped the top.

"Yea, color my black ass surprised when this muthafucka shows up at my office," Jangles answered. "Just one more thing to deal with by the time all of this shit is over with, but for the moment I've learned a few things I'm sure Ms. Fancy ass wasn't expecting me to find out. I've just got control of all of my money once again and now a few deals I had on the low boil I can jump on."

"Cool," Jorge took a big swallow from the bottle. "So what next, Bobby? What do we do from here?"

"We keep our meeting with Jimmy Q and plan out that shit on Uncle Yuen so we can get Jim up and running. Sydney is working on finding Courtney and once we have her in place we're going to get this shit over and done with. I can tell you this, the bitch is my fuckin' kind of woman… she killed Nicky Styles."

"No shit?"

"Yea, from what Syd explained, Nicky was in with him and some white dude keeping Courtney ass in place and when the bitch found out… well she capped both Nick and the white guy.”

"Shit,” Jorge laughed, “I like her already.”

“No kidding…” Jangles fought to keep from laughing. There was something about Courtney that definitely intrigued him but he would never let anyone know that.

“Look, Bobby, I'm pulling up in front of IXion right now… why don’t you head down and we’ll finish talking on our way to the club.”

“Cool,” Jangles walked over to the windows and looked out over the city; everything always looked so peaceful from these upper floors especially with all of the lights off in the room. “I’ll be down in a sec.”

“Hello, Baby,” Nina’s voice startled him enough that he’d pulled his pistol before he realized that it was her. Slowly turning away from the window he could see her silhouette in the door thanks to the light from the reception area.

“You need to learn to give a nigga a bit of notice, Girl,” he laughed shoving the gun back into his shoulder harness. “What the hell are you doing here this time of night?”

“Looking for you… of course.”

“Well I’d say you found me,” Jangles moved back to his seat at the conference table. “So tell me, what can I do you for?”

Nina stepped into the room, but didn’t close the door. Jangles sat at the end of the table allowing his eyes to roam over every curve of her body, and again he was thankful that she’d stop letting herself go. For a while he’d began to fear that he would have to drop her ass like an old habit because she’d sunk so far. He almost laughed as he what she’d look like if she began to gain weight. Even in the darkness of the room the skirt or dress that she was wearing seemed to be painted on her body and all he could think of was grabbing her and tossing her on the table and fucking her brains out.

"I think that the time has come for us to have a little talk," Nina answered, or at least he thought that it was Nina. Something didn't seem right.

Jangles moved to pull out his pistol once more.

"I really wouldn't do that, Jangles," the light to the room switched on and Courtney stood where he'd thought Nina was and in her hand was a gun he'd swear she shouldn't be able to hold up. "If you don't mind pulling that gun of yours out and sliding it across the table to me… please."

Not moving fast enough for her, Jangles was quicker to comply the moment he heard the hammer of the large .44 magnum pulled back. The metal made a rattling, scraping sound as he slid it across the table, and then he sat back and folded his arms across his chest.

"So here we are," he smiled, "back where it all began huh?"

"You're in my chair," Courtney pointed to the seat, "and I'm going to enjoy sitting there again."

"So, should I say, welcome back, Boss Lady?" Jangles hadn't dropped his smile, "Tell me something, Courtney, what are you going to do next, huh? Are you going to kill me like you did good ole Nicky Styles?"

"I don't now, Bobby," Courtney's smile broadened as she stepped around the table. "What do you think I should do?"

"Kiss my a…"

"Watch your fucking mouth." Nick stepped into the room and grinned as Jangles eyes became as big as saucers and the smile faded from his face. "As you can see, I'm not dead, Bobby. It would seem that Sydney isn't the only somebody that can pull off a death trick."

"Goddamn, Nicky Styles, as I live and breathe… no wait, as you live and breathe. I'm not sure what the fuck is going on, but," Jangles reached into his jacket and pulled out a blunt, "this shit is getting interesting."

"This shit is just beginning," Nina stepped into the room and walked up to the table picking up the pistol laying there. "Like I said… I think it's time we had a little talk."

Jangles' smile slowly creased his lips as he lit the blunt and took a big toke. He pushed back in his chair and released the smoke into the conference room before taking another big pull. "I'm really loving this shit. The three muthafuckin' amigos in the muthafuckin' building."

As his phone rang, Jangles slowly reached into his jacket pocket pulling it out and answered.

"Ay, yo, Jangles," he'd hit the speaker button so everyone could hear Jorge's voice, "what's going on? Where you at?"

"I'll be down in a bit," Jangles tried sounding confident even in the face of the odds he faced right now. "I'm just dealing with a little matter and then I'll be down so we can go meet up with Jimmy… shit, we may not need to do too much after this right here."

"Cool, I'm down…"

****

Jackson was watching everything that was taking place in the conference room and he was waiting until just the right moment; that moment came when Nina finally stepped into the room and

351

picked up Jangles gun with a new gleam in her eyes. He'd never worked much with women and as he sat there watching these two in action he wondered why? He was finding that women had a deeper brutality than most of the men he'd ever worked for. The phone call became an added bonus.

Ay yo Jangles, Jorge's voice was loud and clear over the cell phone's speaker, and Jackson smiled. *What's going on?*

I'll be down in a bit, Jangles answered and Jackson noticed that look of faux bravado.

"All teams," he called out into his boom mic, "take out all targets."

I'm just dealing with a little matter and then I'll be down.

As he received responses from his men in the field, Jackson picked up the switch from the dashboard of his truck. He counted down from ten in his head and pressed the red button on the top of the switch.

"Target one… taken out."

So we can go meet up with Jimmy…

"Target two has been taken out."

"Target three has been taken out."

Shit, we may not need to do much after this right here.

"Target four… taken out."

"Everyone to the rendezvous point," Jackson watched the screen as Jangles jumped up from his chair and ran over to the window and looked down upon the street far below.

Cool, I'm down…

Jangles Lagrange smiled as Jorge never got to finish his statement, and he drove off to meet his men.

****

"What the fuck's going on?" Jangles demanded as he stared down at what could be nothing except a car explosion. His mind took a quick trip back to that moment he was sure Sydney had been blown up.

"Jorge?" He was yelling into the phone as he turned to stare at Courtney. "Was that?"

His knees felt weak and he began to realize that he'd completely underestimated this woman. Jangles looked broken and more pitiful than he'd ever been seen. He was standing, leaning over the table trying to keep himself from falling over and as he stood there shaking his head the only thought running through his head was…

How the fuck did I get bested by a goddamn woman?

"What now?" he asked as he dropped into his chair. With his kingdom crumbling around him maybe it was time to toss in the white flag. "Well, what the fuck now, Courtney?"

"Aw," Courtney's smile alone was sarcastic enough, "now where's that cocky son-of-a-bitch we've all come to love?"

"Fuck you, Bitch," Jangles looked up and the smile was gone and replaced by contempt. "And what about you, Nina, where the fuck do you stand with all of this?"

Nina stood holding his pistol on him with nothing but hatred in her eyes. She eased by Courtney and walked the length of the table until she was face to face with him. Leaning over she grabbed the back of his head and pulled him forward until their lips pressed together. Her tongue slipped between his lips and she gave him the kiss of a lifetime.

"I loved you," she whispered as she pulled away. "I don't know why or how, but I loved you, Bobby Johnson. You broke me… for a moment, you had me right where you wanted me and I'd almost lost everything including my soul to you. You tried to kill her and then you lied to me and I was too fucking blind to see it."

"Oh so now you're whining?" Jangles laughed as the woman he'd allowed himself to actually love stood up over him smiling.

"Not whining, Bobby," Nina answered. "Just freeing myself."

"Excuse me, Ms. Vaughn," Jackson's voice was on the room's intercom system.

"Yes, Mr. Lagrange?" Courtney placed her gun on the table and took a seat her eyes never leaving Jangles as he looked around the room.

"The remainder of the Nine has been taken care of."

"What the fuck do you mean… taken care of?" Jangles stared down the table at Courtney and then back up at Nina.

"I've done to you what you've been trying to do to me for the last two years, Mr. Johnson," her smile was completely unnerving and he couldn't keep his eyes on her. "I've taken everything away from you. The money, the business, your family, the woman you loved, and now… every man you thought you could count on. I've taken it all and now it's just you."

"What about Sydney?"

"Sydney's dead," Courtney stated viciously. "But, the man walking around with his face… well I plan on dealing with him very soon, don't you go worrying about that."

"You've become something very cold, Woman." Jangles sat back in the chair and folded his arms over his chest. "I guess Sydney really fucked up with you huh?"

"I wouldn't say he fucked up," Courtney grinned, "but I would say that he is pretty much my Dr. Frankenstein. It all works out in the end. Everything that he trained me for is about to come full circle, and without you and the Nine in my way I'm going to take IXion into a whole new industry and the people working for me… well I intend to make a lot of them some very rich people. That could have been us, Jangles, we could have all been some very rich people, but you had your mind set on trying to kill me.

"So I'm here to return the favor," Courtney stood from the table and turned to leave, "you Son-of-a-bitch."

"I need you to know something, Bobby," Nina was staring in his eyes. He was completely broken, and that made her feel as powerful as she knew he'd always felt. She bathed in as she kissed his lips once more and then slid her face around to his ear to whisper softly. "I'm pregnant, Baby, and this beautiful little child of ours will never know anything about the monster that was his father."

Jangles turned to Nina just as she raised the gun up to his head. As he opened his mouth to beg for his life, the fire from the muzzles blinded him… for only a split second. The bullet ripped through his skull with enough force to knock him and the heavy chair he was sitting in backwards. His body rolled over the back of the chair just as his breathing stopped and he twitched one final time before fading away in a pool of his blood.

"Mr. Lagrange," Nina stood staring at her dead lover's body, "will you have someone clean up this mess and get this office ready for business again… please?"

"Yes, Ms. Carleton," Jackson sat watching with a smile on his face, "I'll have it all taken care of post haste."

"We'll see you in a couple of hours," Courtney said as she and Nick left Nina.

"Will she be ok?" Nick asked glancing back.

"Yes," Courtney smiled… "I've come to find that Nina is a lot stronger than I ever knew so I'm sure she'll be just fine."

Epilogue

"Court?" Nick was sitting on the sofa nursing another glass of coffee. This one had been his fourth or fifth since waking up at about five and not getting back to sleep. He watched as she came ambling from the bedroom with her hair still a mess on top of her head as she bee-lined into the kitchen.

"Courtney?" he was concerned about her and now about Nina after the events at IXion a few days ago. He'd been over to check on Nina a few times, but each time she'd refused to allow him into her condo. He'd left orders with the two men he had watching her place to make certain she ate and to keep a close eye on her.

He heard Courtney in the kitchen moving things around undoubtedly looking for the coffee cup that she preferred to drink from. He made his way into the kitchen and stood in the doorway leaning against the frame. Even in this moment of dishevel she was still absolutely beautiful. The light gown that she was wearing hit at about mid-thigh and was so lacy that he could see clear through it in the kitchen's light. Her hair was a mess of curls tossed all over the place and matted in other areas leaving her looking like she'd just wrestled a hurricane and lost. Her feet were bare and he grinned as she twisted the ball of one foot into the floor as she reached up into the cabinet to grab her cup. He whistled as the hem of the gown showed off the bottom of her ass causing her to jump and pull down on the skimpy material before turning to face him.

"You know," she brushed her hair from her face and glared at him in mock anger, "the least you could do Mr. Nastyass is come over here and get my cup for me."

Nick laughed as he entered the kitchen and retrieved her cup placing it on the counter so she could pour from the fresh pot he'd only made a little bit ago. Stepping back, he watched as she went through the process of adding too much creamer and enough sugar to jump start a dead man's heart and then she stirred it in making certain that the spoon clanged around in the cup as loudly as she could make it.

"You getting an eyeful, Mister?" she took her first sip and added some more sugar.

"More than an eyeful I'd say," he grinned as she looked over at him again and stuck out her tongue. "Damn, I could say something but I'll keep it to myself this time."

"You're incorrigible, Nicholas," she walked by and slapped his arm.

"More than you know." Following her out into the living room and watching the swish of her ass with each step. "One of these days I'm going to get your ass declared a deadly weapon… shit, maybe a weapon of mass destruction."

"Go to hell," she laughed as she dropped down on the sofa. Pulling her feet up under her, Courtney glanced over her shoulder and winked at him before beckoning him to join her.

"How are you?" Nick asked as he sat on the other end of the sofa allowing her to stretch her legs out and placing her feet on his lap.

"I'm really not sure just yet," she honestly answered. "Right now I'm more worried about Nini. I haven't heard from her, and she's not answering her phone."

"Her door neither, but I have a couple of guys there watching out for her."

Courtney nodded her head and switched on the television. For the last couple of days, she'd been expecting to hear something about all of the men she'd had executed, but so far, there'd been nothing of them on any of the news channels. She wanted to relax, but the game still wasn't over and at some point she knew she'd have to face that one final obstacle.

"Have you decided how you're going to handle him?" Nick could easily see that she was thinking about Sydney. He'd tried to talk to her about him, but each time she'd waved him and told him that she wasn't ready… yet.

"Yes I have," she answered. "In the only way that he would understand and respect the person I've become. It has to be direct."

"Yea." Nick sat his cup down on the coffee table and proceeded to softly rub on her feet. "Are you sure you can meet up with him like that and not just…"

"Just what?" her voice was soft and unsure. "Just crumble? I don't know, Nicky, I truly don't know. I have fought with myself back and forth on forgiving him and just walking away, but each time I'm reminded that Sydney used me like I was some kind of lab rat in his little science project. He literally put my life and the life of my child in danger, and he has yet to redeem himself in any manner. As a matter of fact, he's done the exact opposite."

Courtney could no longer waste tears on the fact that not only was her husband alive, but he was a part of his best friend trying to ruin her. In her head she could still see the recording in the conference room of Sydney and Jangles after Sydney had pulled free the bugs in the room that he knew about. A part of her was still very much in love with this man, who she really didn't know, but every ounce of respect she'd had for him had washed out to sea the day Jackson Lagrange had shown her evidence of him being alive; the day in the conference room had only hammered home the final nail in his coffin.

****

"Goddamn, Syd," Jangles watched as the man walked around the large room pulling free small microphones and cameras and tossing them on the table. "Nigga, you've created a monster with this chick."

"Yea, I've been told that… on a few occasions." Sydney pulled out a chair and sat down. "So much shit's going on and I don't even know where to begin."

"The beginning, Muthafucka, the beginning."

Pulling a couple of cigars from his coat pocket, he offered one to Jangles as he cut the butt and lit the tip of his own. He sucked in deep and held the fragrant smoke in his mouth before slowly blowing it towards the ceiling of the room. He'd got this batch of Cubans from a guy he'd met while being treated overseas and he couldn't get over the exquisite taste of them.

"I could never understand why you had to kill Big Fats," he blurted out as Jangles was lighting his cigar. "I mean, he was like the only father either of us had ever known, and he was good to us."

"Man, fuck Big Fats," Jangles spat out. "That nigga ain't do shit for me… he ain't really do shit for either of us."

"He taught us all of this shit, Bobby."

360

"Syd, open your fuckin' eyes… we were
fuckin' pawns for that muthafucka. You know what
he did for us? He made certain that we kept the
streets flowing with that weak ass coke of his and we
made him money. We made a rich nigga… Naw
fuck that, we made him a richer nigga. And what did
you do? You idolized him."

"You're talking nonsense," Sydney couldn't
even look at the man he'd always considered his
brother. "And then you started killing me the same
goddamn way. I didn't recognize it at first, but then
it became obvious that I was being poisoned. Why?"

"I didn't want to," Jangles stood and walked
away from the table, "but the decision had been
made. You forgot about us, Sydney… You forgot
about the Nine and started making plans to do some
stupid shit and well, we wasn't havin' that."

"So it was all of you?"

"Yea… well, almost all. That nigga JC was
always against it but it was easy to work around him.
And, it had to be me… I couldn't let them do shit to
you."

"So where do we stand now, Bobby?"

"Damn good question," Jangles pressed his
back to one of the windows overlooking the city and
puffed on his cigar. "There's a lot of dirty water
flowing under this bridge… can we kiss and make
up like boys and move on from here?"

"Well, Nigga, I ain't kissing you, but I'll give
you a pound and a hug and remember you're my
brother… will that work?"

"Works for me."

Sydney stood and crossed the room with his
hand extended. They quickly met in the middle and
clasped hands before pulling each other into a well-
deserved and much needed hug. Sweeping the past

under the rug the two men were once again brothers and ready to face the world, and Jangles wasted no time.

"So, what we gon' do about your fuckin' wife?" he pulled away staring at his friend. "She's a beast and I know that I've underestimated her."

"Well like I said, I trained her to play this game," Sydney began pacing in front of Jangles thinking. "I guess I'll have to be the one to out think her and end this shit."

"No," Jangles said causing Sydney to stop in his tracks. "We need to deal with her ass… permanently."

"Shit," Sydney couldn't look at Bobby, but he knew that his boy wasn't lying. Courtney was like a dog gone rabid, and she needed to be put down… quick.

"Syd," Jangles knocked on the top of the table. "Sydney, you hear me? Courtney needs to be handled."

"Yea… permanently, I hear you, but I'll have to do it," Sydney answered. "I'll need you and your people to keep her people busy. Without Nicky Styles around I'm sure she'd be all kinds of fucked up and not paying attention to shit like she should be."

"Yea," Jangles broke out in a toothy smile. "I can do that shit. I just need to know when and how."

"I know of a large shipment that she's set up going to three different locations," Sydney explained as he sat back down. "My thoughts is this… if we were to hijack those shipments. Better yet, we need to basically smear her name and then we'll have to just rebuild the IXion trust back up. I'll get you the routes, dates and times and you put the men in play. I need those trucks destroyed, and I'll send some

men that I have out to find a ship I know she has
out."

"If I didn't know any better, Sydney,"
Jangles sat back smoking on his cigar, "I'd almost
think that you've been planning to off your wife for
quite a while."

"No," Sydney responded, "not a while, but
there comes a time when even the most trained of
dogs has to be put down by its Master."

"Now that's some of the coldest shit that I've
ever fuckin' heard."

"Yea," Sydney looked up with the biggest
smile Jangles had ever seen on the man's face, "cold
it may be, but this is Florida, my nigga, and down
here we like to keep this shit hot."

"Stupid ass," the two men began laughing as
Jangles got up and fixed two glasses of Hennessey.
"Here's to keeping shit hot and getting rid of rabid
dogs."

They touched glasses laughing once again.

"Boys will be boys," Courtney murmured as
she walked away from the computer she'd been
watching. Her stomach was in her throat, but at least
now she knew where she stood with Sydney. If she
was going to be a dog to him, then the time had
come for this dog to bite the hand that had been
feeding her. She'd waste no more tears on Sydney or
this fucking company, and when the dust settled he
was going to realize that just like Jangles… he'd
completely underestimated her.

****

The table cloths covering the table were
softer than some sheets she slept on and she couldn't
keep from stroking them as she sat out on the
outdoor patio. This wasn't the first time she'd been
to the Columbia restaurant, but each time was

always like taking a trip back in time. The beautiful colors of the bricks and the designs of the overall setting was magnificent with its Spanish archways and the staccato flooring. The metal chairs were always as comfortable as sitting on her patio looking out over the pool in her backyard, when she had a house. The palms and the potted flowers were a constant reminder that you were in the heart of Florida and right in the heart of Tampa with each refreshing breath you'd take.

Today was simply beautiful as the early evening sun was falling off slowly to the West and the clouds were taking on the colors of the Floridian rainbow in hues of oranges, pinks, and purples. There was a soft breeze passing through the patio that brought with it all of the delicious smells from the kitchen that kept her mouthwatering.

"Good evening, Mrs. Roulette, my name is Nichelle," the waitress stood at her table side with a beautiful smile with a tall glass of iced tea. "I'll be your waitress for the evening, Ma'am. I've got a glass of tea with a lemon wedge, and if you're ready I'll be happy to take your order."

"Thank you, Nichelle, but please call me Ms. Vaughn, and I'm waiting on my company. I'm pretty sure that he'll be along pretty soon." she explained with a smile and then pulled the floppy brim of her hat lower as she returned to her thoughts.

"Yes, Ma'am, just wave to me when the two of you are ready, and I'll be right over. Welcome to the Columbia; enjoy your evening and meal."

She always felt under dressed coming here, and today was no different. She was in a very light summer dress that was a beige color with a pair of coral colored heels on and a large brimmed hat that matched the color of her dress. She could feel people watching her, and it should have unnerved her and a few years ago it would have; but today, everything just seemed to fall over her shoulders barely touching her. Maybe it was due to everything she'd gone through, or maybe it was because she was no longer the little girl from Missouri any longer and thanks to everything she'd gone through she was a completely different woman.

Courtney pulled a picture of her daughter from her purse and sat there staring at it. Her heart was heavy because it had been far too long since she'd last seen her cute, little love bug and she was missing her immensely.

"She's beautiful," the voice came up from behind her and she had to fight to keep from jumping. "You really did a good job."

"I would say that *'We'* did a good job since you did have a hand in making her." Courtney refused to turn and meet his eyes opting to wait for him to make his way around to the chair across from her.

Sydney gently placed his hands on her shoulders hoping for something softer in her than he received. Courtney was so completely different than the woman he'd left just a few years ago, and he could feel it in just the subtleness of his touch. He stood over her for a moment more before walking around the table and taking a seat. He sat back from the table and crossed his legs as he stared at the woman he'd married and pretty much given everything he'd created; she was still the most beautiful woman he'd ever laid eyes on. He watched as she slid the picture across the table to him and he picked it gazing into his little girl's eyes.

"I cannot wait to see her," Sydney stared at the beautiful little girl who was all smiles in the picture before placing it in his pocket assuming she was giving him that one to keep. "I'm looking forward to giving her plenty of hugs and kisses and making up for all of the time that I've missed."

"Somehow," Courtney finally looked up, "I doubt that will ever happen."

"Why would you say that?"

"Because, Mr. McGregor," she responded, "as far as my daughter is concerned… her father is dead. It was such a tragic ordeal, but I'm assuming it was because of the shady business dealings that he was accustomed to. I am all that she's had and I'm all she'll ever need."

"You're awfully bitter, Courtney," Sydney kept his eyes glued on her. "Why the open hostilities?"

"You think this is hostile?" Courtney smiled as she watched his eyes from behind the sunglasses she was wearing. There was something different about this man that she didn't recognize. He was trying remain confident and appeared to be in control, but he wasn't. Courtney could see fear in his eyes and for the first time she could feel this pressure lifting from her shoulders. Without so much as a second thought she signaled for her waitress and sat back waiting for the girl to get there.

"Yes, Ma'am, what can I get you?" Nichelle stood ready with her order pad.

"Nichelle, I think we need wine… something red and semi-sweet," Courtney ordered. "And please bring the bottle."

"Yes, Ms. Vaughn," the girl gave a curt nod and scurried off.

"Ms. Vaughn?" Sydney chuckled as if he'd heard a joke. "So we're going to keep up with this shit are we?"

"I don't see that this is shit, Mr. McGregor." Courtney removed her hat but not her glasses.

"Courtney, I'm your goddamn husband."

"No," she calmly responded. "As I've already said; my husband died in a very violent car explosion that I blamed on his fucking best friend for almost three years. The last time I saw anything of my husband was a box that I could only assume his body was in because his remains were not deemed viewable by the mortician. Burned beyond recognition. You're not my husband… you're the man who has been pretending to help me keep my husband's company, but in truth you're nothing more than an asshole who felt it was good to throw me to the motherfucking wolves and watch me scramble to survive."

"That's not it at all, Courtney…" Sydney began.

"If I didn't know any better, Sydney," Jangles voice spoke clearly thought the recorder's speaker, *"I'd almost think that you've been planning to off your wife for quite a while."*

"No," Sydney responded, *"not a while, but there comes a time when even the most trained of dogs has to be put down by its Master."*

"This is the dog letting you know that I no longer need you as my master," Courtney slid the recorder across the table.

"You had new shit planted in the offices?" Sydney picked it up shaking his head. "Goddamn, Nicky was right wasn't he?"

"I tried to warn your ass," Sydney turned as the familiar voice came from a nearby table. "I told you that what you were doing, that *We* was doing, was going to backfire and I asked who was going to be there to pick up the pieces?"

Nick walked over to the table and pulled up a chair next to Courtney and sat down. The look on Sydney's face was priceless and something he'd been looking forward to seeing since the day Courtney had shot him. He folded his arms over his chest and just stared at the man for a moment.

"I guess in a lot of ways I'm a slow fucking student," Nick finally spoke. "I should have seen what was going on long before I got myself all caught up with you and Jangles, but I saw the money… shit, I think that's all Jangles saw was the money. You played us all, didn't you, Syd?

"How the fuck are you…" Sydney was stumbling over his words.

"It's really not that fucking hard, Sydney, we just did to you what we did to her," Nick said bluntly. "You needed to believe that she'd finally stepped over the ledge so that you would go running to Jangles. We needed to find you and get the two of you together in one place just to find out how the two of you would react. I was actually going more towards the two of you killing one another."

"But," Courtney interjected, "like I've always said… boys will be boys, and you two asses could never remain mad at each other for long. You two, you and Bobby, are worse than most women I know. I knew you two would mend your fences and once that happened I knew I was nothing but a memory to you. I just needed to know how."

"Shit," Sydney rubbed his hand over his bald head laughing at his predicament. "You learned this shit better than I did. Damn, Courtney, Big Fats would be proud as hell right at this moment, you played the shit out of me and Jangles and I didn't even see it."

"The fucked up part about it, Sydney," the sound of his name left a bad taste in her mouth, "I was never playing. I feel like a fool believing that I ever meant anything to you when from the very beginning you had every intention of coming back here and killing me just to get back everything. It was never really about Jangles, for some reason you thought this little experiment was going to break me and what? Did you think that you would be able to just come back to life and I'd fall all over you until you found just the right time to remove me from your life?"

"It wasn't like that," Sydney sat up and leaned over the table as if trying to scare her. "I loved you."

"Loved? Nice," Courtney shook her head. "I loved you too, but that's passed. Now we have a problem."

"And that is?"

"You, of course," Nick answered. "You see we've taken care of the Nine and Jangles and you, Mr. McGregor are the last remaining loose end that needs to be sewn up."

"Taken care of? What the fuck do you mean taken care of?" Sydney's eyes bounced between the two sitting across from him. "Courtney, what have you done?"

"I've done a lot," she took a sip of the wine that had been sitting in front of her.

Sydney pulled out his phone and dialed Bobby's phone and stared at his wife and her new lover as he listened to the ringtone. When the phone was finally answered he breathed in a sigh of relief before he spoke. "Bobby…"

369

"Sorry, Sydney," Nina answered, "but Bobby's never answering this phone ever again. You see, Bobby's dead and if you don't believe that you can check your text message… I've just sent you proof. You take care, you, son-of-a-bitch… I hope that your death is worse than this bastard's was."

Sydney slowly dropped his eyes to the screen of his phone as he pulled it from his ear. As he opened the message, he stared in horror at the picture of his best friend lying on the floor of the conference room of IXion Industries with a hole in the center of his forehead. He tried to blink. He wanted to clear the look of his friend's dead eyes from his vision, but nothing short of shooting himself would ever stop him from seeing that for as long as he lived. He looked up and across the table with a newfound hatred for Courtney and Nick who were both just calmly watching him.

"As you can see, Mr. McGregor, I'll have a lot to answer for but that's something I'll deal with soon enough… but."

"But what?" Sydney couldn't read her face and with her eyes covered he couldn't figure out what she was up to.

"But, I'll not lose a night of sleep over you again," she nodded her head.

"You've become one heartless bitch, Courtney," Sydney leaned across the table to make certain she could see the anger in his eyes. "You'll pay for this… I promise you. I'll make certain that you both will…"

"How?" Courtney removed her sunglass so that he too could see her eyes. Dark. Cold. Uncaring for anything that he had to say. "You have nothing, and I've made certain of that. Everything that you thought you had, any money, in any personal accounts anywhere around the world… I have. I have IXion. I have everything and I have taken everything including that bastard Bobby from you.

"You're fucking dead in the water, Mr. McGregor," Courtney's voice was so calm that it sent a shiver up both Nick and Sydney's spines. "I could let you go right now and never have to worry about you ever again."

Sydney turned just in time to see Everlast walk up holding open his coat to show the butt of his pistol. The big Jamaican placed a hand on Sydney's shoulder to keep him from moving as Jackson Lagrange stepped up and reached into his coat and pull free the pistol he had holstered. Confused he turned back to Courtney.

"You're going to take a ride with these two gentlemen, Mr. McGregor," she explained, "they've arranged a parting for you that I'm sure you'll find satisfactory. It is in your best interest to never let our paths cross again, Evan McGregor, because if they do it will most definitely be our last meeting."

"You cannot do this to me, Bitch," Sydney growled as he tried to rise and E.L. slammed him back down into the chair. "This isn't over, Courtney, not by a long shot is this shit over."

"The funny thing is," Courtney rose from her seat, "for me, all of this shit is over. Thank you for showing me the woman I have become, hell, I've even enjoyed her, but I have a daughter to raise away from all of this craziness. I never want her to know of you or of this Courtney. At this point I just hope that the good I plan to do with all of this bad money that you and Bobby made, our company, and my daughter I can find the redemption that I now seek for all of this shit that I've done.

"You take care of yourself." Just as she stood Nichelle returned with the bottle of wine and Courtney smiled.

"I'm so sorry, Baby, here you do me a big favor." Courtney reached into her purse and pulled out five thousand dollars. "You pull out $300 as your tip for being so quick and prompt and then have your manager use the rest to pay for as many of the customers' meals that it will and have him send the balance for the remainder of the night to IXion Industries and I'll it all taken care of."

"Yes, Ma'am," an excited Nichelle answered as she ran off to get with her manager.

Courtney walked up to her "husband" and leaned over giving him one final kiss upon his lips. Taking a napkin, she wiped her lips and then passed the paper to him as she walked up to Nick and took the crook of his arm and walked off. As they got to the door leading into the restaurant, she turned one last time and stared at him before putting her hat back on and walking away.

Nick stood in the door a moment longer watching as E.L and Jackson helped Sydney to his feet. It was crazy that the few people sitting in the restaurant all continued with their meals as if seeing a scene like this was a normal and natural thing. Several of Jackson's men stood from various tables and the group of them headed off in the opposite direction that he and Courtney had left, and he watched until they were out of sight before he quickly walked to catch her.

"What now?" he asked.

Courtney took a deep breath and stared up into the evening sky. The sun had set and the stars were out dancing around a full moon. The weight of the world was off of her shoulders for the moment and all she wanted to do was scream and cheer and maybe even dance in the street. Ybor City was starting to light up around her as she reached out for his hand and they walked off towards their waiting car.

"Take me to the airport and put me on a plane to go get my daughter," she ordered with a very big smile.

"I figured as much," Nick spun her around and into his arms kissing her hard. "So I called and had one of our pilot's get one of IXion's planes ready. He texted a moment ago, and informed me that it's fueled and waiting. I've also sent word to Nina to meet us there."

"Excellent." She was giggling like a school girl. "Thank you, Nick. I need you to know that I love you and I think I'm ready for a brand new start … if you are?"

"I am ready… hell, I'm very ready," he opened the door and waited for her to get in and sit. Before closing the door Nick knelt down in front of her and reached in to his pocket pulling out a small ring box. "I love you too, Courtney Marie Vaughn."

****

"Ay, Nick St. Cloud, you there?" E.L. asked as he answered the phone.

"What's good, Everlast?" Nick stepped to the back of the plane as Courtney and Nina sat gabbing.

"Just calling to check in, Bossman," E.L. answered. "I wanted to tell you and those ladies to have a safe flight and have fun with that little lady once you get to her."

"Thanks, Bro," Nick glanced up and smiled at Courtney as she sat there showing Nina the ring he'd put on her finger just about an hour ago. "And that other thing?"

373

"Let's just say that between me and my new friend, Mr. Lagrange, you ain't gon' have to worry about that problem ever again."

Nick took a deep breath and thanked his friend before hanging up his phone and stuffing it into his pocket. As he was walking back to the two ladies, he stopped one of the flight attendants and requested a bottle of champagne to be opened once they were airborne and then he took his seat next to Courtney.

"Who was that on the phone?" She asked.

"It was E.L just wishing us a safe flight."

"Is that all?" Courtney was trying to read his eyes, and then he smiled at her.

"We won't have no worries with that ever again," he answered. "You have my word on that."

"Tell the Captain that we're ready," Courtney said to the flight attendant feeling all jittery. "I'm going to see my little baby and I can't wait any longer."

"Right away, Ms. Vaughn," the lady answered, "I'll let him know."

As they buckled in, Courtney stared at her best friends and she thanked them once more being with her through all of the shit she'd been through. She leaned in and she kissed Nick once more.

"You're stuck with me this time, Mr. St. Cloud," she smiled sliding her hand down his face.

"And you with me, Ms. Vaughn… always."

"Good."

The wheels of the plane were bouncing along the tarmac towards the runway and Courtney found herself staring out the window and into the thick clouds overhead. Her lips moved in a silent prayer as she felt the plane lurch forward and she watched the ground slowly disappear beneath them. She knew this would be the first of many, but this first one was only that they made it to her little Sydnee safely… afterwards; she would take the time to ask for forgiveness.

"Mommy's coming to get you, Baby girl."

~FIN

From a very young age Gerald was taught the value of his words. His parents had very high regards for education and impressed upon him the desires to Learn... Succeed... Exceed. Gerald wrote his first full novel at the age of 16 based upon his

participation in the role playing game Dungeons & Dragons. His love of reading had always been great and at any given time he could be found reading books simultaneously. This sparked a new desire and this he combined his joy of reading and a fondness for creating new worlds and characters and he found a love for writing.

Not to be tied to any one genre Gerald loves writing and creating in multiple platforms including Fantasy, Science Fiction, Thriller, Paranormal, and Erotica. The series of books that he's concentrated the most on have been in the Urban Literature genre, and he's extremely proud at how that set of book was written and how well they were received. As a writer,

Gerald's primary desire is to entertain his readers and
fans, and his goal is to one day see his work playing
up on the big screen.

"Writing and seeing my work published; for me, is a
dream come true, and I want to personally thank
each and every one of you who have taken a chance
on my work. I love that you love what I do and that
you keep coming back, and I hope to continue to
bring you the kinds of books that will keep your
minds entertain. Thank you, Thank you all."

Gerald R. Johnson

COMING SOON TWO NEW WORKS
FROM THE MIND OF A WRITER

From Gerald R Johnson
Driven Obsessions

From Damien Darke
Maxine Steele –
The White Chapel Files: The Reaper's Edge

Book excerpt – Driven Obsessions
Gerald R Johnson coming 2016

Chapter 2: That First Encounter

"Mr. Cross, Mr. Cross," Devin Cross had come to love hearing his name screamed out over a crowd. An ocean of faces all looking up at him as he sat in the limelight; he was born for moments like this. "Will you be writing anymore books to add to this current series?"

"That's a damn good question," he smiled looking out over the throng of people crowded around the small wooden table covered with his most current book. "My publisher and I were discussing that very thing just a few days ago, but I'm still unsure which direction I'll be going. I am currently working on a couple of new projects, but nothing's jumped out as my next to-be-completed project."

"Do you plan to continue writing about serial killers, or have you decided to jump off into a totally different genre all together?"

"Well," Devin smiled as everyone seemed to be hanging on his every word, "as I've said, I am working on a few new things, there are a couple of new psychological thrillers in the bunch, but I have been dabbling with a couple of science fiction stories which is something I haven't done in years."

The questions kept coming and he continued answering; over the course of the last couple of years he'd become quite comfortable talking to the press. He loved the questions especially those he'd get from the actual readers because they always gave him new material for anything he'd be working on. The atmosphere in the small book store was pleasant and the owners were extremely delighted with the turn out and the number of new purchases of the Cross soon to be best seller. His publicist had set up this book signing because he'd frequented the store often, and he'd have to remember to thank her for stepping up.

Slowly the hubbub died down to a gentle roar of the book readers holding conversations amongst themselves. Devin was a little thankful as he finally had the opportunity to sit down to begin this long day of signing books and keeping up a smile that was locked upon his lips and stretching his face. He looked back at the young lady standing off to the side of him and nodded his head as a gesture of beginning the second part of this show and she stepped forward as he sat and pulled himself up to the table.

"Ok, ok everyone," she was waving her hand to get everyone's attention. "May I have your attention please? Mr. Cross is ready to begin the signing so if you would… please form a single line to the left of the table. We do ask that your requests be short because as you can see Mr. Cross will be at this for a while."

Devin and everyone chuckled as Aura Daniels continued to go through the pre-requisites of the signing. He had a bad habit of staring at the younger woman whenever she wasn't looking; she was quite a beautiful woman that he'd often wondered if his publisher was up to no good where the publicist was concerned. She was rather short but the heels she always wore gave her the height she commanded, her complexion beautiful up close; it always had this soft glow that gave it this cream look that just went perfectly with those dark brown eyes that could stop any man mid-sentence. It was times like these he loved the most; she was standing with her back to him giving him the perfect angle for his eyes to slowly travel the length of her slender legs disappearing beneath the bottom of that too short skirt leading him right up to the curve of her ass. Devin shook his head as flashes of dreams and fantasies of what he could do with that ass flashed through his head.

We're going to have a long talk about this one, Mishelle, he mumbled as the girl turned and smiled.

"They're ready for you, Mr. Cross."

"Thank you, Aura," he said picking up the first of the five pens laid out for him to use.

Popping his fingers and looking down the line of people Devin smiled. Today was a great showing of people here to see him for his newest book, and that was always thrilling. He glanced down at the table that was stacked with copies and he knew that it was going to be a long day as he waved his first fan up and accepted the receipt for the book purchase.

"I've been a fan since your very first book, Mr. Cross," the man looked like he should be home playing dungeons and dragons or Magic: The Gathering, and this made Devin smile.

"Oh yea?" he said opening the book to where he'd sign. "What was your favorite part?"

"I loved the fight scene between Diana and Captain Bluebeard Morgan," the man quickly answered. "I think I was in love with her flowing red hair and those beautiful green eyes, and that she was just so defiant. It was like being right there as she weaved herself around a much larger man until she

381

was able to get through his guard. The way that you described the blade slipping through his flesh and piercing his spine… wow.”

“I haven’t run into anyone whose read those books in years,” Devin was trying not to sound as excited as his male fan, but he was. “It’s too bad you hadn't bought one of those with you, I would have loved to have signed it for you.”

“The next time you're in town I definitely will.”

A real fan of his writing; Devin was completely beside himself. It had been a long time since anyone had brought up any of his work prior to him being signed to a major label, and for it to be about his lady pirate Diana Linde only solidified that he was always meant to be a writer. He could sit here and talk to this one man all day, but he got the man’s name and wrote him something special to thank him for making the start of his day extremely special.

“Come on up, young lady,” his smile was larger now as he waved up his next book to sign.

The line was moving slowly, but talking to the people only seemed to get better. Each one reminded him of something from his past books. He wasn’t one of those writers who would go and put out ten to twelve books within a year, but little did most people know he had enough books sitting on his laptop to keep his publisher busy for a few years. He did like for his people, his fans, to be itching and begging for something new and thus he’d put out two to three books per year just to satisfy their hunger.

Aura was doing her job going from fan to fan asking them for their opinions about the new book’s cover, for new story ideas, and taking notes that she'd pass on to Devin later after everyone had left. She was definitely good with people and she kept a group of them involved as the line continued to crawl forward; he'd have to talk to Mishelle about getting the young lady some kind of incentive raise to keep her motivated. What pleased him most about her was that she was always looking out for new venues for him to do his book signings, and she was getting rather creative.

"Excuse me, Mr. Cross," Mrs. Beasley, one of the owners of the book store was at his side.

"Yes, Ma'am?" Devin answered not turning around as he continued to sign the book he had in front of him.

"I'd like for you to meet someone, Sir," she smiled pressing her hand in the back of the young lady at her side trying to push her forward. "I know that you're in the middle of signing but this is Elise, she's been a big supporter of our little shop, and she was one of the first to purchase your very first book that we carried. She's been a huge fan ever since and pretty much begged me to introduce her to you."

"Excuse me for just a second," Devin apologized to the next person before turning around in his chair. His eyes felt as if they were about to pop from their sockets as he stared up at the young lady standing beside the elderly woman smiling down at him; he stood almost turning over the table of books and extended his hand.

"Hi," he responded trying to regain his lost composure. "Devin Cross."

"Yes, you are," she almost shrieked as she reached out taking his hand and shaking it frantically. "I'm… I'm Elise, Elise Mannsen, and I cannot believe that I'm finally meeting you. Mr.

Cross, I am your biggest fan… I know that you hear that a lot, but I am being so for real right now."

The heels she wore made her look as tall as he and they were staring into one another's eyes. Smoldering coals of liquid blue ice burned into his skull as he tried to find his footing before tripping and falling all over the woman. She was more than beautiful and the more he looked at her the more he found he couldn't take his eyes off of her. Her long dark hair hung loose down to the middle of hr back. Her lips weren't full but spread into a full smile had him smitten. The dark dress just hugged her like liquid latex had been poured over body to fit her perfectly; the full flare of her hips and the fullness of her breast of her breast with her deeply exposed cleavage. As a writer, the more he looked the further away the words became.

"I'm so glad that you're here," he finally choked out before stepping back to pull a chair over to his table. "Please, sit. Wait… can you sit?"

"Yes," Elise was excited beyond words as she pulled on the back of the dress before easing down into the offered chair."

"Excellent," Devin sat and picked up his pen and waved up the next fan with a renewed smile. "We can get to know each other while I sign some more books."

Devin couldn't help but to cut his eyes to his right just to catch glimpses of the beautiful woman now sitting there. His fans were still his priority and without missing a beat he kept up with the book signing and the plethora of questions as each new person walked up. His hand hurt and the smile was becoming tedious but he was in his zone. He was a people person and could talk to anyone, and being in

these small venues made it easy to feel comfortable
with the fans that showed up the book signing,

After about an hour he asked to take a small
break to allow his hand a moment to rest, and this
would give him a little time with Elise. He couldn't
help noticing Aura and the look on her face; the
beautiful woman had no problem showing that she
did not care for the other woman sitting next to him,
and he grinned. The hour passed quickly and soon
Aura was gesturing that it was time to begin again.
Devin smiled. Picking up his pen he waved for his
next fan to step forward. The woman was a little
older but she still looked nice and she tried to plaster
an amicable smile on her face as she slid her book
across the table.

"Ok so I have to know, what got you into
writing about psychos and killers?" Elise asked as
she smiled at the woman now openly glaring at her.

"I don't really know how to answer that
one," Devin scribbled the woman's name and a
small message to her before scratching his name
boldly across the page. "I guess you can say that I
have a slight love for the macabre. I was a kid who
grew up on old fashion slasher movies and I'm a man
who loves crime dramas… so at some point I
decided to bring them together. I studied serial
killers and even did a little studying into split
personalities and manic psychosis.

"It was fun."

"Now why do I not find that too hard to
believe about you?" Elise responded.

They laughed and continued talking as the
next fan walked up and begged him for a hug and a
kiss. Devin stood and leaned over the table to give
the woman a big hug before pressing his lips to her
cheek. The woman squealed as the girl with her took

their picture on a cell phone. He was quickly caught up in the whirlwind of her excitement as she hung on to his neck and pulling his face down towards her exposed cleavage.

Turning his head, he could see Aura shaking hers as she stood off a ways from the floor show with her arms folded across her chest. He shrugged his shoulders as if to let her know that he had no control over his fans, but the smile on his face told that he loved the attention. Elise was sitting there laughing with the over excited woman as she held him captive into her chest swinging back and forth keeping him smothered in her very abundant breasts.

"Ma'am?" Aura finally stepped forward and placed a hand on the woman's arm. "Could you please release Mr. Cross so that we can continue with the rest of the book signing?"

"I love this man," the woman squealed as she squeezed his head into her breasts once more. "I have wanted to meet you for the longest."

"What's your name?" Devin mumbled from her cleavage.

"Monique," she was kissing the top of his head. "Monique Biscayne, and I am one of your biggest fans. I even have a fanpage set up in your honor on Facebook."

"I'll have to find it and check it out," Devin was laughing as he felt Aura pulling at the woman's arms to release him. "You'll have to release my head and write it down for me."

The woman finally released his head and attempted to kiss him once more but he dropped down into his seat just out of her reach. Her book was sitting on the table and he snatched it up signing it as Aura leaned over asking if he was alright. He passed the woman her book and a business card for hr to write down the Facebook page as he let his publicist know that he was fine. He grinned looking over at Elise who was still laughing almost uncontrollably.

"Why do you continue to make things so difficult for me?" Aura huffed and stomped back off to where she'd been standing. "Ms. Rivers don't pay me enough to keep babysitting you."

"I'd be worried if I knew you didn't love me," Devin blew her a kiss before resuming the book signing once more.

Elise was a tornado of questions and as he wrote he kept up answering as fast as he could. It was so refreshing to just sit and talk to someone who seemed to really know him beyond just his books. From his birthday to where he'd been born right down to the little tidbit of trivia he'd give about his being born the day man walked on the moon. She didn't shy away from any of his questions about where she'd been born, and she was quick about telling him all about her dysfunctional family.

"So are you sure that you're not a stalker?" Devin joked.

"What do you mean?" Elise stopped and her face became quite serious as she stared deeply into his eyes. There was a look there that he didn't recognize, but he quickly dismissed it and laughed.

"I was teasing." Devin began laughing harder because she looked so serious. For a moment he was sure that he'd messed up, but slowly her smile returned and then she was laughing and they were laughing together as well as those in the line close enough to hear bits and parts of the conversation.

They fed off of one another and their stories just filled the book store even as the fans brought their own stories to the mix. Devin had never had a book signing as exciting as this one and he was working out a way to thank Elise for bringing more to his day. One more look at Aura and he knew he'd have to sit her down soon and talk about this new attitude she was showcasing in front of his fans.

The final fan in the line was walking away extremely happy, and before he could turn to address the woman sitting beside him, she was sliding over her book. Her smile was intoxicating and her eyes were hypnotic as he opened the book to his signature page.

"So," he licked his lips, "who would you like for me to make this out to?"

"I'm going to boldly step out on a limb and say… *to my future wife, Elise, I look forward to seeing what tomorrow holds for us.*"

And that is exactly what he wrote.

(to be continued)

Book excerpt from
Maxine Steele – The White Chapel Files:
The Reaper's Edge

Chapter 2

Friday

The buzzing sound of the alarm clock was so annoying that she finally reached over in her sleep and slammed her hand down on the snooze button just to shut it up. Light was softly diffusing into her room through the blinds covering the window taking away the dark that seemed to consume the room only a short time ago. The air conditioning was cold and she pulled the bed spread up tighter around her body and realized it didn't move as freely as usual.

"Shit, not again" Detective Maxine Steele murmured under breath as the events of last night slowly flooded her mind.

Slowly she rolled over and stared at the sleeping form of the man beside her and shook her head. She pushed herself up in the bed and looked over the side for anything she could throw on as clothes before she woke him to get him out. Reaching down she grabbed her panties and a t-shirt and moved to the edge of the bed tossing the shirt over her head and pulling it on before she stood up and pulling her panties up her legs with a grunt of effort. Her head was spinning and her stomach was churning as she lanced back once more to see if was still asleep. She didn't even recognize his face. Shaking her head to clear away last night's cobwebs, Maxine climbed back up onto the bed pressing back against the headboard and she lit a cigarette. Taking a deep breath and then slowly blowing it out she tapped on the man's shoulder a little annoyed at herself and at him for still being in her home.

"Hey, ummm…" she grumbled trying to remember his name. "You need to wake up and go."

"Nick," The man moaned and stirred a bit but did not wake and this began to piss her off. "It's Nick, Baby."

Taking a deep drag from her cigarette and holding it in her lungs she finally blew out the smoke and reached over to shake the man. Finally, he began to come around and rolled over onto his back and stared over at her.

"Ok, whatever. Look, I really need for you to get up, get dressed and get gone."

"What's the hurry?" he smiled at her and licked his lips. "I mean we could… you know."

"No we can't. I think you got more than your share last night," she stared at him as he began to sit up and the covers fell away from his body and she began to remember why she brought him into her house in the first place. His chest was like a chiseled piece of marble that he kept bouncing to show off that he worked out, and that led down to an washboard stomach that was a defined six pack that she honestly wanted to rub her hands over again. He pulled back the covers since he knew she was watching and revealed his slowly growing dick bouncing against his thigh. She could feel the heat in the room rise and the moisture between her thighs building.

"I… umm," she swallowed and then took another drag from her cigarette before looking away, "have some things to do this morning. So, up, up, up. I need for you to go. Now."

Without another word of protest, he rose from her bed naked and searching for his clothes which were strewn about the room. She sat staring as his body rippled and flexed and his equipment continued to come to life; he purposely stood profile so she could watch it stiffen hoping that would change her mind and invite him back into her bed. Maxine looked away with a blushing smile as she realized what he was trying to do by showing off his impressive "morning wood". She could really go for another toss, but if she were to do that it would make him think he could have his way with her again.

"Bastard," she said under her breath as she took the last drag on her cigarette and snuffed out the butt in the ashtray on the nightstand. She got up out of the bed and walked around it towards the door so she could let her nameless tryst out and she could get her day started. As he walked past her, he tried for a kiss on the lips but was met with thin air and a smile as she waited for him to walk on out and into the hallway of her apartment complex.

"Will I get to see you again, Max?"

"Damn, are we that close already?"

"You didn't seem to mind last night," he flashed what he was sure was his most award winning smile. "So, will I?"

She glanced at him and remembered quite suddenly that he was the cute guy from the apartment mailbox area. "I'm sure you will," she flashed him a stunning smile. "If I'm not mistaking, we live in the same complex. Thank you for a wonderful night… umm, Nick."

She quickly closed the door without waiting for him to respond. She rushed back to her room and grabbed another cigarette and lit it and took a deep pull as she fell back on her bed exasperated. She pressed her thighs together tightly to seize the fire now burning there. One of these days… she'd have to get some kind of control over her life.

"What the fuck was I thinking?" she questioned out loud before rolling over to scream into her pillow. The alarm clock's buzzer went off again reminding her that she had things to do, and it was forcing her to get up off her ass and get them started.

Sitting up, Maxine took another long drag from the cigarette and looked at remembering that at the beginning of the year she had made another resolution to quit smoking, and she hadn't yet. She reached over and slapped her hand down on the clock to shut up the alarm and with a groan stood up once more, and walked out towards the kitchen. Coffee was already brewing and she smiled as she sucked in and puffed out the smoke looking through her cabinets for a possible clean cup. Not surprised that she didn't find one, she quickly washed a mug that was lying in the sink and stood waiting for the fresh caffeine to join the nicotine.

With coffee and nicotine in her system she rushed off to the shower to truly get her day started. Once she was under the water she let out a sigh as her mind went back to the events of last night. Maxine grimaced as once again she realized it all began because she had been drinking; a lot of the shit she got into began with her drinking here lately, and that all began after the last undercover case she'd been on. Maxine had spent more than her fair share of time hating herself, but the alcohol helped to take care of a lot of that time. Her intentions always began with just wanting to have a few drinks, but a few became more than just that, and soon after that she would be sent home from the bar. It's always a good thing that the bar she frequented was just down the street from where she lived and she never had to drive or else she would really be fucked – and not literally.

"Hey, Jerry," her words were slurred, even as she stood under the water remembering them, "how's about one more for the road, huh?"

She remembered Jerry, the bartender at Chapel Hill Pub, telling her he wouldn't serve her anymore to drink, and that only served to make her mad. She was sitting on the bar stool trying to savor every last drop of that last glass of vodka and cranberry with the shot of vodka as if it would be her very last drink ever. She was dipping her finger into the glass and wiping along the sides. She could see Jerry staring at her shaking his head and calling her hopeless as begged for one more drink promising to go home. She remembered the string of profane words she spewed out as she slid and stumbled from her bar stool and then headed out the door.

Stepping deeper under the spray of water letting it run through her hair and down over her face rubbing so she could remove any of the remaining makeup. The headache from the booze and sex was slowly dissipating, but the remnants would be there throughout the day. She knew she'd have to apologize to Jerry and his waitress, but she could hear them telling her to forget about it and once again the alcohol would flow as if nothing had happened. She could already taste the alcohol again and already see some naked, faceless man staring up at her…

"Fuck me." She grabbed her loofa and dumped some liquid soap on it and rubbed it to a hurried lather. "What the hell is wrong with you, Maxine?"

Maxine showered and washed her hair and
then hurried from the shower. She brushed her teeth
and was thankful that the steam from her shower
clouded the mirror so she didn't have to look at the
woman who would be staring back at her. She
wrapped a towel about her body and walked into her
bedroom and had set about her new mission of
finding clothes when the phone rang. She walked
over and looked at the caller id and answered with a
look of disgust on her face.

"Good Morning, Ms. Steele, this is White
Chapel Adult Living."

"Yes I could see that on my caller I.D.," she
fought to maintain her temper, "has something
happened with my mother?"

"She's been screaming out to see you all
morning and nothing we do seems to calm her. We
need for you to come here as soon as you possibly
can."

"What's she screaming about?"

"We can't make any sense of it, but in the
end the doctors all feel that you need to come here so
we can get her calm without the use of drugs. When
can we expect you, Ms. Steele?"

"Well," Maxine stood there thinking, "I have
an appointment that I cannot break so it will be
shortly after that. If you have to give her something
to at least make her relax a little until I get there,
then do it."

"I'll let the doctors know you'll be here
soon," there was a snide sound in her response,
"maybe telling her that will calm your mother
enough until you make it."

"Whatever she needs," Maxine answered,
"and I'll be there as soon as I can."

She hung up the phone before the rude little bitch could say anything else and returned to finding clothes for the day. As she sat down at her vanity, she stared at her face completely unblemished with makeup and shook her head. *There's something so fucking wrong with you* she thought to herself as she set to putting on her "face". As she put on her makeup she would stare at her hair and toyed with putting it up in her new wild style hairdo that she had been wearing just to see how it went over with more professional types.

Stepping out of her house and onto the morning streets Maxine took in a deep breath and looked around. She pulled out a cigarette, lit it, and took a deep drag into her lungs before releasing the smoke into the air. She could feel the morning breeze blowing through her spiked and teased hair and she smiled to herself as she walked towards her car sitting patiently at the curb. Since she was on administrative leave from work she had opted for a pair of blue jeans and a light top over which she wore her favorite black leather jacket and a pair of black leather boots to finish the ensemble. It was mid-August and there was just a little nip in the air and she welcomed it.

She tossed away her cigarette before getting into the cherry red Dodge Charger. She turned the key and smiled again at the roar of the motor. Looking at her cell phone she saw that she had missed a call from her Captain and figured he was calling to make certain she didn't miss this newest appointment with her psycho-therapist. She tossed the phone down onto the passenger seat and shook her head.

"Oh Captain my Captain," she glanced in the rear view mirror before pulling out onto the empty street, "yes I'm on the way to see my quack, please no worries."

****

"Good morning," the receptionist tossed around her hair and smiled, "are you here for an appointment?"

"Yes, Det. Maxine Steele," Maxine answered knowing that the woman behind the desk recognized her. It never made any sense to her to be asked the same things with each visit when the one asking the question is the same one who set up the appointment.

"Dr. Castille is still with her current patient, Det. Steele," the girl said still smiling, "if you'll have a seat I'm sure she'll be with you momentarily."

"Thank you."

Maxine sat down in the lobby and glanced around at the couple of other people sitting and waiting as well. The man sitting there was a cop, not that she knew him, but it was the way he was sitting there with his eyes constantly moving around watching everything around him. He sat there with a straight back and a little stiff in the neck and he seemed to favor his left side a bit more than his right; most likely a gunshot wound close to his hip, and probably the reason he was here to discuss the shooting and his injuries. She stared into his eyes and could see he was trying to figure out why she was there and she merely nodded at him to let him know she too was a fellow officer… he returned the nod and they both resumed checking out the other people sitting around them.

She turned her attentions to the lady sitting there holding her head down and looking at her shoes. The woman was definitely a housewife and from the way she was sitting there a very unhappy housewife. She didn't lack money, her husband was probably some big shot defense lawyer and she was reaping the rewards of his cases of defending some of the most ill-reputed criminals of White Chapel; as a criminal profiler, she had a habit of speculating and even stereotyping people. He was most likely cheating on her; Maxine continued sizing the woman up silently, and from the looks of the way she was shaking he was definitely beating on her and he was sending her to see a psychiatrist to help her "deal with it".

She glanced up at the young girl behind the window who asked her to sit down and noticed that the other cop was looking at the girl as well… both of them no doubt going through a full routine of questions mentally. To the naked eye she probably seemed quite the jovial girl, with her ever present smile, but as Maxine stared she was certain that the young assistant had at least one child. Maxine had her still living at home with her parents and giving them the majority of her money for her room and board and to help care for her child. Maxine watched the girl's lips moving telling someone off behind her, that she was ready for the day to be over already and hated being away from little Jacen for such long periods.

Maxine shook her head.

"Detective." the girl was now looking at her. "Excuse me, Det. Steele; the Dr. Castille is ready to see you now. Please come on back."

Maxine glanced at the cop and nodded once more before standing and walking towards the door that led to the back rooms. She took a deep breath and waited for the click of the lock before pulling on the door and walking in. As she walked through,

Maxine did as she always did; she took note of the pristine clean walls and floors. She took note of which doors were open and which were closed. Passing by the closed doors she could hear voices behind them, but there was no time to stop and listen. Her mind worked in circles as she followed the girl ahead of her towards the room she would be sitting in for the next twenty minutes waiting for the doctor and the hour after that talking. She hated coming to this place, she hated it with a passion.

"Doctor Castille will be in with you in a moment."

Maxine stepped inside the room and stared at her for but a moment. She was the girl that she couldn't see the first girl talking to, and she too had that painted on smile as she opened the door and then closed it behind her as she walked back up to her seat in the small office area.

This office was so sub-clinical; it was more like another office than a doctor's patient room. The walls were not a drab and painful white they were more of a soft beige color that as gentle on the eyes, and the floors were covered in a plush carpet instead of the normal linoleum tile. There was a large, comfortable looking leather sofa against one wall and the wall across from it had a large bookshelf full of books ranging from clinical books to differing story books which caused her to wonder just how many of any of these books had the doctor actually read. At the head of the room was a rather modest mahogany desk with an oversized, leather chair behind it. The desk was cluttered with a computer monitor and its peripherals, and the typical patient papers and folders all covering the large desk calendar. There were a few family pictures; mother, father, two brothers and a sister, hanging on the walls or standing on the book shelf, but more prominently displayed were all of her degrees. Maxine made a mental note that there were no pictures of anyone that could be considered a husband… or a wife.

Maxine grinned and took a seat on the sofa and waited patiently. This was her fifth or sixth visit with the doctor since she'd been placed on administrative leave three months ago. This was her punishment after coming back from a deep cover investigation feeling just a little less than normal. There were more investigations to endure from the suits in Internal Affairs, but going this "psyche eval" was her only means of returning to active duty. She pushed herself back into the cushions of the sofa and took a deep breath. She shook her head wishing that she could light up a cigarette, or that the doctor had a bottle of anything alcoholic in this dungeon she could use to get numb.

She laid her head back and tried to relax but there was no comfort only more memories she was longing to forget. She had been working with Dr. Castille to help her come to terms with some of the things she'd gone through while she was undercover, but it seemed that the more they talked the worse she continued to feel about herself. The more they talked the more she longed to leave her couch and find a bar and drink herself into a coma. Dr. Castille's answer to everything was to stop and think and then consider an alternative.

"There are no real alternatives," she hissed out.

"I see you're dwelling on the negatives again, Detective." The voice came from a door opening from the other side of the room, but unlike most of her patients, Maxine Steele did not jump.

"I'm not quite a detective in my current state of mind, Doctor Castille."

Dr. Castille smiled as she stepped around her desk and sat in the chair. As always, Maxine took a moment to apprise the woman who basically could ruin her well-earned career or help her to put it all back on track. The woman was rather short even in extreme heels she always wore. Her long blonde hair she kept in a tightly wound bun at the top of her head and of course she wore the half glasses that she surely thought made her look more educated. Her blue eyes were bright and her face was rather pretty and definitely didn't show her to be the age Maxine knew… what great work plastic surgeons could do.

"So beyond the negative," she smiled as she began to read through the notes in Maxine's folders, "how are you feeling today, Maxine?"

"Not too good, Doc." Maxine settled into to rambling that she was about to deliver. "I woke up this morning to a hangover, another naked man and of course the home called about my mother needing to see me. If that's not enough, my Captain called and I missed his call but I'm sure he was calling to make certain I'd be coming here this morning, and I'm sure I'm going to get an earful when I do call him back. I found myself thinking about my New Year's resolutions again, and yes, I was smoking at the time. So, all in all, it's been a great start to another great day."

"Sounds like a full morning," Castille was unaffected by the spiel and jotted notes on her pad. She glanced over the edge of her glasses evaluating the physical appearance of her patient before she continued. "Did you take the time to work on any of the exercises I asked of you, or did you do as you've been doing and killed more of your precious brain cells with alcohol?"

Maxine sat there a moment and considered lying to the woman just to get a rise out of her, but she was truly trying to make her way back to work. She closed her eyes and pictured herself smoking a cigarette and then slowly opened them exhaling the air before looking back at the other woman. Her body relaxed. Her shoulders dropped just enough to give the impression that she was calmer as she focused on the doctor's eyes.

"Actually," she tried to smile, "I worked on the exercises and for the most part they did seem to help some. But the truth is, there's a lot of shit, damn I mean stuff, I know I need to work through. That operation totally fucked me up, I know it did, but I honestly think that getting shot is still messing with my head. I can't seem to get past any of it."

"The more I try to focus on something… positive; I can suddenly hear the crack of the gunshot. I smell the smoke. I can feel the bullet piercing through my belly and then again out of my back. I can hear the doctors saying I was fortunate that the bullet missed any vital organs. They said that I was… lucky. Lucky."

"Maxine," her stern voice kicked in, "those exercises were not given to you to help you to forget but to accept. I understand completely that you went through a lot when you were undercover, and I understand completely that being under so deep that you were expected to do a lot of things that you were not trained to do or expected to do. I don't completely understand it, but I'm sure there are more than just physical scars that you have to deal with concerning the shooting.

"The way I see it, you're ready to go back to work."

"What do you mean I'm ready to go back to work?" Maxine stared at her doctor raising an eyebrow.

"Yes, you are, Maxine," Castille continued, "but it is you who keeps holding you back."

"Holding me back?"

"Yes," Castille sat back in her chair. "You're holding on so tightly to those repressed memories that they are not allowing you to move forward, Maxine. You were in a traumatic situation; your job is composed of traumatic situations. The question is… are you ready to step away from this One and stare at another?"

"So you're telling me that you could sign the papers for me to get back into the department?" Maxine was battling the urges to jump and shout her excitement. She was looking forward to getting out of her little apartment and back into the world. She couldn't wait to sink her teeth into a fresh case and put all of the shit she'd been through behind her.

"Yes I could do so today," Castille smiled, "and you could be working again as soon as Monday."

"Dr. Castille, I need to get back to work. I mean I really need it because I feel like I'm going stir crazy sitting at home. If I'm out of work much longer I swear I feel I'll get lost in some Facebook nonsense, or I'll wind up finishing what someone else started."

"I'm sure you'll find a way to keep yourself out of such dire dramatic situations, but seriously, how much do you want to go to work?"

"I really need this, Doc," Maxine was sitting up on the edge of her seat. "I can honestly say I'll do almost anything to get my real life back."

"Then I need for you to give me one thing," the Doctor smiled at the raised eyebrow she got and the quizzical look. "One story, it has to be about the most regrettable thing you had to do and what you feel must be done to get over it."

The most regrettable thing? Maxine sat back thinking for a moment. She closed her eyes. Slowly her mind drifted back and there was only one story that even came close. Her stomach grumble and her head was suddenly hurting. She opened her eyes and stared across the room. The most regrettable thing that she's had to do.

It had to be that incident with the young girl.

(To be continued)

9 781943 159055